U0097796

序　言

我國每年選派許多專業人員出國，從事進修或執行有關軍備的採購任務；而選派人員的標準，除了考量專業知識外，便是英語能力，因爲國外大都是以英語爲溝通工具；若語文能力不足，小則影響個人學習進度，大則危害國家安全，不可不慎。

ECL 測驗（English Comprehension Level）是由美國國防語文學院所舉辦，測驗內容分爲聽力和閱測兩部分，全部都是四選一的單選題，出題方向著重於**非正式英語**，也就是口說英語。這項測驗對軍人而言非常重要，軍事學校每年都會定期舉辦 ECL 模擬測驗，作爲甄選軍官或士官的篩選標準；而國防部實際挑選外派或進修人員時，也會設定申請者要通過 ECL 測驗的一定成績標準。

有鑒於 ECL 測驗的專業化，學習出版公司特別針對這項考試推出了系列叢書，包括「如何準備 ECL」、「ECL 字彙」、「ECL 聽力測驗 I」、「ECL 文法題庫 ①」、「ECL 模擬試題詳解」。此外，爲了因應讀者的熱烈迴響，我們花了三年的時間來籌備，推出全新的「**ECL 聽力測驗 II**」，書中試題完全仿照眞正的 ECL 測驗，而且每一道題目都有詳盡的解說，是最具有練習價值的資料。

本書在編審及校對的每一階段，均力求完善，但恐有疏漏之處，誠盼各界先進不吝批評指正。

編者　謹識

CONTENTS

ECL 測驗簡介

◎ 測驗對象：欲前往美國受軍事訓練或進修的軍官將士。

◎ 測驗內容：聽力測驗及閱讀測驗。測驗時間約 60-75 分鐘。滿分為一百分。我國各單位所訂立的篩選標準，大多為八十分。測驗有效期為一〇五天。每月最多可受測一次。

◎ ECL 測驗分數與語言能力對照表：

ECL 測驗分數	適合參與的訓練課程	英語程度描述	字彙量
60-65	薄片金屬構造工 輕型汽車機械工 建築設備操作員	能理解基本句型，以及簡單問答。能看懂由簡單句子及熟悉主題所構成的文章。	約 3000 字
70	醫務人員 後勤人員 基礎電子工程學	能理解大部分的動詞時態、問答及敘述，但若這些句型出現在不熟悉的情況時，可能就會聽不懂。能閱讀短文，但對於不熟悉的內容，常常會誤解文法結構。	約 4000 字
80	專業軍事教育課程 大學飛行課程 危險課程（爆裂物、潛水、水中爆破）	會使用現在、過去、未來式、完成式的時態。能夠閱讀較不複雜的文章，且可依上下文的推敲，理解複雜或技術性的文章。	約 5000 字
85-90	進階飛行課程 安全工程 情報課程	能充分理解一般主題，及與專業相關的內容，能聽懂正常語速的對話或報告。能看懂各種主題的文章，並連結相關概念，推導出結論。	約 6000 字

ECL 測驗答案卷參考範本

STUDENT NAME : ______________________

INSTRUCTOR NAME/TCO : ______________________

COUNTRY/LOC CODE : ______________________

PROJECT : ______________ WCN : ______________

SPONSOR SERVICE : ______________________

TEST DATE : ______________________ (year) (month) (day)

TEST ID : ______________________

RAW SCORE: _______ CONV SCORE: ______ REQ ECL : ____

SCN							TCN		
0	0	0	0	0	0	0	0	0	0
1	1	1	1	1	1	1	1	1	1
2	2	2	2	2	2	2	2	2	2
3	3	3	3	3	3	3	3	3	3
4	4	4	4	4	4	4	4	4	4
5	5	5	5	5	5	5	5	5	5
6	6	6	6	6	6	6	6	6	6
7	7	7	7	7	7	7	7	7	7
8	8	8	8	8	8	8	8	8	8
9	9	9	9	9	9	9	9	9	9

Seat ________ Lab ________

1 ⓐⓑⓒⓓ	21 ⓐⓑⓒⓓ	41 ⓐⓑⓒⓓ	61 ⓐⓑⓒⓓ	81 ⓐⓑⓒⓓ	101 ⓐⓑⓒⓓ
2 ⓐⓑⓒⓓ	22 ⓐⓑⓒⓓ	42 ⓐⓑⓒⓓ	62 ⓐⓑⓒⓓ	82 ⓐⓑⓒⓓ	102 ⓐⓑⓒⓓ
3 ⓐⓑⓒⓓ	23 ⓐⓑⓒⓓ	43 ⓐⓑⓒⓓ	63 ⓐⓑⓒⓓ	83 ⓐⓑⓒⓓ	103 ⓐⓑⓒⓓ
4 ⓐⓑⓒⓓ	24 ⓐⓑⓒⓓ	44 ⓐⓑⓒⓓ	64 ⓐⓑⓒⓓ	84 ⓐⓑⓒⓓ	104 ⓐⓑⓒⓓ
5 ⓐⓑⓒⓓ	25 ⓐⓑⓒⓓ	45 ⓐⓑⓒⓓ	65 ⓐⓑⓒⓓ	85 ⓐⓑⓒⓓ	105 ⓐⓑⓒⓓ
6 ⓐⓑⓒⓓ	26 ⓐⓑⓒⓓ	46 ⓐⓑⓒⓓ	66 ⓐⓑⓒⓓ	86 ⓐⓑⓒⓓ	106 ⓐⓑⓒⓓ
7 ⓐⓑⓒⓓ	27 ⓐⓑⓒⓓ	47 ⓐⓑⓒⓓ	67 ⓐⓑⓒⓓ	87 ⓐⓑⓒⓓ	107 ⓐⓑⓒⓓ
8 ⓐⓑⓒⓓ	28 ⓐⓑⓒⓓ	48 ⓐⓑⓒⓓ	68 ⓐⓑⓒⓓ	88 ⓐⓑⓒⓓ	108 ⓐⓑⓒⓓ
9 ⓐⓑⓒⓓ	29 ⓐⓑⓒⓓ	49 ⓐⓑⓒⓓ	69 ⓐⓑⓒⓓ	89 ⓐⓑⓒⓓ	109 ⓐⓑⓒⓓ
10 ⓐⓑⓒⓓ	30 ⓐⓑⓒⓓ	50 ⓐⓑⓒⓓ	70 ⓐⓑⓒⓓ	90 ⓐⓑⓒⓓ	110 ⓐⓑⓒⓓ
11 ⓐⓑⓒⓓ	31 ⓐⓑⓒⓓ	51 ⓐⓑⓒⓓ	71 ⓐⓑⓒⓓ	91 ⓐⓑⓒⓓ	111 ⓐⓑⓒⓓ
12 ⓐⓑⓒⓓ	32 ⓐⓑⓒⓓ	52 ⓐⓑⓒⓓ	72 ⓐⓑⓒⓓ	92 ⓐⓑⓒⓓ	112 ⓐⓑⓒⓓ
13 ⓐⓑⓒⓓ	33 ⓐⓑⓒⓓ	53 ⓐⓑⓒⓓ	73 ⓐⓑⓒⓓ	93 ⓐⓑⓒⓓ	113 ⓐⓑⓒⓓ
14 ⓐⓑⓒⓓ	34 ⓐⓑⓒⓓ	54 ⓐⓑⓒⓓ	74 ⓐⓑⓒⓓ	94 ⓐⓑⓒⓓ	114 ⓐⓑⓒⓓ
15 ⓐⓑⓒⓓ	35 ⓐⓑⓒⓓ	55 ⓐⓑⓒⓓ	75 ⓐⓑⓒⓓ	95 ⓐⓑⓒⓓ	115 ⓐⓑⓒⓓ
16 ⓐⓑⓒⓓ	36 ⓐⓑⓒⓓ	56 ⓐⓑⓒⓓ	76 ⓐⓑⓒⓓ	96 ⓐⓑⓒⓓ	116 ⓐⓑⓒⓓ
17 ⓐⓑⓒⓓ	37 ⓐⓑⓒⓓ	57 ⓐⓑⓒⓓ	77 ⓐⓑⓒⓓ	97 ⓐⓑⓒⓓ	117 ⓐⓑⓒⓓ
18 ⓐⓑⓒⓓ	38 ⓐⓑⓒⓓ	58 ⓐⓑⓒⓓ	78 ⓐⓑⓒⓓ	98 ⓐⓑⓒⓓ	118 ⓐⓑⓒⓓ
19 ⓐⓑⓒⓓ	39 ⓐⓑⓒⓓ	59 ⓐⓑⓒⓓ	79 ⓐⓑⓒⓓ	99 ⓐⓑⓒⓓ	119 ⓐⓑⓒⓓ
20 ⓐⓑⓒⓓ	40 ⓐⓑⓒⓓ	60 ⓐⓑⓒⓓ	80 ⓐⓑⓒⓓ	100 ⓐⓑⓒⓓ	120 ⓐⓑⓒⓓ

LISTENING TEST ①

- *Directions for questions 1-25. You will hear questions on the test CD. Select the one item A, B, C or D which answers the question correctly, and mark your answer sheet.*

1. A. Yes, I hate it.
   B. Yes, it's far too serious for me.
   C. Yes, it's very good to be outside.
   D. Yes, I'm becoming accustomed to it.

2. A. old people　　B. men and women
   C. mom and dad　　D. boys and girls

3. A. falling rain　　B. colors in the sky
   C. a colorful bowtie　　D. a park ranger

4. A. the price of the jacket
   B. the owner of the broom
   C. the owner of the jacket
   D. the size of the jacket

5. A. the things　　B. the people
   C. the pets　　D. the family

6. A. tomorrow　　B. next year
   C. recently　　D. regularly

7. A. Yes, he phoned in.
   B. No, he planned it carefully.
   C. Yes, I was surprised.
   D. Yes, he planned it carefully.

8. A. It was painted. B. It was sold.
   C. It was stolen. D. It was sacrificed.

9. A. colored B. stared
   C. stuck D. changed

10. A. five days ago B. three days ago
    C. two days ago D. four days ago

11. A. on a bear B. on a horse
    C. on a bike D. on a cow

12. A. movement B. comparatively
    C. cloudburst D. encounter

13. A. slow B. sudden
    C. sometimes D. never

14. A. I haven't made up my mind yet.
    B. I'm mixed up.
    C. Did you think so, too?
    D. I'm not bothering you at all.

15. A. iron it B. unfold it
    C. fetch it D. scan it

16. A. She ate it quickly.
    B. She burned it quickly.
    C. She cooked it quickly.
    D. She looked at it quickly.

17. A. gentle wind B. a cold wind
C. no wind at all D. a dry wind

18. A. to look bad B. to stink bad
C. to smell good D. to look good

19. A. How about going skiing?
B. Terrific! Let's go.
C. Why? Did I do something wrong?
D. Why not try again?

20. A. I didn't know he did.
B. Out of curiosity, I guess.
C. He will buy a good one.
D. I wanted him to do so.

21. A. Yes, it will go up about 10 degrees.
B. Yes, it will go down about 10 degrees.
C. No, it will go up about 10 degrees.
D. No, it will climb about 10 degrees.

22. A. Yes, I like it the best.
B. Yes, I like everything.
C. Yes, it is the blue one.
D. It's OK, isn't it?

23. A. poor eyesight B. good eyesight
C. keen hearing D. poor hearing

24. A. protection B. perfection
C. pardon D. prediction

25. A. the people B. the clothes
C. the weather D. the cars

● *Directions for questions 26-50. You will hear statements on the test CD. Select the one answer A, B, C, or D which comes closest to the meaning of the statement and mark your answer sheet.*

26. A. We saw it flying up.
B. We saw it going down.
C. We saw it going out.
D. We saw it going up.

27. A. He wants to fight.
B. He wants to make a fire.
C. He wants to go out.
D. He wants to fire us.

28. A. He accomplished his mission.
B. He objected to his mission.
C. He failed in his mission.
D. He cherished his mission.

29. A. The parents are looking at the children.
B. The parents are cooking food with their children.
C. The children are looking at their parents.
D. The children cook the food.

30. A. I did his work. B. I saved him.
C. I cared for him. D. I cooked for him

31. A. We should do it whenever.
B. We should do it when we have time.
C. We should do it without delay.
D. We should put it away.

32. A. It was sunny.
B. It never rained.
C. It rained nearly every day.
D. It rained nearly every Friday.

33. A. We didn't give it a try.
B. We didn't give a damn.
C. We didn't give up.
D. We didn't live it up.

34. A. She gave food to people without homes.
B. She gave food to each teacher.
C. She gave food to each home.
D. She gave food to each pet.

35. A. She is dangerous. B. She is careful.
C. She is strange. D. She is driven.

36. A. She took control.
B. She takes the contact.
C. She is taking control.
D. She took cornbread.

37. A. The boy is leaping.
    B. The boy is arriving.
    C. The boy is staying.
    D. The boy is leaving.

38. A. We are angry to meet her.
    B. We are tired to meet her.
    C. We are bored to meet her.
    D. We are eager to meet her.

39. A. It will not be a fine day.
    B. It will not be sunny tomorrow.
    C. It will not be windy tomorrow.
    D. It will not rain tomorrow.

40. A. Lisa is very tired.
    B. Lisa is naughty.
    C. Lisa is ill.
    D. Lisa has been visiting someone.

41. A. He went to get goods.
    B. He has a good back.
    C. He has left permanently.
    D. He has a good city.

42. A. Some people talk too much.
    B. They like to talk for or against something.
    C. They talk too quickly.
    D. Some people are crazy.

43. A. She is beautiful.
    B. She is polite.
    C. She is childish.
    D. She is thin.

44. A. The man will help the police.
    B. The man will not listen to the police.
    C. The man will fight against the police.
    D. The man will stay with the police.

45. A. The heavier the cars are the more accidents happen.
    B. Accidents occur when there are many cars.
    C. There are many accidents when it rains heavily.
    D. Accidents are really serious when there are many vehicles.

46. A. It is clean. B. It is not clean.
    C. It is polished. D. It is new.

47. A. He wanted to recommend the subject.
    B. He wanted to vomit the subject.
    C. He wanted discuss the subject.
    D. He wanted to omit the subject.

48. A. Her score was satisfactory.
    B. Her score was high.
    C. Her score was unsatisfactory.
    D. Her score was average.

49. A. Major Williams should assume control of the pilot.
    B. Major Williams should check the plane.
    C. Major Williams should assume control of the plane.
    D. Major Williams should be friends with the pilot.

50. A. He loves his father.
    B. He respects his father.
    C. He resembles his father.
    D. His father should work less.

- *Directions for questions 51-60. You will hear dialogs on the test CD. Select the correct answer A, B, C, or D and mark your answer sheet.*

51. A. The cost is ninety dollars and fifty cents.
    B. The cost is nineteen dollars and fifty cents.
    C. The cost is nine dollars and fifty cents.
    D. The cost is ninety-five dollars.

52. A. start eating
    B. start beating
    C. start erasing
    D. start drinking

53. A. They could put the packages in two trucks.
    B. They could put the packages in two troupes.
    C. They could put the packages in two groups.
    D. They could put the packages in two boxes.

54. A. The door is knocked.
B. The door is locked.
C. The door is opened.
D. The door is strong.

55. A. the least important treason
B. the least important reason
C. the most important season
D. the most important reason

56. A. She hates it. B. She likes it.
C. She is indifferent to it. D. She takes care of it.

57. A. jogging B. skating
C. playing D. driving

58. A. where he is running
B. when he will arrive
C. the reason he is running
D. when he is coming home

59. A. She publishes a magazine.
B. She is a reporter.
C. She writes stories.
D. She reads the news.

60. A. her medicines B. her instruments
C. her doctor D. her golf clubs

ECL 聽力測驗①詳解

1. (**D**) Are you getting used to the school?
你習慣學校生活了嗎？
(A) 是的，我恨它。
(B) 是的，這對我而言實在太嚴肅了。
(C) 是的，到戶外眞好。
(D) 是的，我變得習慣了。

* ***get used to*** 習慣
far〔 fɑr 〕*adv.* 很；極
serious〔ˈsɪrɪəs 〕*adj.* 嚴肅的
outside〔ˈaʊtˈsaɪd 〕*adv.* 在戶外
accustomed〔 əˈkʌstəmd 〕*adj.* 習慣的

2. (**D**) The kids can watch the movie without paying. Who can watch the movie for free?
這些小孩可以免費看電影。／誰可以免費看電影？
(A) 老人。 (B) 男人跟女人。
(C) 媽媽跟爸爸。 (D) 男孩和女孩。

* kid〔 kɪd 〕*n.* 小孩 pay〔 pe 〕*v.* 付錢
for free 免費地

3. (**B**) The girl was staring at the rainbow. What was she staring at?
這個女孩凝視著彩虹。／她凝視著什麼？
(A) 下雨。
(B) 天空中的顏色。

(C) 一個五顏六色的領結。

(D) 一位公園管理員。

＊ stare〔 stɛr 〕*v.* 凝視　rainbow〔ˈren,bo 〕*n.* 彩虹
colorful〔ˈkʌləfəl 〕*adj.* 五顏六色的
bowtie〔ˈbo,taɪ 〕*n.* 領結
ranger〔ˈrendʒə 〕*n.* 公園管理員

4. (**C**) Renee asked, "Whose jacket is this?" What did she want to know?
芮妮問：「這是誰的夾克？」／她想要知道什麼？

(A) 夾克的價錢。　(B) 掃把的所有人。
(C) 夾克的所有人。　(D) 夾克的尺寸。

＊ price〔 praɪs 〕*n.* 價格　owner〔ˈonə 〕*n.* 所有人
broom〔 brum 〕*n.* 掃帚　size〔 saɪz 〕*n.* 尺寸

5. (**A**) Penny asked Karl about the stuff on the chair. What did she ask about?
珮妮詢問卡羅有關椅子上的東西。／她問了什麼？

(A) 那些東西。　(B) 那個人。
(C) 那些寵物。　(D) 那個家庭。

＊ stuff〔 stʌf 〕*n.* 東西；原料　pet〔 pɛt 〕*n.* 寵物

6. (**C**) She is a new teacher. When did she arrive?
她是位新老師。／她什麼時候抵達的？

(A) 明天。　(B) 明年。
(C) 最近。　(D) 定期地。

＊ arrive〔 əˈraɪv 〕*v.* 抵達　recently〔ˈrisn̩tlɪ 〕*adv.* 最近
regularly〔ˈrɛgjələlɪ 〕*adv.* 定期地

7. (**D**) Did he intend to do this?
他打算這麼做嗎？

(A) 是的，他打電話來。 (B) 不，他小心地計劃著。
(C) 是的，我很驚訝。 (D) 是的，他小心地計劃著。

* intend〔ɪnˈtɛnd〕*v.* 打算做… phone〔fon〕*v.* 打電話
plan〔plæn〕*v.* 計畫 carefully〔ˈkɛrfəlɪ〕*adv.* 小心地
surprised〔səˈpraɪzd〕*adj.* 驚訝的

8. (**C**) A thief walked away with our new bike. What happened to the bike?
小偷偷走了我們的新腳踏車。／這輛腳踏車發生了什麼事？

(A) 它被塗上油漆。 (B) 它被賣掉了。
(C) 它被偷了。 (D) 它被犧牲了。

* thief〔θif〕*n.* 竊賊 ***walk away with*** 順手牽羊
bike〔baɪk〕*n.* 腳踏車 happen〔ˈhæpən〕*v.* 發生
paint〔pent〕*v.* 油漆
sell〔sɛl〕*v.* 賣（過去式及過去分詞皆爲 sold）
steal〔stil〕*v.* 偷竊（三態變化爲：steal-stole-stolen）
sacrifice〔ˈsækrəˌfaɪs〕*v.* 犧牲

9. (**D**) The surgeon said, “I don’t think your eyes need to be altered.” What does the surgeon mean by altered?
外科醫生說：「我不認爲你的眼睛需要改變。」／這名外科醫生所說的改變是什麼意思？

(A) 顏色。 (B) 徽章。
(C) 貼紙。 (D) 改變。

* surgeon〔ˈsɝdʒən〕*n.* 外科醫生 alter〔ˈɔltɚ〕*v.* 改變
mean〔min〕*v.* 意思是 color〔ˈkʌlɚ〕*v.* 染色
stare〔stɛr〕*v.* 瞪眼看 stick〔stɪk〕*v.* 刺
change〔tʃendʒ〕*v.* 改變

10. (**C**) Ms. Lily said, "I haven't seen Tina since the day before yesterday." When was the last time that Ms. Lily saw Tina?
莉莉小姐說：「我從前天就沒看到緹娜了。」／莉莉小姐最後一次看到緹娜是什麼時候？

(A) 五天前。 (B) 三天前。
(C) 兩天前。 (D) 四天前。

* since〔sɪns〕*conj.* 自從…以來
the day before yesterday 前天
last〔læst〕*adj.* 最後的　time〔taɪm〕*n.* 次
ago〔ə'go〕*adv.*（距今）…以前

11. (**B**) Cowboys travel many miles every day. How do they travel? 牛仔每天行進好幾英哩。／他們是如何行進的？

(A) 騎著熊。 (B) 騎著馬。
(C) 騎著腳踏車。 (D) 騎著牛。

* cowboy〔'kaʊ,bɔɪ〕*n.* 牛仔　travel〔'trævḷ〕*v.* 行進；旅行
mile〔maɪl〕*n.* 英哩　cow〔kaʊ〕*n.* 牛

12. (**C**) Many English words are composed of two words put together. Which of these words is made of two words?
許多英文單字，是由兩個合在一起的單字所構成的。／下列哪一個字是由兩個單字所構成的？

(A) 活動。 (B) 比較地。
(C) 豪雨。 (D) 邂逅。

* compose〔kəm'poz〕*v.* 構成 <*of*>　***put together*** 組成
movement〔'muvmənt〕*n.* 活動；移動
comparatively〔kəm'pærətɪvlɪ〕*adv.* 比較地
cloudburst〔'klaʊd,bɝst〕*n.* 豪雨
encounter〔ɪn'kaʊntɚ〕*v.* 邂逅

13. (**B**) There was an abrupt transition in temperature. What kind of transition was it?

氣溫突然轉變。／那是什麼樣的變化？

(A) 緩慢的。 (B) 突然的。 (C) 有時。 (D) 從來沒有。

* abrupt 〔əˈbrʌpt〕*adj.* 突然的
transition 〔trænˈzɪʃən〕*n.* 轉變
temperature 〔ˈtɛmprətʃɚ〕*n.* 氣溫 slow 〔slo〕*adj.* 緩慢的
sudden 〔ˈsʌdn̩〕*adj.* 突然的

14. (**A**) Have you decided when you're going to retire?

你已經決定好什麼時候退休了嗎？

(A) 我還沒決定好。 (B) 我被搞混了。
(C) 你也這麼認爲嗎？ (D) 我一點也不會打擾到你。

* decide 〔dɪˈsaɪd〕*v.* 決定 retire 〔rɪˈtaɪr〕*v.* 退休
make up *one's* ***mind*** 下定決心 yet 〔jɛt〕*adv.* 尙（未）
mix up 使…混亂 bother 〔ˈbɑðɚ〕*v.* 打擾
not at all 全然；一點也不

15. (**B**) The woman told her daughter to spread out the tablecloth on the table. What was the daughter told to do with the tablecloth?

那位女士要她的女兒把桌上的桌布攤開。／女兒被告知要把桌布怎麼樣？

(A) 熨燙。 (B) 攤開。
(C) 去把它拿來。 (D) 仔細查看它。

* daughter 〔ˈdɔtɚ〕*n.* 女兒
spread 〔sprɛd〕*v.* 攤開 ***spread out*** 攤開
tablecloth 〔ˈtebl̩ˌklɔθ〕*n.* 桌布 iron 〔ˈaɪɚn〕*v.* 熨燙
unfold 〔ʌnˈfold〕*v.* 攤開 scan 〔skæn〕*v.* 仔細查看；掃描
fetch 〔fɛtʃ〕*v.* 把…拿來

16. (**D**) Terry glanced through the novel. What did Terry do?
泰莉瀏覽了一下那本小說。／泰莉做了什麼？

(A) 她很快地吃完它。
(B) 她很快地燒完它。
(C) 她很快地把它煮好。
(D) 她很快地看了它一下。

* glance〔glæns〕*v.* 瀏覽　novel〔ˈnɑvl̩〕*n.* 小說
burn〔bɝn〕*v.* 燃燒　cook〔kuk〕*v.* 烹調；煮

17. (**B**) Joe said, "This wind is as sharp as a knife." What kind of wind is it?
喬說：「這陣風跟刀子一樣刺骨。」／那是什麼樣的風？

(A) 和風。
(B) 一陣冷風。
(C) 一點風也沒有。
(D) 一陣乾燥的風。

* wind〔wɪnd〕*n.* 風
sharp〔ʃɑrp〕*adj.* 凜冽的；刺骨的
knife〔naɪf〕*n.* 刀子
gentle〔ˈdʒɛntl̩〕*adj.* 溫和的
at all 一點也（沒有）　dry〔draɪ〕*adj.* 乾燥的

18. (**C**) Why do some men wear cologne?
爲什麼有些男人噴香水？

(A) 難看。　(B) 有難聞的臭味。
(C) 好聞。　(D) 好看。

* wear〔wɛr〕*v.* 噴（香水）；穿戴（衣物）
cologne〔kəˈlon〕*n.* 一種香水的名稱
stink〔stɪŋk〕*v.* 發臭　smell〔smɛl〕*v.* 聞起來

19. (**C**) I have a bone to pick with you.
我對你有所不滿。

(A) 去滑雪怎樣？
(B) 太棒了！我們走吧。
(C) 爲什麼？我做錯了什麼嗎？
(D) 爲什麼不再試一次？

* ***have a bone to pick with*** *sb.* 對某人不滿
ski (ski) *v.* 滑雪　terrific (tə'rɪfɪk) *adj.* 極好的
wrong (rɔŋ) *adj.* 錯誤的

20. (**B**) Why did your brother take the watch apart?
你弟弟爲什麼要把手錶給拆了？

(A) 我不知道他這樣做。
(B) 因爲好奇吧，我猜。
(C) 他會買一個好的。
(D) 我要他這麼做的。

* ***take apart*** 分解　curiosity (ˌkjurɪ'ɑsətɪ) *n.* 好奇心
out of curiosity 出於好奇心　guess (gɛs) *v.* 猜測

21. (**A**) Is the temperature going to rise today?
今天氣溫會上升嗎？

(A) 是的，大概上升十度。
(B) 是的，大概下降十度。
(C) 不，大概會上升十度。
(D) 不，大概會上升十度。

* rise (raɪz) *v.* 上升
go up 上升　about (ə'baut) *prep.* 大約
degree (dɪ'gri) *n.* 度　***go down*** 下降
climb (klaɪm) *v.* 上升

22. (**A**) Is it your favorite? 它是你最喜歡的東西嗎？

(A) 是的，我最喜歡它。

(B) 是的，我什麼都喜歡。

(C) 是的，就是藍色那個。

(D) 還不錯，不是嗎？

* favorite〔ˈfevərɪt〕*n.* 最喜愛的東西

23. (**A**) The collision was caused by the driver's blurred vision. What caused the collision?

這場碰撞是由於駕駛視線模糊所引起的。／造成碰撞的原因是什麼？

(A) 視線不良。 (B) 視線良好。

(C) 聽力好。 (D) 聽力不好。

* collision〔kəˈlɪʒən〕*n.* 碰撞；衝突

cause〔kɔz〕*v.* 導致；引起

blurred〔blɝd〕*adj.* 模糊的 vision〔ˈvɪʒən〕*n.* 視線

poor〔pʊr〕*adj.* 欠佳的 eyesight〔ˈaɪˌsaɪt〕*n.* 視線

keen〔kin〕*adj.* 敏銳的 hearing〔ˈhɪrɪŋ〕*n.* 聽力

24. (**A**) They were concerned about the fence. What concerned them?

他們很擔心籬笆。／他們擔心什麼？

(A) 保護。 (B) 完美。

(C) 原諒。 (D) 預測。

* concerned〔kənˈsɝnd〕*adj.* 擔心的

fence〔fɛns〕*n.* 籬笆 concern〔kənˈsɝn〕*v.* 使擔心

protection〔prəˈtɛkʃən〕*n.* 保護；庇護物

perfection〔pɚˈfɛkʃən〕*n.* 完美

pardon〔ˈpɑrdn̩〕*n.* 原諒

prediction〔prɪˈdɪkʃən〕*n.* 預測

25. (**C**) A lot of people like Florida's climate. What do they like? 許多人喜愛佛羅里達的氣候。／他們喜歡什麼？

(A) 那裡的人。 (B) 那裡的衣服。
(C) <u>那裡的天氣。</u> (D) 那裡的車。

* Florida〔ˈflɔrədə〕*n.* 佛羅里達
climate〔ˈklaɪmɪt〕*n.* 氣候
clothes〔kloz〕*n. pl.* 衣服 weather〔ˈwɛðɚ〕*n.* 天氣

26. (**B**) We saw the dog sinking. 我們看見這隻狗沉下去。

(A) 我們看見牠飛上去。 (B) <u>我們看見牠沉沒。</u>
(C) 我們看見牠離開。 (D) 我們看見牠升上去。

* sink〔sɪŋk〕*v.* 下沉 fly〔flaɪ〕*v.* 飛
go down 沉沒；墜落 ***go out*** 離開 ***go up*** 上升

27. (**B**) Mr. Wilson needs a lighter. 威爾森先生需要一個打火機。

(A) 他想要打架。 (B) <u>他想要生火。</u>
(C) 他想要離開。 (D) 他想要開除我們。

* lighter〔ˈlaɪtɚ〕*n.* 打火機 fight〔faɪt〕*v.* 打架
fire〔faɪr〕*n.* 火 *v.* 解僱 ***make a fire*** 生火

28. (**A**) The soldier carried out his mission.
那名士兵執行了他的任務。

(A) <u>他完成了他的任務。</u> (B) 他不服從他的任務。
(C) 他未能達成任務。 (D) 他珍惜他的任務。

* soldier〔ˈsoldʒɚ〕*n.* 士兵 ***carry out*** 完成；執行
mission〔ˈmɪʃən〕*n.* 任務
accomplish〔əˈkɑmplɪʃ〕*v.* 完成
object〔əbˈdʒɛkt〕*v.* 反對；不服 fail〔fel〕*v.* 失敗
cherish〔ˈtʃɛrɪʃ〕*v.* 珍惜

29. (**C**) The children are watching their parents cook the food.
那些小孩正看著他們的父母做飯。

(A) 這對父母正看著他們的小孩。
(B) 這對父母正和他們的小孩一起煮東西吃。
(C) 孩子們正看著他們的父母。
(D) 孩子們自己煮東西吃。

* parents (ˈpɛrənts) *n. pl.* 父母

30. (**A**) I substituted for my father when he was sick.
我在爸爸生病時代替他。

(A) 我做他的工作。 (B) 我救了他。
(C) 我喜歡他。 (D) 我為他做飯。

* substitute (ˈsʌbstəˌtjut) *v.* 代替；代理
sick (sɪk) *adj.* 生病的 save (sev) *v.* 拯救
care (kɛr) *v.* 喜歡 < *for* >

31. (**C**) When we have an assignment, we should never put off doing it.
當我們有職務在身時，絕不能拖延。

(A) 不論何時我們都應該執行它。
(B) 我們應該在有空時執行它。
(C) 我們應該馬上執行它。
(D) 我們應該把放棄它。

* assignment (əˈsaɪnmənt) *n.* 分派；職務
put off 拖延 whenever (hwɛnˈɛvɚ) *adv.* 無論何時
delay (dɪˈle) *n.* 遲延 ***without delay*** 馬上；即刻
put away 放棄

32. (**C**) It was raining almost every day last week.
上星期幾乎每天下雨。

(A) 天氣是晴天。 (B) 沒下過雨。
(C) 幾乎每天下雨。 (D) 幾乎每星期五都下雨

* almost〔'ɔl,most〕*adv.* 幾乎
last〔læst〕*adj.* 上一個的
sunny〔'sʌnɪ〕*adj.* 晴朗的 nearly〔'nɪrlɪ〕*adv.* 幾乎

33. (**C**) We were victorious because we had resolve.
我們贏了，因爲我們有決心。

(A) 我們沒嘗試過。
(B) 我們一點也不在乎。
(C) 我們沒有放棄。
(D) 我們沒有享受人生。

* victorious〔vɪk'torɪəs〕*adj.* 勝利的
resolve〔rɪ'zalv〕*n.* 決心 ***give it a try*** 嘗試
not give a damn 一點也不在乎 ***give up*** 放棄
live it up 享受人生

34. (**A**) She distributed food to the homeless.
她分送食物給無家可歸的人。

(A) 她分送食物給無家可歸的人。
(B) 她分送食物給每位老師。
(C) 她分送食物給每個家庭。
(D) 她分送食物給每隻寵物。

* distribute〔dɪ'strɪbjut〕*v.* 分送
homeless〔'homlɪs〕*adj.* 無家可歸的
the homeless 無家可歸的人 pet〔pɛt〕*n.* 寵物

35. (**B**) Jane is a good driver. 珍是位好駕駛。

(A) 她很危險。 (B) 她很小心。
(C) 她很奇怪。 (D) 她是逼不得已的。

* dangerous〔ˈdendʒərəs〕*adj.* 危險的
careful〔ˈkɛrfəl〕*adj.* 小心的
strange〔strendʒ〕*adj.* 古怪的
driven〔ˈdrɪvən〕*adj.* 逼不得已的；勢不可擋的

36. (**A**) Helen assumed responsibility for the class.
海倫負起對那個班級的責任。

(A) 她掌管那個班。
(B) 她去聯絡。
(C) 她正掌管那個班。
(D) 她吃了玉米麵包。

* assume〔əˈsjum〕*v.* 假定；承擔
responsibility〔rɪˌspɑnsəˈbɪlətɪ〕*n.* 責任
take〔tek〕*v.* 負責（班級、學科）；採取（某種行動）；吃
control〔kənˈtrol〕*n.* 控制；掌管
contact〔ˈkɑntɛkt〕*n.* 接觸；聯絡
cornbread〔ˈkɔrnˌbrɛd〕*n.* 玉米麵包

37. (**D**) The boy is departing. 那個男孩正要出發。

(A) 那個男孩跳來跳去。
(B) 那個男孩剛到。
(C) 那個男孩留在原地。
(D) 那個男孩正要離開。

* depart〔dɪˈpɑrt〕*v.* 出發；放棄 leap〔lip〕*v.* 跳躍
arrive〔əˈraɪv〕*v.* 抵達 leave〔liv〕*v.* 離開

38. (**D**) We are looking forward to meeting her.
我們正在期盼見到她。

(A) 我們很生氣看到她。 (B) 我們很厭倦看到她。
(C) 我們很厭煩看到她。 (D) 我們很渴望看到她。

* ***look forward to*** 盼望 meet (mit) *v.* 會見；遇見
angry ('æŋgrɪ) *adj.* 生氣的
tired (taɪrd) *adj.* 疲倦的；厭煩的
eager ('igɚ) *adj.* 渴望的

39. (**D**) The weather report predicts no precipitation for tomorrow. 氣象報告預測明天不會下雨。

(A) 明天不會是個晴朗的日子。
(B) 明天不會是晴天。
(C) 明天不會颳風。
(D) 明天不會下雨。

* weather ('wɛðɚ) *n.* 天氣；氣象 report (rɪ'port) *n.* 報告
weather report 天氣預告；氣象報告
predict (prɪ'dɪkt) *v.* 預報；預測
precipitation (prɪˌsɪpə'teʃən) *n.* 降雨；下雪
fine (faɪn) *adj.* 晴朗的
windy ('wɪndɪ) *adj.* 颳風的；多風的

40. (**C**) Lisa is not in the classroom because she has been sick for three weeks.
麗莎不在教室裡，因爲她已經病了三個星期。

(A) 麗莎很累。 (B) 麗莎很淘氣。
(C) 麗莎生病了。 (D) 麗莎已經去拜訪某人了。

* tired ('taɪrd) *adj.* 累的 naughty ('nɔtɪ) *adj.* 淘氣的
ill (ɪl) *adj.* 生病的 visit ('vɪzɪt) *v.* 拜訪

41. (**C**) The man has gone back to his city for good.
這名男子回到他的城市，而且不再離開。

(A) 他去拿東西。
(B) 他的背很健康。
(C) 他永遠地離開了。
(D) 他有座好城市。

* ***for good*** 永遠地　goods (gudz) *n.* 物品；財產
back (bæk) *n.* 背部
leave (liv) *v.* 離開（過去式與過去分詞皆爲 left）
permanently (ˈpɝmənəntlɪ) *adv.* 永久地

42. (**B**) Some people like to argue all the time.
有些人喜歡一直爭論。

(A) 有些人講太多話。
(B) 他們喜歡發表言論來支持或反對某些事。
(C) 他們說得太快了。
(D) 有些人是瘋狂的。

* argue (ˈɑrgjʊ) *v.* 爭論　***all the time*** 一直；經常
for (fɔr) *prep.* 支持　against (əˈgɛnst) *prep.* 反對
crazy (ˈkrezɪ) *adj.* 瘋狂的

43. (**B**) Sandy is a well-behaved girl.
珊蒂是個循規蹈矩的女孩。

(A) 她很漂亮。　(B) 她很有禮貌。
(C) 她很幼稚。　(D) 她很苗條。

* well-behaved (ˈwɛlbɪˈhevd) *adj.* 循規蹈矩的
beautiful (ˈbjutəfəl) *adj.* 美麗的
polite (pəˈlaɪt) *adj.* 有禮貌的
childish (ˈtʃaɪldɪʃ) *adj.* 幼稚的　thin (θɪn) *adj.* 苗條的

44. (**A**) The man will cooperate with the authorities.
這個人將會和有關當局合作。

(A) 這個人會幫助警察。
(B) 這個人不會聽警察的話。
(C) 這個人會和警察對抗。
(D) 這個人會和警察在一起。

* cooperate〔ko'ɑpə,ret〕*v.* 合作
authority〔ə'θɔrətɪ〕*n.* 有關當局　police〔pə'lis〕*n.* 警察
listen〔'lɪsn̩〕*v.* 聽　fight〔faɪt〕*v.* 打架；對抗
against〔ə'gɛnst〕*prep.* 反對；反抗

45. (**B**) Most accidents take place in heavy traffic.
大部份的車禍都發生在交通繁忙時。

(A) 車子越重，就會發生越多交通事故。
(B) 交通事故發生於車流量大時。
(C) 很多交通事故發生在下大雨時。
(D) 車流量大時，交通事故會很嚴重。

* accident〔'æksədənt〕*n.* 意外事故；車禍
take place 發生　heavy〔'hɛvɪ〕*adj.* 繁忙的；重的
heavy traffic 交通繁忙時刻　occur〔ə'kɝ〕*v.* 發生
heavily〔'hɛvɪlɪ〕*adv.* 猛烈地；大大地
vehicle〔'viɪkl̩〕*n.* 車輛

46. (**B**) The vehicle is covered with dust.
這部車上滿是灰塵。

(A) 它很乾淨。　(B) 它不是乾淨的。
(C) 它是有光澤的。　(D) 它是新的。

* cover〔'kʌvɚ〕*v.* 覆蓋
dust〔dʌst〕*n.* 灰塵　clean〔klin〕*adj.* 乾淨的
polished〔'pɑlɪʃt〕*adj.* 有光澤的

47. (**D**) The professor wanted to leave out the old subject.
這名教授想要省略這個古老的議題。

(A) 他想要介紹這個議題。
(B) 他想要洩漏這個問題。
(C) 他想討論這個議題。
(D) 他想省略這個議題。

* professor (prə'fɛsɚ) *n.* 教授　***leave out*** 省略
subject ('sʌbdʒɪkt) *n.* 議題；問題
recommend (ˌrɛkə'mɛnd) *v.* 介紹；推薦
vomit ('vɑmɪt) *v.* 嘔吐；洩漏
discuss (dɪ'skʌs) *v.* 討論　omit (o'mɪt) *v.* 省略

48. (**C**) Melinda failed her last examination.
米蘭達上次的考試不及格。

(A) 她的成績令人滿意。
(B) 她的分數很高。
(C) 她的成績無法令人滿意。
(D) 她的成績很普通。

* fail (fel) *v.* 不及格
examination (ɪgˌzæmə'neʃən) *n.* 考試
score (skor) *n.* 考試成績；分數
satisfactory (ˌsætɪs'fæktərɪ) *adj.* 令人滿意的
unsatisfactory (ˌʌnsætɪs'fæktərɪ) *adj.* 無法令人滿意的
average ('ævərɪdʒ) *adj.* 普通的

49. (**C**) The captain told Major Williams to take over the airplane. 機長要求威廉斯少校接管這架飛機。

(A) 威廉斯少校應該要負起監督飛行員的責任。
(B) 威廉斯少校應該檢查這架飛機。

(C) 威廉斯少校應該要負起控制這架飛機的責任。

(D) 威廉斯少校應該和飛行員交朋友。

* captain (ˈkæptən) *n.* 機長　major (ˈmedʒɚ) *n.* 少校
take over 接管　airplane (ˈɛr,plen) *n.* 飛機
assume (əˈsum) *v.* 擔負（責任）
control (kənˈtrol) *n.* 控制；監督
pilot (ˈpaɪlət) *n.* 駕駛員；飛行員　check (tʃɛk) *v.* 檢查
plane (plen) *n.* 飛機　***be friends with*** 與…做朋友

50. (**C**) Dylan looks like his father.
迪倫長得像他父親。

(A) 他愛他父親。　(B) 他尊敬他父親。

(C) 他酷似他父親。　(D) 他父親應該減少工作量。

* ***look like*** 長得像　respect (rɪˈspɛkt) *v.* 尊敬
resemble (rɪˈzɛmbḷ) *v.* 相似　less (lɛs) *pron.* 較少量

51. (**B**) M：What is the bus fare to Miami?
W：$19.50.
How much does it cost to get to Miami by bus?
男：到邁阿密的車資是多少？
女：十九塊五十分。
搭客運去邁阿密要多少錢？

(A) 要花九十塊五十分。

(B) 要花十九塊五十分。

(C) 要花九塊五十分。

(D) 要花九十五塊。

* fare (fɛr) *n.* 車資　Miami (maɪˈæmɪ) *n.* 邁阿密
cost (kɔst) *v.* 花費　ninety (ˈnaɪntɪ) *adj.* 九十的
cent (sɛnt) *n.* 分　nineteen (ˈnaɪnˈtin) *adj.* 十九的
fifty (ˈfɪftɪ) *adj.* 五十的

52. (**A**) M：Do you feel ready? I really want to try those tomatoes.

W：Sure. My mouth is watering already.

What are the boy and the girl ready to do?

男：妳準備好了嗎？我眞的想試試這些蕃茄。

女：當然。我已經開始流口水了。

這個男孩跟女孩準備好要做什麼？

(A) 開始吃東西。　(B) 開始打。

(C) 開始擦掉。　(D) 開始喝東西。

* ready〔ˈrɛdɪ〕*adj.* 準備好的　tomato〔təˈmeto〕*n.* 番茄
sure〔ʃʊr〕*adv.* 當然　water〔ˈwɑtɚ〕*v.* 流口水
beat〔bit〕*v.* 打；擊敗　erase〔ɪˈres〕*v.* 擦掉

53. (**C**) W：How can we carry the boxes from the truck?

M：We could separate the heavy ones from the light ones.

What did the boy say?

女：我們要怎樣把箱子從貨車上搬下來？

男：我們可以把重的跟輕的分開。

那個男孩說了什麼？

(A) 他們可以把這些包裹放進兩部貨車裡。

(B) 他們可以把這些包裹分成兩隊。

(C) 他們可以把這些包裹分成兩類。

(D) 他們可以把這些包裹分成兩箱。

* carry〔ˈkærɪ〕*v.* 搬運　truck〔trʌk〕*n.* 貨車
separate〔ˈsɛpəˌret〕*v.* 分開　heavy〔ˈhɛvɪ〕*adj.* 重的
light〔laɪt〕*adj.* 輕的　package〔ˈpækɪdʒ〕*n.* 包裹
troupe〔trup〕*n.* 一隊　group〔grup〕*n.* 群；類

54. (**B**) W：It's cold. Why can't you let us in?
M：We forgot the key.
Why can't the girl and the boy go in?
女：好冷。爲什麼不讓我們進去？
男：因爲我們忘了帶鑰匙。
爲什麼女孩跟男孩進不去？

(A) 有人在敲門。 (B) 門被鎖住了。
(C) 門是開的。 (D) 門很堅固。

* knock〔nɑk〕*v.* 敲擊 lock〔lɑk〕*v.* 上鎖
strong〔strɔŋ〕*adj.* 堅固的

55. (**D**) W：What is the prime reason for doing this?
M：I'm not aware of it.
What is it that the man didn't know?
女：這樣做的主要原因是什麼？
男：我也不知道。
這位男士不知道什麼事？

(A) 最不重要的叛亂。 (B) 最不重要的理由。
(C) 最重要的季節。 (D) 最重要的理由。

* prime〔praɪm〕*adj.* 主要的 reason〔'rizn̩〕*n.* 原因
aware〔ə'wɛr〕*adj.* 知道的 least〔list〕*adv.* 最不
treason〔'trizn̩〕*n.* 叛亂 season〔'sizn̩〕*n.* 季節

56. (**B**) M：Have you seen my new cat?
W：Yes, it is very cute.
How does the woman feel about the cat?
男：妳看過我新養的貓了嗎？
女：看過了，它非常可愛。

這位女士對那隻貓的感覺如何？

(A) 她討厭它。　(B) 她喜歡它。
(C) 她不在乎它。　(D) 她照顧它。

＊ cute〔kjut〕*adj.* 可愛的
indifferent〔ɪnˈdɪfrənt〕*adj.* 漠不關心的；不在乎的
take care of 照顧

57. (D) M：Did Jenny use the freeway?
W：Yes, she did.
What was Jenny doing?
男：珍妮有走高速公路嗎？
女：有的。
珍妮正在做什麼？

(A) 慢跑。　(B) 溜冰。
(C) 玩。　(D) 開車。

＊ freeway〔ˈfriˌwe〕*n.* 高速公路　jog〔dʒɑg〕*v.* 慢跑
skate〔sket〕*v.* 溜冰

58. (C) M：Look, Maurice is running down the block.
W：Why would he do that?
What does the woman want to know?
男：看，摩里斯從那個街區跑下來。
女：他爲什麼要這麼做？
這位女士想知道什麼？

(A) 他在哪裡跑步。　(B) 他什麼時候會到。
(C) 他奔跑的原因。　(D) 他什麼時候回家。

＊ ***run down*** 跑下來　block〔blɑk〕*n.* 街區
arrive〔əˈraɪv〕*v.* 抵達

59. (**C**) W：What does Miss Jane do for a living?
M：She writes romances.
What does Miss Jane do?
女：珍小姐是以什麼維生？
男：她寫愛情小說。
珍小姐是做什麼的？

(A) 她出版了一本雜誌。
(B) 她是位新聞記者。
(C) 她撰寫故事。
(D) 她閱讀新聞。

* living〔ˈlɪvɪŋ〕*n.* 生計
romance〔roˈmæns〕*n.* 愛情小說
publish〔ˈpʌblɪʃ〕*v.* 出版
magazine〔ˈmægəˌzin〕*n.* 雜誌
reporter〔rɪˈportɚ〕*n.* 新聞記者　　news〔njuz〕*n.* 新聞

60. (**B**) M：Nurse, can't you help me?
W：I'm sorry. I can't. I don't have my equipment.
What does the nurse need?
男：護士小姐，妳不能幫幫我嗎？
女：對不起。我幫不上忙。我沒有帶我的器材。
這位護士需要什麼？

(A) 她的藥。　　(B) 她的工具。
(C) 她的醫生。　　(D) 她的高爾夫球俱樂部。

* nurse〔nɝs〕*n.* 護士
equipment〔ɪˈkwɪpmənt〕*n.* 設備；器材
medicine〔ˈmɛdəsn̩〕*n.* 藥
instrument〔ˈɪnstrəmənt〕*n.* 儀器；工具
golf〔gɑlf〕*n.* 高爾夫球　　club〔klʌb〕*n.* 俱樂部

LISTENING TEST ②

- *Directions for questions 1-25. You will hear questions on the test CD. Select the one item A, B, C or D which answers the question correctly, and mark your answer sheet.*

1. A. at the newsroom B. at the restaurant
   C. at the hospital D. at the store

2. A. some time ago B. immediately
   C. in a few minutes D. as soon as he can

3. A. stand on the chair B. move across the room
   C. buy a ticket D. say something aloud

4. A. She produces the machines.
   B. She controls the machines.
   C. She controls the department.
   D. She controls the product line.

5. A. What's the question? Of course, it's Smith.
   B. I don't know, Sir. My father didn't tell me.
   C. John, sir.
   D. Mary, I guess.

6. A. in a small city B. in a tall city
   C. in a small pity D. on a farm

7. A. It sounds pretty expensive.
   B. It looks pretty nice. C. It took three hours.
   D. It looks pretty deep.

8. A. about a kilogram
   B. one minute
   C. very far
   D. about two days by car

9. A. at home
   B. at the zoo
   C. at school
   D. at the club

10. A. No, she didn't disturb them.
    B. No, she disturbed him.
    C. No, she disturbed her.
    D. No, she didn't disturb him.

11. A. He will look for new work.
    B. He will quit his job.
    C. He will be fired from his job.
    D. He will be taught how to do the work.

12. A. Yes, here's my credit card.
    B. In two weeks.
    C. No, that's all. Thanks.
    D. I like it.

13. A. She's going to take up cooking classes.
    B. She's going away for a year.
    C. She's going to give him the business.
    D. She's going to study business.

14. A. seventy
    B. sixty
    C. twenty
    D. sixteen

15. A. because she was sick
    B. because she had to
    C. because of the heat
    D. because she wanted to be in a hot place

16. A. Yes, I came just now.
    B. Sorry to have kept you waiting.
    C. No, I just got here.
    D. I was caught in a traffic jam.

17. A. because they weren't clean
    B. because they were clean
    C. because she wanted a refund
    D. because they were expensive

18. A. get some credit B. get some money
    C. get some Mickey D. get some honey

19. A. a rat B. a bat
    C. a cat D. a hat

20. A. I left it on the chair in the train station.
    B. Reading and working in my office.
    C. It cost me over one hundred dollars.
    D. The supermarket is across the road.

21. A. at 11:00. B. at 8:00.
    C. at 10:00. D. at 9:00.

22. A. I want to work at the craft show this year.
    B. Tom is always building models.
    C. I like painting and fishing.
    D. I work five days a week.

23. A. small pieces of metal
    B. small pieces of wood
    C. small pieces of particles
    D. small pieces of food

24. A. contempt
    B. noon
    C. chocolate
    D. breakfast

25. A. He was doing the investigation.
    B. He was a merchant.
    C. He was a detective.
    D. He was a discoverer.

● *Directions for questions 26-50. You will hear statements on the test CD. Select the one answer A, B, C, or D which comes closest to the meaning of the statement and mark your answer sheet.*

26. A. It isn't boring.
    B. It isn't interesting.
    C. It is very short.
    D. It's exciting.

27. A. She went to bed.
    B. She didn't tell a lie.
    C. She told the truth.
    D. She didn't tell the truth.

28. A. He thought the man acted knowingly.
    B. He guessed the man acted seemingly.
    C. He proclaimed the man acted currently.
    D. He thought the man acted unconsciously.

29. A. She loves her supervisor.
    B. She can't tolerate her supervisor.
    C. She fears her supervisor.
    D. She likes her supervisor.

30. A. It's satisfactory to her.
    B. It's prosperous to her.
    C. It's surplus to her.
    D. It's previous to her

31. A. He doesn't care about the strategy.
    B. He rejects the strategy.
    C. He accepts the strategy.
    D. He doesn't like the strategy.

32. A. The party started at 9:00.
    B. The party was interrupted at 9:00.
    C. The party ended at 9:00.
    D. The party was boring by 9:00.

33. A. She asked me to move the plane.
    B. She asked me to walk toward the front.
    C. She asked me to sit down.
    D. She asked me to walk toward the back.

34. A. He had to admire the customs.
    B. He had to adjust to the customs.
    C. He had to adjust the customs.
    D. He had to adorn to the customs.

35. A. Sam is going to be a soccer player.
    B. Sam is going to be a teacher.
    C. Sam is going to be a parent.
    D. Sam is going to be an accountant.

36. A. I can't see very well.
    B. I can see very well.
    C. I can smell very well.
    D. I can't smell very well.

37. A. It was a dry day.
    B. It was a damp day.
    C. It was a long day.
    D. It was a typical day.

38. A. He boarded the bus.
    B. He waited for the bus.
    C. He missed the bus.
    D. He stood up on the bus.

39. A. Both of them speak French.
    B. Eric speaks French; Tom doesn't.
    C. Neither of them speaks French.
    D. Tom speaks French; Eric doesn't.

40. A. She was told to ignore it.
    B. She was told to consider it.
    C. She was considering to tell it.
    D. She was told to forget it.

41. A. He visited a business area.
    B. He visited a campus.
    C. He visited a hospital.
    D. He visited a housing area.

42. A. Don't put up with poor men.
    B. Don't look up to poor men.
    C. Don't look down upon poor men.
    D. Don't look for poor men.

43. A. The house is opposite the bookstore.
    B. The house is around the corner from the bookstore.
    C. The house is opposite the hotel.
    D. The house is opposite the bar.

44. A. The weather is warm today.
    B. The weather is better today.
    C. The weather is the same.
    D. The weather isn't so good today.

45. A. I suddenly reminded her face.
    B. I suddenly ramified her race.
    C. I suddenly remembered her face.
    D. I suddenly reported her face.

46. A. It is the sight rise.
    B. It is the night sign.
    C. It is the right size.
    D. It is the wrong side.

47. A. They have been here only five minutes.
    B. They have been here over five minutes.
    C. They have been here over five days.
    D. They have been here only five hours.

48. A. The clouds were clear last night.
    B. The clouds came last night.
    C. The clouds were dancing last night.
    D. The clouds went home last night.

49. A. He mailed a letter.
    B. He gave his brother a gift.
    C. He received a letter from his brother.
    D. He sent someone to give his brother a letter.

50. A. Be careful before you drive.
    B. Drive on the highway.
    C. Be sure to look around.
    D. Use your car.

● *Directions for questions 51-60. You will hear dialogs on the test CD. Select the correct answer A, B, C, or D and mark your answer sheet.*

51. A. drop down　　B. drop up
    C. drop in　　D. drop out

52. A. Jerry is a philosopher.
    B. Taking pictures is Jerry's duty.
    C. Jerry is responsible for collecting pictures.
    D. Jerry's responsibility is to travel around.

53. A. He wants to ride the bike.
    B. He wants to drive the car.
    C. He wants to drive the war.
    D. He wants to drive over the tar.

54. A. at the department store
B. on the border
C. on the corner
D. at the post office

55. A. Are they wearing anything?
B. Are they going anywhere?
C. Are they wealthy families?
D. Are they worth anything?

56. A. Places are being saved for them.
B. They are too late.
C. They can't be seated.
D. The movie is finished.

57. A. behind the woman
B. at the next table
C. next to the woman
D. in front of the man

58. A. down
B. a money order
C. a post office
D. some mail

59. A. The lady couldn't pay the bill.
B. The lady paid by credit card.
C. The lady was waiting for her friend.
D. The lady gave him a tip.

60. A. It was stolen.
B. It was wrecked.
C. It was repaired.
D. It was taken away.

ECL 聽力測驗②詳解

1. (**D**) Where did she buy the pen?
她在哪裡買這支筆？
(A) 在新聞編輯室。 (B) 在餐廳。
(C) 在醫院。 (D) 在店裡。
* newsroom ('njuzrum) *n.* 新聞編輯室
restaurant ('rɛstərənt) *n.* 餐廳
hospital ('hɑspɪtl̩) *n.* 醫院

2. (**B**) Andy said, "It's 8 a.m., and I'm leaving now." When did he leave?
安迪說：「已經八點了，我現在要走了。」／安迪什麼時候離開的？
(A) 一段時間以前。 (B) 立刻。
(C) 在幾分鐘內。 (D) 儘快。
* immediately (ɪ'midɪɪtlɪ) *adv.* 立刻
as soon as** one **can 儘快

3. (**B**) Uncle John walked over to the chair. What did he do?
約翰叔叔走到椅子那裡去。／他做了什麼？
(A) 站在椅子上。
(B) 到房間的另一邊去。
(C) 買一張票。
(D) 大聲說某件事。
* across (ə'krɔs) *adv.* 從一邊到另一邊
ticket ('tɪkɪt) *n.* 票 aloud (ə'laud) *adv.* 大聲地

4. (**B**) Mrs. Lyndon's job is to watch over the machine. What does Mrs. Lyndon do?
林頓太太的工作是監督機器。／林頓太太是做什麼的？
(A) 她生產機械。 (B) 她管理機械。
(C) 她管理這個部門。 (D) 她管理這條產品線。

* ***watch over*** 監視；保護 machine〔 mə'ʃin 〕*n.* 機器
produce〔 prə'djus 〕*v.* 生產
control〔 kən'trol 〕*v.* 管理
department〔 dɪ'pɑrtmənt 〕*n.* 部門
product line 產品線

5. (**C**) What is your first name, Smith?
史密斯，你的名字叫什麼？
(A) 有什麼問題？當然是叫史密斯。
(B) 老師，我不知道。我父親沒有告訴我。
(C) 老師，我叫約翰。
(D) 我猜是瑪莉。

* ***first name*** 名字 question〔 'kwɛstʃən 〕*n.* 問題
guess〔 gɛs 〕*v.* 猜

6. (**A**) After traveling awhile, Ann stopped to eat in a town. Where did she stop?
在旅行一會兒之後，安在一個城鎮停下來吃東西。／她停在哪裡？
(A) 在一個小城市。 (B) 在一個很高的城市。
(C) 在一個小憐憫。 (D) 在農場裡。

* awhile〔 ə'hwaɪl 〕*adv.* 一會兒
town〔 taʊn 〕*n.* 鎮；市；城 tall〔 tɔl 〕*adj.* 突然的
pity〔 'pɪtɪ 〕*n.* 憐憫

7. (**B**) Jane asked, "How's the weather?" How should you answer her question?
珍問：「天氣怎麼樣？」／你應該如何回答她的問題？

(A) 聽起來很貴。
(B) 看起來很好。
(C) 要三個小時。
(D) 看起來很深。

* pretty〔'prɪtɪ〕*adv.* 相當；頗；非常
expensive〔ɪk'spɛnsɪv〕*adj.* 昂貴的
deep〔dip〕*adj.* 深的

8. (**D**) How long does it take to go from New York to Miami?
從紐約到邁阿密要多久？

(A) 大約一公斤。 (B) 一分鐘。
(C) 非常遠。 (D) 開車大約要兩天。

* kilogram〔'kɪlə,græm〕*n.* 公斤

9. (**D**) The airmen decided to have their celebration at the club where they will have more room for dancing. Where will they have more room?
那些空軍決定在俱樂部舉辦慶祝會，因為那裡有比較多空間可以跳舞。／他們在哪裡有比較多空間？

(A) 家裡。 (B) 動物園裡。
(C) 學校裡。 (D) 俱樂部裡。

* airman〔'ɛrmən〕*n.* 空軍士兵 decide〔dɪ'saɪd〕*v.* 決定
celebration〔,sɛlə'breʃən〕*n.* 慶祝
club〔klʌb〕*n.* 俱樂部
room〔rum〕*n.* 空間

10. (**D**) Did she bother Mr. Jane when she called?

當她打電話來時有打擾到珍先生嗎？

(A) 不，她沒有打擾到他們。

(B) 不，她打擾到他。

(C) 不，她打擾她。

(D) 不，她沒有打擾他。

* bother [ˈbɑðɚ] *v.* 打擾

disturb [dɪˈstɝb] *v.* 擾亂

11. (**D**) Alex will be trained to do this work. What will happen to Alex?

艾力克斯會被訓練去做這項工作。／艾力克斯會怎樣？

(A) 他會去找新工作。

(B) 他會辭職。

(C) 他會被開除。

(D) 他會被教導如何做這項工作。

* train [tren] *v.* 訓練　　***look for*** 尋找

quit [kwɪt] *v.* 停止；放棄

quit one's job 辭職　　fire [faɪr] *v.* 開除

12. (**A**) Do you want to charge it?

你要付帳嗎？

(A) 是的，這是我的信用卡。

(B) 兩個星期內。

(C) 不，那就是全部。謝謝。

(D) 我喜歡。

* charge [tʃardʒ] *v.* 付帳　　***credit card*** 信用卡

13. (**D**) She is going to take up business this year. What is she going to do?
她今年要上商業課程。／她將做什麼？
(A) 她將上烹飪課程。 (B) 她將離開一年。
(C) 她將給他那筆生意。 (D) 她將研習商業課程。
* ***take up*** 上課 business〔ˈbɪznɪs〕*n.* 商業；生意
go away 離開

14. (**B**) Sixty girls attended the beach party last Thursday. How many were at the party?
上星期四有六十個女孩參加海灘派對。／派對有多少人？
(A) 七十個。 (B) 六十個。
(C) 二十個。 (D) 十六個。
* attend〔əˈtɛnd〕*v.* 參加

15. (**C**) Since it was so hot, she stayed at home. Why did she remain at home?
因為天氣很熱，所以她待在家裡。／她為何留在家裡？
(A) 因為她生病了。 (B) 因為她必須要待在家裡。
(C) 因為炎熱。 (D) 因為她想要待在熱的地方。
* remain〔rɪˈmen〕*v.* 留下 heat〔hit〕*n.* 炎熱

16. (**C**) Hello! Have you been waiting long?
哈囉！你已經等很久了嗎？
(A) 是的，我現在才剛到。
(B) 抱歉，讓你久等了。
(C) 不，我剛到這裡。
(D) 我碰到大塞車了。
* ***traffic jam*** 塞車

17. (**A**) Why did Selena wash her clothes?
瑟琳娜爲什麼要洗她的衣服？

(A) 因爲它們不乾淨。 (B) 因爲它們是乾淨的。
(C) 因爲她想要拿到退款。 (D) 因爲它們很貴。

* refund〔ˈriˌfʌnd〕*n.* 退款
expensive〔ɪkˈspɛnsɪv〕*adj.* 昂貴的

18. (**B**) The girl said "I want to cash my check." What did she want to do?
那個女孩說：「我想要兌現我的支票。」／她想要做什麼？

(A) 得到一些信用貸款。 (B) 拿一些錢。
(C) 拿一些米奇。 (D) 拿一些蜂蜜。

* cash〔kæʃ〕*v.* 把（支票）兌現 check〔tʃɛk〕*n.* 支票
credit〔ˈkrɛdɪt〕*n.* 信用貸款；信譽

19. (**D**) Jane wanted something to cover her head. What did Jane want? 珍想要戴個東西在頭上。／珍想要什麼？

(A) 一隻老鼠。 (B) 一隻蝙蝠。
(C) 一隻貓。 (D) 一頂帽子。

* cover〔ˈkʌvɚ〕*v.* 戴上
rat〔ræt〕*n.* 鼠 bat〔bæt〕*n.* 蝙蝠

20. (**B**) How did you spend your weekend?
你怎麼過你的週末？

(A) 我把它留在火車站的椅子上。
(B) 在我的辦公室裡面讀書和工作。
(C) 它花了我一百多塊錢。
(D) 過了馬路就是超級市場。

* leave〔liv〕*v.* 遺留；忘記帶走 ***train station*** 火車站

21. (**A**) Miss Jenny usually goes to sleep at 11:00. Last night she went to bed at 8:00. What time does Miss Jenny usually go to bed?

珍妮小姐通常十一點睡覺。昨晚她在八點鐘上床睡覺。／珍妮小姐通常幾點睡覺？

(A) 十一點。 (B) 八點。
(C) 十點。 (D) 九點。

22. (**C**) What hobbies do you have? 你有什麼嗜好？

(A) 我今年想去飛機展覽會工作。
(B) 湯姆總是在建造模型。
(C) 我喜歡畫畫和釣魚。
(D) 我一週工作五天。

* hobby〔ˈhɑbɪ〕*n.* 興趣；嗜好
craft〔kræft〕*n.* 飛機 show〔ʃo〕*n.* 展覽會
model〔ˈmɑdl̩〕*n.* 模型 painting〔ˈpentɪŋ〕*n.* 畫畫

23. (**A**) Particles of iron were discovered in the water. What was found in the water?

在水裡發現了鐵砂。／在水裡找到了什麼？

(A) 小塊的金屬。 (B) 小塊的木頭。
(C) 小塊的顆粒。 (D) 小塊的食物。

* particle〔ˈpɑrtɪkl̩〕*n.* 顆粒 iron〔ˈaɪɚn〕*n.* 鐵
discover〔dɪˈskʌvɚ〕*v.* 發現 piece〔pis〕*n.* 片；塊
metal〔ˈmɛtl̩〕*n.* 金屬 wood〔wʊd〕*n.* 木材

24. (**D**) Which of these is a meal? 以下何者是正餐？

(A) 輕視。 (B) 中午。
(C) 巧克力。 (D) 早餐。

* meal〔mil〕*n.* 餐；飯 contempt〔kənˈtɛmpt〕*n.* 輕視

25. (D) The Portuguese naval explorer Vasco da Gama was the first to reach India from Europe. What was Vasco da Gama?
葡萄牙海軍的探險者達迦瑪是第一個從歐洲抵達印度的人。／達迦瑪是什麼樣的人？

(A) 他在做調查的工作。 (B) 他是一位商人。
(C) 他是一位偵探。 (D) 他是一位發現者。

* Portuguese〔'portʃə,giz〕*adj.* 葡萄牙的
naval〔'nevḷ〕*adj.* 海軍的
explorer〔ɪk'splorɚ〕*n.* 探險家
Vasco da Gama 達迦瑪【1469-1524；葡萄牙航海家】
investigation〔ɪn,vɛstə'geʃən〕*n.* 調查
merchant〔'mɝtʃənt〕*n.* 商人
detective〔dɪ'tɛktɪv〕*n.* 偵探
discoverer〔dɪs'kʌvərɚ〕*n.* 發現者

26. (B) The article is extremely dull.
這篇文章極度無聊。

(A) 它不無聊。 (B) 它很無趣。
(C) 它非常短。 (D) 它很刺激。

* extremely〔ɪk'strimlɪ〕*adv.* 極度地
dull〔dʌl〕*adj.* 無聊的

27. (D) The big girl lied. 那個年長的女孩說謊。

(A) 她上床睡覺。 (B) 她沒有說謊。
(C) 她說了實話。 (D) 她沒有說實話。

* big〔bɪg〕*adj.* 年長的
lie〔laɪ〕*v.* 說謊【三態變化爲：lie-lied-lied】
truth〔truθ〕*n.* 事實

28. (**A**) The judge declared that the man's actions were deliberate. 法官表示那個男人的行動是有計畫的。

(A) <u>他認爲那個男人是故意地這樣做。</u>
(B) 他猜那個男人是表面上這樣做。
(C) 他宣佈那個男人是普遍地這樣做。
(D) 他認爲那個男人是無意識地這樣做。

* judge〔dʒʌdʒ〕*n.* 法官 declare〔dɪ'klɛr〕*v.* 表示；聲稱
deliberate〔dɪ'lɪbə,ret〕*adj.* 故意的；有計畫的
knowingly〔'noɪŋlɪ〕*adv.* 故意地
seemingly〔'simɪŋlɪ〕*adv.* 表面上
proclaim〔pro'klem〕*v.* 宣佈
currently〔'kɝəntlɪ〕*adv.* 普遍地
unconsciously〔ʌn'kɑnʃəslɪ〕*adv.* 不知不覺地

29. (**B**) Melinda can't stand her supervisor.
梅玲達不能忍受她的主管。

(A) 她愛她的主管。 (B) <u>她不能忍受她的主管。</u>
(C) 她害怕她的主管。 (D) 她喜歡她的主管。

* stand〔stænd〕*v.* 忍受 supervisor〔,supə'vaɪzə〕*n.* 上司
tolerate〔'tɑlə,ret〕*v.* 容忍

30. (**A**) What he did was quite good enough for her.
他所做的事令她非常滿意。

(A) <u>對她來說很滿意。</u> (B) 對她來說很成功。
(C) 對她來說是剩餘的。 (D) 那在她之前。

* quite〔kwaɪt〕*adv.* 相當
satisfactory〔,sætɪs'fæktərɪ〕*adj.* 令人滿意的
prosperous〔'prɑspərəs〕*adj.* 成功的；茂盛的
surplus〔'sɝplʌs〕*adj.* 剩餘的
previous〔'privɪəs〕*adj.* 在前的

31. (**C**) The general says that he approves the strategy.
將軍說他同意這項策略。

(A) 他不在乎這項策略。
(B) 他不同意這項策略。
(C) <u>他接受這項策略。</u>
(D) 他不喜歡這項策略。

* general〔ˈdʒɛnərəl〕*n.* 將軍
approve〔əˈpruv〕*v.* 同意；贊同
strategy〔ˈstrætədʒɪ〕*n.* 戰略
reject〔rɪˈdʒɛkt〕*v.* 不同意　　accept〔əkˈsɛpt〕*v.* 接受

32. (**C**) Everyone left the party at nine o'clock.
每個人都在九點離開宴會。

(A) 這宴會在九點鐘開始。
(B) 這宴會在九點鐘被中斷。
(C) <u>這宴會在九點鐘結束。</u>
(D) 這個宴會到九點鐘以前都很無趣。

* interrupt〔ˌɪntəˈrʌpt〕*v.* 中斷

33. (**B**) The flight attendant asked me to please move forward in the aircraft.
這空服員請我在機艙中往前移動。

(A) 她要求我移動飛機。　　(B) <u>她要我向前走。</u>
(C) 她要我坐下。　　(D) 她要我向後走。

* flight〔flaɪt〕*n.* 班機　　attendant〔əˈtɛndənt〕*n.* 服務生
forward〔ˈfɔrwɚd〕*adv.* 向前
aircraft〔ˈɛrˌkræft〕*n.* 飛機　　plane〔plen〕*n.* 飛機
toward〔təˈwɔrd〕*prep.* 關於；朝向
front〔frʌnt〕*n.* 前面

34. (**B**) The foreigner had to get used to the culture.
外國人必須要逐漸習慣這個文化。

(A) 他必須要仰慕這些習俗。
(B) <u>他必須要適應這些習俗。</u>
(C) 他必須要調整這些習俗。
(D) 他必須要裝飾這些習俗。

* foreigner〔ˈfɔrɪnɚ〕*n.* 外國人　　***get used to*** 逐漸習慣
admire〔ədˈmaɪr〕*v.* 欽佩　　custom〔ˈkʌstəm〕*n.* 習俗
adjust〔əˈdʒʌst〕*v.* 適應；調整
adorn〔əˈdɔrn〕*v.* 裝飾

35. (**B**) Sam wants to be a soccer player, but his parents want him to be a teacher. He always obeys his parents.
山姆想要成爲一位足球員，但是他的父母要他當老師。他總是順從他的父母。

(A) 山姆會成爲足球員。
(B) <u>山姆會成爲老師。</u>
(C) 山姆將爲人父母。
(D) 山姆會成爲會計師。

* soccer〔ˈsɑkɚ〕*n.* 足球　　obey〔oˈbe〕*v.* 順從
accountant〔əˈkaʊntənt〕*n.* 會計師

36. (**A**) My eyesight is weak.
我的視力不太好。

(A) <u>我看不大清楚。</u>　　(B) 我看得很清楚。
(C) 我的嗅覺很好。　　(D) 我的嗅覺不太好。

* eyesight〔ˈaɪˌsaɪt〕*n.* 視力
weak〔wik〕*adj.* 功能不佳的
smell〔smɛl〕*v.* 有嗅覺

37. (**B**) The humidity was ninety-five percent.
溼度是百分之九十五。
(A) 天氣很乾燥。 (B) 天氣很潮濕。
(C) 那是漫長的一天。 (D) 那是很典型的一天。
* humidity (hju'mɪdətɪ) *n.* 溼度 dry (draɪ) *adj.* 乾燥的
damp (dæmp) *adj.* 潮濕的 typical ('tɪpɪkl) *adj.* 典型的

38. (**C**) Cadet Carson was too late to catch the bus.
候補軍官卡爾森因遲到而趕不上公車。
(A) 他搭乘公車。 (B) 他等公車。
(C) 他錯過了公車。 (D) 他站在公車上。
* cadet (kə'dɛt) *n.* 候補軍官 board (bord) *v.* 搭乘

39. (**C**) Eric doesn't speak French, and Tom doesn't either.
艾力克不會講法文，湯姆也不會。
(A) 他們都會說法文。
(B) 艾力克會說法文；湯姆不會。
(C) 他們都不會說法文。
(D) 湯姆會說法文；艾力克不會。
* French (frɛntʃ) *n.* 法語 either ('iðɚ) *adv.* 也（不）
neither ('niðɚ) *pron.* 兩者都不

40. (**B**) She was told to think it through before making a decision. 她被要求在做決定前仔細想清楚。
(A) 她被告知要忽視它。 (B) 她被告知要考慮它。
(C) 她在考慮把它說出去。 (D) 她被告知要忘記它。
* ***think through*** 仔細想清楚
decision (dɪ'sɪʒən) *n.* 決定 ignore (ɪg'nor) *v.* 忽視
consider (kən'sɪdɚ) *v.* 仔細考慮

41. (**D**) Alan visited a residential area of town.
艾倫造訪了鎮上的住宅區。

(A) 他造訪了商業區。 (B) 他造訪校園。
(C) 他造訪醫院。 (D) 他造訪住宅區。

* residential [ˌrɛzəˈdɛnʃəl] *adj.* 住宅的
campus [ˈkæmpəs] *n.* 校園
housing [ˈhaʊzɪŋ] *n.* 住宅

42. (**C**) Don't despise the poor.
不要看不起窮人。

(A) 不要忍受窮人。 (B) 不要尊敬窮人。
(C) 不要看不起窮人。 (D) 不要尋找窮人。

* despise [dɪˈspaɪz] *v.* 輕視　poor [pʊr] *adj.* 貧窮的
the poor 窮人　***put up with*** 忍受
look up to 尊敬　***look down upon*** 輕視；看不起
look for 尋找

43. (**A**) The house is across from the bookstore.
那間房子在書店的對面。

(A) 那間房子在書店的對面。
(B) 那間房子在書店的轉角處。
(C) 那間房子在旅館的對面。
(D) 那間房子在酒吧的對面。

* across [əˈkrɔs] *prep.* 在…對面
across from 在…對面
opposite [ˈɑpəzɪt] *prep.* 在…的對面
corner [ˈkɔrnɚ] *n.* 轉角處
around the corner from 在…轉角處
bar [bɑr] *n.* 酒吧

44. (**D**) The snow is worse today.
今天下雪的情況更惡劣了。

(A) 今天天氣很暖和。
(B) 今天天氣比較好。
(C) 天氣情況一樣。
(D) 今天天氣不太好。

＊ worse〔 wɝs 〕*adj.* 更差的

45. (**C**) Her face immediately came into my mind.
我馬上想到她的臉。

(A) 我突然提醒她的臉。
(B) 我突然使她的臉分叉。
(C) 我突然記起她的臉。
(D) 我突然報導她的臉。

＊ immediately〔 ɪˈmidɪɪtlɪ 〕*adv.* 立即；馬上
mind〔 maɪnd 〕*n.* 記憶　　***come into** one's **mind*** 想到
suddenly〔ˈsʌdn̩lɪ 〕*adv.* 突然
remind〔 rɪˈmaɪnd 〕*v.* 提醒
ramify〔ˈræməˌfaɪ 〕*v.* 使…分叉
report〔 rɪˈpɔrt 〕*v.* 報導

46. (**C**) This cap fits me perfectly. I'll buy it.
這頂帽子很適合我。我要買它。

(A) 它是風景上升。　(B) 它是夜晚告示。
(C) 它是正確的尺寸。　(D) 它是錯的一邊。

＊ cap〔 kæp 〕*n.* 帽子　　fit〔 fɪt 〕*v.* 適合
perfectly〔ˈpɝfɪktlɪ 〕*adv.* 非常　　sight〔 saɪt 〕*n.* 風景
rise〔 raɪz 〕*v.* 上升　　sign〔 saɪn 〕*n.* 告示

47. (**A**) They have been here just five minutes.
他們才到這裡五分鐘。
(A) <u>他們才到這裡五分鐘。</u>
(B) 他們到達這裡超過五分鐘了。
(C) 他們到達這裡超過五天了。
(D) 他們才到這裡五小時。

48. (**B**) The sky was clear yesterday morning, but it got cloudy last night. 昨天早上天空沒有雲，但晚上雲量開始變多。
(A) 昨晚的雲很潔淨。 (B) <u>雲在昨晚出現。</u>
(C) 昨晚的雲在跳舞。 (D) 雲在昨晚回家。

* clear〔klɪr〕*adj.* 無雲的；潔淨的
cloudy〔ˈklaʊdɪ〕*adj.* 多雲的

49. (**A**) General Lee sent his brother a letter.
李將軍寄給他哥哥一封信。
(A) <u>他寄了一封信。</u>
(B) 他給他哥哥一份禮物。
(C) 他收到他哥哥寄來的信。
(D) 他派人送信給他哥哥。

* send〔sɛnd〕*v.* 寄；送 gift〔gɪft〕*n.* 禮物
receive〔rɪˈsiv〕*v.* 收到 send〔sɛnd〕*v.* 派遣

50. (**C**) Be sure to look carefully before you drive onto the highway. 在你開上公路之前，一定要小心留意。
(A) 在開車前一定要小心。 (B) 開在公路上。
(C) <u>一定要到處查看。</u> (D) 用你的車。

* carefully〔ˈkɛrfəlɪ〕*adv.* 小心地
highway〔ˈhaɪˌwe〕*n.* 公路

51. (**A**) M：Did you move the sculptures?

W：Yes, we thought they would fall.

What did the women think the sculptures would do?

男：妳們有移動那些雕像嗎？

女：有，我們認爲它們會掉下來。

那位女士認爲雕像會怎樣？

(A) <u>落下。</u>　　(B) 落上。

(C) 突然造訪。　　(D) 輟學。

＊ sculpture〔ˈskʌlptʃɚ〕*n.* 雕像　drop〔drɑp〕*v.* 落下

drop in 突然造訪　***drop out*** 輟學

52. (**B**) W：What are your duties, Jerry Lee?

M：My responsibility is photography.

What does Jerry Lee do?

女：李傑瑞，你的職責是什麼？

男：我負責攝影。

李傑瑞是做什麼的？

(A) 傑瑞是哲學家。

(B) <u>照相是傑瑞的責任。</u>

(C) 傑瑞負責收集照片。

(D) 傑瑞的責任是四處旅行。

＊ duty〔ˈdjutɪ〕*n.* 責任

responsibility〔rɪˌspɑnsəˈbɪlətɪ〕*n.* 職責

photography〔fəˈtɑgrəfɪ〕*n.* 攝影

philosopher〔fəˈlɑsəfɚ〕*n.* 哲學家

take picture 拍照

responsible〔rɪˈspɑnsəbl̩〕*adj.* 負責的

collect〔kəˈlɛkt〕*v.* 收集

53. (**A**) M：I need a used bike. Do you have any?
W：Yes, I can sell you this one for about 150 dollars.
M：May I try it out?
What does the man want to do?
男：我需要一台二手腳踏車。妳有嗎？
女：是的，我可以用大約一百五十元把這台賣給你。
男：我可以試騎嗎？
那位男士想要做什麼？
(A) 他想要騎那台腳踏車。
(B) 他想要開那部車。
(C) 他想要趕走那戰爭。
(D) 他想要開過柏油。

* used〔juzd〕*adj.* 舊的；二手的
try out 試用　drive〔draɪv〕*v.* 駕駛；趕走
war〔wɔr〕*n.* 戰爭　tar〔tɑr〕*n.* 柏油

54. (**C**) M：Where should we meet next week?
W：I think this corner would be great. I was going to say the club, but now I think we'd better meet right here.
Where will the boy and girl probably meet?
男：我們下個禮拜在哪碰面？
女：我想這個轉角不錯。我本來想說俱樂部，但是我現在認爲我們最好在這裡碰面。
那個男孩和女孩可能在哪裡碰面？
(A) 在百貨公司。　(B) 在國界。
(C) 在轉角。　(D) 在郵局。

* ***had better*** 最好　border〔ˈbɔrdɚ〕*n.* 國界
post office 郵局

55. (**D**) M：He collects stones from all over the world.

W：That's interesting, but do they have any value?

What does the girl want to know?

男：他收集世界各地的石頭。

女：眞有趣，但是它們有任何價值嗎？

那個女孩想要知道什麼？

(A) 它們有穿任何東西嗎？

(B) 它們要去哪裡嗎？

(C) 他們是富裕的家族嗎？

(D) <u>它們值任何東西嗎？</u>

* value〔ˈvælju〕*n.* 價值

wealthy〔ˈwɛlθɪ〕*adj.* 富裕的

worth〔wɝθ〕*adj.* 有…價值的

56. (**A**) M：The movie theater is very crowded.

W：I know, but I made reservations.

What does the woman mean?

男：那家電影院非常擁擠。

女：我知道，我有預約。

那位女士的意思是？

(A) <u>會留位置給他們。</u>

(B) 他們太遲了。

(C) 他們不能入座。

(D) 電影已經結束了。

* theater〔ˈθiətɚ〕*n.* 戲院

crowded〔ˈkraʊdɪd〕*adj.* 擁擠的

reservation〔ˌrɛzɚˈveʃən〕*n.* 預約

save〔sev〕*v.* 留　　seat〔sit〕*v.* 使入座

57. (**C**) W：Why don't you move over here and stand beside me?
M：Thank you. I'd be glad to.
Where will the man stand?
女：你為什麼不過來站在我身邊？
男：謝謝妳。我很樂意。
那位男士將站在哪裡？
(A) 在那位女士的後面。
(B) 隔壁的桌子旁邊。
(C) 那位女士的旁邊。
(D) 那位男士的前面。

＊ glad〔glæd〕*adj.* 高興的

58. (**B**) W：Where can we purchase a money order?
M：Down at the post office.
What did the woman want to purchase?
女：我們可以在哪裡買到匯票？
男：在郵局那裡。
那位女士想要買什麼？
(A) 在那邊。 (B) 一張匯票。
(C) 一家郵局。 (D) 一些信。

＊ purchase〔ˈpɜtʃəs〕*v.* 購買
money order （郵政）匯票
down〔daʊn〕*adv.* 在那邊 *n.* 下降

59. (**D**) W：How much do I owe you?
M：That's five and a half dollars.
W：Here are six one-dollar bills. Keep the change.

What has happened?

女：我欠你多少錢？

男：五塊半。

女：這裡是六張一塊的紙鈔。不用找了。

發生了什麼事？

(A) 那位女士無法付帳。

(B) 那位女士用信用卡付賬。

(C) 那位女士在等她的朋友。

(D) 那位女士給他小費。

＊ owe〔 o 〕*v.* 欠　　half〔 hæf 〕*n.* 五角
bill〔 bɪl 〕*n.* 鈔票；帳單
keep〔 kip 〕*v.* 保留　　change〔 tʃendʒ 〕*n.* 零錢
tip〔 tɪp 〕*n.* 小費

60. (**B**) W：I heard about your accident. I'm glad you weren't hurt. Is your car OK too?

M：No, it was destroyed.

What happened to the car?

女：我聽說你發生意外。我很高興你沒有受傷。你的車子也還好嗎？

男：不，它壞了。

那部車怎麼了？

(A) 它被偷了。　　(B) 它受損了。

(C) 它被整修。　　(D) 它被帶走。

＊ accident〔ˈæksədənt〕*n.* 意外
hurt〔 hɝt 〕*v.* 受傷　　destroy〔 dɪˈstrɔɪ 〕*v.* 毀壞
wreck〔 rɛk 〕*v.* 毀壞　　repair〔 rɪˈpɛr 〕*v.* 修理

LISTENING TEST ③

- *Directions for questions 1-25. You will hear questions on the test CD. Select the one item A, B, C or D which answers the question correctly, and mark your answer sheet.*

1. A. No. My mother bought it for me.
   B. No. I've never been interested in sports.
   C. It must be fun.
   D. You got the ticket?

2. A. explosion under the sun B. exposure to the gun
   C. exposure to the run D. exposure to the sun

3. A. a cavity drilled by the Adventist
   B. a cavity filled by the dinosaur
   C. a cavity filled by the bandits
   D. a cavity filled by the dentist

4. A. The sound is superior. B. The sound is audible.
   C. The sound is genuine. D. The sound is contained.

5. A. making a strip B. taking a trim
   C. taking a trip D. faking a flip

6. A. The wind dies out.
   B. The wind blows stronger.
   C. There is no wind.
   D. It's always windy.

7. A. at nine o'clock B. at midnight
   C. at six o'clock D. at ten o'clock

8. A. to let the cars through B. to clear the road
   C. to block traffic D. to speed up traffic

9. A. Six rooms were ready to be fused.
   B. Six rooms were ready to be used.
   C. Six rooms were ready to be amused.
   D. Six rooms were ready to be abused.

10. A. She's steaming until late every night.
    B. She's studying until late every night.
    C. She's screaming until late every night.
    D. She's streaming until late every night.

11. A. She sold it. B. She tested it.
    C. She painted it. D. She drank it.

12. A. space to keep things in B. rats and mice
    C. a door and windows D. a ceiling and floor

13. A. He is very sensible. B. He is very diligent.
    C. He is very pessimistic. D. He is very successful.

14. A. show the directions B. write the directions
    C. read the directions D. find the dictionary

15. A. Being on time is very important to him.
    B. Being late doesn't bother him.
    C. Being on time is an activity for him.
    D. Being on time is his assistance.

16. A. Its speed became faster. B. It grew bigger.
    C. It looked darker. D. It became softer.

17. A. in April B. on foot
    C. by boat D. by jet plane

18. A. Just before the report
    B. The day before
    C. That afternoon
    D. Earlier in the morning

19. A. 100 years B. 10 years
    C. 1000 years D. a period of time

20. A. It had a very pleasant misery.
    B. It had a very plausible memory.
    C. It had a very pleasant melody.
    D. It had a very pleasant mystery.

21. A. She has a good retribution.
    B. She has a good amputation.
    C. She has a good reputation.
    D. She has a good reason.

22. A. He's talking too much.
    B. He's working while walking.
    C. He's doing fine.
    D. Mr. Grubb likes to work hard.

23. A. I went by bus number 153.
    B. It's two hundred thirty-three.
    C. To a basketball game.
    D. At three o'clock.

24. A. the inside B. the master bedroom
    C. the living room D. the outside

25. A. She cooks us. B. She turns us into food.
    C. She goes to museums. D. She prepares the food.

● *Directions for questions 26-50. You will hear statements on the test CD. Select the one answer A, B, C, or D which comes closest to the meaning of the statement and mark your answer sheet.*

26. A. His first thoughts of the town were bad.
    B. His first thoughts of the town were favorable.
    C. His first thoughts of the town were strange.
    D. His first thoughts of the town were unfavorable.

27. A. She rented my offer.
    B. She raised my offer.
    C. She refused my offer.
    D. She took my offer.

28. A. Chew your food foolishly.
    B. Chew your food quickly.
    C. Chew your food thoroughly.
    D. Chew your food halfway.

29. A. It needs transportation. B. It needs shops.
    C. It needs living quarters. D. It needs hospitals.

30. A. She came this morning.
    B. She left this evening.
    C. She checked her work this morning.
    D. She passed out this evening.

31. A. Some of them will go.
    B. None of them will go.
    C. Only one person will go.
    D. They will all go.

32. A. She is sick and poor.
    B. She is either sick or poor.
    C. She is just sick.
    D. She isn't sick or poor.

33. A. Plastic and nylon are beautiful materials.
    B. Plastic and nylon are useful materials.
    C. Plastic and nylon are natural materials.
    D. Plastic and nylon are man-made materials.

34. A. She knew she could pass it.
    B. She knew he could pass her.
    C. She knew she wouldn't take it.
    D. She knew she could take a makeup test.

35. A. She weeps after lunch.
    B. She sweeps after lunch.
    C. She sleeps after lunch.
    D. She slips after lunch.

36. A. Jeff might go to the dentist.
    B. Jeff might go dancing.
    C. Jeff might go to school.
    D. Jeff might go to the gym.

37. A. He doesn't like sports.
    B. He participates in many types of sports.
    C. He likes to watch sports on television.
    D. He likes basketball better than baseball.

38. A. He's a stupid mechanic.
    B. He's an incompetent mechanic.
    C. He's a skilled mechanic.
    D. He's an angry mechanic.

39. A. She was mad. B. She was busy.
    C. She was anxious. D. She was depressed.

40. A. She has an addiction to flying.
    B. She has an aversion to flying.
    C. She has an affection for flying.
    D. She has an impartiality for flying.

41. A. She likes it. B. She loathes it.
    C. She licks it. D. She lacks it.

42. A. The war is almost unbelievable.
    B. The belief is almost without progress.
    C. The production is almost unpredictable.
    D. The progress is almost unbelievable.

43. A. It's beautiful. B. It's necessary.
    C. It's dangerous. D. It's impossible.

44. A. She is devoted.
    B. She is disclosed.
    C. She is careful.
    D. She is enduring.

45. A. Would you label them?
    B. Would you check them in?
    C. Would you carry them?
    D. Would you watch them?

46. A. We called it. B. We liked it.
    C. We repelled it. D. We stir-fried it.

47. A. They are not paid.
B. They are paid every month.
C. They are telephones.
D. They are bills.

48. A. Everybody will hear tomorrow's discussion.
B. Nobody wants to miss tomorrow's discussion.
C. Nobody will notice that there's a discussion tomorrow.
D. Everybody will give a discussion tomorrow.

49. A. He mortified her.
B. He reduced her.
C. He helped her.
D. He protested her.

50. A. He cast money.
B. He was ordered to go to the post office.
C. He spent his money in the post office.
D. He obtained some money.

● *Directions for questions 51-60. You will hear dialogs on the test CD. Select the correct answer A, B, C, or D and mark your answer sheet.*

51. A. drop it
B. carry it
C. close it
D. trash it

52. A. The electricity isn't flowing properly.
B. There isn't enough fuel.
C. The electricity is flowing properly.
D. The equipment has run too long.

53. A. covering it B. selling it
C. opening it D. filling it

54. A. strange B. boring
C. lively D. tiring

55. A. The Chinese restaurant.
B. The Japanese restaurant.
C. The Mexican restaurant.
D. The Vietnamese restaurant.

56. A. tests B. homework
C. stickers D. pencils

57. A. September B. October
C. January D. December

58. A. They are going to kill the cat.
B. They are going to swallow it.
C. They are going to play with it.
D. They are going to give it to the cat.

59. A. They are the most important.
B. They are the least important.
C. They are the most impossible.
D. They are the most impersonal.

60. A. He couldn't run. B. He couldn't sing.
C. He couldn't hear. D. He couldn't see.

ECL 聽力測驗③詳解

1. (**B**) Did you see the last World Cup final?

你有看上一屆世界盃的決賽嗎？

(A) 不。我媽媽買給我的。

(B) <u>不。我對運動一向沒有興趣。</u>

(C) 一定很好玩。

(D) 你買到票啦？

* last〔 læst 〕*adj.* 上一個

World Cup 世界盃

final〔ˈfaɪnḷ〕*n.* 決賽

interested〔ˈɪntrɪstɪd〕*adj.* 有興趣的

sport〔 sport 〕*n.* 運動　　ticket〔ˈtɪkɪt〕*n.* 票

2. (**D**) The man went to a beach and got severely burned. What caused his burn?

這位男士到海灘去，而且曬得很黑。／什麼原因使他曬黑？

(A) 太陽下的爆炸。

(B) 暴露在槍下。

(C) 暴露在跑步下。

(D) <u>暴露在太陽下。</u>

* beach〔 bitʃ 〕*n.* 海灘

severely〔 səˈvɪrlɪ 〕*adv.* 嚴重地；嚴厲地

burn〔 bɝn 〕*v. n.* 曬黑　　cause〔 kɔz 〕*v.* 造成

explosion〔 ɪkˈsploʒən 〕*n.* 爆炸

exposure〔 ɪkˈspoʒɚ 〕*n.* 暴露　　gun〔 gʌn 〕*n.* 槍

3. (**D**) Andy said that he got a new filling today. What did he get?

安迪說他今天要去補新牙。／他將得到什麼？

(A) 一個被耶穌再生論者鑽的洞。

(B) 一個被恐龍填補的蛀洞。

(C) 一個被強盜填補的蛀洞。

(D) <u>一個被牙醫填補的蛀洞。</u>

* filling〔ˈfɪlɪŋ〕*n.* （補牙的）填充材料
cavity〔ˈkævətɪ〕*n.* 洞；蛀牙（的洞）
drill〔drɪl〕*v.* 鑽孔
Adventist〔ˈædvɛntɪst〕*n.* 耶穌再生論者
fill〔fɪl〕*v.* 填補　　dinosaur〔ˈdaɪnəˌsɔr〕*n.* 恐龍
bandit〔ˈbændɪt〕*n.* 強盜
dentist〔ˈdɛntɪst〕*n.* 牙醫

4. (**B**) This new auditorium assures that the sound is able to be heard. How is the auditorium?

新劇院保證可以聽到聲音。／這個劇院如何？

(A) 聲音很優良。

(B) <u>聽得見聲音。</u>

(C) 聲音很眞實。

(D) 聲音被包括。

* auditorium〔ˌɔdəˈtorɪəm〕*n.* 劇院
assure〔əˈʃʊr〕*v.* 向（人）保證
sound〔saʊnd〕*n.* 聲音
superior〔səˈpɪrɪɚ〕*adj.* 優良的
audible〔ˈɔdəbl̩〕*adj.* 聽得見的
genuine〔ˈdʒɛnjʊɪn〕*adj.* 眞實的
contain〔kənˈten〕*v.* 包括

5. (**C**) They were on a tour when the accident happened. What were they doing when the accident occurred?
發生意外時，他們正在旅行。／意外發生時，他們在做什麼？

(A) 做連環漫畫。　(B) 修剪。
(C) 旅遊。　(D) 假裝輕彈。

* tour (tʊr) *n.* 旅行　accident (′æksədənt) *n.* 意外事故
occur (ə′kɝ) *v.* 發生　strip (strɪp) *n.* 連環漫畫
trim (trɪm) *n.* 修剪　trip (trɪp) *n.* 旅行
fake (fek) *v.* 假裝　flip (flɪp) *n.* 用指頭彈；輕打

6. (**B**) Every night the wind picks up. What happens when the wind picks up?
每晚風速都會變強。／風速變強會發生什麼事？

(A) 風消失了。　(B) 風吹得更強。
(C) 沒有風。　(D) 風總是很大。

* wind (wɪnd) *n.* 風　***pick up*** 增加速度
die out 消失　blow (blo) *v.* 吹
strong (strɔŋ) *adj.* 強烈的
windy (′wɪndɪ) *adj.* 風力強的

7. (**B**) Kevin goes to bed at midnight regularly, but last night he went to bed at nine o'clock. What time does Kevin usually go to bed?
凱文習慣性半夜才睡覺，但昨晚他九點就睡了。／凱文通常何時上床睡覺？

(A) 九點。　(B) 午夜。
(C) 六點。　(D) 十點。

* midnight (′mɪd,naɪt) *n.* 午夜
regularly (′rɛgjələlɪ) *adv.* 規律地；習慣性地

8. (**C**) Why did the army put up a barricade?
為什麼軍隊要設路障？

(A) 讓車通過。　(B) 清理道路。
(C) 封鎖交通。　(D) 加速通行。

* army〔'ɑrmɪ〕*n.* 軍隊　barricade〔,bærə'ked〕*n.* 路障
block〔blɑk〕*v.* 封鎖　traffic〔'træfɪk〕*n.* 交通；通行
speed〔spid〕*v.* 加速 <*up*>

9. (**B**) The receptionist said that there were only six rooms available in the motel. What did the receptionist mean?
櫃檯人員說這家汽車旅館只有六間房間。／櫃檯人員的意思是？

(A) 有六間房間準備好要裝保險絲。
(B) 有六間房間準備好可以使用。
(C) 有六間房間準備好被娛樂。
(D) 有六間房間準備好被濫用。

* receptionist〔rɪ'sɛpʃənɪst〕*n.* 櫃檯人員
available〔ə'veləbḷ〕*adj.* 可獲得的；可用的
motel〔mo'tɛl〕*n.* 汽車旅館　ready〔'rɛdɪ〕*adj.* 準備好的
fuse〔fjuz〕*v.* 給…裝保險絲
amuse〔ə'mjuz〕*v.* 娛樂　abuse〔ə'bjuz〕*v.* 濫用

10. (**B**) Shannon is burning the midnight oil. What is she doing? 雪寧在開夜車。／她在做什麼？

(A) 每晚她都生氣到很晚。
(B) 每晚她都讀書讀到很晚。
(C) 每晚她都尖叫到很晚。
(D) 每晚她都流淚到很晚。

* ***burn the midnight oil*** 熬夜　steam〔stim〕*v.* 生氣
scream〔skrim〕*v.* 尖叫　stream〔strim〕*v.* 淚漣漣；流出

11. (**B**) Jane tried out the motorcycle on the highway. What did she do? 珍在公路上試騎摩托車。／她做了什麼？

(A) 她賣了它。 (B) 她測試它。
(C) 她油漆它。 (D) 她喝了它。

* ***try out*** 徹底試驗 motorcycle〔ˈmotɚˌsaɪkḷ〕*n.* 摩托車
highway〔ˈhaɪˌwe〕*n.* 公路 test〔tɛst〕*v.* 測試
paint〔pent〕*v.* 油漆

12. (**A**) This mansion has lots of storage space. What does the mansion have?
這棟大樓有很多儲藏的空間。／這棟大樓有什麼？

(A) 儲存東西的地方。 (B) 老鼠。
(C) 門窗。 (D) 天花板和地板。

* mansion〔ˈmænʃən〕*n.* 大廈
storage〔ˈstorɪdʒ〕*n.* 貯藏 space〔spes〕*n.* 空間
keep〔kip〕*v.* 存放 rat〔ræt〕*n.* 老鼠
mice〔maɪs〕*n. pl.* 老鼠【單數爲 mouse】
ceiling〔ˈsilɪŋ〕*n.* 天花板 floor〔flor〕*n.* 地板

13. (**B**) Thomas is described as a very industrious writer. What kind of writer is Thomas?
湯瑪斯被形容成非常勤奮的作家。／湯瑪斯是怎樣的作家？

(A) 他非常敏感。 (B) 他非常勤奮。
(C) 他非常悲觀。 (D) 他非常成功。

* describe〔dɪˈskraɪb〕*v.* 形容
industrious〔ɪnˈdʌstrɪəs〕*adj.* 勤奮的
sensible〔ˈsɛnsəbḷ〕*adj.* 敏感的
diligent〔ˈdɪlədʒənt〕*adj.* 勤奮的
pessimistic〔ˌpɛsəˈmɪstɪk〕*adj.* 悲觀的
successful〔səkˈsɛsfəl〕*adj.* 成功的

14. (**C**) Ann doesn't know how to use the vending machine. What should she do first?

安不知道如何使用自動販賣機。／她應該要先做什麼？

(A) 出示說明書。

(B) 寫出使用說明。

(C) 閱讀使用說明。

(D) 找出字典。

* vend (vɛnd) *v.* 販賣 ***vending machine*** 自動販賣機
show (ʃo) *v.* 出示
directions (dəˈrɛkʃənz) *n. pl.* 使用說明；說明書
dictionary (ˈdɪkʃən,ɛrɪ) *n.* 字典

15. (**A**) James has been criticized for placing too much emphasis on being on time. Why has James been criticized?

詹姆士由於太過注重守時而被批評。／詹姆士爲何被批評？

(A) 守時對他來說很重要。

(B) 遲到不會使他感到困擾。

(C) 守時對他來說是個活動。

(D) 守時是他的援助。

* criticize (ˈkrɪtə,saɪz) *v.* 批評 place (ples) *v.* 放置
emphasis (ˈɛmfəsɪs) *n.* 重視 ***on time*** 準時
place (ples) *v.* 把…看成
bother (ˈbɑðɚ) *v.* 困擾 activity (ækˈtɪvətɪ) *n.* 活動
assistance (əˈsɪstəns) *n.* 援助

16. (**A**) As the banana fell, its velocity increased. What happened as the banana fell?

當香蕉落下時，它的速度會增加。／香蕉落下時發生了什麼事？

(A) 它的速度加快。
(B) 它變得比較大。
(C) 它看起來比較黑。
(D) 它變得比較軟。

* banana〔bə'nænə〕*n.* 香蕉
velocity〔və'lɑsətɪ〕*n.* 速度
increase〔ɪn'kris〕*v.* 增加
speed〔spid〕*n.* 速度　grow〔gro〕*v.* 變成
dark〔dɑrk〕*adj.* 黑的　soft〔sɔft〕*adj.* 軟的

17. (**D**) How will they cross the Pacific Ocean in such a short time? 他們將如何在這麼短的時間內橫越太平洋？
(A) 在四月。　(B) 用走的。
(C) 乘船。　(D) 搭飛機。

* cross〔krɔs〕*v.* 橫越　***the Pacific Ocean*** 太平洋
boat〔bot〕*n.* 船　jet〔dʒɛt〕*adj.* 噴射式的
jet plane 噴射機

18. (**D**) A severe earthquake hit central Taiwan early this morning. When did the earthquake occur?
今天早上一個嚴重的地震襲擊中台灣。／地震什麼時候發生的？
(A) 報導之前。　(B) 前一天。
(C) 那天下午。　(D) 早晨稍早。

* severe〔sə'vɪr〕*adj.* 嚴重的
earthquake〔'ɝθ,kwek〕*n.* 地震
hit〔hɪt〕*v.* 襲擊　central〔'sɛntrəl〕*adj.* 中間的
report〔rɪ'pɔrt〕*n.* 報導

19. (**A**) A great man lived a century ago. How long before now was that?

一個偉人活在一百年前。／那是多久以前的事？

(A) <u>一百年前。</u> (B) 十年前。
(C) 一千年前。 (D) 一段時間。

* century〔ˈsɛntʃərɪ〕*n.* 一世紀；百年
period〔ˈpɪrɪəd〕*n.* 期間；一段時間

20. (**C**) How did you like the music? 你覺得那段音樂如何？

(A) 它有一個令人愉快的災禍。
(B) 它有一個似眞實的記憶。
(C) <u>它有一段令人愉悅的旋律。</u>
(D) 它有一個令人愉快的秘密。

* pleasant〔ˈplɛzn̩t〕*adj.* 令人愉快的
misery〔ˈmɪzərɪ〕*n.* 悲慘；災禍
plausible〔ˈplɔzəbl〕*adj.* 似眞實的
memory〔ˈmɛmərɪ〕*n.* 記憶 melody〔ˈmɛlədɪ〕*n.* 旋律
mystery〔ˈmɪstrɪ〕*n.* 謎；秘密

21. (**C**) Miss Pink is a respectable woman. How would you characterize her?

粉紅小姐是位可敬的女士。／你會怎麼描述她的特徵？

(A) 她有好報。 (B) 她的切除技術良好。
(C) <u>她有名聲很好。</u> (D) 她有好理由。

* respectable〔rɪˈspɛktəbl̩〕*adj.* 可尊敬的
characterize〔ˈkærɪktəˌraɪz〕*v.* 描述…的特徵
retribution〔ˌrɛtrəˈbjuʃən〕*n.* 報應
amputation〔ˌæmpjəˈteʃən〕*n.* 切除術
reputation〔ˌrɛpjəˈteʃən〕*n.* 名聲

22. (**C**) How is Mr. Grubb getting along with his new job?
葛拉布先生新工作的進展如何？
(A) 他的話太多了。 (B) 他邊走邊工作。
(C) 他表現得不錯。 (D) 葛拉布先生喜歡努力工作。
* ***get along*** 進展

23. (**C**) Were did you go the day before yesterday?
你前天去哪裡了？
(A) 我搭 153 號公車去。 (B) 兩百三十三元。
(C) 去看籃球賽。 (D) 在三點鐘。

24. (**D**) The agent said, "The exterior of the house was very beautiful". What part of the house was she talking about?
仲介商說：「這間屋子的外觀非常美麗。」／她在說這間屋子的哪個部份？
(A) 內部。 (B) 主臥房。
(C) 客廳。 (D) 外觀。
* agent〔'edʒənt〕*n.* 仲介商
exterior〔ɪk'stɪrɪɚ〕*n.* 外部；外觀
part〔pɑrt〕*n.* 部分 inside〔'ɪn'saɪd〕*n.* 內部
master〔'mæstɚ〕*adj.* 主人的
outside〔'aʊt'saɪd〕*n.* 外觀

25. (**D**) Betty cooks all our food for us. What does she do?
貝蒂爲我們所有人做飯。／她做什麼？
(A) 她煮我們。 (B) 她把我們變成食物。
(C) 她去博物館。 (D) 她準備食物。
* ***turn into*** 變成 museum〔mju'ziəm〕*n.* 博物館
prepare〔prɪ'pɛr〕*v.* 準備

26. (**B**) Eric's first impression of the town was good.
艾力克對這座小鎮的第一印象很好。

(A) 他對這座小鎮的第一印象不好。
(B) <u>他對這座小鎮的第一印象是讚賞的。</u>
(C) 他對這座小鎮的第一印象很奇怪。
(D) 他對這座小鎮的第一印象是令人不快的。

* impression〔ɪmˈprɛʃən〕*n.* 印象
thoughts〔θɔts〕*n. pl.* 看法；見解
favorable〔ˈfevərəbl̩〕*adj.* 讚許的
strange〔strendʒ〕*adj.* 奇怪的
unfavorable〔ʌnˈfevərəbl̩〕*adj.* 令人不快的；不討人喜歡的

27. (**C**) Helen rejected my proposal. 海倫否決了我的提案。

(A) 她租了我的提議。
(B) 她提高了我的提議。
(C) <u>她拒絕了我的提議。</u>
(D) 她拿了我的提議。

* reject〔rɪˈdʒɛkt〕*v.* 否決　　proposal〔prəˈpozl̩〕*n.* 提案
rent〔rɛnt〕*v.* 租　　offer〔ˈɔfɚ〕*n.* 提議
raise〔rez〕*v.* 提高　　refuse〔rɪˈfjuz〕*v.* 拒絕

28. (**C**) Chew your food well. 好好咀嚼你的食物。

(A) 要愚蠢地咀嚼你的食物。
(B) 要迅速咀嚼你的食物。
(C) <u>要徹底咀嚼你的食物。</u>
(D) 不要徹底咀嚼你的食物。

* chew〔tʃu〕*v.* 咀嚼
foolishly〔ˈfulɪʃlɪ〕*adv.* 愚蠢地
thoroughly〔ˈθɝolɪ〕*adv.* 徹底地
halfway〔ˈhæfˈwe〕*adv.* 不徹底地

29. (**C**) This town needs some housing.
這個城鎮需要一些住宅。
(A) 它需要運輸工具。 (B) 它需要商店。
(C) 它需要住宅區。 (D) 它需要醫院。
* housing〔'haʊzɪŋ〕*n.* 住宅
transportation〔,trænspə'teʃən〕*n.* 運輸工具
living〔'lɪvɪŋ〕*adj.* 居住的 quarter〔'kwɔrtə〕*n.* 區域

30. (**B**) Rita checked out this evening. 麗塔今天晚上退房。
(A) 她今天早上來的。
(B) 她今天晚上離開的。
(C) 她今天早上檢查她的工作。
(D) 她今天晚上去世。
* ***check out*** 辦理退房手續 check〔tʃɛk〕*v.* 檢查
pass out 過世

31. (**D**) The entire class is leaving for Japan. 全班要去日本。
(A) 他們之中有一些人要去。
(B) 他們沒有人要去。
(C) 只有一個人要去。
(D) 他們全部都會去。
* entire〔ɪn'taɪr〕*adj.* 全部的 none〔nʌn〕*pron.* 沒人

32. (**D**) She is neither sick nor poor. 她既沒生病，也不窮。
(A) 她又生病，又貧窮。
(B) 她不是生病，就是很窮。
(C) 她剛生病。
(D) 她既沒生病，也不窮。
* ***neither*** A ***nor*** B 不是 A，也不是 B
poor〔pʊr〕*adj.* 貧困的

33. (**D**) Chemists make different kinds of artificial materials like plastic and nylon.
化學家製造各種不同的人造物質，像塑膠和尼龍。

(A) 塑膠和尼龍是漂亮的物質。
(B) 塑膠和尼龍是有用的物質。
(C) 塑膠和尼龍是自然的物質。
(D) 塑膠和尼龍是人造的物質。

* chemist〔ˈkɛmɪst〕*n.* 化學家
different〔ˈdɪfərənt〕*adj.* 不同的
artificial〔ˌɑrtəˈfɪʃəl〕*adj.* 人造的
material〔məˈtɪrɪəl〕*n.* 材料；物質
plastic〔ˈplæstɪk〕*n.* 塑膠　nylon〔ˈnaɪlɑn〕*n.* 尼龍
useful〔ˈjusfəl〕*adj.* 有用的
natural〔ˈnætʃərəl〕*adj.* 自然的
man-made〔ˈmænˌmed〕*adj.* 人造的

34. (**A**) She was sure she would pass the exam.
她確定自己會通過考試。

(A) 她知道自己會通過。　(B) 她知道他會經過她。
(C) 她知道她不會去考。　(D) 她知道她會去補考。

* pass〔pæs〕*v.* 通過；經過　exam〔ɪgˈzæm〕*n.* 考試
makeup test 補考

35. (**C**) The young girl likes to take a nap in the afternoon.
這個年輕女孩喜歡在下午睡午覺。

(A) 她在午餐後哭泣。　(B) 她在午餐後打掃。
(C) 她在午餐後睡覺。　(D) 她在午餐後滑倒。

* nap〔næp〕*n.* 小睡；午睡　***take a nap*** 午睡
weep〔wip〕*v.* 哭泣　sweep〔swip〕*v.* 打掃
slip〔slɪp〕*v.* 滑倒

36. (**A**) Jeff will go to a dentist if his tooth still hurts tomorrow.
如果傑夫的牙齒明天還痛，他就會去看牙醫。

(A) 傑夫可能會去看牙醫。
(B) 傑夫可能會去跳舞。
(C) 傑夫可能會去學校。
(D) 傑夫可能會去健身房。

* hurt (hɜt) *v.* 疼痛　　gym (dʒɪm) *n.* 健身房

37. (**B**) Ted takes part in all kinds of sports.
泰德參與各種運動。

(A) 他不喜歡運動。
(B) 他參加許多不同種類的運動。
(C) 他喜歡看電視上的體育活動。
(D) 他喜歡籃球勝於棒球。

* ***take part in*** 參與
participate (pɑrˈtɪsəˌpet) *v.* 參加

38. (**C**) Fred is an excellent mechanic.
佛來德是個傑出的技工。

(A) 他是個愚笨的技工。
(B) 他是個無能的技工。
(C) 他是個技術精湛的技工。
(D) 他是個生氣的技工。

* excellent (ˈɛksl̩ənt) *adj.* 傑出的
mechanic (məˈkænɪk) *n.* 技工
stupid (ˈstjupɪd) *adj.* 笨的
incompetent (ɪnˈkɑmpətənt) *adj.* 無能的
skilled (skɪld) *adj.* 技術精湛的

39. (**B**) When I called her, she was too occupied to talk.
我打電話給她時，她忙得沒辦法講電話。

(A) 她瘋了。 (B) 她很忙。
(C) 她很不安。 (D) 她很沮喪。

* occupied〔ˈɑkjəˌpaɪd〕*adj.* 忙碌的
mad〔mæd〕*adj.* 瘋的
anxious〔ˈæŋkʃəs〕*adj.* 不安的
depressed〔dɪˈprɛst〕*adj.* 沮喪的

40. (**B**) Sally has such an intense dislike for flying that she must take therapy.
莎莉對飛行的痛恨強烈到必須接受治療。

(A) 她對飛行上癮。 (B) 她厭惡飛行。
(C) 她熱愛飛行。 (D) 她對飛行是公平的。

* intense〔ɪnˈtɛns〕*adj.* 強烈的 dislike〔dɪsˈlaɪk〕*n.* 討厭
flying〔ˈflaɪɪŋ〕*n.* 飛行；搭飛機的旅行
therapy〔ˈθɛrəpɪ〕*n.* 治療
addiction〔əˈdɪkʃən〕*n.* 上癮
aversion〔əˈvɜʒən〕*n.* 厭惡
affection〔əˈfɛkʃən〕*n.* 愛；鍾愛
impartiality〔ˌɪmpɑrˈʃælətɪ〕*n.* 公平無私

41. (**A**) Jenny considers her job wonderful.
珍妮覺得她的工作太棒了。

(A) 她喜歡它。 (B) 她討厭它。
(C) 她舔它。 (D) 她缺少它。

* consider〔kənˈsɪdɚ〕*v.* 覺得
wonderful〔ˈwʌndɚfəl〕*adj.* 極好的
loathe〔loð〕*v.* 討厭 lick〔lɪk〕*v.* 舐；舔
lack〔læk〕*v.* 缺少

42. (**D**) Since World War II, incredible improvements have been made in the development and production of this engine. 自從第二次世界大戰以來，引擎的發展和製造有驚人的進步。

(A) 那戰爭幾乎令人難以置信。

(B) 那種信仰幾乎毫無進展。

(C) 產量幾乎是無法預測的。

(D) 那種進步幾乎令人難以置信。

* incredible〔ɪnˈkrɛdəbl̩〕*adj.* 驚人的
improvement〔ɪmˈpruvmənt〕*n.* 進步
development〔dɪˈvɛləpmənt〕*n.* 發展
production〔prəˈdʌkʃən〕*n.* 製造；生產量
engine〔ˈɛndʒən〕*n.* 引擎
unbelievable〔ˌʌnbəˈlivəbl̩〕*adj.* 難以置信的
belief〔bəˈlif〕*n.* 信仰
progress〔ˈprɑgrɛs〕*n.* 進步；發展
unpredictable〔ˌʌnprɪˈdɪktəbl̩〕*adj.* 無法預測的

43. (**B**) The first part of the mission is essential
這件任務的第一個部分是必要的。

(A) 它是美麗的。

(B) 它是不可或缺的。

(C) 它是危險的。

(D) 它是不可能的。

* mission〔ˈmɪʃən〕*n.* 任務
essential〔əˈsɛnʃəl〕*adj.* 不可缺的；必要的
necessary〔ˈnɛsəˌsɛrɪ〕*adj.* 不可或缺的

44. (**C**) A thorough person, she spent hours waxing the floors before the party.

她是個一絲不苟的人，她在宴會前花了數小時爲地板打蠟。

(A) 她很熱中。　　　(B) 她被揭發。

(C) <u>她很謹慎。</u>　　　(D) 她很耐久。

* thorough〔ˈθɝo〕*adj.* 一絲不苟的
wax〔wæks〕*v.* 打蠟
floor〔flor〕*n.* 地板
devoted〔dɪˈvotɪd〕*adj.* 熱中的
disclose〔dɪsˈkloz〕*v.* 揭發
enduring〔ɪnˈdurɪŋ〕*adj.* 持久的

45. (**D**) Would you keep an eye on our bags for us?

可以請你幫我們看一下背包嗎？

(A) 可以請你把它們貼上標籤嗎？

(B) 可以請你把它們交運嗎？

(C) 可以請你帶著它們嗎？

(D) <u>可以請你留意一下它們嗎？</u>

* ***keep an eye on*** 照料
label〔ˈlebḷ〕*v.* 貼標籤　　***check in*** 交運
carry〔ˈkærɪ〕*v.* 攜帶

46. (**C**) We fought off the surprise attack.

我們擊退了突襲。

(A) 我們呼叫它。　　　(B) 我們喜歡它。

(C) <u>我們擊退它。</u>　　　(D) 我們炒它。

* ***fight off*** 擊退　　surprise〔səˈpraɪz〕*adj.* 突然的
attack〔əˈtæk〕*n.* 攻擊
repel〔rɪˈpɛl〕*v.* 擊退　　stir-fry〔ˈstɝˌfraɪ〕*v.* 炒

47. (**B**) Gas bills are paid monthly.
瓦斯帳單是按月繳納的。

(A) 它們未被付清。
(B) 它們每月被付清。
(C) 它們是電話。
(D) 它們是帳單。

* gas〔 gæs 〕*n.* 瓦斯　bill〔 bɪl 〕*n.* 帳單
monthly〔'mʌnθlɪ〕*adj.* 每月一次的

48. (**A**) Tomorrow's discussion will be heard by everyone.
每個人都會聽見明天的討論。

(A) 每個人都會聽見明天的討論。
(B) 沒有人想錯過明天的討論。
(C) 沒有人會注意到明天有一場討論。
(D) 明天每個人都會進行討論。

* discussion〔 dɪ'skʌʃən 〕*n.* 討論　miss〔 mɪs 〕*v.* 錯過
notice〔'notɪs〕*v.* 注意到

49. (**A**) He has humiliated her beyond endurance.
他對她的羞辱使她無法忍受。

(A) 他羞辱她。
(B) 他減少她。
(C) 他幫助她。
(D) 他抗議她。

* humiliate〔 hju'mɪlɪ,et 〕*v.* 使〈人〉蒙羞
beyond〔 bɪ'jand 〕*prep.* 超過…的範圍
endurance〔 ɪn'djʊrəns 〕*n.* 忍受
mortify〔'mɔrtə,faɪ〕*v.* 使〈人〉感到羞辱
reduce〔 rɪ'djus 〕*v.* 減少　protest〔 prə'tɛst 〕*v.* 抗議

50. (**D**) Lieutenant Michael cashed the money order at the post office. 麥可上尉在郵局兌現匯票。

(A) 他拋掉錢。

(B) 他奉命到郵局去。

(C) 他把他的錢花在郵局。

(D) 他得到一些錢。

* lieutenant〔luˈtɛnənt〕*n.* 上尉
cash〔kæʃ〕*v.* 兌現
money order 匯票　***post office*** 郵局
cast〔kæst〕*v.* 拋　order〔ˈɔrdɚ〕*v.* 命令
obtain〔əbˈten〕*v.* 得到

51. (**B**) M：May I help you?
W：Yes, hold the bag while we are in the mall.
What does the girl want the boy to do with the bag?
男：我可以幫妳嗎？
女：是的，當我們在購物中心時，拿著這個袋子。
這女孩想要男孩怎樣處理包包？

(A) 掉在地上。　(B) 帶著它。

(C) 關起來。　(D) 丟掉。

* hold〔hold〕*v.* 拿住
mall〔mɔl〕*n.* 商場　***do with*** 處置
drop〔drɑp〕*v.* 掉落　close〔kloz〕*v.* 關上
trash〔træʃ〕*v.* 丟棄

52. (**A**) W：Why won't this equipment work?
M：Because there was a short circuit in it.
What did the man mean?

女：爲什麼這個機器不會動？
男：因爲裡面短路。
這位男士的意思是？

(A) 電流不順。　(B) 燃料不足。
(C) 電流流通順暢。　(D) 機器運作太久了。

* equipment (ɪˈkwɪpmənt) *n.* 機器
work (wɝk) *v.* 運轉
circuit (ˈsɝkɪt) *n.* 電路　***short circuit*** 短路
electricity (ɪˌlɛkˈtrɪsətɪ) *n.* 電流
flow (flo) *v.* 流通
properly (ˈprɑpɚlɪ) *adv.* 適當地；正確地
fuel (ˈfjuəl) *n.* 燃料　run (rʌn) *v.* 運轉

53. (**A**) W：When are you going to mail the package?
M：Just as soon as I'm done wrapping it.
What is the man doing to the package?

女：你什麼時候會去寄這個包裹？
男：我一包好就拿去寄。
這位男士在對包裹做什麼？

(A) 包裝它。　(B) 賣了它。
(C) 打開它。　(D) 充滿它。

* package (ˈpækɪdʒ) *n.* 包裹
as soon as 一…就…　wrap (ræp) *v.* 包裹
cover (ˈkʌvɚ) *v.* 包裝　fill (fɪl) *v.* 填滿

54. (**C**) W：Alex is a real live wire, isn't he?
M：He certainly is.
What kind of person is Alex?

女：艾力克斯眞是精力充沛，不是嗎？
男：他確實是。
艾力克斯是怎樣的人？

(A) 奇怪的。　　(B) 無聊。
(C) <u>充滿活力。</u>　　(D) 無聊。

* ***live wire*** 精力充沛的人　certainly〔'sɝtn̩lɪ〕*adv.* 確實
strange〔strendʒ〕*adj.* 奇怪的
lively〔'laɪvlɪ〕*adj.* 充滿活力的
tiring〔'taɪrɪŋ〕*adj.* 無聊的

55. (**B**) W：Where would you like to go for lunch?
M：Why don't we go have some sushi?
W：Good idea.
Which restaurant are they going to?
女：你中午要去吃什麼？
男：我們何不去吃壽司？
女：好主意。
他們要去什麼餐廳？

(A) 中國餐廳。　　(B) <u>日本餐廳。</u>
(C) 墨西哥餐廳。　　(D) 越南餐廳。

* sushi〔'susɪ〕*n.* 壽司　restaurant〔'rɛstərənt〕*n.* 餐廳
Japanese〔,dʒæpə'niz〕*adj.* 日本的
Mexican〔'mɛksɪkən〕*adj.* 墨西哥的
Vietnamese〔vi,ɛtnɑ'miz〕*adj.* 越南的

56. (**B**) W：Does your professor give you a lot to write after class?
M：Sometimes, but he didn't last night.
What does the professor give him to do after class?

女：你的教授在課後給你很多東西寫嗎？
男：有時候，但他昨晚沒有這樣做。
教授在課後給他什麼去做？

(A) 考試。 (B) 作業。
(C) 貼紙。 (D) 鉛筆。

＊ professor (prəˈfɛsɚ) *n.* 教授 sticker (ˈstɪkɚ) *n.* 貼紙

57. (**D**) M：Did you start in November?
W：Yes, and I was done in one month.
When did the woman finish?
男：妳是從十一月開始做的嗎？
女：是的，而且我一個月內就完成了。
這位女士何時做完？

(A) 九月。 (B) 十月。
(C) 一月。 (D) 十二月。

58. (**D**) M：How are we gonna get the cat to take the drug?
W：We are going to inject it.
What are they going to do with the drug?
男：我們要怎樣才能讓這隻貓吃藥？
女：我們要用打針的。
他們要怎麼處理藥？

(A) 他們將殺了這隻貓。
(B) 他們將把藥吞了。
(C) 他們將和它玩。
(D) 他們將把它給貓吃。

＊ gonna (ˈgɔnə) 等於 going to，是口語化的用法。
take (tek) *v.* 吃 drug (drʌg) *n.* 藥
inject (ɪnˈdʒɛkt) *v.* 注射 swallow (ˈswɑlo) *v.* 吞下

59. (**A**) W：Which are the main chapters of the novel?

M：The 3rd and the 4th.

What is special about the 3rd and 4th chapters?

女：這本小說的主要章節是哪些？

男：第三和第四章。

第三和第四章有什麼特別的？

(A) 它們是最重要的。

(B) 它們是最不重要的。

(C) 它們是最不可能的。

(D) 它們是最客觀的。

* main〔men〕*adj.* 主要的
chapter〔ˈtʃæptɚ〕*n.* 章　　novel〔ˈnɑvl̩〕*n.* 小說
least〔list〕*adv.* 最不
impersonal〔ɪmˈpɝsn̩l̩〕*adj.* 客觀的

60. (**B**) M：What happened to Neal?

W：He lost his voice.

What was wrong with Neal?

男：尼爾怎麼了？

女：他失聲了。

尼爾怎麼了？

(A) 他不能跑。

(B) 他不能唱。

(C) 他不能聽。

(D) 他不能看。

* lose〔luz〕*v.* 失去　　voice〔vɔɪs〕*n.* 聲音

LISTENING TEST ④

- *Directions for questions 1-25. You will hear questions on the test CD. Select the one item A, B, C or D which answers the question correctly, and mark your answer sheet.*

1. A. at ten o'clock　　B. at 952 Broadway
   C. in the past　　D. on Mars

2. A. Tony's eyes　　B. Tony's ears
   C. Tony's throat　　D. Tony's teeth

3. A. the people　　B. the food
   C. the weather　　D. the scenery

4. A. next week　　B. after a while
   C. tomorrow　　D. right away

5. A. happy　　B. sad
   C. ecstatic　　D. angry

6. A. Yes, I knew you were arrested.
   B. What did you say was broken?
   C. No, when did that happen?
   D. When will the party begin?

7. A. The weather changed.
   B. May took a shower.
   C. The rained stopped all of a sudden.
   D. The rain lasted for a week.

8. A. Yes, I'd like to see it, too.
   B. If you agree to put it away when you're through.
   C. Great. It's too much for me.
   D. No, I think that's a good idea.

9. A. She used a bar. B. She used a car.
   C. She used a cat. D. She used a cap.

10. A. because it was open B. because it was a holiday
    C. because it was Monday D. because it was ugly

11. A. steak B. salad
    C. apple pie D. meatballs

12. A. No, she liked the food.
    B. Yes, she said she didn't like the food or the people.
    C. Yes, the trip was good.
    D. Yes, she took a trip.

13. A. if Joe had money in a bank
    B. if he needed money
    C. if the bank was open
    D. if Joe was in the bank

14. A. No, he doesn't want to stay.
    B. Yes, he decided to go.
    C. Yes, he often goes there. D. Does he mean it?

15. A. at 7:45 B. at 8:15
    C. at 8:45 D. at 8:30

16. A. pretty B. good-looking
C. handsome D. fine

17. A. There's dirt in the corner.
B. There's dirt everywhere.
C. There's dirt on the ceiling.
D. There's no dirt.

18. A. to the lost and found office
B. to the supermarket
C. to the post office
D. to the travel agent to get a package deal

19. A. Yes, everybody is welcome here.
B. Yes, it is owned by Mr. Collins.
C. No, it's not a place where you can visit.
D. Yes, dogs are allowed here.

20. A. rolling B. shaking
C. ascending D. descending

21. A. the rubber around the headlight
B. the rubber around the wheel
C. the rubber around the gas tank
D. the rubber around the steel

22. A. to destroy tanks B. for long distances
C. only for a short time D. for a long time

23. A. when they want problems
    B. when they want food
    C. when they want cats
    D. when they want help

24. A. He was a crafty person.
    B. He was very shy.
    C. He was a cunning person.
    D. He was a very skillful person.

25. A. He will anticipate the plan.
    B. He will consider the plan.
    C. He will check the plan.
    D. He will renew the plan.

● *Directions for questions 26-50. You will hear statements on the test CD. Select the one answer A, B, C, or D which comes closest to the meaning of the statement and mark your answer sheet.*

26. A. The engine becomes cold.
    B. The engine becomes too hot.
    C. The engine becomes angry.
    D. The engine becomes excited.

27. A. She had less money.
    B. She had fewer friends.
    C. She had less pain.
    D. She had problems.

28. A. They constructed the car.
    B. They took apart the car.
    C. They raced the car.
    D. They designed the car.

29. A. I'm having my bike washed.
B. I'm having trouble with my bike.
C. I'm having my bike sold.
D. I'm having my bike photographed.

30. A. The police took him away.
B. The police gave him a fine.
C. The police let him go.
D. The police put him in prison.

31. A. It helped our plans.
B. It made us change our plans.
C. It made us keep our plans.
D. It made our plans even better.

32. A. They will flip. B. They will spit.
C. They will skip. D. They will slip.

33. A. Decay is gotten rid of with a drill.
B. Decay comes from not brushing properly.
C. Drilling is painful.
D. The tooth has a cavity.

34. A. They can cause a lot of damage.
B. They are no longer used.
C. They are expensive.
D. They are harmless.

35. A. He doesn't have enough.
B. He has a credit card. C. He lost his wallet.
D. He doesn't have any money at all.

36. A. He wanted to buy soft food.
B. He wanted to buy hard drinks.
C. He wanted to buy soft drinks.
D. He wanted to buy bread.

37. A. A lot of people work for Mr. Franklin.
B. Only a few people work for him.
C. Mr. Franklin works hard.
D. Mr. Franklin hired a new worker.

38. A. She never goes to school.
B. She always goes to school.
C. She seldom goes to school.
D. She doesn't like school.

39. A. Simon was going on a trip.
B. Simon was making a bag.
C. Simon was going to wrestle.
D. Simon just came home.

40. A. She is dependent. B. She is dangerous.
C. She is divergent. D. She is diligent.

41. A. Paullina interrogated me.
B. Paullina interested me.
C. Paullina interrupted me. D. Paullina immersed me.

42. A. The dog cannot cook in.
    B. The dog cannot come in.
    C. The dog can come in.
    D. The god cannot hold on.

43. A. Jane doesn't need to fry a ticket.
    B. Jane doesn't need to buy a ticket.
    C. Joe doesn't need to fly a ticket.
    D. Joe doesn't need to lie a ticket.

44. A. He saw a right far away.
    B. He saw a light far away.
    C. He saw a fight far away.
    D. He saw a night far away.

45. A. The cotton is dangerous.
    B. The cotton is expensive.
    C. The cotton is cheap.
    D. The cotton is extraordinary.

46. A. The masked men made away with the money.
    B. The masked men hid it.
    C. The masked men prevented from the money.
    D. The masked men carried on holding money.

47. A. The supermarket never sells milk.
    B. There isn't anymore milk.
    C. The store has plenty of milk.
    D. The store delivers milk.

48. A. He is a horse in a harness.
    B. He was a pig in a pigpen.
    C. He was a bull in a china shop.
    D. He is a man in ski pants.

49. A. They saw land but not the clouds.
    B. They saw planets in orbit.
    C. They saw the clouds but not the water.
    D. They saw aliens flying around.

50. A. He wanted to rest there.
    B. He wanted to live there permanently.
    C. He lives there for a while.
    D. He goes there for a visit.

- *Directions for questions 51-60. You will hear dialogs on the test CD. Select the correct answer A, B, C, or D and mark your answer sheet.*

51. A. She just got back from a short trip.
    B. She is lazy.
    C. She has traveled far.
    D. She is excited about the trip.

52. A. car B. boat
    C. plane D. train

53. A. He does not like women.
    B. He does not like shopping.
    C. He does not like playing.
    D. He does not like to work.

54. A. put the dishes under the table
B. put the dishes on the chair
C. put the dishes on the table
D. put the drinks on the table

55. A. They are about to go out for the evening.
B. The woman is going somewhere with the baby-sitter.
C. The man is not dressed yet.
D. The baby-sitter is about to leave.

56. A. He had better hurry.
B. The flight will leave on time.
C. The flight will not leave on time.
D. The man needs to reconfirm his flight.

57. A. in a florist shop B. in a restaurant
C. in a stadium D. in a supermarket

58. A. in his office B. on vacation
C. at lunch D. in retirement

59. A. 10:00 B. 10:15
C. 11:15 D. 9:45

60. A. He didn't try the assignment at all.
B. The assignment was too difficult for him to complete.
C. He finished the entire homework assignment.
D. He got stuck in the mind.

ECL 聽力測驗④詳解

1. (**B**) Where does Joanna live?

喬安納住在哪裡？

(A) 十點鐘。 (B) 百老匯街 952 號。
(C) 過去。 (D) 火星上。

* live〔 lɪv 〕*v.* 居住
Broadway〔ˈbrɔd,we〕*n.* 百老匯
past〔 pæst 〕*n.* 過去　Mars〔 mɑrz 〕*n.* 火星

2. (**B**) Tony went to the doctor to have his hearing tested. What did the doctor test?

東尼去醫生那裡作聽力測試。／醫生要測試什麼？

(A) 東尼的眼睛。 (B) 東尼的耳朵。
(C) 東尼的喉嚨。 (D) 東尼的牙齒。

* hearing〔ˈhɪrɪŋ〕*n.* 聽力　test〔 tɛst 〕*v.* 測試
throat〔 θrot 〕*n.* 喉嚨　teeth〔 tiθ 〕*n.* 牙齒

3. (**C**) The climate in that country is comfortable. What is comfortable about that country?

那個國家的氣候很舒適。／那個國家的什麼很舒適？

(A) 人民。 (B) 食物。
(C) 天氣。 (D) 風景。

* climate〔ˈklaɪmɪt〕*n.* 氣候
comfortable〔ˈkʌmfɚtəbl̩〕*adj.* 舒適的
country〔ˈkʌntrɪ〕*n.* 國家　weather〔ˈwɛðɚ〕*n.* 天氣
scenery〔ˈsinərɪ〕*n.* 風景

4. (**D**) This problem requires immediate action. When should we act?

必須馬上對這個問題採取行動。／我們應該何時行動？

(A) 下週。 (B) 等一下。

(C) 明天。 (D) 立刻。

* problem〔ˈprɑbləm〕*n.* 問題
require〔rɪˈkwaɪr〕*v.* 需要
immediate〔ɪˈmidɪɪt〕*adj.* 立即的
action〔ˈækʃən〕*n.* 行動 while〔hwaɪl〕*n.* 短暫的時間

5. (**D**) The irritated woman went on her way. How did the woman feel?

這個生氣的女人繼續旅行。／這位女士覺得怎麼樣？

(A) 快樂的。 (B) 難過的。

(C) 欣喜若狂的。 (D) 生氣的。

* irritated〔ˈɪrəˌtetɪd〕*adj.* 發怒的
go on** one's **way 繼續旅行
ecstatic〔ɪkˈstætɪk〕*adj.* 欣喜若狂的

6. (**C**) Did I tell you that a burglar broke into my house?

我有跟你提過有個強盜闖入我家嗎？

(A) 是的，我知道你被逮捕了。

(B) 你說什麼東西破了？

(C) 沒有，什麼時候發生的？

(D) 晚宴什麼時候開始？

* burglar〔ˈbɝglɚ〕*n.* 強盜 ***break into*** 強行進入
arrest〔əˈrɛst〕*v.* 逮捕
broken〔ˈbrokən〕*adj.* 破裂的
happen〔ˈhæpən〕*v.* 發生

7. (**A**) Suddenly, there was a rain shower. What happened?
突然下了場陣雨。／發生什麼事？

(A) 天氣改變了。 (B) 梅沖了澡。
(C) 雨突然停了。 (D) 雨持續下了一星期。

* suddenly〔ˈsʌdn̩lɪ〕*adv.* 突然地
shower〔ˈʃauɚ〕*n.* 陣雨；淋浴 ***all of a sudden*** 突然地
last〔læst〕*v.* 持續

8. (**D**) It's getting dark. Do you mind if I turn on the light?
天黑了。你介意我把燈打開嗎？

(A) 是的，我也想要看看它。
(B) 如果你同意用完後收拾整齊的話。
(C) 太棒了。對我來說太多了。
(D) 不會，我想這是個好主意。

* mind〔maɪnd〕*v.* 介意 ***turn on*** 打開
agree〔əˈgri〕*v.* 同意 ***put away*** 收拾
through〔θru〕*adv.* 完成

9. (**B**) What type of vehicle did she use? 她用那一種交通工具？

(A) 她用一根棒子。 (B) 她開車。
(C) 她用一隻貓。 (D) 她用一頂帽子。

* vehicle〔ˈviɪkl̩〕*n.* 交通工具 bar〔bɑr〕*n.* 棒子
cap〔kæp〕*n.* 帽子

10. (**B**) Why was the office closed today?
今天辦公室爲什麼關著呢？

(A) 因爲它是開的。 (B) 因爲是假日。
(C) 因爲是星期一。 (D) 因爲它很醜。

* closed〔klozd〕*adj.* 關閉的
holiday〔ˈhɑləˌde〕*n.* 假日 ugly〔ˈʌglɪ〕*adj.* 醜陋的

11. (**C**) Jane ate some dessert at dinner. What did she eat?
珍在晚餐時吃了一些點心。／她吃了什麼？

(A) 牛排。 (B) 沙拉。
(C) <u>蘋果派。</u> (D) 肉丸。

* dessert〔dɪ'zɝt〕*n.* 點心 steak〔stek〕*n.* 牛排
salad〔'sæləd〕*n.* 沙拉 pie〔paɪ〕*n.* 派；餡餅
meatball〔'mit,bɔl〕*n.* 肉丸

12. (**B**) Did Anna complain about her trip?
安那有抱怨她的旅行嗎？

(A) 沒有，她喜歡那種食物。
(B) <u>有，她說她不喜歡那裡的食物或人。</u>
(C) 有，那趟旅行很棒。
(D) 有，她有去旅行。

* complain〔kəm'plen〕*v.* 抱怨 trip〔trɪp〕*n.* 旅行

13. (**A**) Mr. Smith asked Mr. Joe, "Do you have a bank account?" What did Mr. Smith want to know?
史密斯先生問喬先生：「你有銀行帳戶嗎？」／史密斯先生想要知道什麼？

(A) <u>喬是否有錢放在銀行。</u> (B) 他是否需要錢。
(C) 銀行是否開著。 (D) 喬是否在銀行裡。

* account〔ə'kaunt〕*n.* 帳戶

14. (**B**) Did he make up his mind to go? 他下定決心要走了嗎？

(A) 不，他不要留下來。 (B) <u>是的，他決定要走。</u>
(C) 是的，他常去那裡。 (D) 他是這個意思嗎？

* ***make up** one's **mind*** 下定決心
decide〔dɪ'saɪd〕*v.* 決定 mean〔min〕*v.* 意謂著

15. (**B**) Jim finished his work at a quarter after eight. When did Jim finish his work?
吉姆在八點十五分時完成他的工作。／吉姆何時完成他的工作？
(A) 七點四十五分。
(B) 八點十五分。
(C) 八點四十五分。
(D) 八點半。

* finish (ˈfɪnɪʃ) *v.* 完成
quarter (ˈkwɔrtɚ) *n.* 十五分鐘

16. (**D**) Tina's feeling pretty good. How does she feel?
緹娜覺得很棒。／她覺得如何？
(A) 漂亮。 (B) 漂亮。
(C) 英俊。 (D) 蠻好的。

* pretty (ˈprɪtɪ) *adv.* 非常；*adj.* 漂亮的
good-looking (ˈgudˈlukɪŋ) *adj.* 漂亮的
handsome (ˈhænsəm) *adj.* 漂亮的；英俊的

17. (**B**) The dirt is all over the place. Where is the dirt?
這個地方到處都是灰塵。／灰塵在哪裡？
(A) 角落有灰塵。
(B) 到處都有灰塵。
(C) 天花板上有灰塵。
(D) 沒有灰塵。

* dirt (dɝt) *n.* 灰塵 corner (ˈkɔrnɚ) *n.* 角落
ceiling (ˈsilɪŋ) *n.* 天花板

18. (**C**) Doreen wants to send a package. Where should she go? 多琳想要寄一個包裹。／她應該去哪裡？

(A) 去失物招領處。
(B) 去超市。
(C) <u>去郵局。</u>
(D) 到旅行社拿套裝行程。

* package〔ˈpækɪdʒ〕*n.* 包裹
the lost and found 失物招領處
office〔ˈɔfɪs〕*n.* 處；所 ***post office*** 郵局
agent〔ˈedʒənt〕*n.* 代理業者 ***travel agent*** 旅行業者
package deal 整套商品；套裝行程

19. (**B**) Is this club private? 這是私人俱樂部嗎？

(A) 是的，歡迎每個人來這裡。
(B) <u>是的，這是柯林斯先生所有。</u>
(C) 不，它不是你可以參觀的地方。
(D) 是的，狗可以進來這裡。

* private〔ˈpraɪvɪt〕*adj.* 私人的
welcome〔ˈwɛlkəm〕*adj.* 受歡迎的
own〔on〕*v.* 擁有 allow〔əˈlaʊ〕*v.* 准許

20. (**B**) She can feel the bus vibrating. What was the bus doing? 她可以感覺到巴士在震動。／巴士在做什麼？

(A) 滾動。 (B) <u>搖晃。</u>
(C) 爬坡。 (D) 下坡。

* vibrate〔ˈvaɪbret〕*v.* 震動 roll〔rol〕*v.* 滾動
shake〔ʃek〕*v.* 震動；搖動 ascend〔əˈsɛnd〕*v.* 上坡
descend〔dɪˈsɛnd〕*v.* 下坡

21. (**B**) The bus lost the left front tire. What did the bus lose?
那台巴士左前方的輪胎掉了。／那台巴士掉了什麼？

(A) 圍繞大燈的橡膠。 (B) 圍繞輪子的橡膠。
(C) 圍繞油箱的橡膠。 (D) 圍繞鋼的橡膠。

* tire (taɪr) *n.* 輪胎 rubber (ˈrʌbɚ) *n.* 橡膠
headlight (ˈhɛd,laɪt) *n.* 車前大燈
wheel (hwil) *n.* 輪子 ***gas tank*** 油箱
steel (stil) *n.* 鋼

22. (**B**) You should use this weapon for long range only.
When should you use it?
你只能在長程射擊時使用這種武器。／你應該何時使用它？

(A) 破壞坦克時。 (B) 長距離時。
(C) 只能用一下子。 (D) 能用很久。

* weapon (ˈwɛpən) *n.* 武器 range (rendʒ) *n.* 範圍；射程
destroy (dɪˈstrɔɪ) *v.* 破壞 tank (tæŋk) *n.* 坦克車
distance (ˈdɪstəns) *n.* 距離

23. (**D**) If the women need aid, they should call the police.
When should the women call the police?
如果那些女人需要幫助，他們應該叫警察。／那些女人應該在什麼時候叫警察？

(A) 當她們想要麻煩時。
(B) 當她們想要食物時。
(C) 當她們想要貓時。
(D) 當她們想要幫助時。

* aid (ed) *n.* 援助 police (pəˈlis) *n.* 警察
problem (ˈprɑbləm) *n.* 問題 help (hɛlp) *n.* 幫助

24. (**D**) Ray became an expert. What was Ray?
雷成爲了專家。／雷是什麼？

(A) 他是個狡猾的人。
(B) 他非常地害羞。
(C) 他是個狡猾的人。
(D) 他是個技術精湛的人。

* expert 〔'ɛkspɝt〕*n.* 專家　crafty 〔'kræftɪ〕*adj.* 狡猾的
shy 〔ʃaɪ〕*adj.* 害羞的　cunning 〔'kʌnɪŋ〕*adj.* 狡猾的
skillful 〔'skɪlfəl〕*adj.* 技術精湛的

25. (**B**) I will think over your plan and give you an answer next week. What will the man do?
我會考慮你的計劃，然後在下星期給你答覆。／這位男士會做什麼？

(A) 他會預先做好這個計劃的準備。
(B) 他會考慮這個計劃。
(C) 他會檢查這個計劃。
(D) 他會更新這個計劃。

* ***think over*** 仔細考慮
anticipate 〔æn'tɪsə,pet〕*v.* 預先做好準備
consider 〔kən'sɪdɚ〕*v.* 考慮　check 〔tʃɛk〕*v.* 檢查
renew 〔rɪ'nju〕*v.* 更新

26. (**B**) The engine sometimes gets overheated.
這部引擎有時候會過熱。

(A) 這部引擎變冷。　(B) 這部引擎太熱。
(C) 這部引擎生氣。　(D) 這部引擎變得很興奮。

* engine 〔'ɛndʒən〕*n.* 引擎
overheated 〔,ovɚ'hitɪd〕*adj.* 過熱的

27. (**C**) The medication brought Jane some relief.
藥物減輕珍的病痛。

(A) 她的錢比較少。 (B) 她的朋友比較少。
(C) <u>她比較不痛了。</u> (D) 她有麻煩。

* medication (ˌmɛdɪ'keʃən) *n.* 藥物
relief (rɪ'lif) *n.* (痛苦、負擔等的) 減輕
pain (pen) *n.* 痛苦

28. (**A**) I saw the guys build a race car.
我看到那些傢伙組了一台賽車。

(A) <u>他們組了這部車。</u>
(B) 他們拆了這部車。
(C) 他們用這部車出賽。
(D) 他們設計了這部車。

* guy (gaɪ) *n.* 傢伙 build (bɪld) *v.* 建造；組合
race car 賽車 construct (kən'strʌkt) *v.* 組合
take apart 拆解
race (res) *v.* 使 (馬、車、遊艇等) 出賽
design (dɪ'zaɪn) *v.* 設計

29. (**B**) I've got to have my bike repaired.
我必須要把我的腳踏車送修。

(A) 我正要把我的腳踏車送洗。
(B) <u>我的腳踏車故障。</u>
(C) 我正要賣掉我的腳踏車。
(D) 我正要拍下我的腳踏車。

* ***have got to*** 必須 (= *have to*)
repair (rɪ'pɛr) *v.* 修理 trouble ('trʌbl̩) *n.* 故障
photograph ('fotəˌgræf) *v.* 拍照

30. (**C**) The burglar was freed by the police.
這個強盜被警察放了。
(A) 警察把他帶走了。 (B) 警察給他罰金。
(C) 警察讓他走。 (D) 警察送他去坐牢。
* free〔fri〕*v.* 釋放　fine〔faɪn〕*n.* 罰金
prison〔ˈprɪzn̩〕*n.* 監牢

31. (**B**) The weather interfered with our plans for a trip.
天氣妨礙了我們去旅行的計劃。
(A) 它對我們的計劃有幫助。
(B) 它使我們改變計劃。 (C) 它使我們維持計劃。
(D) 它使我們的計劃變得更好。
* interfere〔ˌɪntəˈfɪr〕*v.* 妨礙

32. (**D**) The children will slide on the ice. 這些小孩要去溜冰。
(A) 他們會輕彈。 (B) 他們會吐口水。
(C) 他們會蹦蹦跳跳。 (D) 他們會滑行。
* slide〔slaɪd〕*v.* 滑行　flip〔flɪp〕*v.* 輕彈
spit〔spɪt〕*v.* 吐口水　skip〔skɪp〕*v.* 蹦蹦跳跳
slip〔slɪp〕*v.* 滑行

33. (**A**) A drill is used to remove decay from a tooth.
鑽孔機是用來除去牙齒的蛀牙部分。
(A) 蛀牙是用鑽孔機來去除。
(B) 蛀牙是因爲不當的刷牙方式。
(C) 鑽牙很痛。 (D) 牙齒有一個蛀洞。
* drill〔drɪl〕*n.* 鑽孔機　remove〔rɪˈmuv〕*v.* 除去
decay〔dɪˈke〕*n.* 蛀牙　***get rid of*** 去除
brush〔brʌʃ〕*v.* 刷牙　properly〔ˈprɑpəlɪ〕*adv.* 不適當地
drilling〔ˈdrɪlɪŋ〕*n.* 鑽孔　cavity〔ˈkævətɪ〕*n.* 蛀牙產生的洞

34. (**A**) Those weapons are dangerous.
那些武器很危險。

(A) <u>它們能造成很大的損害。</u>
(B) 它們已不再被使用。
(C) 它們很貴。
(D) 它們是無害的。

* dangerous ('dendʒərəs) *adj.* 危險的
cause (kɔz) *v.* 造成
damage ('dæmɪdʒ) *n.* 損害 ***no longer*** 不再
expensive (ɪk'spɛnsɪv) *adj.* 昂貴的
harmless ('hɑrmlɪs) *adj.* 無害的

35. (**D**) Mr. Pell has no money.
沛爾先生沒有錢。

(A) 他的錢不夠。 (B) 他有一張信用卡。
(C) 他的皮夾掉了。 (D) <u>他一點錢都沒有。</u>

* credit ('krɛdɪt) *n.* 信用 ***credit card*** 信用卡
wallet ('wɑlɪt) *n.* 皮夾 ***not at all*** 一點也不

36. (**C**) Paul went to the beverage section of the corner store.
保羅到街角那家商店的飲料區。

(A) 他要買無刺激性的食物。
(B) 他要買酒精飲料。
(C) <u>他要買非酒精飲料。</u>
(D) 他要買麵包。

* beverage ('bɛvərɪdʒ) *n.* (非酒精性)飲料
section ('sɛkʃən) *n.* 區域
soft (sɔft) *adj.* 無刺激性的 ***hard drink*** 酒精性飲料
soft drink 非酒精性飲料

37. (**A**) Mr. Franklin employs a lot of workers.
法蘭克林先生僱用許多員工。

(A) <u>許多人替法蘭克林先生工作。</u>
(B) 只有一些人替法蘭克林先生工作。
(C) 法蘭克林先生很努力工作。
(D) 法蘭克林先生僱用了一位新員工。

* employ〔ɪm'plɔɪ〕*v.* 僱用　hire〔haɪr〕*v.* 僱用

38. (**B**) Barbara has never skipped class.
芭芭拉從不翹課。

(A) 她從不去學校。　(B) <u>她總是去學校。</u>
(C) 她很少去學校。　(D) 她不喜歡學校。

* skip〔skɪp〕*v.* 翹（課）　seldom〔'sɛldəm〕*adv.* 很少

39. (**A**) Simon was packing his bags.
賽門在打包他的袋子。

(A) <u>賽門要去旅行。</u>　(B) 賽門在做袋子。
(C) 賽門要去摔角。　(D) 賽門剛回家。

* pack〔pæk〕*v.* 打包　wrestle〔'rɛsl̩〕*v.* 摔角

40. (**D**) Lucia is attentive and hard-working.
露西亞既專心又勤奮。

(A) 她很依賴。　(B) 她很危險。
(C) 她是分歧的。　(D) <u>她很勤奮。</u>

* attentive〔ə'tɛntɪv〕*adj.* 專心的
hard-working〔'hɑrd'wɝkɪŋ〕*adj.* 勤奮的
dependent〔dɪ'pɛndənt〕*adj.* 依賴的
divergent〔daɪ'vɝdʒənt〕*adj.* 分歧的
diligent〔'dɪlədʒənt〕*adj.* 勤勉的

41. (**C**) I was talking to Tommy when Paullina cut in.
當我和湯米說話時寶琳娜插嘴。

(A) 寶琳娜質問我。
(B) 寶琳娜使我感興趣。
(C) <u>寶琳娜打斷我。</u>
(D) 寶琳娜爲我施洗禮。

* ***cut in*** 插嘴　　interrogate〔ɪn'tɛrə,get〕*v.* 質問
interest〔'ɪntərɪst〕*v.* 使感興趣
interrupt〔,ɪntə'rʌpt〕*v.* 中斷
immerse〔ɪ'mɝs〕*v.* 施洗禮；浸入

42. (**B**) The dog must stay out. 那隻狗必須待在外面。

(A) 那隻狗不能在家煮飯。
(B) <u>那隻狗不能進來。</u>
(C) 那隻狗能進來。
(D) 那位神明無法堅持下去。

* in〔ɪn〕*adv.* 在家　　god〔gɑd〕*n.* 神
hold on 堅持下去

43. (**B**) Jane said that she'd like to go to the movie, but she didn't have enough money. Her roommate told her that it would be OK because the movie is free.
珍說她想要去看電影，但是她沒有足夠的錢。她的室友說沒關係，因爲電影是免費的。

(A) 珍不需要炸一張票。　(B) <u>珍不需要買一張票。</u>
(C) 珍不需要飛一張票。　(D) 珍不需要騙一張票。

* roommate〔'rum,met〕*n.* 室友
fry〔fraɪ〕*v.* 炸　　lie〔laɪ〕*v.* 欺騙

44. (**B**) Mr. Eric saw a light in the distance.
艾立克先生看見遠方有一道光。

(A) 他看見遠方有個右外野手。
(B) 他看見遠方有一道光。
(C) 他看見遠方有打鬥。
(D) 他看見遠方有夜晚。

* distance〔ˈdɪstəns〕*n.* 遠處　right〔raɪt〕*n.* 右外野手
far away 遠方　fight〔faɪt〕*n.* 打架

45. (**C**) This cotton is inexpensive.
這塊棉布不貴。

(A) 這塊棉布很危險。　(B) 這塊棉布很貴。
(C) 這塊棉布很便宜。　(D) 這塊棉布很特別。

* cotton〔ˈkɑtn̩〕*n.* 棉布
inexpensive〔ˌɪnɪkˈspɛnsɪv〕*adj.* 不貴的
cheap〔tʃip〕*adj.* 便宜的
extraordinary〔ɪkˈstɔrdn̩ˌɛrɪ〕*adj.* 特別的

46. (**A**) Two masked men held up the clerks and took away the money.
兩個戴面具的人搶了店員，並奪走錢。

(A) 戴面具的人奪走錢。
(B) 戴面具的人把它藏起來。
(C) 戴面具的人防止錢。
(D) 戴面具的人繼續拿著錢。

* masked〔mæskt〕*adj.* 帶假面具的
hold up 搶奪　clerk〔klɝk〕*n.* 店員
make away with 拿走　hide〔haɪd〕*v.* 藏起來
prevent〔prɪˈvɛnt〕*v.* 防止　***carry on*** 繼續

47. (**B**) The store is out of milk.
那家店沒有牛奶了。

(A) 那家超市從來不賣牛奶。 (B) <u>牛奶一點也不剩。</u>
(C) 那家店有充足的牛奶。 (D) 那家店有外送牛奶。

* ***out of*** 缺乏；沒有 ***plenty of*** 充分的
deliver〔dɪˈlɪvɚ〕*v.* 遞送

48. (**C**) John came in like a tactless person and his rough talk caused the request to be turned down.
約翰進來時像個笨拙的人，他粗魯的言詞使得要求被拒。

(A) 他是戴著馬具的馬。
(B) 他是豬舍裡的豬。
(C) <u>他是笨手笨腳的人。</u>
(D) 他是穿滑雪褲的人。

* ***come in*** 進來 tactless〔ˈtæktlɪs〕*adj.* 笨拙的
rough〔rʌf〕*adj.* 粗魯的 request〔rɪˈkwɛst〕*n.* 要求
turn down 拒絕 harness〔ˈhɑrnɪs〕*n.* 馬具
pigpen〔ˈpɪgˌpɛn〕*n.* 豬棚
a bull in a china shop 笨手笨腳的人
pants〔pænts〕*n. pl.* 褲子

49. (**C**) When they flew over the sea, there were clouds below them. 當他們飛過海，雲在他們下面。

(A) 他們看到陸地但沒看到雲。
(B) 他們看到軌道上的行星。
(C) <u>他們看到雲但沒看到水。</u>
(D) 他們看到外星人到處飛。

* cloud〔klaʊd〕*n.* 雲 land〔lænd〕*n.* 陸地
planet〔ˈplænɪt〕*n.* 行星 orbit〔ˈɔrbɪt〕*n.* 軌道
alien〔ˈeljən〕*n.* 外星人

50. (**B**) He wanted to settle down in the country.

他要在鄉下定居。

(A) 他要在那裡休息。

(B) 他要永遠住在那裡。

(C) 他要在那裡住一會兒。

(D) 他到那裡參觀。

* settle〔ˈsɛtl̩〕*v.* 定居 ***settle down*** 定居
country〔ˈkʌntrɪ〕*n.* 鄉下 rest〔rɛst〕*v.* 休息
permanently〔ˈpɝmənəntlɪ〕*adv.* 永久地
for a while 一會兒

51. (**C**) M：You look exhausted.

W：Well, it was a long trip.

What do you learn about the woman?

男：妳看起來筋疲力竭。

女：是啊，那是一趟漫長的旅行。

你知道關於這位女士的什麼？

(A) 她剛從一個短程的旅行回來。

(B) 她很懶惰。

(C) 她到遙遠的地方旅行。

(D) 她對於這趟旅行很興奮。

* exhausted〔ɪgˈzɔstɪd〕*adj.* 筋疲力竭的
lazy〔ˈlezɪ〕*adj.* 懶惰的
far〔fɑr〕*adv.* 遙遠地

52. (**B**) W：How are you traveling to Asia?

M：I'm traveling by ship.

What vehicle is the man taking?

女：你是怎麼到亞洲旅行的？
男：我乘船旅行。
這位男士是搭乘什麼交通工具？

(A) 汽車。　(B) <u>船。</u>　(C) 飛機。　(D) 火車。

* Asia〔'eʃə〕*n.* 亞洲　ship〔ʃɪp〕*n.* 船
vehicle〔'viɪkl̩〕*n.* 交通工具

53. (**D**) M：I think I will ask Paul to do it.
W：Don't ask him. He is lazy.
What was the woman saying about Paul?
男：我想我會請保羅來做這件事情。
女：不要找他。他很懶。
關於保羅，這位女士說了什麼？

(A) 他不喜歡女人。　(B) 他不喜歡購物。
(C) 他不喜歡玩。　(D) <u>他不喜歡工作。</u>

54. (**C**) W：I'm starving.
M：May I help you with lunch?
W：Oh, thanks. You can put the plates on the table.
What did the woman say to do?
女：我好餓。
男：我可以提供妳午餐嗎？
女：喔，謝謝。你可以把盤子放在桌子上。
這位女士說要做什麼？

(A) 把食物放在桌子下面。
(B) 把食物放在椅子上面。
(C) <u>把食物放在桌子上面。</u>
(D) 把飲料放在桌子上面。

* starve〔starv〕*v.* 飢餓　plate〔plet〕*n.* 盤子
dish〔dɪʃ〕*n.* 食物；菜餚　drink〔drɪŋk〕*n.* 飲料

55. (**A**) M : The baby-sitter should be here any minute.

W : I'll hurry up and get dressed.

What is about to happen?

男：褓母應該隨時會到。

女：我會趕快穿好衣服。

將要發生什麼事？

(A) 他們晚上將要出去。

(B) 那位女士要跟褓母去某處。

(C) 這男士還沒有穿好衣服。

(D) 那褓母將要離開。

* ***baby-sitter*** 褓母　***any minute*** 隨時；馬上

hurry up 趕快　dressed〔drɛst〕*adj.* 穿衣服的

be about to 即將　for〔fɔr〕*prep.* 在…時候

deliver〔dɪˈlɪvɚ〕*v.* 遞送

56. (**A**) M : I hope the flight leaves on time.

W : Well, if you don't step on it, it won't matter.

What does the woman mean?

男： 我希望班機會準時起飛。

女： 嗯，如果你不快一點，飛機是否準時起飛就無關緊要了。

這位女士是什麼意思？

(A) 他最好趕快。

(B) 飛機將會準時離開。

(C) 飛機將不會準時離開。

(D) 那男士必須再次確認班次。

* flight〔flaɪt〕*n.* 班機　***on time*** 準時

step on it 趕快　matter〔ˈmætɚ〕*v.* 關係重要

had better 最好　hurry〔ˈhɝɪ〕*v.* 加快

reconfirm〔ˌrikənˈfɝm〕*v.* 再確認

57. (**D**) M：Where are the vegetables?
W：They're behind the juices on aisle 3.
Where does the conversation take place?
男：蔬菜放在哪裡？
女：在第三排走道，果汁的後面。
這段對話發生在什麼地方？
(A) 在花店。 (B) 在餐廳。
(C) 在運動場。 (D) 在超級市場。

* aisle (aɪl) *n.* 走道
conversation (ˌkɑnvɚˈsɛʃən) *n.* 對話
take place 發生 florist (ˈflorɪst) *n.* 花卉
stadium (ˈstedɪəm) *n.* 運動場

58. (**B**) W：When can I see Dr. Smith about my arm?
M：I'm sorry he is off this month, but Dr. Mason can take you.
Where is Dr. Smith?
女：我什麼時候可以請史密斯醫生看我的手臂？
男：很抱歉，他這個月休假，不過梅森醫生可以幫你看。
史密斯醫生在那裡？
(A) 在他的辦公室。 (B) 休假中。
(C) 在吃午餐。 (D) 退休了。

* off (ɔf) *adj.* 休息的 take (tek) *v.* 檢查
vacation (veˈkeʃən) *n.* 休假
on vacation 在休假中
retirement (rɪˈtaɪrmənt) *n.* 退休

59. (**A**) M：Gee, I wonder what's keeping Keith? He said he'd be here at 10:00, and it's already a quarter after.

W：He's always an hour late.

What time does the man expect Keith to appear?

男：咦！不知道基斯被什麼事耽擱了？他說他十點會到，而現在已經十點十五分了。

女：他向來都遲到一小時。

這位男士預計基斯何時會出現？

(A) 十點。　(B) 十點十五分。

(C) 十一點十五分。　(D) 九點四十五分。

＊ gee〔dʒi〕*interj.* 咦　keep〔kip〕*v.* 使…停留

quarter〔ˈkwɔrtɚ〕*n.* 十五分鐘

expect〔ɪkˈspɛkt〕*v.* 預計　appear〔əˈpɪr〕*v.* 出現

60. (**B**) W：Did you complete the homework assignment?

M：I tried, but I got stuck on number three.

What is the man's problem?

女：你的家庭作業做完了嗎？

男：我試著要寫，但是我被第三題難倒了。

這位男士的問題爲何？

(A) 他完全沒有試著要寫作業。

(B) 作業太難了，以致於他無法完成。

(C) 他已經完成全部的家庭作業。

(D) 他的腦中遇到難題。

＊ complete〔kəmˈplit〕*v.* 完成

assignment〔əˈsaɪnmənt〕*n.* 指定作業

get stuck 遇到難題　***not at all*** 完全不

difficult〔ˈdɪfəˌkʌlt〕*adj.* 困難的

entire〔ɪnˈtaɪr〕*adj.* 全部的

LISTENING TEST ⑤

- *Directions for questions 1-25. You will hear questions on the test CD. Select the one item A, B, C or D which answers the question correctly, and mark your answer sheet.*

1. A. tennis B. sailing
   C. golf D. Ping-Pong

2. A. paying fines B. explanations
   C. driving regulations D. group dynamics

3. A. unite them B. utilize them
   C. scatter them D. separate them

4. A. guns and ammunition B. milk and bread
   C. cats and dogs D. nails and hammers

5. A. catch the ball B. feel sleepy
   C. understand D. stand up

6. A. They'll explode the truck.
   B. They'll exploit the truck.
   C. They'll examine the truck.
   D. They'll exterminate the car.

7. A. Which track is the right one?
   B. How can she reach the train station?
   C. What time does the next train leave?
   D. When will the train arrive?

8. A. That perhaps he would come to visit her.
   B. That he wouldn't come to visit her.
   C. That they were going to get married.
   D. That she loved him.

9. A. He will gun the elevator.
   B. He will run the elevator.
   C. He will run the escalator.
   D. He will walk the elevator.

10. A. He directed the movie.
    B. He directed the dimension.
    C. He directed the discussion.
    D. He directed the illusion.

11. A. She commemorated with them.
    B. She communicated with them.
    C. She complicated them.
    D. She compromised with them.

12. A. Ensure that his ideas are new.
    B. Ensure that his ideas are old.
    C. Ensure that his ideas are refused.
    D. Ensure that his ideas are used.

13. A. to a contest   B. to a social gathering
    C. to a game   D. to a movie

14. A. It's used to sweep the room.
    B. It's used to make toast.
    C. It's used to kill flies.
    D. It's used to turn on the motor.

15. A. sixteen B. fourteen and eighteen
    C. fourteen D. eighteen

16. A. her weight B. her height
    C. her density D. her length

17. A. before we arrived B. when we arrived
    C. after we arrived D. raining heavily

18. A. tell them what to do B. watch them
    C. pay them D. help them

19. A. daydreaming B. fooling around
    C. thinking D. watching

20. A. because he is angry B. because he is cold
    C. because he is tired D. because he is hot

21. A. Yes, I'll finish it quickly.
    B. Yes, I'll start it soon.
    C. Yes, I won't finish it tomorrow.
    D. Yes, it's very difficult.

22. A. a check B. money
C. gas D. a new bike

23. A. because the wind will shift
B. because the wine will disappear
C. because the wind will slow
D. because the wind will stop

24. A. Yes, but never when I'm in a hurry.
B. No, only when I'm in a hurry.
C. No, never when I drive.
D. Yes, only when I'm furry.

25. A. They were in the supermarket this morning.
B. They were from Eastern Taiwan.
C. She lives in Taipei.
D. They will migrate to America.

● *Directions for questions 26-50. You will hear statements on the test CD. Select the one answer A, B, C, or D which comes closest to the meaning of the statement and mark your answer sheet.*

26. A. Let's forget it. B. Let's finish it.
C. Let's abandon it. D. Let's try it.

27. A. It has a new method.
B. It has a new school.
C. It has a new type.
D. It has some news.

28. A. She did what she liked to do.
    B. She did what she always does.
    C. She did what she couldn't do.
    D. She did what she was supposed to do.

29. A. They are gone. B. They are worn.
    C. They are old. D. They are sold.

30. A. He can't hear. B. He can't see.
    C. He can't run. D. He can't speak.

31. A. He made the best tool.
    B. He bought the best tool.
    C. He chose the best tool.
    D. He ordered the best tool.

32. A. People were listening to the radio broadcast.
    B. Everyone watched the rocket take off.
    C. People were watching the movie.
    D. The racket landed.

33. A. She is waiting to travel.
    B. She has agreed to travel.
    C. She is whining to travel.
    D. She is armed to travel.

34. A. The head has the power to give rises.
    B. The head is not able to make a decision.
    C. The organization never gives rises.
    D. The authority of the head doesn't work.

35. A. They like it.
B. They wouldn't try it.
C. They prefer cake.
D. They don't like it.

36. A. He doesn't like the lettuce at all.
B. He wants to know where he can get some.
C. He thinks the lettuce is too crispy to take.
D. He never had lettuce before.

37. A. I got six hours of sleep per night.
B. I got six hours of sleep last night.
C. I don't stay in bed after 6:00.
D. I like to read in bed.

38. A. He must fly early in the morning.
B. He must have a co-pilot.
C. He must pay attention to flying.
D. He must not drink.

39. A. She wrote her notes.
B. She reviewed her notes.
C. She showed her notes.
D. She hid her notes.

40. A. They did not understand the regulations.
B. They broke the regulations.
C. They didn't like the regulations.
D. They made the rules.

41. A. We encountered traffic.
B. We exterminated traffic.
C. We were extremely tragic.
D. We extinguished traffic.

42. A. He removed his jacket.
    B. He repossessed his jacket.
    C. He rearranged his jacket.
    D. He reimbursed his jacket.

43. A. He will agree with the suggestion.
    B. He will disagree with the suggestion.
    C. He will agree with the selection.
    D. He will argue with the suggestion.

44. A. He drives every time.
    B. He drives sometimes.
    C. He drives anytime.
    D. He drives every night.

45. A. The mechanic examines Laura's car every 3 hours.
    B. The mechanic breaks Laura car every 3 months.
    C. The mechanic examines Laura's car every 3 months.
    D. The mechanic examines Laura's car every 3 years.

46. A. We don't know if she will come.
    B. We don't know why she will come.
    C. We don't know when she will come.
    D. We don't know how she will come.

47. A. Stop your studies.
    B. Continue your studies.
    C. Do your best in your studies.
    D. Your studies won't help you at all.

48. A. You will be certain of having a seat.
    B. You don't need to reserve a seat.
    C. You can always have a seat.
    D. The seats are already reserved.

49. A. Altogether, there were 20 girls on the trip.
    B. Altogether, there were 20 students on the trip.
    C. Altogether, there were 5 girls on the trip.
    D. Altogether, there were 65 girls on the trip.

50. A. Students will eat their identification.
    B. Students will eat spaghetti.
    C. Students will eat in the clubs.
    D. Students will eat in the mess hall.

- *Directions for questions 51-60. You will hear dialogs on the test CD. Select the correct answer A, B, C, or D and mark your answer sheet.*

51. A. because he studied   B. because he likes to eat
    C. because he was cooking   D. because he had a date

52. A. a museum exhibition   B. a sports contest
    C. a theater show   D. a movie

53. A. The man will not take the bus.
    B. The man will go shopping.
    C. The man will go to the bus station.
    D. The man will change to another bus.

54. A. She wants to go to school.
    B. She wants to work.
    C. She wants a boyfriend.
    D. She wants to get somewhere fast.

55. A. She has just had an accident.
    B. She is seeing a doctor.
    C. She is physically incapable.
    D. She is moving to a new apartment.

56. A. a rock B. a man
    C. a fire D. a barbecue

57. A. because it was too rare
    B. because it didn't care
    C. because it was unfair
    D. because it was bare

58. A. buy some helicopters B. buy some water
    C. buy some medicine D. buy computer games

59. A. how fast the plane was flying
    B. how long the plane was
    C. how high the plane was flying
    D. how big the plane was

60. A. He ate too many sandwiches and it made him sick.
    B. He doesn't like pizza.
    C. He's bored of eating sandwiches.
    D. He wants to eat pizza every day.

ECL 聽力測驗⑤詳解

1. (**B**) Ping-Pong, tennis, and golf are popular sports, but lately sailing has become popular. What has become popular recently?

桌球、網球和高爾夫是很受歡迎的運動，但是最近划船也變得很受歡迎。／近來什麼變得很受歡迎？

(A) 網球。 (B) 划船。
(C) 高爾夫。 (D) 乒乓球。

* ping-pong〔ˈpɪŋˌpɑŋ〕*n.* 桌球
tennis〔ˈtɛnɪs〕*n.* 網球
popular〔ˈpɑpjələ˞〕*adj.* 受歡迎的
lately〔ˈletlɪ〕*adv.* 最近 sailing〔ˈselɪŋ〕*n.* 划船
recently〔ˈrisn̩tlɪ〕*adv.* 最近

2. (**C**) The police officer talked about traffic laws to the group. What did he talk about?

警官跟這個團體講解交通規則。／他講解什麼？

(A) 繳付罰金。 (B) 解釋。
(C) 駕駛規定。 (D) 團體動力學。

* ***police officer*** 警官
traffic〔ˈtræfɪk〕*adj.* 交通的 law〔lɔ〕*n.* 法規
pay〔pe〕*v.* 支付 fine〔faɪn〕*n.* 罰金
explanation〔ˌɛkspləˈneʃən〕*n.* 解釋
driving〔ˈdraɪvɪŋ〕*adj.* 駕駛的
regulation〔ˌrɛgjəˈleʃən〕*n.* 法規
dynamics〔daɪˈnæmɪks〕*n.* 動力學

3. (**A**) He will put the pieces together. What will he do?
他會把這些零件組合起來。／他會做什麼？

(A) 組合它們。　　(B) 利用它們。
(C) 分散他們。　　(D) 分開它們。

* ***put together*** 組合
piece [pis] *n.* (機器) 零件
unite [juˈnaɪt] *v.* 組合　　utilize [ˈjutḷˌaɪz] *v.* 利用
scatter [ˈskætɚ] *v.* 分散
separate [ˈsɛpəˌret] *v.* 分開

4. (**B**) She's heading to the grocery store. What will she buy? 她正前往雜貨店。／她會買什麼？

(A) 槍跟彈藥。
(B) 牛奶和麵包。
(C) 貓跟狗。
(D) 釘子和榔頭。

* head [hɛd] *v.* 前往　　grocery [ˈgrosɚɪ] *n.* 雜貨店
ammunition [ˌæmjəˈnɪʃən] *n.* 彈藥
bread [brɛd] *n.* 麵包　　nail [nel] *n.* 釘子
hammer [ˈhæmɚ] *n.* 榔頭

5. (**C**) Bonnie is just starting to catch on. What's Bonnie just starting to do?
邦妮才剛開始明白這件事。／邦妮才開始做什麼？

(A) 接球。　　(B) 想睡覺。
(C) 了解。　　(D) 站起來。

* ***catch on*** 明白；領會　　sleepy [ˈslipɪ] *adj.* 想睡的
understand [ˌʌndɚˈstænd] *v.* 了解

6. (**C**) The mechanics will inspect your truck tomorrow. What will they do?

技師明天會檢查你的卡車。／他們將做什麼？

(A) 他們會炸掉這台卡車。 (B) 他們會利用這台卡車。

(C) 他們會檢查這台車。 (D) 他們會消滅這部車。

＊ mechanic (mə'kænɪk) *n.* 技師
inspect (ɪn'spɛkt) *v.* 檢查 truck (trʌk) *n.* 卡車
explode (ɪk'splod) *v.* (使) 爆炸
exploit (ɪk'splɔɪt) *v.* 利用
examine (ɪg'zæmɪn) *v.* 檢查
exterminate (ɪk'stɝmə,net) *v.* 消滅

7. (**B**) Can you tell me where the train station is ? What is this woman asking?

你能告訴我火車站在哪裡嗎？／這位女士問什麼？

(A) 哪一條鐵軌是對的？

(B) 她要怎樣才能到火車站？

(C) 下一班火車何時出發？

(D) 火車何時抵達？

＊ station ('steʃən) *n.* 車站 track (træk) *n.* 鐵軌
reach (ritʃ) *v.* 抵達 leave (liv) *v.* 出發
arrive (ə'raɪv) *v.* 到達

8. (**A**) Monica said that Hector might come to visit her. What did Monica say ?

莫妮卡說赫克特可能會來拜訪她。／莫妮卡說什麼？

(A) 也許他會來拜訪她。 (B) 他不會來拜訪她。

(C) 他們要結婚了。 (D) 她愛他。

＊ visit ('vɪzɪt) *v.* 拜訪 perhaps (pɚ'hæps) *adv.* 也許
married ('mærɪd) *adj.* 結婚的

9. (**B**) The boss said that Joe would operate the elevator tomorrow. What will Joe do?

老闆說喬明天會使電梯運轉。／喬將要做什麼？

(A) 他要開槍射擊電梯。 (B) <u>他要使電梯運轉。</u>

(C) 他要使電扶梯運轉。 (D) 他要在電梯裡面走。

* operate〔ˈɑpəˌret〕*v.* 使運轉
elevator〔ˈɛləˌvetɚ〕*n.* 電梯
gun〔gʌn〕*v.* 開槍射擊 run〔rʌn〕*v.* 運轉
escalator〔ˈɛskəˌletɚ〕*n.* 電扶梯

10. (**C**) General Longoria guided the discussion. What did he do?

隆戈里亞將軍指導這次的討論。／他做什麼？

(A) 他導演這部電影。 (B) 他指導這個尺寸。

(C) <u>他指導這次的討論。</u> (D) 他指導這個錯覺。

* general〔ˈdʒɛnərəl〕*n.* 將軍
guide〔gaɪd〕*v.* 指導 discussion〔dɪˈskʌʃən〕*n.* 討論
direct〔dəˈrɛkt〕*v.* 導演；指導
dimension〔dəˈmɛnʃən〕*n.* 尺寸
illusion〔ɪˈljuʒən〕*n.* 錯覺；幻想

11. (**B**) I contacted our family. What did this woman do?

我聯絡了我們的家人。／這位女士做了什麼？

(A) 她紀念他們。 (B) <u>她和他們聯繫。</u>

(C) 她把他們複雜化。 (D) 她和他們和解。

* contact〔ˈkɑntækt〕*v.* 聯絡
commemorate〔kəˈmɛməˌret〕*v.* 紀念
communicate〔kəˈmjunəˌket〕*v.* 聯絡
complicate〔ˈkɑmpləˌket〕*v.* 複雜化
compromise〔ˈkɑmprəˌmaɪz〕*v.* 妥協；和解

12. (**D**) Joe has a great deal of influence at this university. What can Joe do?

喬在這所大學很有影響力。／喬能做什麼？

(A) 確保他的想法是新的。
(B) 確保他的想法是舊的。
(C) 確保他的想法被拒絕。
(D) 確保他的想法被採用。

* ***a great deal*** 許多
influence〔ˈɪnfluəns〕*n.* 影響力
university〔ˌjunəˈvɝsətɪ〕*n.* 大學
ensure〔ɪnˈʃur〕*v.* 確保　refuse〔rɪˈfjuz〕*n.* 拒絕

13. (**B**) Colonel Grover went to a party. Where did he go?

格佛上校參加了一場宴會。／他去了那裡？

(A) 比賽。　(B) 社交聚會。
(C) 遊戲。　(D) 看電影。

* colonel〔ˈkɝnl̩〕*n.* 上校　contest〔ˈkɑntɛst〕*n.* 競賽
social〔ˈsoʃəl〕*adj.* 社交上的
gathering〔ˈgæðərɪŋ〕*n.* 聚會
social gathering 社交聚會

14. (**D**) What is the purpose of this knob?

那個球形把手是做什麼用的？

(A) 它是用來打掃房間的。　(B) 它是用來做吐司的。
(C) 它是用來殺蒼蠅的。　(D) 它是用來開馬達的。

* purpose〔ˈpɝpəs〕*n.* 目的　knob〔nɑb〕*n.* 球形把手
sweep〔swip〕*v.* 清掃　toast〔tost〕*n.* 吐司
fly〔flaɪ〕*n.* 蒼蠅　***turn on*** 打開
motor〔ˈmotɚ〕*n.* 馬達

15. (**A**) Which number is between 15 and 17?
哪一個數字介於 15 和 17 之間？

(A) 16。　　(B) 14 和 18。
(C) 14。　　(D) 18。

* between〔bə'twin〕*prep.* 介於…之間

16. (**B**) The doctor knew how tall she was. What did the doctor know about her?
醫生知道她有多高。／關於她，醫生知道什麼？

(A) 她的體重。　　(B) 她的身高。
(C) 她的密度。　　(D) 她的長度。

* weight〔wet〕*n.* 體重　　height〔haɪt〕*n.* 身高
density〔'dɛnsətɪ〕*n.* 密度　　length〔lɛŋθ〕*n.* 長度

17. (**B**) As soon as we arrived the rain began to fall. When did it start raining?
當我們一抵達就開始下雨。／何時開始下的雨？

(A) 在我們抵達之前。　　(B) 當我們抵達時。
(C) 我們抵達後。　　(D) 雨下得很大。

* ***as soon as*** 一…就…　　arrive〔ə'raɪv〕*v.* 抵達
heavily〔'hɛvɪlɪ〕*adv.* 猛烈地

18. (**B**) Bob is going to observe the plumbers. What is he going to do?
鮑伯將去監視水管工／他要去做什麼？

(A) 告訴他們要做什麼。　　(B) 監視他們。
(C) 付他們錢。　　(D) 協助他們。

* observe〔əb'zɜv〕*v.* 監視　　plumber〔'plʌmɚ〕*n.* 水管工
watch〔wɑtʃ〕*v.* 監視　　pay〔pe〕*v.* 支付

19. (**C**) Fred has lots of new ideas. What has he been doing?
佛瑞德有很多新點子。／他一直在做什麼？

(A) 作白日夢。 (B) 遊手好閒。
(C) 思考。 (D) 觀看。

* daydream (ˈdeˈdrim) *v.* 做白日夢
fool around 遊手好閒

20. (**B**) Why does Joe have the chills?
喬爲什麼全身發冷？

(A) 因爲他生氣了。 (B) 因爲他很冷。
(C) 因爲他很累。 (D) 因爲他很熱。

* chill (tʃɪl) *n.* 發冷 angry (ˈæŋgrɪ) *adj.* 生氣的
tired (taɪrd) *adj.* 疲倦的

21. (**A**) Will you be done with your work soon?
你的工作很快就可以完成嗎？

(A) 是的，我將迅速完成它。
(B) 是的，我快要開始做了。
(C) 是的，我明天做不完。
(D) 是的，它很困難。

* finish (ˈfɪnɪʃ) *v.* 完成 quickly (ˈkwɪklɪ) *adv.* 快速地
difficult (ˈdɪfəˌkʌlt) *adj.* 困難的

22. (**B**) Ron wanted cash for his bike when he sold it. What did he want?
榮恩想要把他的腳踏車賣掉變現。／他想要什麼？

(A) 支票。 (B) 錢。
(C) 瓦斯。 (D) 一台新的腳踏車。

* check (tʃɛk) *n.* 支票

23. (**A**) Last night the wind came from the south and it was hot. Tomorrow the wind will be from the north and it'll be cold. Why will it be cold tomorrow?

昨晚風從南方吹過來，而且是熱風。明天風會從北方吹來，而且是冷風。／為何明天會冷？

(A) 因為風會轉向。　　(B) 因為酒會不見。
(C) 因為風速會降低。　　(D) 因為風會停了。

* south〔sauθ〕*n.* 南方　north〔nɔrθ〕*n.* 北方
shift〔ʃɪft〕*v.* 變換　wine〔waɪn〕*n.* 酒
disappear〔ˌdɪsəˈpɪr〕*v.* 消失

24. (**B**) Do you often drive so fast?

你常開這麼快嗎？

(A) 是的，但我趕時間時從不會這樣。
(B) 不，只有當我趕時間時才會。
(C) 不，我開車時從來不會這樣。
(D) 是的，只有當我毛茸茸時。

* ***in a hurry*** 匆忙　furry〔ˈfɝɪ〕*adj.* 毛茸茸的

25. (**B**) Where did your ancestors come from?

你的祖先從哪裡來？

(A) 他們今天早上在超級市場。
(B) 他們來自東台灣。
(C) 她住在台北。
(D) 他們要移民到美國。

* ancestor〔ˈænsɛstɚ〕*n.* 祖先
supermarket〔ˈsupɚˌmɑrkɪt〕*n.* 超級市場
eastern〔ˈistɚn〕*adj.* 東部的
migrate〔ˈmaɪgret〕*v.* 移民

26. (**B**) Let's wrap up this task as soon as possible.
讓我們儘快結束這份工作吧。

(A) 讓我們忘了它。 (B) 讓我們完成它。
(C) 讓我們拋棄它。 (D) 讓我們試試。

* wrap〔ræp〕*v.* 包裹　***wrap up*** 完成
task〔tæsk〕*n.* 任務；工作　***as soon as possible*** 儘快
forget〔fɚ'gɛt〕*v.* 忘記　finish〔'fɪnɪʃ〕*v.* 完成
abandon〔ə'bændən〕*v.* 拋棄

27. (**A**) The university has a new system for training students how to type.
這所大學有套新的系統可以用來訓練學生打字。

(A) 它有新方法。 (B) 它有新學校。
(C) 它有新樣式。 (D) 它有一些新聞。

* system〔'sɪstəm〕*n.* 系統　train〔tren〕*v.* 訓練
type〔taɪp〕*v.* 打字　*n.* 樣式　method〔'mɛθəd〕*n.* 方法

28. (**D**) The woman did her duty.
這位女士盡她的本份。

(A) 她做她喜歡做的事。 (B) 她做她總是做的事。
(C) 她做她不能做的事。 (D) 她做她應該做的事。

* duty〔'djutɪ〕*n.* 本分　***do one's duty*** 盡某人的本分
supposed〔sə'pozd〕*adj.* 認爲應該的

29. (**A**) My shoes have disappeared. 我的鞋子不見了。

(A) 它們不見了。 (B) 它們磨損了。
(C) 它們舊了。 (D) 它們被賣掉了。

* gone〔gɔn〕*adj.* 失去的　worn〔worn〕*adj.* 磨損的

30. (**A**) Mario is deaf. 馬利歐聽不見。

(A) 他聽不到。　(B) 他看不到。
(C) 他不能跑。　(D) 他不能說話。

* deaf (dɛf) *adj.* 聽不見的

31. (**C**) Mr. Johnson picked out the best tool for his work.
強森先生替他的工作選擇最好的工具。

(A) 他製作最好的工具。　(B) 他買最好的工具。
(C) 他選擇最好的工具。　(D) 他訂購最好的工具。

* pick (pɪk) *v.* 選擇　***pick out*** 選出
tool (tul) *n.* 工具　choose (tʃuz) *v.* 選擇
order (ˈɔrdɚ) *v.* 訂購

32. (**B**) The entire nation saw the rocket take off on TV.
全國國民都在電視上看見火箭升空。

(A) 人們在聽收音機廣播。
(B) 每個人都看著火箭升空。
(C) 人們在看電影。
(D) 火箭降落。

* entire (ɪnˈtaɪr) *adj.* 全部的　nation (ˈneʃən) *n.* 國民
rocket (ˈrɑkɪt) *n.* 火箭　***take off*** 升空；起飛
listen (ˈlɪsn̩) *v.* 聽　broadcast (ˈbrɔdˌkæst) *n.* 廣播
land (lænd) *v.* 降落

33. (**B**) She's willing to take the trip. 她樂於去旅行。

(A) 她等著去旅行。　(B) 她已經同意去旅行。
(C) 她抱怨要去旅行。　(D) 她全副武裝去旅行。

* willing (ˈwɪlɪŋ) *adj.* 樂意的
agree (əˈgri) *v.* 同意　whine (hwaɪn) *v.* 發牢騷
armed (ɑrmd) *adj.* 武裝的

34. (**A**) The head of the organization has the authority to give raises.

該組織的主管有權加薪。

(A) 主管有權加薪。　(B) 主管不能做決定。

(C) 該組織從不加薪。　(D) 那位主管的權力無效。

* head〔 hɛd 〕*n.* 主管
organization〔ˌɔrgənəˈzeʃən〕*n.* 組織
authority〔əˈθɔrətɪ〕*n.* 權力　raise〔 rez 〕*n.* 加薪
decision〔dɪˈsɪʒən〕*n.* 決定
work〔 wɝk 〕*v.* 有效；產生作用

35. (**A**) The children enjoy chocolate candy.

孩子們喜歡巧克力糖。

(A) 他們喜歡它。　(B) 他們不會試試它。

(C) 他們比較喜歡蛋糕。　(D) 他們不喜歡它。

* prefer〔prɪˈfɝ〕*v.* 比較喜歡

36. (**B**) This lettuce is especially crispy. You'll have to show me where you buy it.

這個萵苣特別脆。你一定要告訴我在哪裡買的。

(A) 他一點都不喜歡這萵苣。

(B) 他想知道他可以去哪裡買一些萵苣。

(C) 他覺得這萵苣太脆了，他不想吃。

(D) 他以前沒吃過萵苣。

* lettuce〔ˈlɛtɪs〕*n.* 萵苣
especially〔əˈspɛʃəlɪ〕*adv.* 特別地
crispy〔ˈkrɪspɪ〕*adj.* 脆的　show〔ʃo〕*v.* 告知
not at all 一點也不　***too…to*** 太…以致於不…
have〔hæv〕*v.* 吃；喝

37. (**C**) I get up every morning at six.
我每天早上六點起床。
(A) 我每晚睡六個小時。
(B) 我昨晚睡了六個小時。
(C) 六點後我就沒有待在床上了。
(D) 我喜歡在床上閱讀。

* ***get up*** 起床　per〔 pɚ 〕*prep.* 每
stay in 停留

38. (**C**) The pilot of an airplane must concentrate on his flying. 飛機駕駛員必須專心飛行。
(A) 他必須一大早就去開飛機。
(B) 他必須有一個副駕駛。
(C) 他必須注意飛行。
(D) 他不能喝酒。

* pilot〔'paɪlət〕*n.* 駕駛員　airplane〔'ɛr,plen〕*n.* 飛機
concentrate〔'kɑnsn̩,tret〕*v.* 專注 < *on* >
flying〔'flaɪɪŋ〕*n.* 飛行　co-pilot〔ko'paɪlət〕*n.* 副駕駛
pay attention to 注意

39. (**B**) She looked over her notes.
她瀏覽了一下她的筆記。
(A) 她記筆記。
(B) 她復習她的筆記。
(C) 她展示她的筆記。
(D) 她把她的筆記藏起來。

* ***look over*** 瀏覽　note〔not〕*n.* 筆記
review〔rɪ'vju〕*v.* 複習　show〔ʃo〕*v.* 展示
hide〔haɪd〕*v.* 藏

40. (**A**) The employees were confused by the regulations.
員工被那些規定搞糊塗了。

(A) 他們不了解那些規定。
(B) 他們違反規定。
(C) 他們不喜歡那些規定。
(D) 他們制定規則。

* employee ﹝ˌɛmplɔɪˈi﹞*n.* 員工
confuse ﹝kənˈfjuz﹞*v.* 使…困惑
break ﹝brek﹞*v.* 違反　　make ﹝mek﹞*v.* 制定

41. (**A**) We came across a lot of traffic.
我們碰到車流量大的時刻。

(A) 我們遇到車流量大的時刻。
(B) 我們消滅交通。
(C) 我們非常悲慘。
(D) 我們撲滅交通。

* ***come across*** 碰到　　traffic ﹝ˈtræfɪk﹞*n.* 車流量；交通
encounter ﹝ɪnˈkaʊntɚ﹞*v.* 遇到
exterminate ﹝ɪkˈstɝməˌnet﹞*v.* 消滅
extremely ﹝ɪkˈstrimlɪ﹞*adv.* 極度地
tragic ﹝ˈtrædʒɪk﹞*adj.* 悲慘的
extinguish ﹝ɪkˈstɪŋgwɪʃ﹞*v.* 撲滅

42. (**A**) He took off his jacket. 他脫下他的夾克。

(A) 他脫掉他的夾克。　　(B) 他收回他的夾克。
(C) 他重新整理他的夾克。　　(D) 他償還他的夾克。

* ***take off*** 脫下　　remove ﹝rɪˈmuv﹞*v.* 脫掉
repossess ﹝ˌripəˈzɛs﹞*v.* 收回
rearrange ﹝ˌriəˈrendʒ﹞*v.* 重新整理
reimburse ﹝ˌriɪmˈbɝs﹞*v.* 償還

43. (**A**) Paul will go along with her suggestion.
保羅會同意她的建議。

(A) 他同意那個建議。 (B) 他不同意那個建議。
(C) 他同意那個選擇。 (D) 他會和那個建議爭論。

* ***go along with*** 同意 suggestion (səˈdʒɛstʃən) *n.* 建議
agree (əˈgri) *v.* 同意 < *with* >
disagree (ˌdɪsəˈgri) *v.* 不同意 < *with* >
selection (səˈlɛkʃən) *n.* 選擇 argue (ˈɑrgjʊ) *v.* 爭論

44. (**B**) Mr. Lee drives occasionally. 李先生偶爾才開車。

(A) 他每次都開車。 (B) 他有時開車。
(C) 他總是開車。 (D) 他每晚開車。

* occasionally (əˈkeʒənl̩ɪ) *adv.* 偶爾
anytime (ˈɛnɪˌtaɪm) *adv.* 在任何時候；總是

45. (**C**) Every three months, Ms. Laura takes her car to the mechanic for an inspection.
蘿拉小姐每三個月把她的車開去技師那裡做檢查。

(A) 技師每三個小時檢查蘿拉的車一次。
(B) 技師每三個月弄壞蘿拉的車一次。
(C) 技師每三個月檢查蘿拉的車一次。
(D) 技師每三年檢查蘿拉的車一次。

* mechanic (məˈkænɪk) *n.* 技師
inspection (ɪnˈspɛkʃən) *n.* 檢查 break (brek) *v.* 弄壞

46. (**A**) We don't know whether she will come.
我們不知道她是否會來。

(A) 我們不知道她是否會來。 (B) 我們不知道她爲何要來。
(C) 我們不知道她何時要來。 (D) 我們不知道她要怎麼過來。

* whether (ˈhwɛðɚ) *conj.* 是否

47. (**B**) Stay in school. 待在學校裡。

(A) 停止學習。 (B) <u>繼續學習。</u>

(C) 在課業方面盡力。

(D) 你的課業對你一點幫助也沒有。

* continue〔kən'tɪnjʊ〕*v.* 繼續 ***do one's best*** 盡力

48. (**A**) You will be sure of a place on an airplane if you make a reservation. 如果你有預約的話，就保證會有機位。

(A) <u>你一定會有一個座位。</u> (B) 你不需要訂位。

(C) 你隨時都有座位。 (D) 座位已被預訂了。

* place〔ples〕*n.* 座位 reservation〔,rɛzə'veʃən〕*n.* 預約
certain〔'sɝtn̩〕*adj.* 確定的 seat〔sit〕*n.* 座位
reserve〔rɪ'zɝv〕*v.* 預訂

49. (**A**) There were twenty girls in all who took the trip to the museum. 總共有二十個女孩參加去博物館的旅行。

(A) <u>總共有二十個女孩參加旅行。</u>

(B) 總共有二十個學生參加旅行。

(C) 總共有五個女孩參加旅行。

(D) 總共有六十五個女孩參加旅行。

* ***in all*** 合計 museum〔mju'ziəm〕*n.* 博物館
altogether〔,ɔltə'gɛðɚ〕*adv.* 全部地

50. (**C**) The cafeteria will be closed for repairs for eight days due to yesterday's fire. Arrangements have been made for university students to eat without charge in their respective clubs for the next eight days.

因爲昨天的火災，自助餐廳將休息八天以進行整修。在未來的八天裡，已經爲大學生做好安排，他們將免費在各自的俱樂部裡吃飯。

(A) 學生會吃他們的身分證。 (B) 學生會吃義大利麵。
(C) 學生將在俱樂部裡吃飯。 (D) 學生將在餐廳裡吃飯。

* cafeteria [ˌkæfəˈtɪrɪə] *n.* 自助餐廳
repair [rɪˈpɛr] *v.* 修理 ***due to*** 由於
arrangement [əˈrendʒmənt] *n.* 安排
charge [tʃɑrdʒ] *n.* 費用
respective [rɪˈspɛktɪv] *adj.* 各自的
identification [aɪˌdɛntəfəˈkeʃən] *n.* 身分證
spaghetti [spəˈgɛtɪ] *n.* 義大利麵 ***mess hall*** 餐廳

51. (**D**) W : Did you finish your homework yesterday?
M : No, I didn't. I had a date last night.
Why didn't the student finish his homework?
女：你昨天有寫完家庭作業嗎？
男：不，我沒有。我昨晚有約會。
爲什麼那位學生沒有完成他的家庭作業？
(A) 因爲他在讀書。 (B) 因爲他喜歡吃東西。
(C) 因爲他在煮東西。 (D) 因爲他有約會。

* date [det] *n.* 約會

52. (**B**) W : Where have they gone?
M : They went to watch a game.
What did the people see?
女：他們去哪了？
男：他們去看一場比賽。
那些人看到什麼？
(A) 博物館展覽。 (B) 運動比賽。
(C) 戲劇表演。 (D) 電影。

* museum [mjuˈziəm] *n.* 博物館
exhibition [ˌɛksəˈbɪʃən] *n.* 展覽
contest [ˈkɑntɛst] *n.* 比賽 theater [ˈθiətɚ] *n.* 劇院
show [ʃo] *n.* 表演

53. (**D**) M：Does bus No.38 go to the airport?

W：No, but I can give you a transfer.

M：All right, I'll take it.

What will the man do?

男：三十八號公車有到機場嗎？

女：沒有，但是我可以給你一張轉乘票。

男：好的，我會收下它。

那位男士將做什麼？

(A) 那位男士不會搭乘這班公車。

(B) 那位男士將去購物。

(C) 那位男士將去公車站。

(D) <u>那位男士將轉乘另一輛公車。</u>

註：在外國搭公車時，若需要轉搭別的公車，跟公車司機說，他就會在你的票上蓋個章或打個洞之類的。這時他會說：I will give you a transfer. 這樣你搭下一班公車只要給那班車的司機看看票就行了。)

＊ airport〔ˈɛr,pɔrt〕*n.* 機場　　transfer〔ˈtrænsfɝ〕*n.* 轉乘票
change〔tʃendʒ〕*v.* 換車

54. (**D**) M：What's wrong?

W：I'm in a rush.

What do we know about the girl?

男：怎麼了？

女：我在趕時間。

我們知道那個女孩的什麼事？

(A) 她想要去學校。　　(B) 她想要去工作。

(C) 她想要有一個男朋友。

(D) <u>她想要很快抵達某個地方。</u>

＊ ***in a rush*** 趕時間

55. (**A**) W：Oh, I can't get up. My leg hurts.
M：Don't worry. We've called an ambulance already.
W：Thanks. I guess I broke a bone.
What has happened to this woman?
女：喔，我站不起來。我的腳好痛。
男：不用擔心。我們已經叫了救護車。
女：謝謝。我猜我骨折了。
這位女士發生了什麼事？

(A) 她剛才發生了意外。
(B) 她正在看醫生。
(C) 她是肢體障礙。
(D) 她正搬到新的公寓。

* ***get up*** 站起來　hurt〔 hɝt 〕*v.* 疼痛
worry〔'wɝɪ〕*v.* 擔心
ambulance〔'æmbjələns〕*n.* 救護車
guess〔 gɛs 〕*v.* 猜測　break〔 brek 〕*v.* 折斷
bone〔 bon 〕*n.* 骨頭　happen〔'hæpən〕*v.* 發生
accident〔'æksədənt〕*n.* 意外
physically〔'fɪzɪkḷɪ〕*adv.* 身體上
incapable〔 ɪn'kepəbḷ 〕*adj.* 不能的
apartment〔 ə'pɑrtmənt 〕*n.* 公寓

56. (**C**) W：What started all this?
M：There was something highly flammable in the storage room.
What are they talking about?
女：是什麼引起這件事的？
男：倉庫裡有一些非常易燃的東西。
他們在說什麼？

(A) 一塊石頭。 (B) 一個男人。
(C) 一場火災。 (D) 一場烤肉聚餐。

＊ highly〔ˈhaɪlɪ〕*adv.* 非常
flammable〔ˈflæməbl̩〕*adj.* 易燃的
storage〔ˈstorɪdʒ〕*n.* 倉庫
barbecue〔ˈbɑrbɪˌkju〕*n.* 烤肉聚餐

57. (**A**) W：Waiter, I ordered the hamburger well done.
M：I'll take it back and cook it longer.
Why does the meat need to be cooked longer?
女：服務生，我點的是全熟的漢堡。
男：我會把它拿回去再煮久一點。
爲什麼那塊肉要再煮久一點？

(A) 因爲它太生了。 (B) 因爲它不在乎。
(C) 因爲它不公平。 (D) 因爲它是赤裸的。

＊ waiter〔ˈwetɚ〕*n.* 服務生 order〔ˈɔrdɚ〕*v.* 點菜
hamburger〔ˈhæmbɝgɚ〕*n.* 漢堡
well done 全熟的 rare〔rɛr〕*adj.* 三分熟的；半生不熟的
unfair〔ʌnˈfɛr〕*adj.* 不公平的 bare〔bɛr〕*adj.* 赤裸的

58. (**C**) W：I'll meet you at 11:30. Where?
M：I have to go to the pharmacy. Let's meet there.
What does the man have to do?
女：我在十一點半和你見面。約哪裡？
男：我必須去藥局，我們在那裡見面。
那位男士必須做什麼？

(A) 買一些直昇機。 (B) 買一些水。
(C) 買一些藥。 (D) 買一些電腦遊戲。

＊ pharmacy〔ˈfɑrməsɪ〕*n.* 藥房
helicopter〔ˈhɛlɪˌkaptɚ〕*n.* 直昇機
medicine〔ˈmɛdəsn̩〕*n.* 藥

59. (**C**) W : Did you see the aircraft?
M : Yes. At what altitude do you think it is?
What does the man want to know?
女：你有看見那一架飛機嗎？
男：有。妳猜它飛得多高？
那位男士想要知道什麼？
(A) 那架飛機飛得多快。
(B) 那架飛機有多長。
(C) 那架飛機飛得多高。
(D) 那架飛機有多大。

* aircraft ('ɛr,kræft) *n.* 飛機
altitude ('æltə,tjud) *n.* 高度
plane (plen) *n.* 飛機

60. (**C**) M : I'm sick of eating sandwiches for lunch every day.
W : Me too. Let's order a pizza.
What does the man mean?
男：每天午餐吃三明治煩死了。
女：我也是。我們訂比薩好了。
這位男士是什麼意思？
(A) 他吃了太多了三明治而使他生病。
(B) 他不喜歡比薩。
(C) 他厭煩了吃三明治。
(D) 他每天都想要吃比薩。

* ***be sick of*** 對…覺得厭煩
sandwich ('sændwɪtʃ) *n.* 三明治
order ('ɔrdɚ) *v.* 訂購 ***be bored of*** 對…覺得厭煩

LISTENING TEST ⑥

- *Directions for questions 1-25. You will hear questions on the test CD. Select the one item A, B, C or D which answers the question correctly, and mark your answer sheet.*

1. A. musical weather B. unusual weather
   C. typical weather D. regular weather

2. A. beers B. beard
   C. cheer D. fear

3. A. a light bulb B. a book
   C. a drink D. a comb

4. A. every night B. every week
   C. every year D. every Friday

5. A. to fold things together
   B. to mold things together
   C. to scold things together
   D. to hold things together

6. A. aerobics B. basic drama
   C. baseless stuff D. basic substances

7. A. a hook B. a book
   C. a crook D. a nook

8. A. not move
   B. move toward the major
   C. move faster
   D. move away from the major

9. A. in his ear B. in his foot
   C. in his lung D. in his toes

10. A. steel B. paper
    C. cotton D. wool

11. A. to protect his knight B. to protect his might
    C. to protect his flight D. to protect his sight

12. A. It was sent off. B. It was sold out.
    C. It was sent down. D. It was eaten up.

13. A. $9,000 or less B. $9,000 exactly
    C. at least $9,000 D. $7,000 or more

14. A. They worked out.
    B. They rested.
    C. They exercised.
    D. They broke something.

15. A. keep away from people
    B. keep away from school
    C. keep away from work
    D. keep away from the crash

16. A. The students are at the soccer field.
    B. It's raining at the soccer field.
    C. It's certain that they will go.
    D. It is not certain that they will go.

17. A. eggs B. bread
    C. cookies D. leftovers

18. A. She pays no attention to them.
    B. She is grateful for them.
    C. She is always losing friends.
    D. She doesn't take care of them.

19. A. an informal request B. a command
    C. a polite invitation D. an argument

20. A. sunny B. strong winds
    C. blue skies D. possible rain

21. A. an animal B. a place
    C. a person D. a metal

22. A. names B. their jobs
    C. their hours D. their descriptions

23. A. It was clean.
    B. It was very big.
    C. It was ready for use.
    D. It was occupied.

24. A. the author of a book
    B. a part of a book
    C. a sentence of a book
    D. a place to go have fun

25. A. She is very dirty.
    B. She is too lazy.
    C. She is busy cleaning the house.
    D. She is occupied.

- *Directions for questions 26-50. You will hear statements on the test CD. Select the one answer A, B, C, or D which comes closest to the meaning of the statement and mark your answer sheet.*

26. A. She boiled it. B. She slept outside of it.
    C. She walked towards it. D. She rode on it.

27. A. I will do it with you. B. I will do it alone.
    C. I will do it with her. D. I will do it with him.

28. A. He couldn't open his eyes.
    B. He couldn't see very clearly.
    C. He couldn't find his glasses.
    D. He could see very clearly.

29. A. She does the typing.
    B. She cleans the office.
    C. She manages the staff.
    D. She handles the money.

30. A. He found fault with the exam.
    B. He gave the lie to preparing the exam.
    C. He kept an eye on the exam.
    D. He went to great lengths to prepare for the exam.

31. A. He wanted it in blank.
    B. He wanted it in black and white.
    C. He wanted it in the mail.
    D. He wanted it in coincidence.

32. A. She lost her job.
    B. She doesn't have to go to work.
    C. She doesn't have to go to waste.
    D. She doesn't have to get on welfare.

33. A. Her new furniture was expensive.
    B. She ran out of food.
    C. She ate in the restaurant.
    D. She provided it.

34. A. He handled the car in an easy way.
    B. He drove in a zigzag.
    C. He went carefully.
    D. He gave caution to driving.

35. A. It was nursed back to health.
    B. It was taken to the vet.
    C. It lay down.
    D. It died.

36. A. Sergeant Bond can't leave at nine.
    B. Sergeant Bond can leave at nine.
    C. Sergeant Bond can't live at nine.
    D. Sergeant Bond can leave at seven.

37. A. They prepared the dinner with the children.
    B. The children don't know how to cook.
    C. The children help the parents cook the dinner.
    D. The children prepared the dinner by themselves.

38. A. She must go to die.
    B. She must know tonight.
    C. She must go today.
    D. She must go tomorrow.

39. A. He could not broadcast his choice.
    B. He could not balance his voice.
    C. He could not broadcast his voice.
    D. He could not show his photo.

40. A. The quarterback jumped the track.
    B. The quarterback called the shots.
    C. The quarterback pulled his gun.
    D. The quarterback stuck to his pistol.

41. A. She quickly jotted down what the manager said.
    B. She took the manager's word.
    C. She scrawled out what the manager directed.
    D. She scribed incessantly what the manager said.

42. A. Janet will serve food to the newcomers.
    B. Janet will amuse the newcomers.
    C. Janet will welcome the newcomers.
    D. Janet will talk to all the newcomers.

43. A. This is the one ruler I really like.
    B. The first ruler is longer than the second.
    C. The rulers are similar.
    D. The rulers are different.

44. A. She is lazy and idle.
    B. She's late and rude.
    C. She does her work quickly and well.
    D. She likes other workers.

45. A. We wish it would start.
    B. We wish you a merry Christmas.
    C. We wish it would end.
    D. We wish you a happy birthday.

46. A. His success led to his diligence.
    B. His success ended in his diligence.
    C. His success was caused by his diligence.
    D. His success brought about his diligence.

47. A. The student doesn't care about the test.
    B. He is worried about being nervous.
    C. He likes tests.
    D. He is worried about the test.

48. A. She becomes confused.
    B. She forgets everything.
    C. She recalls his words.
    D. She dresses up to see him.

49. A. She took a long walk.
    B. She went on horseback.
    C. She took a bicycle ride.
    D. She went swimming.

50. A. He isn't rigid. B. He is rigid.
    C. He is strange. D. He flexes his knees.

● *Directions for questions 51-60. You will hear dialogs on the test CD. Select the correct answer A, B, C, or D and mark your answer sheet.*

51. A. She listened to it on the radio.
    B. She watched it on the radio.
    C. She asked her mother.
    D. She asked the TV.

52. A. His jacket got cold. B. His goat got old.
    C. His ears got cold. D. His jacket got old.

53. A. something to eat
    B. something to wear
    C. something to read
    D. something strange

54. A. to relax and enjoy herself
    B. to work and make money
    C. to lecture at a convention center
    D. to retire

55. A. She wants to walk home.
    B. Her father will take her home.
    C. She lives too far away.
    D. She still has work to do.

56. A. to make her go crazy
    B. to make her less tense
    C. to make her hungry
    D. to make her sing

57. A. string
    B. boxes
    C. wires
    D. tubes

58. A. their schedules
    B. their professions
    C. their families
    D. their dreams

59. A. She wants to give money for the book.
    B. She wants to give it to a shop.
    C. She wants to give it as a present.
    D. She wants to get money for the book.

60. A. Steve is smart enough to quit his job.
    B. Steve is crazy to quit his job.
    C. He doesn't mind if Steve quits his job.
    D. It is right for Steve to quit his job.

ECL 聽力測驗⑥詳解

1. (**B**) We are experiencing abnormal weather for this part of the world. What is happening?

我們體驗到這部分的世界的反常天氣。／發生了什麼事？

(A) 音樂的天氣。 (B) 異常的天氣。
(C) 典型的天氣。 (D) 規律的天氣。

* experience [ɪk'spɪrɪəns] *v.* 體驗
abnormal [æb'nɔrml̩] *adj.* 反常的
weather ['wɛðɚ] *n.* 天氣 happen ['hæpən] *v.* 發生
musical ['mjuzɪkl̩] *adj.* 音樂的
unusual [ʌn'juʒuəl] *adj.* 異常的
typical ['tɪpɪkl̩] *adj.* 典型的
regular ['rɛgjəlɚ] *adj.* 規律的

2. (**A**) May I ask what are you getting in?

可以請問你在買什麼嗎？

(A) 啤酒。 (B) 鬍鬚。
(C) 喝采。 (D) 恐懼。

* ***get in*** 購買 beer [bɪr] *n.* 啤酒
beard [bɪrd] *n.* 鬍鬚 cheer [tʃɪr] *n.* 喝采
fear [fɪr] *n.* 恐懼

3. (**D**) Which of these is most likely to be made of plastic?

這些東西中，哪個最可能是塑膠做的？

(A) 燈泡。 (B) 書。
(C) 飲料。 (D) 梳子。

* ***be made of*** 由…製成 plastic ['plæstɪk] *adj.* 塑膠的
bulb [bʌlb] *n.* 電燈泡 comb [kom] *n.* 梳子

4. (**A**) Each night I read sixty pages of my novel. When do I read my novel?

我每天晚上讀六十頁小說。／我什麼時候讀小說？

(A) 每晚。　(B) 每週。
(C) 每年。　(D) 每星期五。

＊ page〔 pedʒ 〕*n.* 頁　novel〔ˈnɑvl̩〕*n.* 小說

5. (**D**) What is the purpose of screws?

螺絲的用途是什麼？

(A) 把東西摺疊在一起。
(B) 把東西鑄造在一起。
(C) 責罵放在一起的東西。
(D) 把東西固定在一起。

＊ purpose〔ˈpɝpəs〕*n.* 用途　screw〔 skru 〕*n.* 螺絲
fold〔 fold 〕*v.* 摺疊　mold〔 mold 〕*v.* 鑄造
scold〔 skold 〕*v.* 責罵　hold〔 hold 〕*v.* 固定

6. (**D**) Emma's studying chemistry at the university. What is she studying?

艾瑪在大學裡唸化學。／她在唸什麼？

(A) 有氧運動。　(B) 基礎戲劇。
(C) 沒有根據的資料。　(D) 基礎物質。

＊ chemistry〔ˈkɛmɪstrɪ〕*n.* 化學
university〔ˌjunəˈvɝsətɪ〕*n.* 大學
aerobics〔ˌeəˈrobɪks〕*n.* 有氧運動
basic〔ˈbesɪk〕*adj.* 基本的
drama〔ˈdrɑmə〕*n.* 戲劇
baseless〔ˈbeslɪs〕*adj.* 沒有根據的
stuff〔 stʌf 〕*n.* 資料　substance〔ˈsʌbstəns〕*n.* 物質

7. (**B**) The young lady looked at the novel. What did she look at? 這位年輕的女士看著那本小說。／她在看什麼？

(A) 鉤子。 (B) 書。
(C) 曲柄枴杖。 (D) 角落。

* hook〔 hʊk 〕*n.* 鉤子
crook〔 krʊk 〕*n.* 曲柄枴杖 nook〔 nʊk 〕*n.* 角落

8. (**B**) The major ordered him to approach. What should the soldier do? 少校命令他過來。／那名士兵應該怎麼做？

(A) 不要動。 (B) 朝少校移動。
(C) 移動快一點。 (D) 遠離少校。

* major〔ˈmedʒɚ 〕*n.* 少校 approach〔 əˈprotʃ 〕*v.* 走近
soldier〔ˈsoldʒɚ 〕*n.* 士兵 toward〔 təˈwɔrd 〕*prep.* 朝向

9. (**C**) He has a problem with his respiratory system. Where is the problem? 他的呼吸系統有問題。／問題在哪裡？

(A) 他的耳朵裡。 (B) 他的腳裡。
(C) 他的肺裡。 (D) 他的腳趾裡。

* respiratory〔 rɪˈspaɪrəˌtorɪ 〕*adj.* 呼吸的
system〔ˈsɪstəm 〕*n.* 系統
lung〔 lʌŋ 〕*n.* 肺 toe〔 to 〕*n.* 腳趾

10. (**A**) What type of metal is this case made of? 這個箱子是用哪種金屬做成的？

(A) 鋼。 (B) 紙。
(C) 棉花。 (D) 羊毛。

* metal〔ˈmɛtl̩ 〕*n.* 金屬 case〔 kes 〕*n.* 箱子
steel〔 stil 〕*n.* 鋼 cotton〔ˈkɑtn̩ 〕*n.* 棉花
wool〔 wʊl 〕*n.* 羊毛

11. (**D**) Why did the swimmer use goggles?

爲什麼那個游泳的人使用泳鏡？

(A) 以保護他的騎士。

(B) 以保護他的優勢。

(C) 以保護他的飛行。

(D) 以保護他的視力。

* goggle〔ˈgɑgḷ〕*n.* 泳鏡　protect〔prəˈtɛkt〕*v.* 保護
knight〔naɪt〕*n.* 騎士　might〔maɪt〕*n.* 優勢
flight〔flaɪt〕*n.* 飛行　sight〔saɪt〕*n.* 視力

12. (**A**) The merchandise was shipped last night. What happened to the merchandise?

那些商品昨天用船運走了。／那些商品怎麼了？

(A) 被運走了。　(B) 被賣光了。

(C) 被下降了。　(D) 被吃光了。

* merchandise〔ˈmɝtʃən,daɪz〕*n.* 商品
ship〔ʃɪp〕*v.* 船運　***send off*** 寄運出去
sell out 賣光　***eat up*** 吃光　***send down*** 下降

13. (**C**) A new SUV will cost $9,000 or higher. How much will the SUV cost?

一輛新的休旅車要價美金九千塊以上。／休旅車要多少錢？

(A) 九千塊以下。　(B) 剛好九千塊。

(C) 至少九千塊。　(D) 七千塊以上。

* ***SUV*** 休旅車（= *sport utility vehicle*）
cost〔kɔst〕*v.* 要價
exactly〔ɪgˈzæktlɪ〕*adv.* 剛好地　***at least*** 至少

14. (**B**) The workers had a 10 minute break. What did they do?
那些工人有十分鐘的休息時間。／他們做什麼？

(A) 他們運動。 (B) 他們休息。
(C) 他們運動。 (D) 他們打破東西。

* break〔brek〕*n.* 休息 *v.* 打破 ***work out*** 運動
rest〔rɛst〕*v.* 休息 exercise〔'ɛksɚ,saɪz〕*v.* 運動

15. (**D**) She tried to avoid the collision. What did she try to do?
她試著避免碰撞。／她試著做什麼？

(A) 避開人群。 (B) 遠離學校。
(C) 遠離工作。 (D) 避開相撞。

* avoid〔ə'vɔɪd〕*v.* 避免 collision〔kə'lɪʒən〕*n.* 碰撞
keep away from 遠離；避開 crash〔kræʃ〕*n.* 相撞

16. (**D**) If it rains, the children may not go to the soccer field. What's going on?
如果下雨的話，孩子們或許就不會去足球場了。／發生了什麼事？

(A) 學生們在足球場。 (B) 足球場在下雨。
(C) 他們確定會去。 (D) 他們不確定是否會去。

* soccer〔'sɑkɚ〕*n.* 足球 field〔fild〕*n.* 球場
go on 發生 certain〔'sɜtn̩〕*adj.* 確定的

17. (**B**) My mother made toast for a snack. What did she use?
我的母親做了一份吐司當點心。／她用了什麼？

(A) 蛋。 (B) 麵包。
(C) 餅乾。 (D) 剩飯。

* toast〔tost〕*n.* 吐司 snack〔snæk〕*n.* 點心
leftovers〔'lɛft,ovɚz〕*n. pl.* 剩飯

18. (**B**) Maria appreciates her family. How does she feel about her family?
瑪莉亞很感謝她的家人。／她對她的家人感覺如何？

(A) 她不注重他們。 (B) <u>她很感激他們。</u>
(C) 她總是失去朋友。 (D) 她不照顧他們。

* appreciate〔əˈpriʃɪˌet〕*v.* 感激 ***pay attention to*** 注意
grateful〔ˈgretfəl〕*adj.* 心懷感激的
lose〔luz〕*v.* 失去 ***take care of*** 照顧

19. (**B**) She was given an order to report to headquarters. What was she given? 她被命令要向總部報告。／她被給予什麼？

(A) 一個非正式的要求。 (B) <u>一道命令。</u>
(C) 一個禮貌的邀請。 (D) 一項爭執。

* report〔rɪˈport〕*v.* 報告
headquarters〔ˈhɛdˈkwɔrtɚz〕*n. pl.* 總部
informal〔ɪnˈfɔrml̩〕*adj.* 非正式的
request〔rɪˈkwɛst〕*n.* 要求 command〔kəˈmænd〕*n.* 命令
polite〔pəˈlaɪt〕*adj.* 禮貌的
invitation〔ˌɪnvəˈteʃən〕*n.* 邀請
argument〔ˈɑrgjəmənt〕*n.* 爭執

20. (**D**) The weather report said, "It might rain today." What is the weather outlook for today?
氣象報告說：「今天可能會下雨。」／今天的天氣預告如何？

(A) 晴朗的。 (B) 強風。
(C) 藍天。 (D) <u>可能會下雨。</u>

* report〔rɪˈport〕*n.* 報告
outlook〔ˈaʊtˌlʊk〕*n.* 預測 ***weather outlook*** 天氣預測
sunny〔ˈsʌnɪ〕*adj.* 晴朗的 strong〔strɔŋ〕*adj.* 強烈的
wind〔wɪnd〕*n.* 風 possible〔ˈpɑsəbl̩〕*adj.* 可能的

21. (**D**) What kind of element is "lead"? 「鉛」是哪一種元素？

(A) 動物。 (B) 場所。

(C) 人物。 (D) 金屬。

＊ element ('ɛləmənt) *n.* 元素 lead (lɛd) *n.* 鉛
place (ples) *n.* 地方；場所

22. (**B**) He made a list of their duties. What was on the list?
他把他們的任務列成一張表。／那張表上面有什麼？

(A) 名字。 (B) 他們的工作。

(C) 他們的辦公時間。 (D) 他們的描述。

＊ list (lɪst) *n.* 表 duties ('djutɪz) *n.pl.* 任務
job (dʒɑb) *n.* 工作 hours (aʊrz) *n.pl.* 辦公時間
description (dɪ'skrɪpʃən) *n.* 描述

23. (**C**) Tanya said that the place was available. What did Tanya say? 坦雅說可以使用這個地方。／坦雅說什麼？

(A) 它是乾淨的。 (B) 它很大。

(C) 隨時都可以使用它。 (D) 它被佔據了。

＊ available (ə'veləbl̩) *adj.* 可利用的
clean (klin) *adj.* 乾淨的
ready ('rɛdɪ) *adj.* 準備好的；隨時可以的
occupy ('ɑkjə,paɪ) *v.* 佔據

24. (**B**) The novel has numerous chapters. What is a chapter?
這部小說有許多章。／什麼是章？

(A) 書的作者。 (B) 書的一部分。

(C) 書中的一句話。 (D) 一個可以去玩樂的地方。

＊ numerous ('njumərəs) *adj.* 許多的
chapter ('tʃæptɚ) *n.* 章 author ('ɔθɚ) *n.* 作者
sentence ('sɛntəns) *n.* 句子
fun (fʌn) *n.* 樂趣 ***have fun*** 玩樂

25. (**B**) She is too indolent to clean the house. How is the woman? 她懶得打掃屋子。／這位女士如何？

(A) 她很髒。 (B) 她太懶了。
(C) 她忙著打掃屋子。 (D) 她沒空。

* ***too…to*** 太…以致於不能
indolent〔ˈɪndələnt〕*adj.* 懶惰的
clean〔klin〕*v.* 打掃 house〔haʊs〕*n.* 房子
dirty〔ˈdɝtɪ〕*adj.* 髒的 lazy〔ˈlezɪ〕*adj.* 懶惰的
occupied〔ˈɑkjəˌpaɪd〕*adj.* 無空閒的

26. (**D**) She was a passenger on the train.
她是火車上的乘客。

(A) 她在煮火車。 (B) 她睡在火車外面。
(C) 她走向火車。 (D) 她搭乘火車。

* passenger〔ˈpæsn̩dʒɚ〕*n.* 乘客
boil〔bɔɪl〕*v.* 烹煮 ***outside of*** 在外面
towards〔tɔrdz〕*prep.* 朝向
ride〔raɪd〕*v.* 搭乘（過去式及過去分詞皆爲 rode〔rod〕）

27. (**B**) I'll work independently on this concept.
我會獨立研究這個理論。

(A) 我會和你一起做。
(B) 我會獨自做這件事。
(C) 我會和她一起做。
(D) 我會和他一起做。

* work〔wɝk〕*v.* 研究
independently〔ˌɪndɪˈpɛndəntlɪ〕*adv.* 獨立地
concept〔ˈkɑnsɛpt〕*n.* 理論
alone〔əˈlon〕*adv.* 獨自

28. (**B**) After the doctor put drops in Jimmy's eyes, his vision became blurred. 醫生把眼藥水滴進吉米的眼睛之後，他的視線就變得很模糊。

(A) 他的眼睛睜不開。 (B) 他沒有辦法看得很清楚。
(C) 他找不到他的眼鏡。 (D) 他可以看得很清楚。

* drops〔drɑps〕*n.*（眼藥水等）滴劑
vision〔ˈvɪʒən〕*n.* 視力 blurred〔blɝd〕*adj.* 模糊不清的
clearly〔ˈklɪrlɪ〕*adv.* 清楚地 glasses〔ˈglæsɪz〕*n.pl.* 眼鏡

29. (**D**) Melanie is the cashier in our company.
美樂妮是我們公司的出納。

(A) 她是打字的。 (B) 她打掃辦公室。
(C) 她管理職員。 (D) 她管理金錢。

* cashier〔kæˈʃɪr〕*n.* 出納員；會計
company〔ˈkʌmpənɪ〕*n.* 公司
do〔du〕*v.* 做；處理 typing〔ˈtaɪpɪŋ〕*n.* 打字
clean〔klɪn〕*v.* 打掃 manage〔ˈmænɪdʒ〕*v.* 管理
staff〔stæf〕*n.* 職員 handle〔ˈhændḷ〕*v.* 管理

30. (**D**) Bill did everything he could to prepare for the exam.
比爾盡全力來準備這次考試。

(A) 他挑這次考試的毛病。
(B) 他證明準備這次考試是錯的。
(C) 他留意這次考試。
(D) 他不辭辛勞地準備這次考試。

* prepare〔prɪˈpɛr〕*v.* 準備 exam〔ɪgˈzæm〕*n.* 考試
fault〔fɔlt〕*n.* 錯誤 ***find fault with*** 挑…的毛病；責備
give the lie to 證明（某事）是虛假（錯誤）的
keep an eye on 留意 length〔lɛŋθ〕*n.* 範圍；程度
go to great lengths 不辭辛勞

31. (**B**) The merchant insisted on having the agreement written down. 這名商人堅持要把協議寫下來。

(A) 他想要契約是空白的。
(B) 他想要書面形式的契約。
(C) 他要把它在郵遞過程。
(D) 他希望它是一致的。

* merchant (ˈmɝtʃənt) *n.* 商人　insist (ɪnˈsɪst) *v.* 堅持
agreement (əˈgrimənt) *n.* 協議；契約
write down 把…寫下來；記錄　blank (blæŋk) *n.* 空白
in blank 空白著　***black and white*** 書面形式
in the mail 在郵遞過程
coincidence (koˈɪnsədəns) *n.* 相同；一致

32. (**B**) Melissa is on a holiday break. 瑪麗莎正在休假中。

(A) 她失業了。　(B) 她不必去上班。
(C) 她不必被浪費掉。　(D) 她不必接受生活救濟。

* holiday (ˈhɑləˌde) *adj.* 假日的　break (brek) *n.* 休假
lose (luz) *v.* 失去　***lose one's job*** 失業
waste (west) *n.* 浪費　***go to waste*** 被浪費掉；糟蹋掉
welfare (ˈwɛlˌfɛr) *n.* 福利；生活救濟
on welfare 接受生活救濟

33. (**D**) Mrs. Cohen furnished all the food for the birthday party. 寇漢太太提供了生日宴會的所有食物。

(A) 她的新傢俱很貴。　(B) 她的食物用完了。
(C) 她在餐廳吃飯。　(D) 她提供食物。

* furnish (ˈfɝnɪʃ) *v.* 提供　food (fud) *n.* 食物
furniture (ˈfɝnɪtʃɚ) *n.* 傢俱　***run out of*** 用完
restaurant (ˈrɛstərənt) *n.* 餐廳
provide (prəˈvaɪd) *v.* 提供

34. (**C**) After nightfall the driver drove ahead with care.
黃昏之後，這名駕駛人小心地往前開。

(A) 他很輕鬆地駕駛這部車。
(B) 他蛇行。　　(C) 他小心地走。
(D) 他給予駕駛警告。

* nightfall ['naɪt,fɔl] *n.* 傍晚；黃昏
ahead [ə'hɛd] *adv.* 向前　　care [kɛr] *n.* 注意
with care 小心地　　handle ['hændḷ] *v.* 駕駛起來
zigzag ['zɪgzæg] *n.* Z字形
carefully ['kɛrfəlɪ] *adv.* 小心地
caution ['kɔʃən] *n.* 警告　　driving ['draɪvɪŋ] *n.* 駕駛

35. (**D**) The animal's wound was fatal.
那隻動物所受的傷是致命傷。

(A) 牠在經過治療之後恢復健康。
(B) 牠被帶去看獸醫。
(C) 牠躺下來。　　(D) 牠死掉了。

* wound [waʊnd] *n.* 傷口　　fatal ['fetḷ] *adj.* 致命的
nurse [nɝs] *v.* 治療　　health [hɛlθ] *n.* 健康
vet [vɛt] *n.* 獸醫（= *veterinarian*）
lie [laɪ] *v.* 躺；臥（三態變化爲：lie-lay-lain）
die [daɪ] *v.* 死掉

36. (**B**) Sergeant Bond said "May I leave for town at 9?" The commanding officer said, "Yes."
龐德中士說：「我可以在九點時前往那個小鎮嗎？」。
指揮官說：「可以」。

(A) 龐德中士不能在九點時離開。
(B) 龐德中士可以在九點時離開。

(C) 九點鐘時，龐德中士不能活著。

(D) 龐德中士可以在七點時離開。

＊ sergeant〔ˈsɑrdʒənt〕*n.* 中士
leave〔liv〕*v.* 離開（某地）前往…<*for*>
town〔taʊn〕*n.* 城鎮
commanding〔kəˈmændɪŋ〕*adj.* 指揮的
officer〔ˈɔfəsɚ〕*n.* 軍官　live〔lɪv〕*v.* 居住；活著

37. (**D**) The kids cooked their own dinner tonight. We didn't help them. 今晚孩子們自己煮了晚餐。我們沒有幫他們。

(A) 他們和孩子們一起準備晚餐。

(B) 孩子們不知道如何煮飯。

(C) 孩子們幫忙父母煮晚餐。

(D) 孩子們自己準備晚餐。

＊ kid〔kɪd〕*n.* 小孩　cook〔kʊk〕*v.* 烹調；煮
parents〔ˈpɛrənts〕*n.pl.* 父母　***by oneself*** 獨自；靠自己

38. (**C**) Miss Jane has to go to work today.
珍小姐今天必須去上班。

(A) 她必須去死。　(B) 她今晚一定要知道。

(C) 她今天一定要去。　(D) 她明天一定要去。

39. (**C**) The teacher broke the speaker. 老師把擴音器弄壞了。

(A) 他無法廣播他的選擇。　(B) 他無法使聲音保持平衡。

(C) 他無法廣播他的聲音。　(D) 他無法展示他的相片。

＊ break〔brek〕*v.* 弄壞　speaker〔ˈspikɚ〕*n.* 擴音器
broadcast〔ˈbrɔdˌkæst〕*v.* 廣播　choice〔tʃɔɪs〕*n.* 選擇
balance〔ˈbæləns〕*v.* 使…保持平衡　voice〔vɔɪs〕*n.* 聲音
show〔ʃo〕*v.* 展示　photo〔ˈfoto〕*n.* 相片

40. (**B**) The quarterback gave orders and the team won the game. 在四分衛的命令下，那支隊伍贏得了比賽。

(A) 那名四分衛出軌了。

(B) 那名四分衛下了命令。

(C) 那名四分衛拔出他的槍。

(D) 那名四分衛堅持己見。

* quarterback〔'kwɔrtə,bæk〕*n.* 四分衛
order〔'ɔrdə〕*n.* 命令　***give orders*** 下令
team〔tim〕*n.* 隊伍　win〔wɪn〕*v.* 贏；獲勝
track〔træk〕*n.* 常軌；行爲方式
jump the track 出軌　***call the shots*** 命令；指揮
pull〔pʊl〕*v.* 拔（槍、刀等）　gun〔gʌn〕*n.* 槍
stick〔stɪk〕*v.* 堅持　pistol〔'pɪstḷ〕*n.* 手槍
stick to *one's* ***pistol*** 堅持己見（= *stick to one's gun*）

41. (**A**) Kelly wrote quickly what the manager dictated. 凱莉很快地把經理所說的話寫下來。

(A) 她很快地把經理說的話記下來。

(B) 她相信經理所說的話。

(C) 她把經理的命令塗掉。

(D) 她不停地把經理所說的話寫下來。

* manager〔'mænɪdʒə〕*n.* 經理
dictate〔'dɪktet〕*v.* 口述
jot〔dʒɑt〕*v.* 匆匆記下 < *down* >
take *one's* ***word*** 相信某人的話
scrawl〔skrɔl〕*v.* 塗掉 < *out* >
direct〔də'rɛkt〕*v.* 命令；指示
scribe〔skraɪb〕*v.* 繕寫
incessantly〔ɪn'sɛsṇtlɪ〕*adv.* 不停地

42. (**B**) Janet will entertain the newcomers.
珍妮特會招待新來的人。

(A) 珍妮特把食物端給新來的人。
(B) <u>珍妮特會使新來的人開心。</u>
(C) 珍妮特會歡迎新來的人。
(D) 珍妮特會跟全部的新人說話。

* entertain〔ˌɛntɚˈten〕*v.* 招待
newcomer〔ˈnjuˈkʌmɚ〕*n.* 新來的人
serve〔sɝv〕*v.* 端出　　amuse〔əˈmjuz〕*v.* 使高興
welcome〔ˈwɛlkəm〕*v.* 歡迎

43. (**C**) This ruler is like that one.
這把尺跟那把尺一樣。

(A) 這是我很喜歡的那把尺。
(B) 第一把尺比第二把尺長。
(C) <u>這兩把尺很相似。</u>
(D) 這兩把尺不一樣。

* ruler〔ˈrulɚ〕*n.* 尺　　similar〔ˈsɪmələ〕*adj.* 相似的
different〔ˈdɪfərənt〕*adj.* 不同的

44. (**C**) Judy is an efficient worker.
茱蒂是位有效率的員工。

(A) 她很懶惰又遊手好閒。
(B) 她遲到又沒禮貌。
(C) <u>她工作做得快又好。</u>
(D) 她喜歡其他員工

* efficient〔əˈfɪʃənt〕*adj.* 有效率的
idle〔ˈaɪdl̩〕*adj.* 遊手好閒的
rude〔rud〕*adj.* 無禮的

45. (**C**) We hope the dry season will be over soon.
我們希望乾季快點結束。

(A) 我們希望乾季開始。
(B) 我們祝你聖誕快樂。
(C) 我們希望乾季結束。
(D) 我們祝你生日快樂。

* dry〔draɪ〕*adj.* 乾燥的　wish〔wɪʃ〕*v.* 希望；祝
merry〔ˈmɛrɪ〕*adj.* 快樂的
Christmas〔ˈkrɪsməs〕*n.* 聖誕節　end〔ɛnd〕*v.* 結束

46. (**C**) His success was due to his diligence.
他的成功要歸功於勤勉。

(A) 他的成功導致他的勤勉。
(B) 他的成功以勤勉收場。
(C) 勤勉是他成功的原因。
(D) 他的成功導致勤勉。

* success〔səkˈsɛs〕*n.* 成功　due〔dju〕*adj.* 歸因於
diligence〔ˈdɪlədʒəns〕*n.* 勤勉　***lead to*** 導致
end〔ɛnd〕*v.* 以…收場 < *in* >
cause〔kɔz〕*v.* 成爲…的原因　***bring about*** 導致

47. (**D**) The new student is nervous about the test.
新來的學生對於考試感到緊張。

(A) 那名學生不在乎考試。　(B) 他擔心會緊張。
(C) 他喜歡考試。　(D) 他擔心考試。

* nervous〔ˈnɝvəs〕*adj.* 緊張的
care〔kɛr〕*v.* 擔心 < *about* >
worry〔ˈwɝɪ〕*v.* 擔心

48. (**A**) You speak so fast that she gets mixed up.
你講太快了，以致於她感到混淆。

(A) 她變得困惑。 (B) 她忘記所有的事。
(C) 她回想起他的話。 (D) 她盛裝打扮去見他。

* get〔gɛt〕*v.* 變得　***mix up*** 使混淆
confused〔kənˈfjuzd〕*adj.* 困惑的
recall〔rɪˈkɔl〕*v.* 回想
words〔wɝdz〕*n. pl.* 言語；話　***dress up*** 盛裝

49. (**A**) The girl took a long hike on her first morning at camp.
那個女孩在露營的第一天早上，健行了很長一段路。

(A) 她走了很長一段路。
(B) 她去騎馬。
(C) 她去騎腳踏車。
(D) 她去游泳。

* hike〔haɪk〕*n.* 健行　camp〔kæmp〕*n.* 露營生活
horseback〔ˈhɔrs,bæk〕*n.* 馬背
on horseback 騎在馬背上　ride〔raɪd〕*n.* 乘騎

50. (**A**) Mr. King is a flexible man.
金恩先生是個會隨機應變的人。

(A) 他不固執。 (B) 他很固執。
(C) 他很奇怪。 (D) 他彎曲膝蓋。

* flexible〔ˈflɛksəbl̩〕*adj.* 有彈性的；可變通的
rigid〔ˈrɪdʒɪd〕*adj.* 固執的；死板的
strange〔strendʒ〕*adj.* 奇怪的
flex〔flɛks〕*v.* 使（肌肉、關節）彎曲
knee〔ni〕*n.* 膝蓋

51. (**A**) M：How did you hear about the news?
W：There was a broadcast.
How did the woman find out about the news?
男：妳怎麼知道這個消息的？
女：有廣播。
這位女士如何得知這個消息？
(A) 她從收音機中聽到這個消息。
(B) 她從收音機看到這個消息。
(C) 她問她媽媽。
(D) 她問電視。
* ***hear about*** 聽說；得知　news〔njuz〕*n.* 消息
broadcast〔ˈbrɔd,kæst〕*n.* 廣播　***find out*** 查知

52. (**D**) W：What happened to your jacket?
M：It wore out.
What does the man mean?
女：你的夾克怎麼回事？
男：舊了。
這位男士的意思是？
(A) 他的夾克變冷。　(B) 他的山羊變老。
(C) 他的耳朵變冷。　(D) 他的夾克變舊。
* happen〔ˈhæpən〕*v.* 發生　jacket〔ˈdʒækɪt〕*n.* 夾克
wear out 穿破；磨損　mean〔min〕*v.* 意思是
goat〔got〕*n.* 山羊　ear〔ɪr〕*n.* 耳朵

53. (**B**) M：What did you purchase?
W：Some clothes.
What did the woman buy?
男：妳買了什麼？
女：一些衣服。

那位女士買了什麼？

(A) 吃的東西。 (B) 穿的東西。
(C) 看的東西。 (D) 奇怪的東西。

* purchase ('pɝtʃəs) *v.* 購買 clothes (kloðz) *n. pl.* 衣服

54. (**A**) M：Why are you leaving?
W：To have fun.
Why is the woman going away?
男：妳爲什麼要離開？
女：去玩。
爲什麼這名女士要走？
(A) 去放鬆一下，好好享受。
(B) 去工作賺錢。
(C) 到會議中心演講。
(D) 退休。

* ***go away*** 離開
relax (rɪ'læks) *v.* 放鬆 ***enjoy*** *oneself* 好好享受
make money 賺錢 lecture ('lɛktʃɚ) *v.* 演講
convention (kən'vɛnʃən) *n.* 會議
retire (rɪ'taɪr) *v.* 退休

55. (**B**) W：Oh no! I just missed the last bus!
M：I can give you a ride if you like.
W：Thank you. But my dad will come pick me up.
Why did the girl refuse the offer of a ride home?
女：噢不！我剛錯過最後一班公車！
男：如果妳願意的話，我可以載妳。
女：謝謝。但是我爸會來接我。
爲什麼那女孩拒絕搭便車回家？

(A) 她想要走路回家。
(B) 她爸爸會來帶她回家。
(C) 她住太遠了。
(D) 她還有工作要做。

＊ miss〔 mɪs 〕*v.* 錯過　***give** sb. **a ride*** 載某人
pick up 搭載　refuse〔 rɪ'fjuz 〕*v.* 拒絕
offer〔'ɔfɚ 〕*n.* 提供　take〔 tek 〕*v.* 把…帶往
far away 遙遠

56. (**B**) W：Was Tina injured in the accident?
M：No, the nurse gave her some medicine to relax her.
Why did the nurse give Tina medicine?
女：緹娜在那場意外中受傷了嗎？
男：沒有，護士給了她一些放鬆的藥。
爲什麼護士要給緹娜藥？

(A) 使她發瘋。　(B) 使她比較不緊張。
(C) 使她肚子餓。　(D) 使她唱歌。

＊ injured〔'ɪndʒɚd 〕*adj.* 受傷的
accident〔'æksədənt 〕*n.* 意外
nurse〔 nɝs 〕*n.* 護士
medicine〔'mɛdəsn̩ 〕*n.* 藥
go crazy 發瘋　tense〔 tɛns 〕*adj.* 緊張的
hungry〔'hʌŋgrɪ 〕*adj.* 飢餓的

57. (**D**) W：How do they get the diesel from the storage container to the vessel?
M：They use pipes.
What do they use?

女：他們是怎麼把柴油從貯存的容器運上船的？
男：用導管。
他們使用什麼？

(A) 線。 (B) 盒子。
(C) 電線。 (D) 管子。

＊ diesel〔ˈdizl̩〕*n.* 柴油 storage〔ˈstorɪdʒ〕*n.* 貯存
container〔kənˈtenɚ〕*n.* 容器
vessel〔ˈvɛsl̩〕*n.* 船 pipe〔paɪp〕*n.* 導管
string〔strɪŋ〕*n.* 線 wire〔waɪr〕*n.* 電線
tube〔tjub〕*n.* 管子

58.(**B**) W：What do you do?
M：I'm a flight controller in the air force. What is your job?
W：I'm a professor at the university.
What are they discussing?
女：你做什麼工作？
男：我在空軍擔任航空管制員。妳的工作是？
女：我是大學教授。
他們在討論什麼？

(A) 他們的時間表。 (B) 他們的職業。
(C) 他們的家人。 (D) 他們的夢想。

＊ flight〔flaɪt〕*n.* 飛行；航空
controller〔kənˈtrolɚ〕*n.* 管制員
air force 空軍 professor〔pɚˈfɛsɚ〕*n.* 教授
university〔ˌjunəˈvɝsətɪ〕*n.* 大學
discuss〔dɪˈskʌs〕*v.* 討論
schedule〔ˈskɛdʒul〕*n.* 時間表
profession〔prəˈfɛʃən〕*n.* 職業

59. (**D**) M：Are you gonna give that novel away?
W：No, I want to sell it.
What did the woman say?
男：妳要把那本小說送人嗎？
女：不，我要把它賣掉。
那位女士說什麼？

(A) 她想要花錢買這本書。
(B) 她想要將這本書送給一家商店。
(C) 她想把這本書當作禮物送人。
(D) 她想要把這本書拿去換錢。

* gonna〔'gɔnə〕等於 going to，是口語化的用法。
give away 贈送　　present〔'prɛznt〕*n.* 禮物

60. (**B**) W：I can't believe Steve is quitting his job.
M：I know. He's not in his right mind.
What is the man's opinion of Steve?
女：我無法相信史帝夫辭職了。
男：我知道。他頭腦不清醒。
這位男士對史帝夫的看法是？

(A) 史帝夫很聰明，把工作辭掉。
(B) 史帝夫瘋了才會辭掉工作。
(C) 他不在意史帝夫要不要辭掉工作。
(D) 史帝夫辭掉工作是正確的。

* quit〔kwɪt〕*v.* 辭職
in *one's* ***right mind*** 神志清醒
opinion〔ə'pɪnɪən〕*n.* 意見；看法
crazy〔'krezɪ〕*adj.* 發瘋的
mind〔mɪnd〕*v.* 在意

LISTENING TEST ⑦

● *Directions for questions 1-25. You will hear questions on the test CD. Select the one item A, B, C or D which answers the question correctly, and mark your answer sheet.*

1. A. more time to study B. more help
   C. more money D. more information

2. A. The mangoes are not good.
   B. The mangoes are cooked.
   C. The mangoes look good.
   D. The mangoes look good, but they are not good.

3. A. It stopped.
   B. It fell apart.
   C. It dropped out of the plane.
   D. It made an awful noise.

4. A. her lungs B. her voice
   C. her reactions D. her heartbeat

5. A. I wanted to watch some basketball games.
   B. I had an accident while driving to the park three days ago.
   C. I had to clean the bedroom.
   D. I wanted to finish my work.

6. A. weapons B. food
   C. tools D. beverages

7. A. something that's good to eat
   B. something to wear
   C. something that burns easily
   D. something to play with

8. A. He can find the umbrella easily.
   B. He can preserve the umbrella for you.
   C. He can show you where the umbrella is.
   D. He can't recognize the umbrella easily.

9. A. I'm worrying about working in a bank.
   B. I'm thinking about working in the bed.
   C. I'm thinking about working in a bank.
   D. I'm thinking about working out in a gym.

10. A. He doesn't like any money.
    B. He doesn't have any honey.
    C. He doesn't have any money.
    D. He doesn't have any bunny.

11. A. He'll need some ice cream.
    B. He'll need some sugar.
    C. He'll eat some sugar.
    D. He'll need some air.

12. A. The teacher learned about the trip.
    B. The teacher forgot about the trip.
    C. The student learned about the trip.
    D. The student forgot about the trip.

13. A. stand up from her chair
    B. finish eating the noodles
    C. finish her drink
    D. put on her coat

14. A. A stamp is more expensive.
    B. It'll take a week.
    C. That will be 10 dollars.
    D. It will be shipped out tonight.

15. A. Yes, we can buy a lighter in this shop.
    B. No, we can't find any fire stations.
    C. Yes, we can use two rocks to make a fire.
    D. No, we can't start a fire with a lighter.

16. A. war must be made more important
    B. war must be made less important
    C. war must be made more interesting
    D. war must be made less boring

17. A. the floor　　B. the cell
    C. the ceiling　　D. the computer

18. A. in a shoe store　　B. in a factory
    C. near the river　　D. in a supermarket

19. A. I usually walk, but I cracked my heel today.
    B. I think we have to take number 83.
    C. Yes, it really is a sunny day.
    D. I think I'll drive.

20. A. Because I have a job interview.
    B. Your apartment really suits you.
    C. Everything is on sale now.
    D. We offer several choices here.

21. A. happy B. excited
    C. worried D. bored

22. A. every month B. at 3 in the afternoon
    C. at 4 p.m. D. once a week

23. A. It came by express mail.
    B. I recommend a package tour.
    C. I used Federal express.
    D. How big is the package?

24. A. only those who live there
    B. only those who work there
    C. only those who know the password
    D. only those with official approval

25. A. get seat assignments B. buy their tickets
    C. leave the plane D. board the plane

- *Directions for questions 26-50. You will hear statements on the test CD. Select the one answer A, B, C, or D which comes closest to the meaning of the statement and mark your answer sheet.*

26. A. I'll forget it. B. I'll learn it.
    C. I'll remember it. D. I'll study it.

27. A. His pain comes and goes.
    B. He has it some of the time.
    C. He doesn't feel anything.
    D. He has it all the time.

28. A. Some workers didn't get fired.
    B. Some workers were happy.
    C. Some workers were injured.
    D. Some workers got fired.

29. A. She likes to work very quickly.
    B. She must work very quickly.
    C. She must work very slowly.
    D. She must wake very quickly.

30. A. Very well.
    B. The children are five years old.
    C. The principal likes the kindergarten.
    D. There are 100 kids in that kindergarten.

31. A. They were behind themselves.
    B. They were in front of us.
    C. They were between us.
    D. They were behind us.

32. A. He will put them in hot water.
    B. He will eat some potatoes in the morning.
    C. He will boil them in soup.
    D. He will put them in hot oil.

33. A. It has no curves. B. It has many turns.
    C. It is in need of repair. D. It goes in zigzags.

34. A. I see a storm receding.
B. A storm is here.
C. A storm is coming.
D. A storm was big.

35. A. The trip will be formed.
B. The results will be heard.
C. The results will be reported.
D. The results will be known.

36. A. She likes food.
B. She is eating food.
C. She is going to eat out.
D. She is fasting today.

37. A. He makes iron shoes for horses.
B. He is a shoemaker.
C. He likes iron.
D. He is new in town.

38. A. Food may go bad in the fridge.
B. Food may be kept in the fridge.
C. Food may be kept warm in the fridge.
D. Food may be forgotten in the fridge.

39. A. She will come.
B. She won’t come.
C. She may come.
D. She will definitely not come.

40. A. It will start at five o’clock.
B. It will smart at five o’clock.
C. It will squat at five o’clock.
D. It will spark at five o’clock.

41. A. I set a table for eight.
    B. I bought a table at eight.
    C. I booked a table for eight.
    D. I put a table at eight.

42. A. The accused went to a party.
    B. The accused was let go.
    C. The accused likes salad.
    D. The accused was found in the country.

43. A. They don't mind it. B. They don't like it.
    C. They don't eat it. D. They don't cook it.

44. A. Their clothing must be long-sleeved.
    B. Their clothing must be fireproof.
    C. Their clothing must be waterproof.
    D. Their clothing must be mothproof.

45. A. It's beginning to get sunny.
    B. It's beginning to rain.
    C. It's beginning to sink.
    D. It's beginning to float.

46. A. It was cloudy. B. There was a downpour.
    C. It was warm. D. There was a drizzle.

47. A. You must first get permission.
    B. You must check your balance.
    C. You must write the date on it.
    D. You must sign your name on the back.

48. A. They work on weekends.
    B. They work by themselves.
    C. They are operated manually.
    D. They work by the lake.

49. A. It is heavy.
    B. It cannot be seen.
    C. It is necessary.
    D. It moves quickly.

50. A. She has a bit of energy.
    B. She has no energy now.
    C. She never has energy.
    D. She has a lot of energy.

- *Directions for questions 51-60. You will hear dialogs on the test CD. Select the correct answer A, B, C, or D and mark your answer sheet.*

51. A. She will go there when it leaves.
    B. She neither knows nor cares when it leaves.
    C. She doesn't know when it leaves.
    D. She knows when it leaves.

52. A. mechanical problems
    B. human error
    C. improper care
    D. the age of the engine

53. A. The man did not plan to take any pictures.
    B. The man did not take any pictures.
    C. The man bought a new camera.
    D. The man took lots of pictures.

54. A. He has enough.
    B. He has too much.
    C. He has something else.
    D. He doesn't like soup.

55. A. 4:45 p.m. B. 5:00 a.m.
    C. 6:05 p.m. D. 5:05 p.m.

56. A. Michael was late to class.
    B. Michael was absent from class.
    C. Michael answered the question.
    D. Michael doesn't know what the question means.

57. A. if the patient slept well
    B. if the patient is eating all right
    C. if the patient took his medicine
    D. if the patient is going home from the hospital

58. A. from Monday to Friday
    B. in an automobile factory
    C. near his home
    D. from nine to five

59. A. It is broken. B. It has no feeling in it.
    C. It's bleeding. D. It itches.

60. A. a bookstore B. a student council office
    C. a hotel D. a library

ECL 聽力測驗⑦詳解

1. (**D**) Before she can do anything else, Jenny needs more data. What does she need?

在珍妮做其他事之前，她需要更多資料？／她需要什麼？

(A) 更多時間唸書。

(B) 更多幫助。

(C) 更多錢。

(D) <u>更多資訊。</u>

* else〔ɛls〕*adj.* 其他的　　data〔ˈdetə〕*n.* 資料
information〔ˌɪnfəˈmeʃən〕*n.* 資料

2. (**A**) Carol said, "These mangoes are spoiled." What did she say about the mangoes?

卡洛說：「這些芒果爛掉了。」／關於芒果，她說了些什麼？

(A) <u>這些芒果不好。</u>

(B) 這些芒果被煮過。

(C) 這些芒果看起來不錯。

(D) 這些芒果看起來不錯，但其實並不好。

* mango〔ˈmæŋgo〕*n.* 芒果　　spoil〔spɔɪl〕*v.* 腐爛
cook〔kuk〕*v.* 烹調；煮

3. (**A**) His motor cut out when he was at 6000 feet. What happened to his motor?

他的車子在六千英呎的地方熄火了。／他的車子怎麼了？

(A) <u>他的車子停下來。</u>

(B) 他的車子分裂了。

(C) 他的車子從飛機上掉出來。

(D) 他的車子發出可怕的聲音。

* motor〔'motɚ〕*n.* 汽車　***cut out***（引擎）熄火
foot〔fʊt〕*n.* 英呎【複數為 feet〔fit〕】
fall apart 散開；分裂　***drop out*** 掉落
plane〔plen〕*n.* 飛機　awful〔'ɔfʊl〕*adj.* 可怕的
noise〔nɔɪz〕*n.* 聲音

4. (**D**) The nurse wants to monitor Jenny's pulse. What does the nurse want to monitor?

護士要測量珍妮的脈搏。／護士要測量什麼？

(A) 她的肺。　(B) 她的聲音。

(C) 她的反應。　(D) 她的心跳。

* nurse〔nɝs〕*n.* 護士　monitor〔'mɑnətɚ〕*v.* 檢測
pulse〔pʌls〕*n.* 脈搏　lung〔lʌŋ〕*n.* 肺
voice〔vɔɪs〕*n.* 聲音　reaction〔rɪ'ækʃən〕*n.* 反應
heartbeat〔'hɑrt,bit〕*n.* 心跳

5. (**D**) Why did you stay so late at the office last Tuesday?

你上星期二為什麼在辦公室待到那麼晚？

(A) 我想要看一些籃球比賽。

(B) 我三天前開車到公園時出車禍。

(C) 我必須打掃臥室。

(D) 我要把工作做完。

* accident〔'æksədənt〕*n.* 意外；車禍

6. (**C**) The man is going to build a house. What will he use?

這位男士將要蓋一間房子。／他會使用什麼？

(A) 武器。　(B) 食物。　(C) 工具。　(D) 飲料。

* build〔bɪld〕*v.* 建造　weapon〔'wɛpən〕*n.* 武器
tool〔tul〕*n.* 工具　beverage〔'bɛvərɪdʒ〕*n.* 飲料

7. (**C**) The bottle in the cupboard is labeled flammable. What does that mean?

碗櫥裡的瓶子上有貼易燃的標籤。／那是什麼意思？

(A) 好吃的東西。　(B) 穿的東西。

(C) <u>容易燃燒的東西。</u>　(D) 玩樂的東西。

* bottle〔ˈbɑtl̩〕*n.* 瓶子　cupboard〔ˈkʌbɚd〕*n.* 碗櫥
label〔ˈlebl̩〕*v.* 在…上貼標籤
flammable〔ˈflæməbl̩〕*adj.* 易燃的
mean〔min〕*v.* 意思是　burn〔bɝn〕*v.* 燃燒

8. (**D**) It's not easy for me to identify your umbrella among a hundred others. What does this man say?

對我來說， 要在一百支雨傘中認出你的傘並不容易。
／這位男士說什麼？

(A) 他輕易就能找到那把傘。

(B) 他可以替你保留那把雨傘。

(C) 他可以告訴你那把傘在哪。

(D) <u>他無法輕易認出那把傘。</u>

* identify〔aɪˈdɛntəfaɪ〕*v.* 認明；分辨
umbrella〔ʌmˈbrɛlə〕*n.* 雨傘
among〔əˈmʌŋ〕*prep.* 在…之中
preserve〔prɪˈzɝv〕*v.* 保留　show〔ʃo〕*v.* 告知
recognize〔ˈrɛkəgˌnaɪz〕*v.* 認出

9. (**C**) What type of work do you have in mind?

你心裡想要哪一種工作？

(A) 我擔心要在銀行工作。　(B) 我想在床上工作。

(C) <u>我想在銀行工作。</u>　(D) 我想到健身房運動。

* ***have…in mind*** 把…記在心理　worry〔ˈwɝɪ〕*v.* 擔心
bank〔bæŋk〕*n.* 銀行　***work out*** 運動
gym〔dʒɪm〕*n.* 健身房

10. (**C**) Vincent is broke. What's his problem?
文森破產了。／他有什麼問題？
(A) 他不喜歡任何錢。 (B) 他沒有蜂蜜。
(C) 他沒錢。 (D) 他沒有小兔子。
* broke〔 brok 〕*adj.* 破產的 honey〔ˈhʌnɪ〕*n.* 蜂蜜
bunny〔ˈbʌnɪ〕*n.* 小兔子

11. (**B**) Marc is going to bake some cookies. What will he need? 馬克要烤一些餅乾。／他需要什麼？
(A) 他將需要一些冰淇淋。 (B) 他將需要一些糖。
(C) 他將吃一些糖。 (D) 他將需要一些空氣。
* bake〔 bek 〕*v.* 烘烤 sugar〔ˈʃʊgɚ〕*n.* 糖

12. (**A**) The teacher found out about the field trip today. What happened today?
那位老師今天去弄清楚戶外教學的事。／今天發生什麼事？
(A) 老師去了解這次旅行。 (B) 老師忘了這次旅行。
(C) 學生去了解這次旅行。 (D) 學生忘了這次旅行。
* ***find out*** 查明；弄清楚 trip〔 trɪp 〕*n.* 旅行
field trip 實地考察旅行；校外教學
learn about 獲悉；了解

13. (**C**) Bonnie said to her friend, "Drink up, and let's go home." What did Bonnie want her friend to do?
邦妮對她的朋友說：「乾杯，然後我們回家去。」／邦妮要她的朋友做什麼？
(A) 從她的椅子上站起來。 (B) 把麵條吃完。
(C) 把飲料喝完。 (D) 穿上她的外套。
* drink〔 drɪŋk 〕*v.* 喝 *n.* 飲料 ***drink up*** 喝光；乾杯
chair〔 tʃɛr 〕*n.* 椅子 noodle〔ˈnudḷ〕*n.* 麵條
put on 穿上 coat〔 kot 〕*n.* 外套

14. (**C**) Can you tell me how much it will cost to mail this package?
你可以告訴我寄這個包裹要花多少錢嗎？
(A) 一張郵票會比較貴。
(B) 要花一個星期。
(C) <u>要花十元。</u>
(D) 今晚就會用船運出去。
* mail〔mel〕*v.* 郵寄　package〔ˈpækɪdʒ〕*n.* 包裹
stamp〔stæmp〕*n.* 郵票
expensive〔ɪkˈspɛnsɪv〕*adj.* 昂貴的
take〔tek〕*v.* 花費　ship〔ʃɪp〕*v.* 用船運

15. (**C**) Can we start a fire with two rocks?
我們可以用兩塊石頭來生火嗎？
(A) 是的，我們可以在這家店買到打火機。
(B) 不行，我們找不到任何消防站。
(C) <u>是的，我們可以用兩塊石頭來生火。</u>
(D) 不行，我們無法用打火機來生火。
* lighter〔ˈlaɪtɚ〕*n.* 打火機　***fire station*** 消防站
make a fire 生火

16. (**B**) War must be de-emphasized. What must be done?
我們必須降低戰爭的重要性。／我們必須做什麼？
(A) 把戰爭變得更重要。
(B) <u>把戰爭變得比較不重要。</u>
(C) 把戰爭變得更有趣。
(D) 把戰爭變得比較不無聊。
* de-emphasize〔diˈɛmfəˌsaɪz〕*v.* 降低重要性

17. (**C**) Which is the highest part of a room?

房間最高的部份是哪個部份？

(A) 地板。 (B) 細胞。

(C) 天花板。 (D) 電腦。

＊ floor〔 flor 〕*n.* 地板 cell〔 sɛl 〕*n.* 細胞

ceiling〔ˈsilɪŋ〕*n.* 天花板

18. (**B**) This is an industrial city. Where do most of the people work?

這是個工業城市。／大多數的人在哪裡工作？

(A) 在鞋店 (B) 在工廠

(C) 在河流附近 (D) 在超級市場

＊ industrial〔 ɪnˈdʌstrɪəl 〕*adj.* 工業的

shoe〔 ʃu 〕*n.* 鞋子 factory〔ˈfæktrɪ 〕*n.* 工廠

19. (**A**) Do you often take the bus, or is today an exception?

你常常搭公車嗎，還是今天是例外？

(A) 我通常用走的，但是我的腳跟今天裂開了。

(B) 我想我們必須搭八十三號公車。

(C) 是的，今天眞是個大晴天。

(D) 我想我會開車。

＊ take〔 tek 〕*v.* 搭乘 exception〔 ɪkˈsɛpʃən 〕*n.* 例外

crack〔 kræk 〕*v.* 使裂開 heel〔 hil 〕*n.* 腳跟

20. (**D**) Does this department sell wool hats?

這個部門有賣羊毛帽嗎？

(A) 因爲我有個工作面試。

(B) 你的公寓眞的很適合你。

(C) 現在所有東西都在特價。

(D) 我們這裡提供幾種選擇。

* department〔dɪ'pɑrtmənt〕*n.* 部門
sell〔sɛl〕*v.* 出售　wool〔wʊl〕*adj.* 羊毛的
interview〔'ɪntə,vju〕*n.* 面試
apartment〔ə'pɑrtmənt〕*n.* 公寓
suit〔sut〕*v.* 適合　***on sale*** 特價
offer〔'ɔfə〕*v.* 提供　several〔'sɛvərəl〕*adj.* 幾個的
choice〔tʃɔɪs〕*n.* 選擇

21. (**C**) Lieutenant Dan was preoccupied about the health of his soldiers. How did he feel about their health?

丹上尉一直想著關於士兵健康的事。／他對他們的健康有何感受？

(A) 高興。　(B) 興奮。

(C) 擔心。　(D) 無聊。

* lieutenant〔lu'tɛnənt〕*n.* 上尉
preoccupy〔pri'ɑkjə,paɪ〕*v.* 使全神貫注
health〔hɛlθ〕*n.* 健康　soldier〔'soldʒə〕*n.* 士兵

22. (**C**) Billy has football practice every afternoon at 4:00. When does he have football practice?

比利每天下午四點都要練橄欖球。／比利何時要練橄欖球？

(A) 每個月。　(B) 下午三點。

(C) 下午四點。　(D) 一週一次。

* football〔'fʊt,bɔl〕*n.* 橄欖球
practice〔'præktɪs〕*n.* 練習
once〔wʌns〕*adv.* 一次

23. (**C**) How did you send the package?
你用什麼方法寄這個包裹？

(A) 它是用限時郵件寄來的。
(B) 我推薦一個套裝行程。
(C) 我用聯邦快遞寄。
(D) 這個包裹有多大？

* send〔sɛnd〕*v.* 寄送
express〔ɪk'sprɛs〕*adj.* 快遞的；限時的 *n.* 快遞
express mail 限時郵件
recommend〔,rɛkə'mɛnd〕*v.* 推薦
package tour 包辦旅行；套裝行程
federal〔'fɛdərəl〕*adj.* 聯邦的

24. (**D**) Only authorized personnel may step into that complex.
Who may enter?
只有經授權的人員才能踏進那個工業區。／誰可能會進入？

(A) 只有住在那裡的那些人。
(B) 只有在那裡工作的那些人。
(C) 只有知道密碼的那些人。
(D) 只有得到官方認可的那些人。

* authorized〔'ɔθə,raɪzd〕*adj.* 經授權的
personnel〔,pɝsn̩'ɛl〕*n.* 人員
step〔stɛp〕*v.* 踏入
complex〔'kɑmplɛks〕*n.* 工業區；聯合企業
password〔'pæs,wɝd〕*n.* 密碼
official〔ə'fɪʃəl〕*adj.* 官方的
approval〔ə'pruvl̩〕*n.* 認可

25. (**D**) Attention all passengers. The flight to Taipei is now boarding at gate number 21. What does she ask people to do?

所有乘客注意。飛往台北的班機現在正在二十一號登機門登機。／她要求人們做什麼？

(A) 取得座位分配。　(B) 買他們的票。
(C) 離開飛機。　(D) 登機。

* attention〔ə'tɛnʃən〕*n.* 注意
passenger〔'pæsn̩dʒɚ〕*n.* 乘客　flight〔flaɪt〕*n.* 班機
board〔bord〕*v.* 上（飛機、車、船等）
gate〔get〕*n.* 登機門　seat〔sit〕*n.* 座位
assignment〔ə'saɪnmənt〕*n.* 分配　ticket〔'tɪkɪt〕*n.* 票

26. (**C**) I'll keep your opinion in mind.

我會記住你的意見。

(A) 我會忘記它。　(B) 我會把它學會。
(C) 我會記住它。　(D) 我會研究它。

* ***keep in mind*** 記住　opinion〔ə'pɪnɪən〕*n.* 意見
remember〔rɪ'mɛmbɚ〕*v.* 記住
study〔'stʌdɪ〕*v.* 研究

27. (**D**) Milton has a constant toothache.

米爾頓時常牙痛。

(A) 他的疼痛瞬息即逝。　(B) 他某些時候會牙痛。
(C) 他沒有任何感覺。　(D) 他經常牙痛。

* constant〔'kɑnstənt〕*adj.* 時常的
toothache〔'tuθ,ek〕*n.* 牙痛　pain〔pen〕*n.* 疼痛
come and go 來來去去；瞬息即逝
some of the time 某些時候　***all the time*** 經常

28. (**C**) There was an accident at the factory.
工廠發生了一場意外。

(A) 有些工人沒有被開除。　(B) 有些工人很開心。
(C) 有些工人受傷了。　(D) 有些工人被開除了。

* fire〔faɪr〕*v.* 開除　injured〔ˈɪndʒɚd〕*adj.* 受傷的

29. (**B**) She must hurry with these jobs.
她必須趕快做這些工作。

(A) 她喜歡快速地工作。　(B) 她必須快速工作。
(C) 她必須很慢地工作。　(D) 她必須很快地醒來。

* hurry〔ˈhɝɪ〕*v.* 趕快進行　wake〔wek〕*v.* 醒來

30. (**A**) How is the English teaching at the kindergarten coming along? 幼稚園的英語教學進行得如何？

(A) 很棒。　(B) 這些孩子們五歲。
(C) 校長喜歡這所幼稚園。
(D) 那所幼稚園有一百個孩子。

* kindergarten〔ˈkɪndɚˌgɑrtn̩〕*n.* 幼稚園
come along 進展；進行
principal〔ˈprɪnsəpl̩〕*n.* 校長　kid〔kɪd〕*n.* 小孩

31. (**D**) Five people followed us yesterday.
昨天有五個人跟著我們。

(A) 他們在自己身後。　(B) 他們在我們前面。
(C) 他們在我們中間。　(D) 他們在我們後面。

* follow〔ˈfɑlo〕*v.* 跟隨
behind〔bɪˈhaɪnd〕*prep.* 在…後面
in front of 在前面　between〔bəˈtwin〕*prep.* 在中間

32. (**D**) Dave will fry potatoes for dinner.
戴夫將炸馬鈴薯來當晚餐。

(A) 他會把馬鈴薯放在熱水裡。
(B) 他早上會吃一些馬鈴薯。
(C) 他會把馬鈴薯拿來煮湯。
(D) 他會把馬鈴薯放進熱油裡。

* fry [fraɪ] *v.* 油炸　potato [pə'teto] *n.* 馬鈴薯
boil [bɔɪl] *v.* 煮　soup [sup] *n.* 湯

33. (**A**) That road is very straight. 那條路很直。

(A) 它沒有彎曲。　(B) 它有很多轉彎。
(C) 它需要修理。　(D) 它是呈 Z 字型走向。

* straight [stret] *adj.* 直的　curve [kɝv] *n.* 彎曲
turn [tɝn] *n.* 轉彎處　***be in need of*** 需要
repair [rɪ'pɛr] *n.* 修理　zigzag ['zɪgzæg] *n.* Z 字型

34. (**C**) I see a big storm approaching.
我看到一個大風暴正在接近當中。

(A) 我看到風暴正遠離。　(B) 風暴在這裡。
(C) 風暴正要來臨。　(D) 那是個大風暴。

* storm [stɔrm] *n.* 風暴
approach [ə'protʃ] *v.* 接近
recede [rɪ'sid] *v.* 後退；遠離

35. (**C**) The results of the trip will be announced immediately.
旅遊的結果將立即宣布。

(A) 旅遊即將形成。
(B) 我們將會聽到結果。

(C) 結果將被報告出來。

(D) 我們將得知結果。

* result〔rɪˈzʌlt〕*n.* 結果　announce〔əˈnaʊns〕*v.* 宣布
immediately〔ɪˈmidɪɪtlɪ〕*adv.* 立即
form〔fɔrm〕*v.* 形成　report〔rɪˈpɔrt〕*v.* 報告

36. (**C**) Mary is dining out this evening.
瑪莉今晚在外面吃飯。

(A) 她喜歡食物。　(B) 她正在吃東西。

(C) 她將要外出用餐。　(D) 她今天禁食。

* ***dine out*** 在外面吃飯　out〔aʊt〕*adv.* 在外面
fast〔fæst〕*v.* 禁食

37. (**A**) Mr. Reed is a blacksmith in our town.
里德先生是我們鎮上的鐵匠。

(A) 他替馬做鐵鞋。　(B) 他是個鞋匠。

(C) 他喜歡鐵。　(D) 他是剛來鎮上的人。

* blacksmith〔ˈblæk,smɪθ〕*n.* 鐵匠
iron〔ˈaɪɚn〕*adj.* 鐵的　*n.* 鐵　horse〔hɔrs〕*n.* 馬
shoemaker〔ˈʃu,mekɚ〕*n.* 鞋匠　new〔nju〕*adj.* 剛來的

38. (**B**) You can store leftovers in the fridge.
你可以把剩菜剩飯存放在冰箱裡。

(A) 食物可能會在冰箱裡變壞。

(B) 食物可以存放在冰箱裡。

(C) 食物可以放在冰箱裡保溫。

(D) 食物可能被忘在冰箱裡。

* store〔stor〕*v.* 儲存
leftovers〔ˈlɛft,ovɚz〕*n. pl.* 吃剩的飯菜
fridge〔frɪdʒ〕*n.* 冰箱　keep〔kip〕*v.* 保存

39. (**A**) I invited her to my house, and she accepted.

我邀請她來我家，而她接受了。

(A) 她會來。
(B) 她不會來。
(C) 她可能會來。
(D) 她一定不會來。

* invite〔ɪn'vaɪt〕*v.* 邀請　accept〔ək'sɛpt〕*v.* 接受
definitely〔'dɛfənɪtlɪ〕*adv.* 一定

40. (**A**) The show will commence at five o'clock.

表演將在五點鐘開始。

(A) 它將在五點鐘開始。
(B) 它將在五點鐘感到劇痛。
(C) 它將在五點鐘蹲下。
(D) 它將在五點鐘發出火花。

* show〔ʃo〕*n.* 表演
commence〔kə'mɛns〕*v.* 開始
smart〔smɑrt〕*v.* 感到劇痛
squat〔skwɑt〕*v.* 蹲下　spark〔spɑrk〕*v.* 發出火花

41. (**C**) I reserved a table for two, at eight o'clock.

我訂了一張兩個人的桌子，八點鐘。

(A) 我爲了八點鐘開飯而擺好餐具。
(B) 我在八點鐘買了一張桌子。
(C) 我預訂八點鐘的一張桌子。
(D) 我在八點鐘時放了一張桌子。

* reserve〔rɪ'zɝv〕*v.* 預定
set〔sɛt〕*v.* 擺好（餐具）　book〔bʊk〕*v.* 預訂

42. (**B**) The accused was found not guilty. 被告被判無罪。

(A) 被告去參加舞會。 (B) 被告被釋放。

(C) 被告喜歡吃沙拉。 (D) 被告在鄉下被找到。

* accused〔ə'kjuzd〕*adj.* 被告發的
the accused 被告　find〔faɪnd〕*v.* 判定；發現
guilty〔'gɪltɪ〕*adj.* 有罪的　***let go*** 釋放
salad〔'sæləd〕*n.* 沙拉　country〔'kʌntrɪ〕*n.* 鄉下

43. (**A**) They do not object to the food in the cafeteria.
他們不討厭自助餐廳的食物。

(A) 他們不反對那些食物。

(B) 他們不喜歡那些食物。

(C) 他們不吃那些食物。

(D) 他們不煮那些食物。

* object〔əb'dʒɛkt〕*v.* 討厭
cafeteria〔,kæfə'tɪrɪə〕*n.* 自助餐廳
mind〔maɪnd〕*v.* 介意；反對

44. (**B**) The firemen must not wear flammable clothes.
消防員一定不能穿易燃的衣服。

(A) 他們的衣服必須是長袖的。

(B) 他們的衣服必須要防火。

(C) 他們的衣服必須要防水。

(D) 他們的衣服必須要防蟲。

* fireman〔'faɪrmən〕*n.* 消防員
clothes〔kloðz〕*n.pl.* 衣服　clothing〔'kloðɪŋ〕*n.* 衣服
long-sleeved〔'lɔŋ'slivd〕*adj.* 長袖的
fireproof〔'faɪr'pruf〕*adj.* 防火的
waterproof〔'wɔtə'pruf〕*adj.* 防水的
mothproof〔'mɔθ'pruf〕*adj.* 防蟲的

45. (**B**) We'd better hurry. It's sprinkling a bit now.
我們最好快一點。現在有點開始下小雨了。

(A) 現在開始放晴。 (B) 現在開始下雨。
(C) 現在開始沉沒。 (D) 現在開始漂浮。

* ***had better*** 最好 hurry〔ˈhɝɪ〕*v.* 趕快
sprinkle〔ˈsprɪŋkl̩〕*v.* 下小雨 ***a bit*** 有點
sink〔sɪŋk〕*v.* 沉沒 float〔flot〕*v.* 漂浮

46. (**B**) It rained hard all morning yesterday.
昨天一整個早上都在下大雨。

(A) 昨天是多雲。 (B) 昨天下了傾盆大雨。
(C) 昨天很溫暖。 (D) 昨天下毛毛雨。

* hard〔hɑrd〕*adv.* 猛烈地
cloudy〔ˈklaʊdɪ〕*adj.* 多雲的
warm〔wɔrm〕*adj.* 溫暖的
downpour〔ˈdaʊnˌpor〕*n.* 傾盆大雨
drizzle〔ˈdrɪzl̩〕*n.* 毛毛雨

47. (**D**) If you want to cash a check, you must endorse it.
如果你要兌現一張支票，你必須要在後面背書。

(A) 你必須先得到允許。
(B) 你必須查看你的存款餘額。
(C) 你必須把日期寫上去。
(D) 你必須在支票後面簽名。

* cash〔kæʃ〕*v.* 兌現 check〔tʃɛk〕*n.* 支票 *v.* 查看
endorse〔ɪnˈdɔrs〕*v.* 背書
permission〔pɚˈmɪʃən〕*n.* 允許
balance〔ˈbæləns〕*n.* 存款餘額 sign〔saɪn〕*v.* 簽名

48. (B) These machines are automatic.
這些機器是自動化的。

(A) 它們在週末工作。 (B) 它們自己會工作。
(C) 要用手操作它們。 (D) 它們在湖邊工作。

* machine〔 mə'ʃin 〕*n.* 機器
automatic〔ˌɔtə'mætɪk 〕*adj.* 自動的
weekend〔'wik'ɛnd 〕*n.* 週末
operate〔'ɑpəˌret 〕*v.* 操作；使運轉
manually〔'mænjuəlɪ 〕*adv.* 用手地
lake〔 lek 〕*n.* 湖

49. (B) Air is invisible. 空氣是看不到的。

(A) 它是重的。 (B) 我們看不到它們。
(C) 它是不可或缺的。 (D) 它移動快速。

* invisible〔 ɪn'vɪzəbl̩ 〕*adj.* 看不見的
heavy〔'hɛvɪ 〕*adj.* 重的
necessary〔'nɛsəˌsɛrɪ 〕*adj.* 必要的；不可或缺的
move〔 muv 〕*v.* 移動

50. (D) Our professor has an abundance of energy.
我們教授的精力充沛。

(A) 她只有一點點活力。
(B) 她現在沒有活力。
(C) 她從來不曾有活力。
(D) 她活力充沛。

* professor〔 prə'fɛsɚ 〕*n.* 教授
abundance〔 ə'bʌndəns 〕*n.* 豐富
an abundance of 大量的
energy〔'ɛnɚdʒɪ 〕*n.* 精力 ***a bit of*** 一點點

51. (**C**) M：Lisa doesn't know when the train leaves.
W：Neither do we.
What did the woman say?
男：麗莎不知道火車何時開走？
女：我們也不知道。
這位女士說什麼？
(A) 當火車離開時，她會到那裡去。
(B) 她不知道也不在乎火車何時開走。
(C) 她不知道火車何時開走。
(D) 她知道火車何時開走。

* neither〔ˈniðɚ〕*adv.* 也不
neither A ***nor*** B 既不 A，也不 B　　care〔kɛr〕*v.* 在乎

52. (**C**) M：What caused the motor to fail?
W：It failed because of inadequate maintenance.
What did the woman blame the failure on?
男：是什麼使這部車停下來？
女：它會停下來是因爲維修不當。
這位女士認爲故障要歸咎於？
(A) 機械問題。　(B) 人爲疏失。
(C) 不當的保養。　(D) 引擎的產出年數。

* cause〔kɔz〕*v.* 使得　　fail〔fel〕*v.* 停止轉動
inadequate〔ɪnˈædəkwɪt〕*adj.* 不適當的
maintenance〔ˈmɛntənəns〕*n.* 維修管理
blame〔blem〕*v.* 歸咎於　　failure〔ˈfeljɚ〕*n.* 停止；故障
mechanical〔məˈkænɪkḷ〕*adj.* 機械的
error〔ˈɛrɚ〕*n.* 失誤
improper〔ɪmˈprɑpɚ〕*adj.* 不適當的
care〔kɛr〕*v.* 照料；保養
age〔edʒ〕*n.* 年齡；產出年數　　engine〔ˈɛndʒən〕*n.* 引擎

53. (**B**) W：Did you plan to take photos on your trip?

M：Yes, but my camera was not working.

What do you learn from this conversation?

女：你打算在旅行中拍照嗎？

男：是的，但是我的相機壞了。

你從這段對話得知什麼？

(A) 那位男士不打算拍任何照片。

(B) 那位男士沒有拍任何照片。

(C) 那位男士買了新相機。

(D) 那位男士拍了許多照片。

* plan〔plæn〕*v.* 打算　photo〔ˈfoto〕*n.* 照片

take a photo 拍照　camera〔ˈkæmərə〕*n.* 相機

work〔wɝk〕*v.* 運轉　learn〔lɝn〕*v.* 得知

conversation〔ˌkɑnvəˈseʃən〕*n.* 對話

54. (**A**) W：Would you like more soup?

M：This is adequate, thank you.

What did the man mean?

女：你要不要再多喝一點湯？

男：這樣就夠了，謝謝妳。

這位男士的意思是？

(A) 他喝夠了。

(B) 他喝太多了。

(C) 他要吃其他東西。

(D) 他不喜歡湯。

* adequate〔ˈædəkwɪt〕*adj.* 足夠的

has〔hæs〕*v.* 吃；喝

55. (**D**) W：Do you know what time we're supposed to arrive in Taichung?

M：It's a thirty-five minute flight, and we left at 4:30 p.m., so…

What time will the plane be landing?

女：你知道我們應該會在幾點抵達台中嗎？

男：要飛三十五分鐘，然後我們是下午四點半離開的，所以…

這班飛機何時降落？

(A) 下午四點四十五分。 (B) 早上五點鐘。

(C) 下午六點零五分。 (D) 下午五點零五分。

* supposed (sə'pozd) *adj.* 認爲應該的

arrive (ə'raɪv) *v.* 抵達 flight (flaɪt) *n.* 飛行

plane (plen) *n.* 飛機

land (lænd) *v.* 著陸；降落

56. (**D**) M：Michael can't answer the question.

W：It's because he doesn't even understand it.

What does the woman mean?

男：麥克無法回答這個問題。

女：那是因爲他甚至不了解這個問題。

這位女士的意思是？

(A) 麥克上課遲到。

(B) 麥克翹課。

(C) 麥克回答了這個問題。

(D) 麥克不知道這個問題的意思。

* even ('ivən) *adv.* 甚至；連

absent ('æbsn̩t) *adj.* 缺席的

57. (**B**) W：She looks better today, doctor.

M：Good, but how is her appetite?

What does the doctor want to know?

女：醫生，她今天看起來好多了。

男：很好，她的食慾如何？

醫生想知道什麼？

(A) 病患是否睡得好。

(B) 病患在進食方面是否沒問題。

(C) 病患是否有吃藥。

(D) 病患是否已經出院回家了。

* appetite〔'æpə,taɪt〕*n.* 食慾　patient〔'peʃənt〕*n.* 病患

all right 沒問題的　medicine〔'mɛdəsn̩〕*n.* 藥

hospital〔'hɑspɪtl̩〕*n.* 醫院

58. (**D**) W：Where does Frank work?

M：In an automobile factory.

W：What are his duty hours?

M：He works from 9 to 5.

When does Frank work?

女：法蘭克在哪裡工作？

男：在汽車工廠。

女：他的值班時間是？

男：他從九點工作到五點。

法蘭克何時工作？

(A) 星期一到星期五。　(B) 在汽車工廠。

(C) 在他家附近。　(D) 從九點到五點。

* automobile〔,ɔtə'mobil〕*n.* 汽車

duty〔'djutɪ〕*adj.* 值班的　hour〔aʊr〕*n.* 固定時間

59. (**B**) W：Why are you holding your arm like that?
M：It's numb.
What did he say about his arm?
女：你為什麼要像那樣抓著你的手臂？
男：它麻掉了。
他說他的手臂怎麼了？

(A) 他的手臂骨折了。 (B) 他的手臂沒有感覺。
(C) 他的手臂在流血。 (D) 他的手臂在癢。

* hold〔 hold 〕*v.* 抓住 arm〔 ɑrm 〕*n.* 手臂
numb〔 nʌm 〕*adj.* 麻木的；無感覺的
broken〔ˈbrokən 〕*adj.* 骨折的
bleed〔 blid 〕*v.* 流血 itch〔 ɪtʃ 〕*v.* 搔癢

60. (**D**) M：Can you tell me the procedure for checking out books here?
W：Sure. You just take your books and your student card to the check-out desk, and they'll do it for you.
Where does this conversation probably take place?
男：妳能告訴我從這裡把書借走的手續嗎？
女：好的。你只要拿著你要借的書和學生證到借書櫃台，他們就會幫你辦手續了。
這段對話最有可能發生在哪裡？

(A) 書店。 (B) 學生自治辦公室。
(C) 旅館。 (D) 圖書館。

* procedure〔 prəˈsidʒɚ 〕*n.* 手續 ***check out*** 辦理借書手續
sure〔 ʃʊr 〕*adv.* 好 ***student card*** 學生證
the check-out desk 辦理借書手續的櫃檯
probably〔ˈprɑbəblɪ 〕*adv.* 可能 ***take place*** 發生
council〔ˈkaʊnsḷ 〕*n.* 會議 ***student council*** 學生自治會
library〔ˈlaɪbrɛrɪ 〕*n.* 圖書館

LISTENING TEST ⑧

- *Directions for questions 1-25. You will hear questions on the test CD. Select the one item A, B, C or D which answers the question correctly, and mark your answer sheet.*

1. A. in an area of low income housing
   B. in an area of private homes
   C. in an area of private detectives
   D. in an area of mobile homes

2. A. Many bones were broken.
   B. Fingers were lost. C. Nails were lost.
   D. There was a lot of blood.

3. A. to drive nails B. to extract a tooth
   C. to boil water D. to cut wool

4. A. drive crazy B. ride dangerously
   C. drive carefully D. drive completely

5. A. It was strong. B. It was sad.
   C. I was small. D. A long time.

6. A. at 1415 B. at 1315
   C. at 1215 D. at 1450

7. A. She did a check. B. She checked a hotel.
   C. She ate at the hotel.
   D. She arrived and registered at the hotel.

8. A. The weather will become hot.
   B. The weather will become moderate.
   C. The weather will become old.
   D. The weather will become cold.

9. A. Raise the prices.
   B. Lower the prices.
   C. Keep prices the same.
   D. Keep the items in the storage room.

10. A. a lot of deals B. a lot of money
    C. a lot of time D. a lot of work

11. A. because it is beautiful
    B. because it is dangerous
    C. because it is a good color
    D. because it is durable

12. A. gasoline B. pigs
    C. stones D. sticks

13. A. come back B. go back
    C. come front D. come down

14. A. He went there to play on-line games.
    B. He went there to eat.
    C. He went there to change his outfit.
    D. He went there because he likes cute animals.

15. A. an animal B. an object
C. a person D. a virus

16. A. Yes, he would like to correct it.
B. Yes, he would like to write it.
C. Yes, he would like to type it.
D. No, he would like to correct it.

17. A. It is far from the toy store.
B. It is close to fast food restaurant.
C. It is closer than toy store.
D. It is close to the toy store.

18. A. permit her to go B. go to town with her
C. give her an allowance D. ground her

19. A. She had a host.
B. She had a visitor.
C. She had a ghost.
D. She had a very big party for the holiday.

20. A. next to his thighs
B. between his shoulders and his hands
C. between his shoulders and his stomach
D. between his shoulders and his head

21. A. between the engine and the radiator
B. in the trunk
C. behind the engine
D. under the engine

22. A. neither B. both
C. a steak D. a pizza

23. A. at four B. at two
C. at six D. at three

24. A. hanging on the mall B. hanging on the wall
C. hanging on the tree D. hanging on the fence

25. A. yesterday
B. a day before the plane took off
C. six hours before the plane took off
D. an hour before the plane took off

- *Directions for questions 26-50. You will hear statements on the test CD. Select the one answer A, B, C, or D which comes closest to the meaning of the statement and mark your answer sheet.*

26. A. Please, stop talking.
B. Please, start talking.
C. Please, keep walking.
D. Please, repeat walking.

27. A. This new magazine is different from the old magazine.
B. This new magazine replaces the old one.
C. This new magazine is the same as the old magazine.
D. This new magazine is much better than the old magazine.

28. A. He filled the cup with tea.
    B. He filled the cup with coffee.
    C. He filled the cup with juice.
    D. He filled the cup with wine.

29. A. The motor was replaced.
    B. The motor landed.
    C. The motor failed.
    D. The motor stop.

30. A. He has a good lab. B. He has a good jar.
    C. He has a good job. D. He has a good jaw.

31. A. She is furious. B. She is indifferent.
    C. She is confident. D. She is placid.

32. A. The water moves.
    B. The water becomes dirty.
    C. The water becomes ice.
    D. The water evaporates.

33. A. She will put them in the oven.
    B. She will put them in cold oil.
    C. She will poach them.
    D. She will put them in hot oil.

34. A. She won't be in today.
    B. She will be in tomorrow.
    C. She won't be absent tomorrow.
    D. She won't be in tomorrow.

35. A. He can't be used.
    B. It can't be used.
    C. She can't be used.
    D. They can't be used.

36. A. We don't know if she will come.
    B. We don't know if we will come.
    C. We don't know if they will come.
    D. We don't know if he will come.

37. A. Mary is a moon walker.
    B. Mary is a bad worker.
    C. Mary wants to change jobs.
    D. Mary is a good worker.

38. A. That woman represents freedom.
    B. That woman governs representatives.
    C. That woman represents the government.
    D. That woman has presents for your official.

39. A. Everything was present and so was Julia.
    B. Everyone bought a present but Julia.
    C. Everything was a present but Julia.
    D. Everyone was present but Julia.

40. A. He always does much better work.
    B. He usually does much better work.
    C. He seldom does much better work.
    D. He sometimes does much better work.

41. A. We watched the games.
    B. We patched the games.
    C. We listened to the games.
    D. We went to the games.

42. A. Their friends took them out to lunch.
    B. They arrived at four o'clock.
    C. They were special guests.
    D. They invited four friends to lunch.

43. A. They are ready to go to Tainan.
    B. They will not go to Tainan.
    C. They went to Tainan yesterday.
    D. They will go to Tainan next week.

44. A. She told me she would cry for me in her car.
    B. She told me she would come for me in her car.
    C. She told me she would cane me in her car.
    D. She said she would sell me her car.

45. A. They hate her. B. They saved her.
    C. They jailed her. D. They painted her.

46. A. He is hot. B. He is cold.
    C. He is angry. D. He is friendly.

47. A. We can give some money to Tina.
    B. We can borrow money from Tina.
    C. We can buy something from Tina.
    D. We will sell you something.

48. A. She collected them quickly.
    B. She collected most of them.
    C. She collected them in order.
    D. She collected them in no fixed order.

49. A. He looks down upon them.
    B. He figures out those people.
    C. He sympathizes with homeless people.
    D. He is very pitiful.

50. A. He might know how it was fired.
    B. He might know when it was burning.
    C. He might know how it exploded.
    D. He might know how it began to burn.

● *Directions for questions 51-60. You will hear dialogs on the test CD. Select the correct answer A, B, C, or D and mark your answer sheet.*

51. A. in a hospital B. in a school
    C. in a hotel D. in an apartment

52. A. She's going to change all the colors and furniture.
    B. She's going to empty the apartment.
    C. She's going to clean the apartment thoroughly.
    D. She's going to change some of the furniture.

53. A. She did not like it.
    B. She did not expect it.
    C. She did not look forward to it.
    D. She did not see him.

54. A. She wants to go to the theater.
    B. She wants to go to the theater, but she can't.
    C. She's going to the theater, but she doesn't want to.
    D. She was invited to go to the theater a long time ago.

55. A. finding their way B. crossing the road
    C. checking the map
    D. finding a convenient store

56. A. a plan B. a program
    C. a secret test D. a movie

57. A. Write the titles of the files on these covers.
    B. Arrange the files in some orderly way.
    C. Arrange the files from smallest to largest.
    D. Stack the files neatly.

58. A. His house is very big. B. His house is very old.
    C. His house is very modern.
    D. His house is very small.

59. A. The boss told him to go away.
    B. The boss told him to return.
    C. The boss told him to enter.
    D. The boss told him to wait.

60. A. He should take a bath.
    B. He needs a break.
    C. He must go west.
    D. He should lose weight.

ECL 聽力測驗⑧詳解

1. (**B**) Terry lives in a high-class suburban area. Where does he live? 泰瑞住在高級郊區。／他住在哪裡？

(A) 在低收入戶區。
(B) 在私人住宅區。
(C) 在私家偵探區。
(D) 在移動式房屋區。

* ***high-class*** 高級的
suburban〔sə'bɝbən〕*adj.* 郊外的
area〔'ɛrɪə〕*n.* 地區　low〔lo〕*adj.* 低的
income〔'ɪn,kʌm〕*n.* 收入　housing〔'haʊzɪŋ〕*n.* 住宅
private〔'praɪvɪt〕*adj.* 私人的
detective〔dɪ'tɛktɪv〕*n.* 偵探
mobile〔'mobḷ〕*adj.* 可移動的

2. (**A**) Fred's hand was crushed in the incident. What happened to his hand?
弗瑞德的手在一場意外中被壓碎了。／他的手怎麼了？

(A) 很多根骨頭碎了。
(B) 失去幾根手指。
(C) 指甲掉了。
(D) 流了很多血。

* crush〔krʌʃ〕*v.* 壓　incident〔'ɪnsədənt〕*n.* 事件
bone〔bon〕*n.* 骨頭
broken〔'brokən〕*adj.* 破碎的；骨折的
finger〔'fɪŋgɚ〕*n.* 手指　lost〔lɔst〕*adj.* 失去的
nail〔nel〕*n.* 指甲　blood〔blʌd〕*n.* 血

3. (**A**) What do you use a hammer for? 你用鐵鎚來作什麼？

(A) 釘釘子。　(B) 拔牙齒。
(C) 煮開水。　(D) 剪毛線。

＊ hammer ('hæmɚ) *n.* 鐵鎚
drive (draɪv) *v.* 把（鐵釘）打入　nail (nel) *n.* 釘子
extract (ɪk'strækt) *v.* 拔　tooth (tuθ) *n.* 牙齒
boil (bɔɪl) *v.* 煮沸　cut (kʌt) *v.* 剪斷
wool (wʊl) *n.* 毛線

4. (**C**) There are plenty of caution signs along the freeway. What is the meaning of these signs?
高速公路沿途有很多警告標誌。／這些標誌的含義是什麼？

(A) 使人抓狂。　(B) 要以危險的方式騎車。
(C) 要小心駕駛。　(D) 要完整地駕駛。

＊ plenty ('plɛntɪ) *n.* 大量　caution ('kɔʃən) *n.* 警告
sign (saɪn) *n.* 標誌　along (ə'lɔŋ) *prep.* 沿著
freeway ('fri,we) *n.* 高速公路
meaning ('minɪŋ) *n.* 含義　drive (draɪv) *v.* 迫使；駕駛
crazy ('krezɪ) *adj.* 瘋狂的　ride (raɪd) *v.* 騎；乘
dangerously ('dendʒərəslɪ) *adv.* 危險地
carefully ('kɛrfəlɪ) *adv.* 小心地
completely (kəm'plitlɪ) *adv.* 完整地

5. (**D**) How long did it take you to get accustomed to the weather? 你花了多久時間習慣這種天氣？

(A) 很強。　(B) 很傷心。
(C) 我很小。　(D) 很長一段時間。

＊ take (tek) *v.* 花費
accustomed (ə'kʌstəmd) *adj.* 習慣的
weather ('wɛðɚ) *n.* 天氣　strong (strɔŋ) *adj.* 強大的

6. (**A**) Lieutenant Flower was told to report to the general at 2:15 p.m. When does she have to be there?
弗羅爾上尉被告知要在下午兩點十五分的時候向將軍報告。／她必須在何時到達那裡？

(A) 下午兩點十五分。
(B) 下午一點十五分。
(C) 中午十二點十五分。
(D) 下午兩點五十分。

* lieutenant〔luˈtɛnənt〕*n.* 上尉
report〔rɪˈport〕*v.* 報告 general〔ˈdʒɛnərəl〕*n.* 將軍

7. (**D**) Donna checked into the hotel yesterday. What did she do? 唐娜昨天在旅館辦了住宿登記。／她做了什麼？

(A) 她做了確認。
(B) 她檢查了旅館。
(C) 她在旅館用餐。
(D) 她到達旅館並辦理登記。

* ***check into*** 到達並登記 check〔tʃɛk〕*n.* 確認 *v.* 檢查
arrive〔əˈraɪv〕*v.* 到達 register〔ˈrɛdʒɪstɚ〕*v.* 登記

8. (**D**) The weather report indicates it will freeze today. What does that mean?
氣象報告指出，今天會很冷。／那是什麼意思？

(A) 天氣會變熱。 (B) 天氣會變溫和。
(C) 天氣會變老。 (D) 天氣會變冷。

* report〔rɪˈport〕*n.* 報告 indicate〔ˈɪndəˌket〕*v.* 指出
freeze〔friz〕*v.* 變得極冷 mean〔min〕*v.* 意謂著
moderate〔ˈmɑdərɪt〕*adj.* 溫和的

9. (**B**) The shop put a number of items on sale. What did they do?

那家店有很多東西在特價。／它們做了什麼？

(A) 漲價。　　(B) 降價。
(C) 維持原價。　　(D) 將東西放在倉庫。

* ***a number of*** 許多　　item〔ˈaɪtəm〕*n.* 項目；東西
on sale 廉價出售　　raise〔rez〕*v.* 提高
price〔praɪs〕*n.* 價錢　　lower〔ˈloɚ〕*v.* 降低
keep〔kip〕*v.* 維持；把…存放
same〔sem〕*adj.* 相同的　　storage〔ˈstorɪdʒ〕*n.* 倉庫

10. (**C**) Rita spent a great deal of time in the West. How much time did she spend?

麗塔在美國西岸待了很長一段時間。／她花了多久的時間待在那裡？

(A) 很多交易。　　(B) 很多錢。
(C) 很多時間。　　(D) 很多工作。

* ***a great deal of*** 許多　　***the West*** 美國西岸
deal〔dil〕*n.* 數量；交易

11. (**D**) Why are some freeways constructed of concrete?

爲什麼有些高速公路是用混凝土建成的呢？

(A) 因爲很美觀。　　(B) 因爲很危險。
(C) 因爲顏色好看。　　(D) 因爲很耐用。

* construct〔kənˈstrʌkt〕*v.* 建造
concrete〔ˈkɑnkrit〕*n.* 混凝土
beautiful〔ˈbjutəfəl〕*adj.* 美觀的
durable〔ˈdjʊrəbl̩〕*adj.* 耐用的

12. (**A**) Which one of these is kept in a tank?
哪一樣是存放在油槽裡的？

(A) 汽油。　　(B) 豬。
(C) 石頭。　　(D) 棍子。

* tank〔tæŋk〕*n.* 油槽　　gasoline〔ˈgæsəˌlin〕*n.* 汽油
stone〔ston〕*n.* 石頭　　stick〔stɪk〕*n.* 棍子

13. (**A**) Jenny is going to return from her trip tomorrow. What is she going to do?
珍妮明天就要從旅途中歸來了。／她將要做什麼？

(A) 回來。　　(B) 回去。
(C) 往前。　　(D) 下來。

* return〔rɪˈtɝn〕*v.* 返回　　trip〔trɪp〕*n.* 旅行
come back 回來　　***go back*** 回去
front〔frʌnt〕*adv.* 向前
down〔daʊn〕*adv.*（從樓上）到樓下
come down 下來

14. (**B**) Herbie went to a restaurant. Why did he go there?
賀比去一家餐廳。／他為什麼去那裡？

(A) 他去那裡玩線上遊戲。
(B) 他去那裡吃東西。
(C) 他去那裡換衣服。
(D) 他去那裡是因為他喜歡可愛的動物。

* restaurant〔ˈrɛstərənt〕*n.* 餐廳
on-line〔ˈɑnˌlaɪn〕*adj.* 線上的　　change〔tʃendʒ〕*v.* 更換
outfit〔ˈaʊtˌfɪt〕*n.*（特定場合穿的）全套服裝
cute〔kjut〕*adj.* 可愛的

15. (**C**) Sunny saw a friend yesterday. What did Sunny see?
桑妮昨天看到一位朋友。／桑妮看到了什麼？

(A) 一隻動物。　(B) 一個物體。
(C) 一個人。　(D) 一種病毒。

* object〔'ɑbdʒɪkt〕*n.* 物體；東西　virus〔'vaɪrəs〕*n.* 病毒

16. (**A**) Would he like to revise this essay?
他會想要修改這篇文章嗎？

(A) 是的，他想修改它。　(B) 是的，他想寫它。
(C) 是的，他想把它打出來。　(D) 不，他想修改它。

* ***would like to V.*** 想要　revise〔rɪ'vaɪz〕*v.* 修改
essay〔'ɛse〕*n.* 散文　correct〔kə'rɛkt〕*v.* 修改
type〔taɪp〕*v.* 用打字機打

17. (**D**) The laundry is near the toy store. Where is it?
洗衣店在玩具店附近。／洗衣店在哪裡？

(A) 它離玩具店很遠。　(B) 它離速食餐廳很近。
(C) 它比玩具店還近。　(D) 它離玩具店很近。

* laundry〔'lɔndrɪ〕*n.* 洗衣店　toy〔tɔɪ〕*n.* 玩具
far〔fɑr〕*adv.* 遙遠地　***far from*** 遠離
close〔klos〕*adj.* 接近的　***fast food*** 速食

18. (**A**) He will allow his daughter to go to town. What will he do? 他會准許他女兒去鎮上。／他會做什麼？

(A) 准許她去。　(B) 和她一起去鎮上。
(C) 給她零用錢。　(D) 把她禁足。

* allow〔ə'laʊ〕*v.* 准許　daughter〔'dɔtɚ〕*n.* 女兒
town〔taʊn〕*n.* 市鎮　permit〔pɚ'mɪt〕*v.* 准許
allowance〔ə'laʊəns〕*n.* 零用錢
ground〔graʊnd〕*v.* 禁止外出

19. (**B**) She had a guest over for the holiday. What did she have? 她假日時有位客人來訪。／她有什麼？

(A) 她有位主人。

(B) 她有位訪客。

(C) 她有個鬼。

(D) 她在假日時舉辦了一場盛大的派對。

* guest ﹝gɛst﹞*n.* 客人　over ﹝'ovɚ﹞*adv.* 過來
holiday ﹝'hɑlə,de﹞*n.* 假日　host ﹝host﹞*n.* 主人
visitor ﹝'vɪzɪtɚ﹞*n.* 訪客　ghost ﹝gost﹞*n.* 鬼
party ﹝'pɑrtɪ﹞*n.* 派對

20. (**D**) Where is a person's neck located? 人的脖子位於何處？

(A) 在他的大腿旁邊。　(B) 在肩膀和手之間。

(C) 在肩膀和胃之間。　(D) 在肩膀和頭中間。

* neck ﹝nɛk﹞*n.* 脖子　locate ﹝lo'ket﹞*v.* 位於…
next to 緊鄰著　thigh ﹝θaɪ﹞*n.* 大腿
between ﹝bə'twin﹞*prep.* 在…之間
shoulder ﹝'ʃoldɚ﹞*n.* 肩膀　stomach ﹝'stʌmək﹞*n.* 胃
head ﹝hɛd﹞*n.* 頭

21. (**C**) The wires were hidden in the back of the engine. Where were the wires hidden?
電線藏在引擎的後面。／電線藏在哪裡？

(A) 在引擎和散熱器中間。　(B) 在行李箱裡。

(C) 在引擎後面。　(D) 在引擎下面。

* wire ﹝waɪr﹞*n.* 電線
hide ﹝haɪd﹞*v.* 隱藏【三態變化為：hide-hid-hidden】
back ﹝bæk﹞*n.* 後面　engine ﹝'ɛndʒən﹞*n.* 引擎
radiator ﹝'redɪ,etɚ﹞*n.* 散熱器　trunk ﹝trʌŋk﹞*n.* 行李箱
behind ﹝bɪ'haɪnd﹞*prep.* 在…後面

22. (**D**) James would rather have a pizza than a steak. What would he rather have?

與其吃牛排，詹姆士寧可吃比薩。／他寧可吃什麼？

(A) 兩者都不要。 (B) 兩者都要。

(C) 牛排。 (D) 比薩。

* rather〔'ræðɚ〕*adv.* 寧可

would rather A ***than*** B 與其 B 不如 A

have〔hæv〕*v.* 吃 pizza〔'pitsə〕*n.* 比薩

steak〔stek〕*n.* 牛排 neither〔'niðɚ〕*pron.* 兩者都不

both〔boθ〕*pron.* 兩者（都）

23. (**B**) The barber was shaving Mr. Johnson at two o'clock yesterday afternoon. At what time was Mr. Johnson getting a shave?

昨天下午兩點的時候，理髮師正在爲強森先生剃頭。／強森先生在什麼時候剃頭？

(A) 四點。 (B) 兩點。

(C) 六點。 (D) 三點。

* barber〔'bɑrbɚ〕*n.* 理髮師

shave〔ʃev〕*v. n.* 剃毛髮

24. (**B**) There's a clock attached to the wall. Where is the clock? 牆上有個時鐘。／時鐘在哪裡？

(A) 掛在購物中心上。 (B) 掛在牆上。

(C) 掛在樹上。 (D) 掛在籬笆上。

* clock〔klɑk〕*n.* 時鐘 attach〔ə'tætʃ〕*v.* 裝；附

wall〔wɔl〕*n.* 牆壁 hang〔hæŋ〕*v.* 懸掛

mall〔mɔl〕*n.* 購物中心 fence〔fɛns〕*n.* 籬笆

25. (**D**) Tanya arrived at the airport at seven. The plane departed at eight. When did Tanya arrive at the airport?
坦亞在七點的時候抵達機場。飛機在八點的時候起飛。／坦亞何時抵達機場？

(A) 昨天。
(B) 飛機起飛的前一天。
(C) 飛機起飛前六個小時。
(D) 飛機起飛前一個小時。

* ***arrive at*** 抵達　airport〔ˈɛrˌport〕*n.* 機場
plane〔plen〕*n.* 飛機　depart〔dɪˈpɑrt〕*v.* 啓程；離開
take off 起飛

26. (**A**) Can you knock it off, please?
能不能請你閉嘴？

(A) 請你停止說話。　(B) 請你開始說話。
(C) 請你繼續走路。　(D) 請你重走。

* ***knock off*** 住口　keep〔kip〕*v.* 繼續
repeat〔rɪˈpit〕*v.* 重做

27. (**C**) This magazine is a reprint of an out of print magazine.
這本雜誌是絕版雜誌的再版。

(A) 這本新雜誌與舊雜誌不同。
(B) 這本新雜誌取代了舊的那本。
(C) 這本新雜誌與舊的那本一樣。
(D) 這本新雜誌比舊的那本好很多。

* magazine〔ˌmægəˈzin〕*n.* 雜誌
reprint〔ˈriˌprɪnt〕*n.* 再版　***out of print*** 絕版的
different〔ˈdɪfərənt〕*adj.* 不同的　replace〔rɪˈples〕*v.* 取代
same〔sem〕*adj.* 相同的　***the same as*** 跟…一樣

28. (**A**) Simon filled the tea into the cup.
賽門將茶注入茶杯中。

(A) <u>他將茶杯裝滿茶。</u>　(B) 他將茶杯裝滿咖啡。
(C) 他將茶杯裝滿果汁。　(D) 他將茶杯裝滿葡萄酒。

* fill (fɪl) *v.* 裝入；注滿　tea (ti) *n.* 茶
cup (kʌp) *n.* 杯子　coffee (ˈkɔfɪ) *n.* 咖啡
juice (dʒus) *n.* 果汁　wine (waɪn) *n.* 葡萄酒

29. (**C**) Something wasn't right with the motor, and we had to make an emergency stop.
車子有點不對勁，我們必須緊急停車。

(A) 車子被換掉了。　(B) 車子著陸了。
(C) <u>車子故障了。</u>　(D) 車子停了。

* motor (ˈmotɚ) *n.* 汽車　***make a stop*** 停車
emergency (ɪˈmɝdʒənsɪ) *adj.* 緊急的
land (lænd) *v.* 登陸　fail (fel) *v.* 失靈

30. (**C**) Monica's husband has an excellent position in the air force. 莫妮卡的先生在空軍擔任很好的職位。

(A) 他有一間不錯的實驗室。
(B) 他有一個不錯的瓶子。
(C) <u>他有一份好工作。</u>
(D) 他有一個好看的下巴。

* husband (ˈhʌzbənd) *n.* 丈夫
excellent (ˈɛksl̩ənt) *adj.* 極好的
position (pəˈzɪʃən) *n.* 職位　***air force*** 空軍
lab (læb) *n.* 實驗室 (= *laboratory*)
jar (dʒɑr) *n.* (寬口的) 瓶　jaw (dʒɔ) *n.* 下巴

31. (**C**) She is a very self-assured young lady.
她是個很有自信的年輕小姐。

(A) 她很憤怒。 (B) 她很冷漠。
(C) 她很有自信。 (D) 她很溫和。

* self-assured (ˌsɛlfəˈʃurd) *adj.* 有自信的
furious (ˈfjurɪəs) *adj.* 狂怒的
indifferent (ɪnˈdɪfrənt) *adj.* 冷淡的
confident (ˈkɑnfədənt) *adj.* 自信的
placid (ˈplæsɪd) *adj.* 溫和的

32. (**C**) The water in this pond often freezes.
這個池塘裡的水經常結冰。

(A) 水在流動。 (B) 水變髒了。
(C) 水變成冰。 (D) 水蒸發了。

* pond (pɑnd) *n.* 池塘　freeze (friz) *v.* 結冰
move (muv) *v.* 移動　become (bɪˈkʌm) *v.* 變成
dirty (ˈdɝtɪ) *adj.* 髒的
evaporate (ɪˈvæpəˌret) *v.* 蒸發

33. (**D**) Tina will fry eggs for lunch.
蒂娜將會煎蛋當午餐。

(A) 她會將蛋放進烤箱裡。
(B) 她會將蛋放進冷油裡。
(C) 她會煮水煮蛋。
(D) 她會將蛋放進熱油裡。

* fry (fraɪ) *v.* 油煎　oven (ˈʌvən) *n.* 烤箱
oil (ɔɪl) *n.* 油　poach (potʃ) *v.* 水煮

34. (**D**) The teacher said, "I will be absent tomorrow."
老師說：「我明天不會來。」

(A) 她今天不會在。　(B) 她明天會在。
(C) 她明天不會缺席。　(D) 她明天不會在。

* absent〔ˈæbsn̩t〕*adj.* 缺席的

35. (**B**) That rule is not applicable to this situation.
那個規定不適用於這個情況。

(A) 他無法被使用。　(B) 它無法被使用。
(C) 她無法被使用。　(D) 他們無法被使用。

* rule〔rul〕*n.* 規定
applicable〔ˈæplɪkəbl̩〕*adj.* 適用的
situation〔ˌsɪtʃuˈeʃən〕*n.* 情況

36. (**A**) We don't know whether she will come.
我們不知道她是否會來。

(A) 我們不知道她是否會來。
(B) 我們不知道我們是否會來。
(C) 我們不知道他們是否會來。
(D) 我們不知道他是否會來。

* whether〔ˈhwɛðɚ〕*conj.* 是否

37. (**D**) Mary did her job with care. 瑪莉小心地工作。

(A) 瑪莉是在月球漫步的人。
(B) 瑪莉是個差勁的員工。
(C) 瑪莉想要換工作。
(D) 瑪莉是個好員工。

* ***with care*** 小心地　moon〔mun〕*n.* 月球
walker〔ˈwɔkɚ〕*n.* 散步的人

38. (**C**) That woman is a government official.
那位女士是政府官員。

(A) 那位女士是自由的象徵。
(B) 那位女士管理衆議員。
(C) 那位女士代表政府。
(D) 那位女士要送禮給你的高級職員。

* government〔'gʌvənmənt〕*adj.* 政府的
official〔ə'fɪʃəl〕*n.* 官員；高級職員
represent〔,rɛprɪ'zɛnt〕*v.* 象徵；代表
freedom〔'fridəm〕*n.* 自由　govern〔'gʌvən〕*v.* 管理
representative〔,rɛprɪ'zɛntətɪv〕*n.* 衆議員
present〔'prɛznt〕*n.* 禮物

39. (**D**) Except for Julia, everyone was present.
除了茱麗亞之外，每個人都有出席。

(A) 每樣東西都在，茱麗亞也是。
(B) 除了茱麗亞，每個人都買了禮物。
(C) 除了茱麗亞，每樣東西都是禮物。
(D) 除了茱麗亞，每個人都有出席。

* except〔ɪk'sɛpt〕*prep.* 除了…以外
except for 除了…以外
present〔'prɛznt〕*adj.* 出席的 *n.* 禮物
but〔bʌt〕*prep.* 除了…之外

40. (**D**) At times, he does much better work.
有時候，他的表現更加優秀。

(A) 他總是表現得更加優秀。　(B) 他通常表現得更加優秀。
(C) 他很少表現得更加優秀。　(D) 他有時表現得更加優秀。

* ***at times*** 有時；偶爾　seldom〔'sɛldəm〕*adv.* 很少

41. (**A**) During the soccer season, my children and I enjoyed watching the games.

在足球季期間，我的孩子和我喜歡一起收看球賽。

(A) 我們收看球賽。
(B) 我們解決球賽爭端。
(C) 我們收聽球賽。
(D) 我們去看球賽。

* soccer〔ˈsɑkɚ〕*n.* 足球　　season〔ˈsizn̩〕*n.* 季節
patch〔pætʃ〕*v.* 暫時解決（爭端）

42. (**D**) Colonel and Mrs. Franks had four guests for lunch.

上校和法蘭克太太與四位客人共進午餐。

(A) 他們的朋友帶他們出去吃午餐。
(B) 他們在四點鐘到達。
(C) 他們是特別來賓。
(D) 他們邀請四位朋友共進午餐。

* colonel〔ˈkɝnl〕*n.* 陸軍上校
take sb. out 帶某人出去
special〔ˈspɛʃəl〕*adj.* 特別的
invite〔ɪnˈvaɪt〕*v.* 邀請

43. (**A**) They are all set to go to the air show in Tainan.

他們都準備好要去台南看飛行表演。

(A) 他們準備好要去台南了。
(B) 他們不會去台南。
(C) 他們昨天去台南。
(D) 他們下禮拜會去台南。

* set〔sɛt〕*adj.* 準備好的　　***air show*** 飛行表演

44. (**B**) She said that she would pick me up in her car.
她說她會開車來接我。
(A) 她告訴我她會在車裡爲我哭泣。
(B) 她告訴我她會爲了我開車過來。
(C) 她告訴我她會在車裡鞭打我。
(D) 她說她會把她的車賣給我。
＊ ***pick up*** 開車去接（人） cane〔ken〕*v.* 鞭打

45. (**B**) The workers rescued the trapped corporal.
工人們把受困住的下士救出來。
(A) 他們恨她。 (B) 他們救了她。
(C) 他們監禁她。 (D) 他們爲她化妝。
＊ rescue〔ˈrɛskju〕*v.* 解救
trapped〔træpt〕*adj.* 陷入困境的
corporal〔ˈkɔrpərəl〕*n.* 下士 save〔sev〕*v.* 解救
jail〔dʒel〕*v.* 監禁 paint〔pent〕*v.* 化妝

46. (**B**) Tom needs another sweater. 湯姆需要再加一件毛衣。
(A) 他很熱。 (B) 他很冷。
(C) 他很生氣。 (D) 他很友善。
＊ another〔əˈnʌðɚ〕*adj.* 再一的
sweater〔ˈswɛtɚ〕*n.* 毛衣 angry〔ˈæŋgrɪ〕*adj.* 生氣的
friendly〔ˈfrɛndlɪ〕*adj.* 友善的

47. (**B**) Tina will send us some cash. 蒂娜會給我們一些現金。
(A) 我們可以給蒂娜一些錢。 (B) 我們可以跟蒂娜借錢。
(C) 我們可以跟蒂娜買東西。 (D) 我們會賣東西給你。
＊ send〔sɛnd〕*v.* 寄；送 cash〔kæʃ〕*n.* 現金
borrow〔ˈbɑro〕*v.* 借（入）

48. (**C**) Fanny collected the students' reports in sequence.
芬妮依序收學生的報告。

(A) 她迅速地收報告。

(B) 她將大部份的報告收集起來。

(C) 她將報告依序收集起來。

(D) 她沒有按照一定的順序來收報告。

* collect [kə'lɛkt] *v.* 收集　report [rɪ'port] *n.* 報告
sequence ['sikwəns] *n.* 順序　***in sequence*** 依序地
order ['ɔrdɚ] *n.* 順序　***in order*** 按順序
fixed [fɪkst] *adj.* 固定的

49. (**C**) Tom takes pity on those who are homeless.
湯姆同情那些無家可歸的人。

(A) 他輕視他們。　(B) 他了解那些人。

(C) 他同情無家可歸的人。　(D) 他很可憐。

* pity ['pɪtɪ] *n.* 憐憫；同情　***take pity on***… 對…憐憫
homeless ['homlɪs] *adj.* 無家的
look down upon 輕視　figure ['fɪgjɚ] *v.* 想
figure out 了解　sympathize ['sɪmpə,θaɪz] *v.* 同情
pitiful ['pɪtɪfəl] *adj.* 可憐的

50. (**D**) That old man seems to know how the building caught fire. 那位老先生似乎知道那棟建築物是怎麼起火的。

(A) 他可能知道它是如何燒掉的。

(B) 他可能知道它何時燃燒。

(C) 他可能知道它是如何爆炸的。

(D) 他可能知道它如何開始燃燒。

* seem [sim] *v.* 似乎　building ['bɪldɪŋ] *n.* 建築物
catch [kætʃ] *v.* 著（火）　***catch fire*** 著火
burn [bɝn] *v.* 燃燒　explode [ɪk'splod] *v.* 爆炸

51. (**A**) W：How are your patients?
M：They are doing very well, except the woman in room 414.
Where is this conversation most likely taking place?
女：你的病人怎麼樣？
男：他們的復原情況良好，除了 414 號房的那位女士以外。
這段對話最有可能在哪裡發生？
(A) 在醫院。 (B) 在學校。
(C) 在旅館。 (D) 在公寓。

* patient〔'peʃənt〕*n.* 病人 ***do well*** 進展良好
conversation〔,kɑnvə'seʃən〕*n.* 對話
likely〔'laɪklɪ〕*adv.* 可能 ***take place*** 發生
apartment〔ə'pɑrtmənt〕*n.* 公寓

52. (**A**) M：Are you going to do this apartment too?
W：Yes, and I'm going to transform it totally.
What will the woman do?
男：妳也要佈置這間公寓嗎？
女：是的，而且我要徹底改造它。
這位女士要做什麼？
(A) 她要把所有的顏色和傢俱都換掉。
(B) 她要把公寓清空。
(C) 她要徹底地打掃這間公寓。
(D) 她要換掉一些傢俱。

* gonna〔'gɔnə〕等於 going to，是口語化的用法。
do〔du〕*v.* 佈置 transform〔træns'fɔrm〕*v.* 改造
totally〔'totl̩ɪ〕*adv.* 完全地 furniture〔'fɝnɪtʃə〕*n.* 傢俱
empty〔'ɛmptɪ〕*v.* 使變空
thoroughly〔'θɝolɪ〕*adv.* 徹底地

53. (**B**) M：I hear that Don is in town.

W：Yes, his visit was a real surprise.

What did the woman say about Don's return?

男：我聽說唐在鎮上。

女：是阿，他的造訪眞令人意外。

關於唐的歸來，那位女士說了什麼？

(A) 她不喜歡。

(B) 她沒有預料到。

(C) 她並不期待。

(D) 她沒有看到他。

* visit (ˈvɪzɪt) *n.* 拜訪　surprise (səˈpraɪz) *n.* 意外的事
return (rɪˈtɝn) *n.* 返回　expect (ɪkˈspɛkt) *v.* 預期
look forward to 期待

54. (**A**) M：Are you going to the theater?

W：I'm looking forward to it.

What does the woman mean?

男：妳要去看電影嗎？

女：我很期待。

這位女士的意思是？

(A) 她想要去看電影。

(B) 她想去看電影，但是她不能去。

(C) 她將去看電影，但是她並不想去。

(D) 很久以前有人邀她去看電影。

* theater (ˈθiətɚ) *n.* 電影院
go to the theater 去看電影
a long time ago 很久以前

55. (**A**) W：These directions have me thoroughly confused.
M：Me, too. Let's stop here at this convenience store and ask for help.
What are they having difficulty doing?

女：這些方位把我完全搞糊塗了。
男：我也是。我們先在這個便利商店停下來，然後請人幫忙。
他們遇到什麼困難？

(A) 找路。　　(B) 穿越馬路。
(C) 查地圖。　　(D) 找便利商店。

* direction〔dəˈrɛkʃən〕*n.* 方位
confused〔kənˈfjuzd〕*adj.* 混亂的
convenience〔kənˈvinjəns〕*adj.* 便利的
convenience store 便利商店　　***ask for help*** 求援
difficulty〔ˈdɪfəˌkʌltɪ〕*n.* 困難　　cross〔krɔs〕*v.* 穿越
check〔tʃɛk〕*v.* 察看　　map〔mæp〕*n.* 地圖

56. (**A**) W：Did you see the new fighter jet?
M：No, but I saw the design for it.
What did the man see?

女：你看過新型的戰鬥噴射機嗎？
男：沒有，不過我看過它的設計圖。
這位男士看過什麼？

(A) 一張設計圖。　　(B) 一個節目。
(C) 一項祕密測試。　　(D) 一部電影。

* fighter〔ˈfaɪtɚ〕*adj.* 戰鬥的　　jet〔dʒɛt〕*n.* 噴射機
design〔dɪˈzaɪn〕*n.* 設計圖　　plan〔plæn〕*n.* 設計圖
program〔ˈprogræm〕*n.* 節目
secret〔ˈsikrɪt〕*adj.* 祕密的

57. (**B**) W：Do you need a hand?

M：Yes, will you please catalog these files so we can find what we want?

What did the man ask the woman to do?

女：你需要幫忙嗎？

男：是的，請妳把這些檔案分類，這樣我們才可以找到我們要的檔案。

這位男士請那位女士做什麼？

(A) 在這些封面上寫下檔案的名稱。

(B) 把檔案照某種順序排好。

(C) 把檔案從小排到大。

(D) 把檔案整齊地堆好。

* hand〔hænd〕*n.* 幫助
catalog〔ˈkætḷˌɔg〕*v.* 爲…編目；分類
file〔faɪl〕*n.* 檔案　　title〔ˈtaɪtḷ〕*n.* 名稱
cover〔ˈkʌvɚ〕*n.* 封面　　arrange〔əˈrendʒ〕*v.* 整理；排列
orderly〔ˈɔrdɚlɪ〕*adj.* 井然有序的
stack〔stæk〕*v.* 把…疊成堆　　neatly〔ˈnitlɪ〕*adv.* 整潔地

58. (**A**) W：What's Andy's house like?

M：It's huge.

What did he say about the house?

女：安迪的房子怎麼樣？

男：很大。

他說房子怎麼樣？

(A) 他的房子很大。　　(B) 他的房子很老舊。

(C) 他的房子很時髦。　　(D) 他的房子很小。

* huge〔hjudʒ〕*adj.* 巨大的
modern〔ˈmɑdɚn〕*adj.* 現代的；時髦的

59. (**B**) W：What did the boss tell you?
M：To come back.
What did the man say about the boss?
女：老闆跟你說什麼？
男：叫我回來。
這位男士說老闆怎麼樣？
(A) 老闆叫他離開。
(B) 老闆叫他回來。
(C) 老闆叫他進去。
(D) 老闆叫他等。

* boss〔 bɔs 〕*n.* 老闆　***come back*** 回來
go away 離開　enter〔'ɛntɚ〕*v.* 進入

60. (**B**) M：I've lost my appetite and I have the chills.
W：Why don't you get some rest?
What does the woman suggest?
男：我沒有食慾而且渾身發冷。
女：你爲什麼不休息一下呢？
這位女士建議什麼？
(A) 他應該洗個澡。　(B) 他需要休息。
(C) 他必須往西走。　(D) 他應該減重。

* lose〔 luz 〕*v.* 失去
appetite〔'æpə,taɪt〕*n.* 食慾　chill〔 tʃɪl 〕*n.* 寒意
have the chills 渾身發冷　rest〔 rɛst 〕*n.* 休息
suggest〔 sə'dʒɛst 〕*v.* 建議
bath〔 bæθ 〕*n.* 洗澡　***take a bath*** 洗澡
break〔 brek 〕*n.* 休息　weight〔 wet 〕*n.* 體重
lose weight 減輕體重

LISTENING TEST ⑨

- *Directions for questions 1-25. You will hear questions on the test CD. Select the one item A, B, C or D which answers the question correctly, and mark your answer sheet.*

1. A. low B. bored
   C. tired D. fine

2. A. climb B. live
   C. grow food D. ski

3. A. to contain the water
   B. to get the water out of the cup
   C. to get the water out of the well
   D. to measure the water

4. A. attentive B. attributive
   C. attractive D. attracted

5. A. under the ground floor B. on the top floor
   C. in the middle D. above the attic

6. A. attractive B. efficient
   C. dumb D. lazy

7. A. a pleasant one. B. a neutral one.
   C. a serious one. D. an annoyed one.

8. A. work harder. B. relax for a while.
   C. stand longer. D. be reminded of his work.

9. A. She was explaining it to professionals.
   B. She was enjoying herself.
   C. She was supporting it.
   D. She was explaining it with pictures.

10. A. atmospheric pollution
    B. very high temperatures
    C. aerodynamic theory
    D. atmospheric discharge

11. A. They must be dependent on their parents.
    B. They must stand on ceremony.
    C. They must stay at home.
    D. They must be independent.

12. A. count B. jump
    C. wash D. pray

13. A. import money B. employ money
    C. suggest money D. deposit money

14. A. She was hollowed out. B. She was taken in.
    C. She was out. D. She was laid waste.

15. A. He passed through. B. He came to.
    C. He kicked the bucket. D. He was struck out.

16. A. walk for exercise B. walk the dog
C. rest D. have dessert

17. A. slow B. sudden
C. sluggish D. strange

18. A. When is the movie starting?
B. The entrance price was expensive.
C. He asked for a ticket.
D. He asked the entrance price.

19. A. No, he gave me his watch instead.
B. Yes, he liked my show a lot, so he clapped his hands.
C. No, he couldn't make it to the party.
D. Yes, he gave me his consent.

20. A. at the amusement park B. at the laundry
C. at the pawn shop D. at the circus

21. A. in the morning B. in the evening
C. she never returned D. in the afternoon

22. A. at 1600 hours B. at 1500 hours
C. at 2000 hours D. at 1400 hours

23. A. behavior B. math test
C. her lessons D. her PE test

24. A. pay his bill B. plan a party
C. plan a meal D. order a meal

25. A. tired, but relieved
    B. in a stolen car
    C. with a small amount of gasoline
    D. with no lights

- *Directions for questions 26-50. You will hear statements on the test CD. Select the one answer A, B, C, or D which comes closest to the meaning of the statement and mark your answer sheet.*

26. A. Wood may be kept in a refrigerator.
    B. Food may be kept in a refrigerator.
    C. Wood may be burned in a refrigerator.
    D. Wood may be kept in a reconstruction.

27. A. She continued attending class.
    B. She stopped attaining class.
    C. She stopped attending class.
    D. She kept attending class.

28. A. The dog must come in.
    B. The dog can not go out.
    C. The dog cannot stay in.
    D. The hat can not count in.

29. A. He doesn't need his jacket.
    B. It's warm outside.
    C. Allow me to get my jacket.
    D. Bring me my coat.

30. A. Where's the salt? B. Is that the salt?
C. The fish tastes salty. D. Please hand me the salt.

31. A. He didn't see him at the meeting.
B. He didn't run to him.
C. He didn't phone him back.
D. He didn't get together with the general.

32. A. We hate tea. B. We like tea.
C. We prefer coffee. D. We prefer tea.

33. A. He is angry. B. He is sick.
C. He is short. D. He is fine.

34. A. The clouds passed by this morning.
B. This clouds arrived this morning.
C. The clouds were not visible this morning.
D. The clouds ran away this morning.

35. A. The bike was cleaned by his sister.
B. The bike was cleaned by his brother.
C. The bike was cleaned by his mother.
D. The bike was cleaned by his father.

36. A. The collision of the President is important.
B. The procedure of the President is important.
C. The safety of the President is very important.
D. The anxiety of the President is important.

37. A. He arrived on a trip. B. He arrived on a ship.
C. He arrested a ship. D. He arranged a chip.

38. A. She's somewhat tired of this weather.
B. She's very tired of this weather.
C. She is not tired of this weather.
D. She is extremely tired of this weather.

39. A. He took the job for five years.
B. He took the job he likes.
C. He took the job he doesn't like.
D. He took the job for only a limited time.

40. A. You ought to burn them.
B. You can mail them.
C. You ought to save them.
D. You can throw them away.

41. A. You look awful. B. You look great.
C. You look tired. D. You look terrible.

42. A. He went at the bottom. B. He went on top.
C. He went in front. D. He walked to the rear.

43. A. She stopped learning French.
B. She started to loathe French.
C. She started to yearn for French.
D. She started to learn French.

44. A. It makes the view more beautiful.
    B. It's nothing.
    C. It should become part of the view.
    D. It will block the view

45. A. It leaves the airport at nine.
    B. It gets checked in time.
    C. It needs maintenance.
    D. It departed on the ninth.

46. A. She anticipated losing her job.
    B. She couldn't think about the loss of her job.
    C. She couldn't deal with the loss of her job.
    D. She was informed of the loss of the job.

47. A. He has concluded to go sightseeing.
    B. He has decided to study overseas this year.
    C. He has determined not to go abroad this year.
    D. He has thought not to study abroad.

48. A. He deleted the last line.
    B. He passed out.
    C. He delayed the paper.
    D. He postponed the paper.

49. A. They disappeared gradually.
    B. They passed away together.
    C. They were killed for a thousand years.
    D. They were dead a long time ago.

50. A. We don't know who damaged it.
    B. One might know who destroyed it.
    C. No one knows who demolished it.
    D. We don't know who started the fire.

- *Directions for questions 51-60. You will hear dialogs on the test CD. Select the correct answer A, B, C, or D and mark your answer sheet.*

51. A. He is upset that she's getting divorced.
    B. He is worried about her.
    C. He is relieved that she's getting divorced.
    D. He is surprised that she made such a decision.

52. A. The son didn't continue his father's business.
    B. The son worked for his father's firm.
    C. The father didn't want his son to work.
    D. The father solved his son's problems.

53. A. at a library
    B. at a bank
    C. at a travel agency
    D. at an amusement park

54. A. The ice cream is not good.
    B. The ice cream is quite tasty.
    C. The ice cream tastes good.
    D. The woman doesn't like any ice cream.

55. A. As soon as possible.
B. Before he finishes school.
C. When he can afford law school.
D. After the man graduates.

56. A. She may have forgotten to turn it off.
B. She turned it off before setting the table.
C. She didn't pour the wine.
D. The man already turned it off.

57. A. a concert
B. a birthday party
C. a darkroom
D. an auditorium

58. A. She doesn't believe him.
B. She thinks he's serious.
C. She is scared.
D. She is unhappy.

59. A. She is doubtful that he bought the magazine.
B. She thinks he remembered to buy the magazine.
C. She wonders if Jeff told her to buy the magazine.
D. She remembers that he bought the magazine.

60. A. She would rather eat at home.
B. She thinks they should go out every night.
C. She really wants to eat out tonight.
D. She isn't sure what to do.

ECL 聽力測驗⑨詳解

1. (**D**) Fanny's feeling pretty good. How does she feel?
芬妮精神很好。／她感覺如何？

(A) 沒有精神。
(B) 很無聊。
(C) 很疲倦。
(D) 精神很好。

* pretty〔'prɪtɪ〕*adv.* 非常 ***feel good*** 感覺舒服
low〔lo〕*adj.* 沒有精神的 bored〔bord〕*adj.* 感到無聊的
tired〔taɪrd〕*adj.* 疲倦的

2. (**B**) Birds are able to survive at very high altitudes. What can they do there?
鳥可以在很高的地方生存。／牠們可以在那裡做什麼？

(A) 登山。 (B) 生活。
(C) 種植糧食。 (D) 滑雪。

* survive〔sɚ'vaɪv〕*v.* 生存 altitude〔'æltə,tjud〕*n.* 高度
climb〔klaɪm〕*v.* 攀爬 grow〔gro〕*v.* 種植
ski〔ski〕*v.* 滑雪

3. (**C**) Why do we need a water pump?
爲什麼我們需要抽水機？

(A) 裝水。 (B) 把水從杯中取出來。
(C) 把水從井裡取出來。 (D) 測量水量。

* pump〔pʌmp〕*n.* 抽水機 contain〔kən'ten〕*v.* 裝入
well〔wɛl〕*n.* 井 measure〔'mɛʒɚ〕*v.* 測量

4. (**C**) Marc is very handsome. How does he look?
馬克很英俊。／他看起來怎麼樣？

(A) 很專心。　(B) 表示屬性的。
(C) 很有吸引力。　(D) 被吸引的。

* handsome ('hænsəm) *adj.* 英俊的
attentive (ə'tɛntɪv) *adj.* 專心的
attributive (ə'trɪbjətɪv) *adj.* 表示屬性的
attractive (ə'træktɪv) *adj.* 有吸引力的
attract (ə'trækt) *v.* 吸引

5. (**A**) Where is the basement of a building?
建築物的地下室在哪裡？

(A) 在一樓底下。　(B) 在頂樓。
(C) 在中間。　(D) 在閣樓上面。

* basement ('besmənt) *n.* 地下室
building ('bɪldɪŋ) *n.* 建築物
ground (graʊnd) *adj.* 地面的　floor (flɔr) *n.* 樓
ground floor 一樓　top (tɑp) *adj.* 最上面的
middle ('mɪdḷ) *n.* 中間　above (ə'bʌv) *prep.* 在…之上
attic ('ætɪk) *n.* 閣樓

6. (**B**) Private Pauline performs her duties well. What kind of person is she?
二等兵寶琳執行任務非常出色。／她是個什麼樣的人？

(A) 有吸引力的。　(B) 有效率的。
(C) 愚笨的。　(D) 懶惰的。

* private ('praɪvɪt) *n.* 二等兵　perform (pɚ'fɔrm) *v.* 執行
duty ('djutɪ) *n.* 任務；職責
efficient (ɪ'fɪʃənt) *adj.* 有效率的
dumb (dʌm) *adj.* 愚笨的　lazy ('lezɪ) *adj.* 懶惰的

7. (**C**) He managed to keep an earnest expression on his face even though he wanted to smile. What expression did he have?

他設法保持嚴肅的表情，即使他很想笑。／他有什麼表情？

(A) 愉快的表情。

(B) 沒什麼表情。

(C) 嚴肅的表情。

(D) 煩惱的表情。

* manage〔ˈmænɪdʒ〕*v.* 設法　　keep〔kip〕*v.* 維持
earnest〔ˈɝnɪst〕*adj.* 嚴肅的
expression〔ɪkˈsprɛʃən〕*n.* 表情
even though 即使
pleasant〔ˈplɛzn̩t〕*adj.* 愉快的
neutral〔ˈnjutrəl〕*adj.* 不顯著的；不明確的
serious〔ˈsɪrɪəs〕*adj.* 嚴肅的
annoyed〔əˈnɔɪd〕*adj.* 煩惱的

8. (**B**) Steve, you're working too hard. Sit down and take it easy for a while. What should Steve do?

史蒂夫，你太拼命了。坐下來放鬆一下。／史蒂夫應該做什麼？

(A) 更努力工作。

(B) 放鬆一下。

(C) 站久一點。

(D) 使他想起他的工作。

* hard〔hɑrd〕*adv.* 努力地　　***work hard*** 努力工作
take it easy 放輕鬆　　***for a while*** 暫時
relax〔rɪˈlæks〕*v.* 放鬆
remind〔rɪˈmaɪnd〕*v.* 使想起

9. (**D**) The professor was illustrating the new technique. What was she doing?

教授正在用圖說明這項新技術。／她正在做什麼？

(A) 她正向專家說明它。
(B) 她正樂在其中。
(C) 她正在支持它。
(D) 她正在用圖講解它。

* professor ﹝prəˈfɛsɚ﹞ *n.* 教授
illustrate ﹝ɪˈlʌstret﹞ *v.* （用圖、實例等）說明
technique ﹝tɛkˈnik﹞ *n.* 技術
explain ﹝ɪkˈsplen﹞ *v.* 講解；說明
professional ﹝prəˈfɛʃənḷ﹞ *n.* 專家
enjoy oneself 過得快樂；好好享受
support ﹝səˈport﹞ *v.* 支持

10. (**B**) One of the many devices used by a weatherman is a pyrometer. What does a pyrometer measure?

氣象預報員使用的衆多儀器之一是高溫計。／高溫計是用來測量什麼？

(A) 大氣污染。　(B) 很高的溫度。
(C) 氣體力學理論。　(D) 大氣放電。

* device ﹝dɪˈvaɪs﹞ *n.* 儀器
weatherman ﹝ˈwɛðɚˌmæn﹞ *n.* 氣象預報員
pyrometer ﹝paɪˈrɑmɪtɚ﹞ *n.* 高溫計
atmospheric ﹝ˌætməsˈfɛrɪk﹞ *adj.* 大氣的
pollution ﹝pəˈluʃən﹞ *n.* 污染
temperature ﹝ˈtɛmpərətʃɚ﹞ *n.* 溫度
aerodynamic ﹝ˌɛrodaɪˈnæmɪk﹞ *adj.* 氣體力學的
theory ﹝ˈθiərɪ﹞ *n.* 理論
discharge ﹝dɪsˈtʃɑrdʒ﹞ *n.* 放電

11. (**D**) Adults must learn to stand on their own two feet. What does the statement mean?
成年人必須學著自食其力。／這段敘述是什麼意思？

(A) 他們必須依賴父母。 (B) 他們必須拘於禮節。
(C) 他們必須待在家裡。 (D) 他們必須獨立。

* adult〔əˈdʌlt〕*n.* 成年人 feet〔fit〕*n. pl.* 腳（foot 的複數）
stand on** one's **own feet 自食其力
statement〔ˈstetmənt〕*n.* 敘述 mean〔min〕*v.* 意謂著
dependent〔dɪˈpɛndənt〕*adj.* 依賴的
parents〔ˈpɛrənts〕*n. pl.* 父母
ceremony〔ˈsɛrəˌmonɪ〕*n.* 客套
stand on ceremony 拘於禮節
independent〔ˌɪndɪˈpɛndənt〕*adj.* 獨立的

12. (**C**) Jenna wants to clean herself up. What does she want to do? 珍娜想梳洗一下。／她想做什麼？

(A) 計算。 (B) 跳。
(C) 洗臉洗手。 (D) 祈禱。

* ***clean up*** 梳洗 count〔kaʊnt〕*v.* 計算
pray〔pre〕*v.* 祈禱

13. (**D**) What can people do at the bank in a savings account?
人們可以在銀行的存款戶頭裡做什麼？

(A) 輸入錢。 (B) 雇用錢。
(C) 建議錢。 (D) 存錢。

* bank〔bæŋk〕*n.* 銀行 savings〔ˈsevɪŋz〕*adj.* 存款的
account〔əˈkaʊnt〕*n.* 帳戶
savings account 儲蓄存款戶頭
import〔ɪmˈpɔrt〕*v.* 輸入 employ〔ɪmˈplɔɪ〕*v.* 雇用
suggest〔səˈdʒɛst〕*v.* 建議 deposit〔dɪˈpɑzɪt〕*v.* 存（錢）

14. (**B**) The policewoman was deceived by the boy's innocent manner. What happened to the policewoman?
女警被男孩無辜的樣子騙了。／這位女警怎麼了？

(A) 她被挖空了
(B) 她被騙了。
(C) 她出去了。
(D) 她被毀損。

* policewoman〔pə'lis,wʊmən〕*n.* 女警
deceive〔dɪ'siv〕*v.* 欺騙
innocent〔'ɪnəsn̩t〕*adj.* 無辜的
manner〔'mænɚ〕*n.* 舉止；樣子
happen〔'hæpən〕*v.* 發生
hollow〔'hɑlo〕*v.* 挖空　***hollow out*** 挖空
be taken in 受騙　out〔aʊt〕*adv.* 不在；出去
lay〔le〕*v.* 使處於（某種狀態）
lay waste 毀損

15. (**C**) Old Mr. Jones died just two days before his birthday. What happened to him?
老瓊斯先生在他生日前兩天過世了。／他怎麼了？

(A) 他經過了。　(B) 他醒過來了。
(C) 他死了。　(D) 他被三振了。

* die〔daɪ〕*v.* 死亡　pass〔pæs〕*v.* 經過
through〔θru〕*prep.* 穿過
pass through 經過　***come to*** 甦醒過來
kick〔kɪk〕*v.* 踢　bucket〔'bʌkɪt〕*n.* 水桶
kick the bucket 翹辮子；死
strike〔straɪk〕*v.* 打擊　***strike out*** 三振

16. (**A**) Joe and Andrew like to take a walk after lunch. What do they like to do after lunch? 喬和安得烈喜歡在午餐後散步。／他們喜歡在午餐後做什麼？

(A) 走路運動。　(B) 蹓狗。
(C) 休息。　(D) 吃點心。

* ***take a walk*** 散步　exercise〔'ɛksɚ,saɪz〕*n.* 運動
rest〔rɛst〕*v.* 休息　have〔hæv〕*v.* 吃
dessert〔dɪ'zɝt〕*n.* 點心

17. (**B**) There was an abrupt variation in the temperature. What kind of variation was there?
氣溫突然變了。／發生了什麼樣的變化？

(A) 緩慢的。　(B) 突然的。
(C) 遲緩的。　(D) 奇怪的。

* abrupt〔ə'brʌpt〕*adj.* 突然的
variation〔,vɛrɪ'eʃən〕*n.* 變化
temperature〔'tɛmpərətʃɚ〕*n.* 溫度
slow〔slo〕*adj.* 緩慢的　sudden〔'sʌdn̩〕*adj.* 突然的
sluggish〔'slʌgɪʃ〕*adj.* 遲緩的
strange〔strendʒ〕*adj.* 奇怪的

18. (**D**) Mr. Cool asked, "How much is the admission price to the movies?" What did he ask?
庫爾先生問：「電影入場券多少錢？」／他問什麼？

(A) 電影何時開始？　(B) 入場費很貴。
(C) 他要一張門票。　(D) 他詢問入場費。

* admission〔əd'mɪʃən〕*n.* 費；入場券
price〔praɪs〕*n.* 價格　entrance〔'ɛntrəns〕*adj.* 入場的
expensive〔ɪk'spɛnsɪv〕*adj.* 昂貴的　***ask for*** 要求
ticket〔'tɪkɪt〕*n.* 門票

19. (**D**) Did he give you his permission?
他有允許你嗎？

(A) 沒有，他給我他的錶作爲替代。
(B) 有的，他非常喜歡我的表演，所以他鼓掌了。
(C) 沒有，他沒有趕上派對。
(D) 有的，他有同意。

* permission〔pə'mɪʃən〕*n.* 允許
instead〔ɪn'stɛd〕*adv.* 作爲替代
show〔ʃo〕*n.* 表演　clap〔klæp〕*v.* 拍擊
make it 趕上　consent〔kən'sɛnt〕*n.* 同意

20. (**B**) Where do you wash your dirty socks?
你在哪裡洗你的髒襪子？

(A) 在遊樂園。　(B) 在洗衣店。
(C) 在當舖。　(D) 在馬戲團。

* dirty〔'dɝtɪ〕*adj.* 髒的　socks〔sɑks〕*n. pl.* 襪子
amusement〔ə'mjuzmənt〕*adj.* 娛樂的
amusement park 遊樂園
laundry〔'lɔndrɪ〕*n.* 洗衣店
pawn〔pɔn〕*adj.* 典當的　***pawn shop*** 當舖
circus〔'sɝkəs〕*n.* 馬戲團

21. (**D**) Helen returned home at 16:35. When did she return?
海倫下午四點三十五分回家。／她何時回來？

(A) 早上。　(B) 晚上。
(C) 她從來沒有回來過。　(D) 下午。

* return〔rɪ'tɝn〕*v.* 返回

22. (**B**) The train arrived at exactly three o'clock. When did the train arrive?
火車在三點整到達。／火車何時到達？

(A) 在下午四點。　　(B) 在下午三點。
(C) 在晚上八點。　　(D) 在下午兩點。

* arrive (əˈraɪv) *v.* 到達
exactly (ɪgˈzæktlɪ) *adv.* 整
hours (aʊrz) *n.* (以二十四個小時所表示的)時刻

23. (**A**) Sherry got a good mark in conduct. What did she get a good mark in?
雪莉的品行成績很好。／她在哪一方面得到好成績？

(A) 品行。　　(B) 數學測驗。
(C) 她的課業。　　(D) 她的體育測驗。

* mark (mɑrk) *n.* 成績　conduct (ˈkɑndʌkt) *n.* 品行
behavior (bɪˈhevjɚ) *n.* 品行
math (mæθ) *adj.* 數學的　lesson (ˈlɛsn̩) *n.* 課業
PE 體育 (= *physical education*)

24. (**A**) The customer waited for the cashier. What does the customer want to do?
顧客在等收銀員。／這位顧客想要做什麼？

(A) 付他的帳。　　(B) 籌畫一個派對。
(C) 計畫一頓飯。　　(D) 點餐。

* customer (ˈkʌstəmɚ) *n.* 顧客　wait (wet) *v.* 等待
cashier (kæˈʃɪr) *n.* 收銀員　bill (bɪl) *n.* 帳單
meal (mil) *n.* 餐；飯　order (ˈɔrdɚ) *v.* 點菜

25. (**C**) The driver reached the city with very little gasoline in his tank. How did he arrive there?
司機用油箱裡的一點汽油，開到城裡。／他如何到達那裡？

(A) 疲累但放心的。 (B) 在一輛贓車裡。
(C) 用很少的汽油。 (D) 在沒有燈光的情況下。

* driver〔ˈdraɪvɚ〕*n.* 司機　reach〔ritʃ〕*v.* 到達
little〔ˈlɪtl̩〕*adj.* 少許的　gasoline〔ˈgæsl̩ˌin〕*n.* 汽油
tank〔tæŋk〕*n.* 油箱　relieved〔rɪˈlivd〕*adj.* 放心的
stolen〔ˈstolən〕*adj.* 偷來的
amount〔əˈmaʊnt〕*n.* 數量

26. (**B**) You can keep food in the fridge.
你可以把食物存放在冰箱裡。

(A) 木柴可以放在冰箱裡。
(B) 食物可以放在冰箱裡。
(C) 木柴可以在冰箱裡燃燒。
(D) 木柴可以放在重建物中。

keep〔kip〕*v.* 保存；存放　fridge〔frɪdʒ〕*n.* 冰箱
wood〔wʊd〕*n.* 木柴
refrigerator〔rɪˈfrɪdʒəˌretɚ〕*n.* 冰箱
burn〔bɝn〕*v.* 燃燒
reconstruction〔ˌrikənˈstrʌkʃən〕*n.* 重建物

27. (**C**) Jane dropped out of gym class. 珍退出體育課。

(A) 她繼續上課。 (B) 她停止得到課程。
(C) 她停止上課。 (D) 她繼續去上課。

* drop〔drɑp〕*v.* 退出；中斷　***drop out*** 退出；退學
gym〔dʒɪm〕*n.* 體育　continue〔kənˈtɪnjʊ〕*v.* 繼續
attend〔əˈtɛnd〕*v.* 上（學）　attain〔əˈten〕*v.* 獲得
keep〔kip〕*v.* 繼續

28. (**B**) The dog must stay in. 狗必須待在家裡。

(A) 狗必須進來。 (B) 狗不可以出門。
(C) 狗不可以待在家裡。 (D) 帽子不可以算進去。

* stay〔ste〕*v.* 留下 ***stay in*** 待在家裡
come in 進來 ***go out*** 出門
hat〔hæt〕*n.* 帽子 ***count in*** 算入

29. (**C**) Let me get my jacket, Selena.
席琳娜，讓我拿一下我的夾克。

(A) 他不需要他的夾克。 (B) 外面很暖和。
(C) 讓我拿一下我的夾克。 (D) 把我的外套帶來給我。

* jacket〔ˈdʒækɪt〕*n.* 夾克 warm〔wɔrm〕*adj.* 溫暖的
outside〔ˈautˈsaɪd〕*adv.* 在外面 allow〔əˈlaʊ〕*v.* 允許；讓
bring〔brɪŋ〕*v.* 帶來 coat〔kot〕*n.* 外套

30. (**D**) Please pass the salt. 請把鹽遞過來。

(A) 鹽在哪裡？ (B) 那是鹽嗎？
(C) 魚吃起來鹹鹹的。 (D) 請把鹽遞給我。

* pass〔pæs〕*v.* 傳遞 salt〔sɔlt〕*n.* 鹽
taste〔test〕*v.* 嚐起來 salty〔ˈsɔltɪ〕*adj.* 鹹的
hand〔hænd〕*v.* 傳遞

31. (**D**) Mr. Ed didn't meet the general.
艾德先生沒有與將軍會面。

(A) 他沒有在會議上見到他。
(B) 他沒有跑向他。 (C) 他沒有回他電話。
(D) 他沒有和將軍見面。

* meet〔mit〕*v.* 會面 general〔ˈdʒɛnərəl〕*n.* 將軍
meeting〔ˈmitɪŋ〕*n.* 會議 phone〔fon〕*v.* 打電話
back〔bæk〕*adv.* 回覆 ***get together*** 會面

32. (**C**) We would rather have coffee.
我們寧可喝咖啡。

(A) 我們討厭茶。
(B) 我們喜歡茶。
(C) <u>我們比較喜歡咖啡。</u>
(D) 我們比較喜歡茶。

* ***would rather*** 寧可　coffee〔ˈkɔfɪ〕*n.* 咖啡
prefer〔prɪˈfɝ〕*v.* 比較喜歡

33. (**B**) Ken has to take five different medications.
肯必須吃五種不同的藥。

(A) 他生氣了。　(B) <u>他生病了。</u>
(C) 他很矮。　(D) 他很好。

* take〔tek〕*v.* 服用　different〔ˈdɪfərənt〕*adj.* 不同的
medication〔ˌmɛdɪˈkeʃən〕*n.* 藥物
angry〔ˈæŋgrɪ〕*adj.* 生氣的　sick〔sɪk〕*adj.* 生病的

34. (**B**) The sky was clear yesterday evening, but it got cloudy this morning.
昨晚天空晴朗無雲，但今天早上雲很多。

(A) 今天早上雲飄過去了。
(B) <u>今天早上雲來了。</u>
(C) 今天早上看不見雲。
(D) 今天早上雲跑走了。

* clear〔klɪr〕*adj.* 晴朗無雲的　get〔gɛt〕*v.* 變得
cloudy〔ˈklaʊdɪ〕*adj.* 多雲的　cloud〔klaʊd〕*n.* 雲
pass by 過去　visible〔ˈvɪzəbl̩〕*adj.* 看得見的
run away 跑開

35. (**B**) The bike was washed by his brother.

他哥哥洗了腳踏車。

(A) 他姐姐把腳踏車洗乾淨。

(B) 他哥哥把腳踏車洗乾淨。

(C) 他媽媽把腳踏車洗乾淨。

(D) 他爸爸把腳踏車洗乾淨。

* bike (baɪk) *n.* 腳踏車　　clean (klin) *v.* 把…洗乾淨

36. (**C**) The security of a President is very important.

總統的安全非常重要。

(A) 總統的碰撞很重要。

(B) 總統的程序很重要。

(C) 總統的安全非常重要。

(D) 總統的焦慮很重要。

* security (sɪ'kjurətɪ) *n.* 安全
President ('prɛzədənt) *n.* 總統
important (ɪm'pɔrtn̩t) *adj.* 重要的
collision (kə'lɪʒən) *n.* 碰撞
procedure (prə'sidʒɚ) *n.* 程序　　safety ('seftɪ) *n.* 安全
anxiety (æŋ'zaɪətɪ) *n.* 焦慮

37. (**B**) Jonas came by boat.

瓊納斯坐船過來。

(A) 他在旅程中到達。　　(B) 他搭船到達。

(C) 他逮捕了一艘船。　　(D) 他把一個碎片排好。

* boat (bot) *n.* 船　　trip (trɪp) *n.* 旅程
ship (ʃɪp) *n.* 船　　arrest (ə'rɛst) *v.* 拘捕
arrange (ə'rendʒ) *v.* 排列　　chip (tʃɪp) *n.* 碎片

38. (**A**) Ann is a little tired of the weather.
安對這種天氣感到有點厭煩。

(A) 她對這種天氣感到有點厭煩。
(B) 她對這種天氣感到非常厭煩。
(C) 她對這種天氣不會感到厭煩。
(D) 她對這種天氣感到極度厭煩。

* ***a little*** 稍微；有一點　***be tired of*** 厭煩的
weather ['wɛðɚ] *n.* 天氣
somewhat ['sʌm,hwɑt] *adv.* 有點
extremely [ɪk'strimlɪ] *adv.* 極度地

39. (**D**) Jack has temporary work. 傑克暫時有工作。

(A) 他接下這份工作五年了。
(B) 他接下他喜歡的工作。
(C) 他接下他不喜歡的工作。
(D) 他這份工作只做了一小段時間。

* **temporary** ['tɛmpə,rɛrɪ] *adj.* 暫時的
take [tek] *v.* 承擔；接下　limited ['lɪmɪtɪd] *adj.* 不多的

40. (**C**) You should keep those envelopes.
你應該把那些信封留下來。

(A) 你應該把它們燒掉。
(B) 你可以把它們寄出去。
(C) 你應該把它們保存起來。
(D) 你可以把它們丟掉。

* **keep** [kip] *v.* 保留　envelope ['ɛnvə,lop] *n.* 信封
ought to V. 應該　mail [mel] *v.* 寄
save [sev] *v.* 保存　throw [θro] *v.* 丟
throw away 丟掉

41. (**B**) Boy, you sure look sharp today! That must be a new suit. 哇，你今天看起來眞時髦！那一定是新套裝。

(A) 你看起來很糟。 (B) 你看起來很棒。

(C) 你看起來很累。 (D) 你看起來很可怕。

* boy (bɔɪ) *interj.* 哇！【表示驚訝或愉快等的感嘆辭】
sure (ʃur) *adv.* 確實地
sharp (ʃɑrp) *adj.* 時髦的；漂亮的
suit (sut) *n.* 套裝 awful (ˈɔful) *adj.* 很糟的
terrible (ˈtɛrəbl̩) *adj.* 可怕的

42. (**D**) The mailman walked to the back of the campus. 郵差走到校園後面。

(A) 他進攻底部。 (B) 他去上面。

(C) 他去前面。 (D) 他走到後面。

* mailman (ˈmel͵mæn) *n.* 郵差 back (bæk) *n.* 後面
campus (ˈkæmpəs) *n.* 校園 ***go at*** 進攻；撲向
bottom (ˈbɑtəm) *n.* 底部
front (frʌnt) *n.* 前面 rear (rɪr) *n.* 後面

43. (**D**) Ann took a French class. 安修了一門法文課。

(A) 她停止學法文。 (B) 她開始厭惡法文。

(C) 她開始渴望法文。 (D) 她開始學法文。

* take (tek) *v.* 修課
French (frɛntʃ) *adj.* 法語的 *n.* 法語
loathe (loð) *v.* 厭惡 yearn (jɝn) *v.* 渴望
yearn for 渴望

44. (**D**) The tent will obstruct the view. 帳篷會擋到視線。

(A) 它使風景更美。

(B) 它沒什麼影響。

(C) 它應該會變成風景的一部份。

(D) 它會擋住視線。

* tent〔tɛnt〕*n.* 帳篷　　obstruct〔əb'strʌkt〕*v.* 阻擋
view〔vju〕*n.* 視線；風景
beautiful〔'bjutəfəl〕*adj.* 美麗的
nothing〔'nʌθɪŋ〕*n.* 微不足道的事（或人）
block〔blɑk〕*v.* 阻擋

45. (**A**) The airplane departs at nine o'clock. 飛機九點起飛。

(A) 它九點飛離機場。　(B) 它準時被檢查。

(C) 它需要保養。　(D) 它在九號那天起飛了。

* airplane〔'ɛr,plen〕*n.* 飛機
depart〔dɪ'pɑrt〕*v.* 啓程；離開　　leave〔liv〕*v.* 離開
airport〔'ɛr,port〕*n.* 機場　　get〔gɛt〕*v.* 被
check〔tʃɛk〕*v.* 檢查
maintenance〔'mentənəns〕*n.* 維修保養
ninth〔naɪnθ〕*n.*（月的）九日

46. (**C**) Mary found it difficult to cope with the loss of her job.
瑪莉發現要處理失業這件事很困難。

(A) 她有預料到會失業。

(B) 她無法想像失去她的工作。

(C) 她無法應付失業這件事。

(D) 她被通知她失業了。

* difficult〔'dɪfə,kʌlt〕*adj.* 困難的
cope〔kop〕*v.* 妥善地處理
cope with 處理；應付　　loss〔lɔs〕*n.* 喪失
anticipate〔æn'tɪsə,pet〕*v.* 預料　　lose〔luz〕*v.* 失去
deal〔dil〕*v.* 處理；應付　　***deal with*** 處理；應付
inform〔ɪn'fɔrm〕*v.* 通知

47. (**C**) William has made up his mind not to study abroad this year. 威廉已經下定決心今年不出國留學了。

(A) 他已經決定要去觀光。

(B) 他已經決定今年要出國唸書。

(C) 他已經決定今年不出國。

(D) 他已經想過不要出國留學。

* mind〔maɪnd〕*n.* 主意　***make up one's mind*** 下定決心
abroad〔ə'brɔd〕*adv.* 在國外　***study abroad*** 留學
conclude〔kən'klud〕*v.* 決定；決心（做）
sightseeing〔'saɪt,siɪŋ〕*n.* 觀光
overseas〔'ovɚ'siz〕*adv.* 在海外；在國外
determine〔dɪ'tɝmɪn〕*v.* 決定　***go abroad*** 出國

48. (**A**) The professor crossed out the last line of the paper. 教授把報告的最後一行刪掉。

(A) 他刪去最後一行。　(B) 他昏倒了。

(C) 他遲交報告。　(D) 他延後交報告。

* cross〔krɔs〕*v.* 畫十字　***cross out*** 刪掉；劃掉
line〔laɪn〕*n.* 行　paper〔'pepɚ〕*n.* 報告
delete〔dɪ'lit〕*v.* 刪除　***pass out*** 昏倒
delay〔dɪ'le〕*v.* 延遲　postpone〔post'pon〕*v.* 延後

49. (**D**) The dinosaurs died out hundreds of thousands of years ago. 恐龍在幾千萬年前就滅絕了。

(A) 牠們逐漸消失。　(B) 牠們一起過世。

(C) 牠們被殺死一千年了。　(D) 牠們很久以前就死了。

* dinosaur〔'daɪnə,sɔr〕*n.* 恐龍
die out 滅絕　hundred〔'hʌndrəd〕*n.* 百
thousand〔'θaʊzn̩d〕*n.* 千

hundreds of thousands of 成千上萬的；好幾千萬的
ago〔ə'go〕*adv.* 以前
disappear〔,dɪsə'pɪr〕*v.* 消失
gradually〔'grædʒuəlɪ〕*adv.* 逐漸地
pass away 去世　　kill〔kɪl〕*v.* 殺死
dead〔dɛd〕*adj.* 死的　　***a long time ago*** 很久以前

50.（**D**）No one knows who set fire to the restaurant.
沒有人知道是誰在那間餐廳縱火的。

(A) 我們不知道誰弄壞它。
(B) 可能有人知道誰弄壞它。
(C) 沒有人知道誰破壞它。
(D) 我們不知道是誰放火的。

＊ ***set fire*** 縱火　　restaurant〔'rɛstərənt〕*n.* 餐廳
damage〔'dæmɪdʒ〕*v.* 損壞
destroy〔dɪ'strɔɪ〕*v.* 毀壞
demolish〔dɪ'mɑlɪʃ〕*v.* 破壞

51.（**C**）W：My sister told me she's thinking about getting a divorce.
M：It's about time!
How does the man feel about the divorce of his friend's sister?
女：我姊姊告訴我她在考慮要離婚。
男：是時候了！
對於他朋友的姊姊要離婚，這位男士覺得如何？
(A) 對於她要離婚，他很心煩。
(B) 他很擔心她。

(C) 對於她要離婚，他鬆了一口氣。

(D) 他很驚訝她做了這樣的決定。

* ***think about*** 考慮　divorce〔dəˈvɔrs〕*n.* 離婚
get a divorce 離婚　about〔əˈbaʊt〕*adv.* 差不多
time〔taɪm〕*n.* 時機　upset〔ʌpˈsɛt〕*adj.* 心煩的
get〔gɛt〕*v.* 使成爲某種狀態
divorced〔dəˈvɔrst〕*adj.* 離婚的　worry〔ˈwɝɪ〕*v.* 擔憂
surprised〔səˈpraɪzd〕*adj.* 驚訝的
decision〔dɪˈsɪʒən〕*n.* 決定　***make a decision*** 下決定

52. (**A**) W：I understand he wanted his son to inherit the family business.

M：Yes, it's true he did, but it just didn't work out. Shame!

What does the man state?

女：我能理解他想要兒子繼承家族事業的心情。
男：是的，他眞的很想，但事情就是無法如願。眞可惜！
這位男士說什麼？

(A) 兒子沒有繼續經營父親的事業。

(B) 兒子爲父親的公司效力。

(C) 父親不要他兒子去工作。

(D) 父親解決了兒子的問題。

* understand〔ˌʌndɚˈstænd〕*v.* 了解（他人）的心情
inherit〔ɪnˈhɛrɪt〕*v.* 繼承　family〔ˈfæməlɪ〕*adj.* 家族的
business〔ˈbɪznɪs〕*n.* 事業　***work out*** 進行順利
shame〔ʃem〕*n.* 遺憾的事
Shame! 眞可惜！　state〔stet〕*v.* 陳述
continue〔kənˈtɪnjʊ〕*v.* 繼續做；延續　***work for*** 效力
firm〔fɝm〕*n.* 公司　solve〔sɑlv〕*v.* 解決

53. (C) M：Well. We can book it for you. You'll have to pay a deposit of one night.

W：That's fair enough. Can you also get me a hotel in Atlanta?

Where does the conversation most probably take place?

男：嗯，我們可以幫妳預訂。妳必須付一個晚上的訂金。

女：那很合理。你可不可以也幫我在亞特蘭大訂一間旅館？

這段對話最有可能在哪裡發生？

(A) 在圖書館。 (B) 在銀行。

(C) <u>在旅行社。</u> (D) 在遊樂園。

＊ well〔 wɛl 〕*interj.* 嗯【用以繼續原來的話題或引入新話題】

book〔 bʊk 〕*v.* 預訂 pay〔 pe 〕*v.* 付款

deposit〔 dɪ'pɑzɪt 〕*n.* 訂金 fair〔 fɛr 〕*adj.* 公道的；合理的

enough〔 ə'nʌf 〕*adv.* 充分地 get〔 gɛt 〕*v.* 爲（某人）弄到

Atlanta〔 ət'læntə 〕*n.* 亞特蘭大【美國喬治亞州首府】

conversation〔,kɑnvə'seʃən 〕*n.* 對話

probably〔'prɑbəblɪ 〕*adv.* 可能 ***take place*** 發生

library〔'laɪ,brɛrɪ 〕*n.* 圖書館 travel〔'trævl̩ 〕*adj.* 旅行的

agency〔'edʒənsɪ 〕*n.* 代辦處 ***travel agency*** 旅行社

54. (A) M：I don't like this ice cream.

W：It's kind of tasteless, isn't it?

What does the woman think of the ice cream?

男：我不喜歡這種冰淇淋。

女：吃起來沒什麼味道，不是嗎？

這位女士認爲冰淇淋怎麼樣？

(A) <u>冰淇淋不好吃。</u> (B) 冰淇淋非常美味。

(C) 冰淇淋很好吃。 (D) 這位女士不喜歡任何冰淇淋。

＊ ice cream〔'aɪs'krim 〕*n.* 冰淇淋 ***kind of*** 有點兒

tasteless〔'testlɪs 〕*adj.* 沒味道的

quite〔 kwaɪt 〕*adv.* 非常 tasty〔'testɪ 〕*adj.* 美味的

55. (**D**) M：Is it true what I hear? They're going to get married?
W：Yes, but not until he finishes law school. They can't afford it now.
When will the couple get married?
男：我聽到的是眞的嗎？他們要結婚了嗎？
女：是的，但要等到他從法學院畢業。他們現在還負擔不起。
這對情侶何時會結婚？
(A) 儘快。 (B) 他畢業之前。
(C) 當他負擔得起唸法學院的時候。
(D) 男方畢業之後。

* married ('mærɪd) *adj.* 結婚的 ***get married*** 結婚
until (ən'tɪl) *prep.* 直到…爲止 finish ('fɪnɪʃ) *v.* 完成
law (lɔ) *adj.* 法律的 school (skul) *n.* 學院
law school 法學院 afford (ə'fɔrd) *v.* 負擔得起
couple ('kʌpl̩) *n.* 情侶 ***as soon as possible*** 儘快
finish school 畢業 graduate ('grædʒʊ,et) *v.* 畢業

56. (**A**) W：The table is set. All we have to do is pour the wine.
M：Did you remember to turn off the oven?
Why is the man concerned about the oven?
女：桌子準備好了。我們所需要做的就是倒酒。
男：妳有記得關烤箱嗎？
這位男士爲什麼擔心烤箱？
(A) 她可能忘記關烤箱。
(B) 她在擺好餐具之前就把烤箱關了。
(C) 她沒有倒酒。 (D) 這位男士已經把烤箱關了。

* set (sɛt) *adj.* 準備好的 *v.* 擺好（餐具）
pour (pɔr) *v.* 倒 wine (waɪn) *n.* 葡萄酒
remember (rɪ'mɛmbɚ) *v.* 記得 ***turn off*** 關掉
oven ('ʌvən) *n.* 烤箱 concerned (kən'sɝnd) *adj.* 擔心的

57. (**B**) W：Hurry up. He's about to blow out the candles.
M：Is the flashbulb ready?
What is the setting of this conversation?
女：快點。他要吹蠟燭了。
男：閃光燈準備好了嗎？
這段對話的背景是什麼？

(A) 音樂會。　　(B) 生日派對。
(C) 暗房。　　(D) 禮堂。

* ***hurry up*** 趕快　***be about to*** 即將
blow〔blo〕*v.* 吹　***blow out*** 吹熄
candle〔ˈkændḷ〕*n.* 蠟燭　flashbulb〔ˈflæʃˌbʌlb〕*n.* 閃光燈
ready〔ˈrɛdɪ〕*adj.* 準備好的
setting〔ˈsɛtɪŋ〕*n.*（故事的）背景
concert〔ˈkɑnsɝt〕*n.* 音樂會
darkroom〔ˈdɑrkˈrum〕*n.*（沖洗底片的）暗房
auditorium〔ˌɔdəˈtorɪəm〕*n.* 禮堂

58. (**A**) M：Can you believe I won a prize in the speech contest?
W：You expect me to believe that?
How does the woman feel about what the man said?
男：妳相信我在演講比賽得了獎嗎？
女：你認爲我會相信嗎？
對於這位男士說的話，這位女士覺得如何？

(A) 她不相信他。　　(B) 她認爲他是認眞的。
(C) 她嚇到了。　　(D) 她不高興。

* win〔wɪn〕*v.* 贏得　prize〔praɪz〕*n.* 獎賞
speech〔spitʃ〕*adj.* 演講的　contest〔ˈkɑntɛst〕*n.* 比賽
expect〔ɪkˈspɛkt〕*v.* 預期；認爲
serious〔ˈsɪrɪəs〕*adj.* 認眞的　scared〔skɛrd〕*adj.* 嚇著的
unhappy〔ʌnˈhæpɪ〕*adj.* 不快樂的

59. (**A**) M：I told Jeff to buy the magazine at the store on his way home.
W：I don't think he remembered.
Is the woman confident that Jeff bought the magazine?
男：我叫傑夫在回家的路上到店裡買雜誌。
女：我不認爲他會記得。
這位女士確信傑夫會買雜誌嗎？
(A) 她懷疑他會買雜誌。
(B) 她認爲他會記得要買雜誌。
(C) 她懷疑傑夫是不是叫她去買雜誌。
(D) 她記得他買了雜誌。

* magazine (ˌmægəˈzin) *n.* 雜誌
on one's way home 在回家途中
confident (ˈkɑnfədənt) *adj.* 確信的
doubtful (ˈdaʊtfəl) *adj.* 懷疑的
wonder (ˈwʌndɚ) *v.* 感到懷疑

60. (**C**) M：How would you like to go out for dinner tonight?
W：What a wonderful idea! We always eat at home.
What is the woman's reaction to the man's suggestion?
男：妳今晚想不想出去吃晚餐？
女：眞是個好主意！我們總是在家裡吃飯。
對於這位男士的提議，這位女士的反應是什麼？
(A) 她寧願在家吃。 (B) 她認爲他們每天晚上都應該出門。
(C) 她今晚眞的很想在外面吃飯。
(D) 她不確定要做什麼。

* wonderful (ˈwʌndɚfəl) *adj.* 極好的
idea (aɪˈdiə) *n.* 主意 reaction (rɪˈækʃən) *n.* 反應
suggestion (səˈdʒɛstʃən) *n.* 提議
really (ˈrilɪ) *adv.* 眞正地 ***eat out*** 在外面吃飯
sure (ʃʊr) *adj.* 確定的

LISTENING TEST ⑩

- *Directions for questions 1-25. You will hear questions on the test CD. Select the one item A, B, C or D which answers the question correctly, and mark your answer sheet.*

1. A. He made both ends meet.
   B. He rested up overnight.
   C. He brushed day in and day out.
   D. He burned the candle at both ends.

2. A. the meter B. the journey
   C. the airplane D. the test

3. A. be reminded of his manners.
   B. remember the best regards.
   C. know from a to z.
   D. mind his p's and q's.

4. A. $25.00 B. $25.90
   C. $26.10 D. None of the above.

5. A. monkeys B. racing cars
   C. juices and snacks D. plants

6. A. She would learn enough. B. She would find one.
   C. She would earn enough. D. She would burn enough.

7. A. close to the suburbs B. close to Los Angeles
   C. close to New York D. close to his mom

8. A. $85.00 B. $32.00
   C. $75.00 D. $95.00

9. A. He billed the house. B. He brought the house.
   C. He built the house. D. He bought the house.

10. A. check herself in B. visit her friend
    C. give some help D. eat lunch

11. A. how to move the lab
    B. how to get a good grade
    C. how to change the lab
    D. how to study effectively

12. A. a lubricant B. an ice cream soda
    C. a lullaby D. a lollipop

13. A. I'll be on the first flight out.
    B. I'll be gone for over two weeks.
    C. Yes. I've never been out of the country.
    D. I'll arrive at three.

14. A. to go free a dentist B. to go be a dentist
    C. to go see the dentist D. to go see the director

15. A. They had already discussed the dates.
    B. Her schedule hasn't been confirmed yet, so I don't know.
    C. No, she'll take a first class flight.
    D. I'm sure that she knows the road.

16. A. a broom of her own B. a groom of her own
    C. a room of her own D. a gloomy room

17. A. a pair of shoes B. town
    C. to his friend's house D. by bus

18. A. call it a day. B. call it off.
    C. give up sleeping. D. keep awake.

19. A. I had to buy a new shirt.
    B. Yes, if you can pay me back this week.
    C. No, I'm sorry I can't help you.
    D. No, it's on sale now.

20. A. see spirits B. see herself
    C. see himself D. see ourselves

21. A. Yes. He went home at three.
    B. He's transferring to your office.
    C. He's a supervisor now.
    D. No. He left about three.

22. A. bright B. fat
    C. short D. small

23. A. He is going for a boat ride.
    B. He is going to have a picnic.
    C. He is going to fly an airplane.
    D. He is going to go very fast.

24. A. introductions
    B. introspection
    C. instructions
    D. installations

25. A. He looked away from the building.
    B. He stopped at the building.
    C. He slipped and fell at the building.
    D. He quickly looked at the building.

● *Directions for questions 26-50. You will hear statements on the test CD. Select the one answer A, B, C, or D which comes closest to the meaning of the statement and mark your answer sheet.*

26. A. He glanced at his notes before the quiz.
    B. The quiz was postponed.
    C. He did the quiz over.
    D. He glanced at the notes during the quiz.

27. A. She didn't answer the phone.
    B. She was making a local phone call.
    C. She just came home.
    D. She was about to go out when she received a phone call.

28. A. The trip is delayed.
    B. The trip is cancelled.
    C. People will get sick on this trip.
    D. Everyone feels good about the trip.

29. A. The object remained in the sky.
    B. The object suddenly vanished.
    C. The object suddenly appeared.
    D. The object suddenly exploded.

30. A. The ship can sail across the Pacific Ocean.
    B. The ship sank because of the storm.
    C. The ship vanished.
    D. The ship can endure terrible storms.

31. A. He needs more money.
    B. He needs more workers.
    C. He needs more uniforms.
    D. He needs a life.

32. A. There is very little water.
    B. There is just enough water.
    C. There is too much water.
    D. There is plenty water.

33. A. They took on the enemy and won.
    B. They attempted to fight off the enemy.
    C. They gave in to the enemy.
    D. They kept away from the enemy.

34. A. Kimberly should eat more grapes.
    B. Kimberly should eat more oranges.
    C. Kimberly should eat more spinach.
    D. Kimberly should eat more apples.

35. A. The learning took place in spite of the exercises.
    B. They all had to learn in the classroom.
    C. The course was in regard to the exercises.
    D. The learning took place in the course of the exercises.

36. A. You couldn't see the sun.
    B. You couldn't see me.
    C. You couldn't see the world.
    D. You couldn't see ghosts.

37. A. This is the correct street.
    B. This is the wrong street.
    C. This is the right street.
    D. This is the left street.

38. A. The soldiers fought very hard against the enemy.
    B. The soldier was defeated.
    C. The enemy gained the victory in the face of the soldier.
    D. The enemy resisted the forces.

39. A. She ate one. B. She made one.
    C. She sold one. D. She gave one.

40. A. We have little money now.
    B. We have a lot of money now.
    C. We hear a low noise now.
    D. We have a present now.

41. A. They gave in. B. They died down.
    C. They fought off. D. They resisted.

42. A. It's beginning to vanish.
    B. It's beginning to rain.
    C. It's beginning to be stained.
    D. It's beginning to pain.

43. A. The location was constant.
    B. The location was vague.
    C. The location was highly populated.
    D. The location was remote.

44. A. There were empty seats on the train.
    B. They had to stand at the train station.
    C. All seats were on the way to the train.
    D. All the seats on the train were taken.

45. A. Their price is high.
    B. They are poor quality.
    C. They are plentiful.
    D. It is a long story.

46. A. The movie wasn't sold out.
    B. There weren't any seats left.
    C. The tickets were expensive.
    D. He bought reserved seats.

47. A. The people were passed over.
    B. The people were forgotten.
    C. They didn't like their people.
    D. They remembered their people.

48. A. He thinks it's too simple.
    B. He thinks it's very hard to learn.
    C. He thinks it's too easy.
    D. He thinks it's too funny.

49. A. It hit and broke the door.
    B. It landed on the car.
    C. It hit and broke the window.
    D. It landed in my neighbor's yard.

50. A. There is something that interests him.
    B. There is someone who misunderstands him.
    C. There is someone who yells at him.
    D. There is something wrong with him.

- *Directions for questions 51-60. You will hear dialogs on the test CD. Select the correct answer A, B, C, or D and mark your answer sheet.*

51. A. It's as glamorous as it sounds.
    B. It's taken up too much of her time.
    C. It's only in the early stages.
    D. It's already led to a few job offers.

52. A. in a classroom B. in a bookstore
    C. in a courtroom D. in a sheriff's office

53. A. 12:30 B. 2:30
    C. 12:00 D. 9:30

54. A. Beth will get a raise.
 B. Beth is stupid.
 C. Beth will not get a raise.
 D. Beth is overweight.

55. A. She hurt her neck.
 B. She is too busy.
 C. She can't read.
 D. Reading is her job.

56. A. Stay at home tonight.
 B. Leave the house tonight.
 C. Cook dinner tonight.
 D. Take a vacation.

57. A. at a library B. at a post office
 C. at a gymnasium D. at a stationery store

58. A. It will be cooler during the week.
 B. It will be very humorous.
 C. It will not be good for viewing.
 D. The weather will be the same for a while.

59. A. at a fire station B. at a supermarket
 C. at a pharmacy D. at a library

60. A. a season B. the climate
 C. clothes D. food

ECL 聽力測驗⑩詳解

1. (**D**) The researcher worked without enough rest. What does the statement mean?

   這名研究人員在沒有充分的休息的情況下工作。／這段敘述是什麼意思？

   (A) 他量入爲出。
   (B) 他整夜休息以恢復精神。
   (C) 他日以繼夜地刷。
   (D) <u>他耗盡精力。</u>

   * researcher〔ˈrisɝtʃɚ〕*n.* 研究人員
   rest〔rɛst〕*n.* 休息　　statement〔ˈstetmənt〕*n.* 敘述
   mean〔min〕*v.* 意思是
   make both ends meet 使收支平衡；量入爲出
   rest up 休息以恢復精神
   overnight〔ˈovɚˈnaɪt〕*adv.* 整夜地
   brush〔brʌʃ〕*v.* 刷　　***day in and day out*** 日以繼夜
   candle〔ˈkændḷ〕*n.* 蠟燭
   burn the candle at both ends 蠟燭兩頭燒；耗盡精力

2. (**B**) The trip was extremely long. What was long?

   這是趟很漫長的旅行。／什麼東西很長？

   (A) 公尺。　　(B) <u>旅行。</u>
   (C) 飛機。　　(D) 考試。

   * trip〔trɪp〕*n.* 旅行
   extremely〔ɪkˈstrimlɪ〕*adv.* 非常
   meter〔ˈmitɚ〕*n.* 公尺　　journey〔ˈdʒɝnɪ〕*n.* 旅行
   airplane〔ˈɛrˌplen〕*n.* 飛機

3. (**D**) Anyone who wishes to succeed must do and say the right things. What should one do to be successful?
想要成功的人，必須做還有說正確的事。／一個人要成功的話，應該做什麼？

(A) 有人使他注意到他的禮貌。
(B) 記得最適合的問候方式。
(C) 從頭到尾都知道。
(D) 注意言行。

* wish〔 wɪʃ 〕*v.* 希望；想　　succeed〔 sək'sid 〕*v.* 成功
successful〔 sək'sɛsfəl 〕*adj.* 成功的
remind〔 rɪ'maɪnd 〕*v.* 提醒；使注意到
manners〔'mænɚz 〕*n. pl.* 禮貌
remember〔 rɪ'mɛmbɚ 〕*v.* 記得
regard〔 rɪ'gɑrd 〕*n.*（書信等的）問候
from A to Z 從頭到尾　　mind〔 maɪnd 〕*v.* 注意
mind** one's **p's and q's 注意言行

4. (**A**) Maria bought a pair of boots for 25 dollars plus 90 cents tax. How much did the boots cost without the tax?
瑪莉亞花了二十五元，加上九十分的稅，買了一雙靴子。／靴子不含稅要價多少？

(A) 二十五元。　　(B) 二十五元九十分。
(C) 二十六元十分。　　(D) 以上皆非。

* pair〔 pɛr 〕*n.* 雙　　boots〔 buts 〕*n. pl.* 長靴
plus〔 plʌs 〕*prep.* 加上
cent〔 sɛnt 〕*n.* 分【美國貨幣單位】
tax〔 tæks 〕*n.* 稅　　none〔 nʌn 〕*pron.* 完全沒有
above〔 ə'bʌv 〕*adj.* 上列的

5. (**A**) The students went to the zoo trip on Tuesday. What did they see?
學生們星期二到動物園旅行。／他們看到了什麼？

(A) 猴子。　　(B) 賽車。
(C) 果汁和點心。　　(D) 植物。

* racing [ˈresɪŋ] *adj.* 賽跑的
juice [dʒus] *n.* 果汁　　snack [snæk] *n.* 點心
plant [plænt] *n.* 植物

6. (**C**) How would a new job enable her to buy a boat?
新工作是如何使她買得起一艘船的？

(A) 她會學到足夠的東西。
(B) 她會找到一個。
(C) 她會賺到足夠的錢。
(D) 她會燒掉足夠的東西。

* enable [ɪnˈebl̩] *v.* 使能夠　　boat [bot] *n.* 船
earn [ɝn] *v.* 賺取　　burn [bɝn] *v.* 燃燒

7. (**B**) John lives in Palos Verdes, which is a suburb of Los Angeles. Where does John live?
約翰住在帕洛斯弗迪斯，那是洛杉磯的郊區。／約翰住在哪？

(A) 接近郊區。　　(B) 接近洛杉磯。
(C) 接近紐約。　　(D) 接近他媽媽。

* suburb [ˈsʌbɝb] *n.* 郊區
Los Angeles [lɔsˈændʒələs] *n.* 洛杉磯【美國加州西南部港市】
close [klos] *adj.* 接近的
New York [njuˈjɔrk] *n.* 紐約【美國東北部一州】

8. (**B**) The only book I liked cost $95. Each of the others was a third of that price. What was the price of the other books?

我唯一喜歡的書要九十五元。其他每一本書都賣三分之一的價格。／其他書的價格是多少？

(A) 八十五元。 (B) <u>三十二元。</u>
(C) 七十五元。 (D) 九十五元。

* ***a third of*** 三分之一的
price (praɪs) *n.* 價格

9. (**C**) Mr. Thomas constructed his home by himself. What did Mr. Thomas do?

湯瑪士先生自己蓋房子。／湯瑪士做了什麼？

(A) 他在房子上貼廣告。
(B) 他帶來這棟房子。
(C) <u>他蓋了這棟房子。</u>
(D) 他買下這棟房子。

* construct (kənˈstrʌkt) *v.* 建造
by oneself 靠自己 bill (bɪl) *v.* 貼廣告於
build (bɪld) *v.* 建築

10. (**C**) Doreen wants to serve in the hospital. What does she want to do in the hospital?

朵莉想要在這家醫院服務。／她想要在這家醫院做什麼？

(A) 投宿在這家醫院。 (B) 拜訪她的朋友。
(C) <u>給予某些協助。</u> (D) 吃午餐。

* serve (sɝv) *v.* 工作；服務
check in 辦理投宿手續

11. (**C**) The teacher showed us how to transform the lab. What did he show us?
老師告訴我們要如何改造這間實驗室。／他告訴我們什麼？
(A) 如何把實驗室遷走。 (B) 如何得到好成績。
(C) 如何改變實驗室。 (D) 如何有效地讀書。
＊ show〔 ʃo 〕*v.* 告知 transform〔 træns'fɔrm 〕*v.* 改造
lab〔 læb 〕*n.* 實驗室（= *laboratory*）
grade〔 gred 〕*n.* 成績
effectively〔 ə'fɛktɪvlɪ 〕*adv.* 有效地

12. (**A**) She got grease all over her shirt. What was on her shirt?
她的襯衫沾滿油。／她的襯衫上面有什麼？
(A) 潤滑油。 (B) 冰淇淋汽水。
(C) 搖籃曲。 (D) 棒棒糖。
＊ grease〔 gris 〕*n.* 油脂 ***all over*** 遍及；在整個…上
shirt〔 ʃɜt 〕*n.* 襯衫 lubricant〔'lubrɪkənt〕*n.* 潤滑油
soda〔'sodə〕*n.* 汽水 lullaby〔'lʌlə,baɪ〕*n.* 搖籃曲
lollipop〔'lɑlɪ,pɑp〕*n.* 棒棒糖

13. (**C**) Are you excited about your trip to Tokyo?
你對於要去東京旅行這件事感到興奮嗎？
(A) 我會搭第一班飛機出去。
(B) 我會去兩個多禮拜。
(C) 是的。我從來沒有出過國。
(D) 我會在三點鐘抵達。
＊ excited〔 ɪk'saɪtɪd 〕*adj.* 興奮的
Tokyo〔'tokɪ,o〕*n.* 東京【日本首都】
flight〔 flaɪt 〕*n.* 班機 out〔 aʊt 〕*adv.* 向外；離開國家
gone〔 gɑn 〕*adj.* 離去的；暫時不在的
over〔'ovɚ〕*prep.* 超過 arrive〔 ə'raɪv 〕*v.* 抵達

14. (**C**) Gary said, "Remember your appointment with the dentist." What did Gary want me to remember?
蓋瑞說：「記得你和牙醫的約會。」／蓋瑞要我記得什麼？
(A) 讓牙醫自由。 (B) 去當個牙醫。
(C) 去看牙醫。 (D) 去看導演。
* appointment〔əˈpɔɪntmənt〕*n.* 約會
dentist〔ˈdɛntɪst〕*n.* 牙醫 ***go free*** 放…自由
director〔dəˈrɛktɚ〕*n.* 導演

15. (**B**) Will she be coming to Taipei on this trip?
她這趟旅行會到台北來嗎？
(A) 他們已經討論過日期了。
(B) 她的時間表還不確定，所以我也不知道。
(C) 不，她會搭頭等艙。
(D) 我確定她知道路。
* discuss〔dɪˈskʌs〕*v.* 討論 date〔det〕*n.* 日期
schedule〔ˈskɛdʒul〕*n.* 時間表
confirm〔kənˈfɝm〕*v.* 確定
yet〔jɛt〕*adv.* 尚（未） ***first class*** 頭等的

16. (**C**) Each of the girls has an individual room. What does each girl have?
每個女孩都有自己的房間。／每個女孩都有什麼？
(A) 自己的掃帚。 (B) 自己的新郎。
(C) 自己的房間。 (D) 陰暗的房間。
* individual〔ˌɪndəˈvɪdʒuəl〕*adj.* 個別的
broom〔brum〕*n.* 掃帚 ***of one's own*** 自己的
groom〔grum〕*n.* 新郎 gloomy〔ˈglumɪ〕*adj.* 陰暗的

17. (**B**) Jim went to town yesterday with his friend to buy a pair of shoes. Where did he go?
吉姆昨天和他朋友到城裡去買了一雙鞋子。／他去哪裡？
(A) 一雙鞋子。 (B) <u>城鎮。</u>
(C) 到他朋友家。 (D) 搭公車。

18. (**A**) The mother decided to quit work and go to bed. What did the mother do?
那位母親決定停止工作上床睡覺。／那位母親做什麼？
(A) <u>結束一天的工作。</u> (B) 取消它。
(C) 放棄睡覺。 (D) 保持清醒。

* decide〔dɪ'saɪd〕*v.* 決定 quit〔kwɪt〕*v.* 停止
call it a day 結束一天的工作 ***call off*** 取消
give up 放棄 awake〔ə'wek〕*adj.* 醒著的

19. (**C**) Excuse me, do you have change for 100 dollars?
抱歉，你有一百塊的零錢嗎？
(A) 我必須買一件新襯衫。
(B) 是的，如果你可以在這星期還我錢的話。
(C) <u>沒有，很抱歉我幫不上忙。</u>
(D) 沒有，現在正在特價。

* change〔tʃendʒ〕*n.* 零錢 ***pay back*** 還錢
on sale 特價

20. (**C**) Ray broke his mirror. What can't he do?
雷打破他的鏡子。／他無法做什麼？
(A) 看見幽靈。 (B) 看見她自己。
(C) <u>看見他自己。</u> (D) 看到我們。

* mirror〔'mɪrɚ〕*n.* 鏡子 spirit〔'spɪrɪt〕*n.* 幽靈

21. (**A**) Has Mike already left for the day?

麥克已經走了嗎？

(A) <u>是的。他三點鐘就回家了。</u>
(B) 他到你的辦公室去了。
(C) 他現在是主管。
(D) 不。他大概三點走的。

* leave (liv) *v.* 離開　***for the day*** 當天
transfer (træns′fɝ) *v.* 移動
supervisor (′supɚˏvaɪzɚ) *n.* 主管

22. (**A**) Which best describes the sun at noon on a clear day?

何者最適合描述晴天中午的太陽？

(A) <u>明亮的。</u>　(B) 肥胖的。
(C) 短的。　(D) 小的。

* describe (dɪ′skraɪb) *v.* 描述
noon (nun) *n.* 中午　clear (klɪr) *adj.* 晴朗的
bright (braɪt) *adj.* 明亮的

23. (**A**) Mike is going sailing. What is he going to do?

麥克將要出海。／他將要做什麼？

(A) <u>他將要去搭船。</u>
(B) 他將要去野餐。
(C) 他將要去開飛機。
(D) 他很快就會過去。

* sailing (′selɪŋ) *n.* 航海
ride (raɪd) *n.* 搭乘　picnic (′pɪknɪk) *n.* 野餐
fly (flaɪ) *v.* 駕駛（飛機）

24. (**C**) The instructor wrote the directions on the whiteboard. The students wrote them in their notebooks. What did the students write in their notebooks?
老師把指示寫在白板上。學生們把它抄在筆記本上。／學生們把什麼寫在筆記本上？

(A) 介紹。 (B) 反省。
(C) 指示。 (D) 安裝。

* instructor (ɪn'strʌktɚ) *n.* 教師
directions (də'rɛkʃənz) *n. pl.* 命令；指示
whiteboard ('hwaɪt,bord) *n.* 白板
notebook ('not,bʊk) *n.* 筆記本
introduction (,ɪntrə'dʌkʃən) *n.* 介紹
introspection (,ɪntrə'spɛkʃən) *n.* 反省
instructions (ɪn'strʌkʃənz) *n. pl.* 命令；指示
installation (,ɪnstə'leʃən) *n.* 安裝

25. (**D**) As the taxi drove down Fifth Avenue, Tom glanced at the Empire State Building. What did he do?
當計程車沿著第五大道行駛時，湯姆看了帝國大廈一眼。／他做了什麼？

(A) 他不看那棟建築物。
(B) 他在那棟建築物停下來。
(C) 他在那棟建築物滑倒。
(D) 他很快地看了一眼那棟建築物。

* taxi ('tæksɪ) *n.* 計程車 ***drive down…*** 沿著…行駛
avenue ('ævə,nju) *n.* 大道 glance (glæns) *v.* 看一眼
empire ('ɛmpaɪr) *adj.* 帝國的
the Empire State Building 帝國大廈（= *ESB*）
look away from… 把眼睛轉向別處，不看…
slip (slɪp) *v.* 滑倒

26. (**A**) Major Garza looked quickly at his notes before taking the book quiz.
加薩少校在參加書籍測驗之前，很快地看了一下筆記。
(A) 他在測驗之前，看了一下筆記。
(B) 測驗延期了。 (C) 他把測驗重做一次。
(D) 他在測驗時，看了一下筆記。
* Major (ˈmedʒɚ) *n.* 陸軍少校 notes (nots) *n. pl.* 筆記
quiz (kwɪz) *n.* 小測驗 postpone (postˈpon) *v.* 延期
do over 重做

27. (**D**) Cindy was ready to go out when she received a long distance phone call.
辛蒂接到長途電話時，就準備好要出門了。
(A) 她沒有接電話。 (B) 她打了一通市內電話。
(C) 她剛回到家。 (D) 她接到電話時，正要出門。
* ready (ˈrɛdɪ) *adj.* 準備好的 receive (rɪˈsiv) *v.* 收到
receive a phone call 接到電話
distance (ˈdɪstəns) *n.* 距離
answer (ˈænsɚ) *v.* 接（電話）
make a phone call 打電話
local (ˈlokḷ) *adj.* 市內的 about (əˈbaʊt) *adj.* 正打算…的

28. (**A**) We'll have to postpone our trip until next weekend because I don't feel very well.
我們必須把旅行延到下週末，因為我覺得不太舒服。
(A) 旅行延期了。 (B) 旅行取消了。
(C) 人們會在這趟旅行中生病。
(D) 每個人都覺得這趟旅行很不錯。
* weekend (ˈwikˈɛnd) *n.* 週末 delay (dɪˈle) *v.* 延期
cancel (ˈkænsḷ) *v.* 取消

29. (**B**) We saw the shining object moving across the sky. But then it suddenly disappeared.

我們看到有個發亮的物體劃過天空。但是它突然就消失了。

(A) 那個物體還在天空中。 (B) <u>那個物體突然消失了。</u>

(C) 那個物體突然出現了。 (D) 那個物體突然爆炸了。

* shining〔'ʃaɪnɪŋ〕*adj.* 發光的
object〔'ɑbdʒɪkt〕*n.* 東西；物體
suddenly〔'sʌdn̩lɪ〕*adv.* 突然地
disappear〔,dɪsə'pɪr〕*v.* 消失 remain〔rɪ'men〕*v.* 依然
vanish〔'vænɪʃ〕*v.* 消失 appear〔ə'pɪr〕*v.* 出現
explode〔ɪk'splod〕*v.* 爆炸

30. (**D**) That new ship can withstand terrible storms at sea.

那艘新船可以抵抗海上的可怕暴風雨。

(A) 這艘船可以橫渡太平洋。

(B) 這艘船因爲暴風雨而沉沒了。

(C) 這艘船消失了。

(D) <u>這艘船可以忍受可怕的暴風雨。</u>

* ship〔ʃɪp〕*n.* 船 withstand〔wɪθ'stænd〕*v.* 經得起；抵抗
terrible〔'tɛrəbl̩〕*adj.* 劇烈的 storm〔stɔrm〕*n.* 暴風雨
sail〔sel〕*v.* 航行 Pacific〔pə'sɪfɪk〕*adj.* 太平洋的
ocean〔'oʃən〕*n.* 海洋 ***the Pacific Ocean*** 太平洋
sink〔sɪŋk〕*v.* 沉沒 endure〔ɪn'djur〕*v.* 忍受

31. (**B**) The director of the factory needs more personnel.

這座工廠的管理者需要更多員工。

(A) 他需要更多錢。 (B) <u>他需要更多工人。</u>

(C) 他需要更多制服。 (D) 他需要一個活人。

* director〔də'rɛktɚ〕*n.* 管理者 factory〔'fæktrɪ〕*n.* 工廠
personnel〔,pɝsn̩'ɛl〕*n.* 【集合名詞】員工
uniform〔'junə,fɔrm〕*n.* 制服 life〔laɪf〕*n.* 活人

32. (**A**) There is a scarcity of water. 這裡缺水。

(A) 水很少。 (B) 水剛好夠用。
(C) 水太多。 (D) 水很多。

* scarcity (ˈskɛrsətɪ) *n.* 缺乏
little (ˈlɪtl̩) *adj.* 少許的
plenty (ˈplɛntɪ) *adj.* 很多的

33. (**B**) The troops tried to prevent the enemy invasion.
軍隊設法阻止敵軍入侵。

(A) 他們接受敵人的挑戰，而且打贏了。
(B) 他們試著擊退敵人。
(C) 他們向敵人投降。
(D) 他們遠離敵人。

* troops (trups) *n. pl.* 軍隊 prevent (prɪˈvɛnt) *v.* 阻止
enemy (ˈɛnəmɪ) *n.* 敵人 ***the enemy*** 敵軍
invasion (ɪnˈveʒən) *n.* 侵入 ***take on*** 接受…的挑戰
attempt (əˈtɛmpt) *v.* 嘗試 ***fight off*** 作戰而擊退
give in to 屈服；投降 ***keep away from*** 遠離

34. (**C**) The nutritionist told Kimberly to eat more vegetables.
營養學家告訴金百莉說要多吃一點蔬菜。

(A) 她應該多吃一點葡萄。
(B) 她應該多吃一點橘子。
(C) 她應該多吃一點菠菜。
(D) 她應該多吃一點蘋果。

* nutritionist (njuˈtrɪʃənɪst) *n.* 營養學家
vegetable (ˈvɛdʒətəbl̩) *n.* 蔬菜
grape (grep) *n.* 葡萄
spinach (ˈspɪnɪtʃ) *n.* 菠菜

35. (**D**) The commanders, as well as the troops, learned during the practice operations.
指揮官和軍隊都在軍事演習期間學到東西。

(A) 儘管是在演習，他們還是學到東西。
(B) 他們全都必須在教室裡學習。
(C) 這個課程和軍事演習有關。
(D) 他們在軍事演習的過程中學到東西。

＊ commander〔kəˈmændɚ〕*n.* 指揮官
as well as 和　practice〔ˈpræktɪs〕*n.* 練習；演習
operations〔ˌɑpəˈreʃənz〕*n.* 軍事行動
take place 發生　***in spite of*** 儘管
exercises〔ˈɛksɚˌsaɪzɪz〕*n.* 軍事演習
course〔kors〕*n.* 課程；過程　***in regard to*** 關於

36. (**A**) The thermometer indicated about 28 degrees, and it was a foggy day.
溫度計指出溫度大約是二十八度，而且是個有霧的日子。

(A) 你看不到太陽。　(B) 你看不到我。
(C) 你看不到這個世界。　(D) 你看不到鬼。

＊ thermometer〔θəˈmɑmətɚ〕*n.* 溫度計
indicate〔ˈɪndəˌket〕*v.* 指示；標示
degree〔dɪˈgri〕*n.* 度數　foggy〔ˈfɑgɪ〕*adj.* 有霧的
ghost〔gost〕*n.* 鬼

37. (**B**) This is not the right street. 這條街不對。

(A) 這條街是對的。　(B) 這條街是錯的。
(C) 這是右邊的那條街。　(D) 這是左邊的那條街。

＊ correct〔kəˈrɛkt〕*adj.* 正確的
wrong〔rɔŋ〕*adj.* 錯誤的
right〔raɪt〕*adj.* 右邊的　left〔lɛft〕*adj.* 左邊的

38. (**A**) When up against the enemy, the soldiers excelled.
遇到敵軍時，這些士兵打贏了。

(A) 這些士兵和敵軍奮勇作戰。
(B) 這些士兵被打敗了。
(C) 敵軍在面對這些士兵時打了勝仗。
(D) 敵軍擋住軍隊。

* against (əˈgɛnst) *prep.* 對著；反抗　***up against*** 遭遇
soldier (ˈsoldʒɚ) *n.* 士兵
excel (ɪkˈsɛl) *v.* 勝過　fight (faɪt) *v.* 作戰
defeat (dɪˈfit) *v.* 打敗　gain (gen) *v.* 獲得
victory (ˈvɪktrɪ) *n.* 勝利　***in the face of*** 面對
resist (rɪˈzɪst) *v.* 抵擋；擋開　forces (ˈfɔrsɪz) *n. pl.* 軍隊

39. (**B**) I watched the woman build a racing bike.
我看著那位女士組一輛賽車用的腳踏車。

(A) 她吃掉一輛。　(B) 她做了一輛。
(C) 她賣了一輛。　(D) 她送了一輛。

* build (bɪld) *v.* 建造　bike (baɪk) *n.* 腳踏車

40. (**A**) We're running low on cash at present.
目前我們的現金快要用完了。

(A) 我們現在沒什麼錢。
(B) 我們現在有很多錢。
(C) 我們現在聽到低沉的聲音。
(D) 我們現在有一個禮物。

* run (rʌn) *v.* 保持在特定水平
low (lo) *adj.* 少的；低沉的
be running low 快要用完了
present (ˈprɛzn̩t) *n.* 現在；禮物　***at present*** 目前
hear (hɪr) *v.* 聽到　noise (nɔɪs) *n.* 聲音

41. (**A**) The enemy force withdrew and stopped opposing the army troops. 敵軍撤退了，並且停止和軍隊對抗。

(A) 他們投降了。　(B) 他們逐漸停止。
(C) 他們擊退了。　(D) 他們抵擋住。

* withdraw〔wɪð'drɔ〕*v.* 撤退
oppose〔ə'poz〕*v.* 使對抗
army〔'ɑrmɪ〕*adj.* 軍隊的　***army troops*** 軍隊
give in 投降　***die down*** 逐漸停止

42. (**B**) We'd better hurry up. It's gently sprinkling on my head. 我們最好趕快。小雨緩緩下在我的頭上。

(A) 開始消失了。　(B) 開始下雨了。
(C) 開始被弄髒了。　(D) 開始痛了。

* ***had better*** 最好　***hurry up*** 趕快
gently〔'dʒɛntlɪ〕*adv.* 逐漸地；緩慢地
sprinkle〔'sprɪŋkḷ〕*v.* 下小雨　stain〔sten〕*v.* 弄髒
pain〔pen〕*v.* 給予痛苦

43. (**D**) The action took place far away from populated areas. 這個活動在遠離人口稠密的區域舉辦。

(A) 地點是不變的。
(B) 地點不明確。
(C) 這個地點的人口密度很高。
(D) 地點很偏僻。

* ***take place*** 舉辦　far〔fɑr〕*adv.* 遙遠地
populated〔'pɑpjə,letɪd〕*adj.* 人口稠密的
area〔'ɛrɪə〕*n.* 地區　location〔lo'keʃən〕*n.* 地點
constant〔'kɑnstənt〕*adj.* 不變的
vague〔veg〕*adj.* 不明確的　highly〔'haɪlɪ〕*adv.* 高度地
remote〔rɪ'mot〕*adj.* 偏僻的

44. (**D**) They had to stand up in the train on the way to town.
他們在到城裡的火車上必須站著。

(A) 火車上有空位。

(B) 他們必須站在火車站。

(C) 所有座椅都在送上火車的途中。

(D) 火車上的所有座位都有人坐。

* ***on the way to…*** 邁向…之路
empty〔'ɛmptɪ〕*adj.* 空的　　seat〔sit〕*n.* 座位；座椅
station〔'steʃən〕*n.* 車站　　take〔tek〕*v.* 佔（位子）

45. (**C**) Fruits are abundant in this country.
這個國家盛產水果。

(A) 它們的價格很高。

(B) 它們的品質不好。

(C) 它們的數量很多。

(D) 那是個很長的故事。

* abundant〔ə'bʌndənt〕*adj.* 豐富的；盛產的
poor〔pur〕*adj.* 欠佳的　　quality〔'kwalətɪ〕*n.* 品質
plentiful〔'plɛntɪfəl〕*adj.* 很多的

46. (**B**) There weren't any seats available for the movie.
買不到這部電影的位子。

(A) 這部電影的票還沒賣完。

(B) 一個座位都不剩。

(C) 電影票很貴。

(D) 他預購座位。

* available〔ə'veləbḷ〕*adv.* 可獲得的　　***sell out*** 賣光
left〔lɛft〕*adj.* 剩下的　　ticket〔'tɪkɪt〕*n.* 票
expensive〔ɪk'spɛnsɪv〕*adj.* 昂貴的
reserved〔rɪ'zɝvd〕*adj.* 預訂的

47. (**D**) They kept their people in mind.
他們把人民記在心裡。

(A) 人民全死了。
(B) 人民被忘記了。
(C) 他們不喜歡他們的人民。
(D) <u>他們記得他們的人民。</u>

* ***keep…in mind*** 把…記在心裡　　***pass over*** 死

48. (**B**) James thinks Russian is a difficult language.
詹姆士認爲俄語是一種困難的語言。

(A) 他認爲俄語太簡單。
(B) <u>他認爲俄語很難學。</u>
(C) 他認爲俄語太簡單。
(D) 他認爲俄語太好笑。

* Russian〔ˈrʌʃən〕*n.* 俄語
difficult〔ˈdɪfə,kʌlt〕*adj.* 困難的
language〔ˈlæŋgwɪdʒ〕*n.* 語言
simple〔ˈsɪmpḷ〕*adj.* 簡單的
funny〔ˈfʌnɪ〕*adj.* 好笑的

49. (**C**) The ball smashed through the window.
那顆球擊穿窗戶。

(A) 它擊中並打破門。
(B) 它落在車上。
(C) <u>它擊中並打破窗戶。</u>
(D) 它落在我鄰居的院子裡。

* smash〔smæʃ〕*v.* 打碎；猛撞　　hit〔hɪt〕*v.* 擊中
break〔brek〕*v.* 打破　　land〔lænd〕*v.* 落下
neighbor〔ˈnebɚ〕*n.* 鄰居　　yard〔jɑrd〕*n.* 院子

50. (**D**) There must be something the matter with Tom.
一定有事情困擾著湯姆。

(A) 有使他感興趣的事。 (B) 有人誤會他。
(C) 有人對他大吼。 (D) 他不太對勁。

* matter〔ˈmætɚ〕*n.* 困擾的事；麻煩的事
interest〔ˈɪntrɪst〕*v.* 使感興趣
misunderstand〔ˌmɪsʌndɚˈstænd〕*v.* 誤會
yell〔jɛl〕*v.* 大吼　wrong〔rɔŋ〕*adj.* 情況不好的

51. (**C**) M：I heard you've begun a modeling career. That sounds pretty glamorous.
W：I've only taken a few workshops so far. There haven't been any job offers yet.
What does the woman say about her new career?
男：我聽說妳已經開始從事模特兒的工作。那聽起來很吸引人。
女：我到現在只是參加了一些研討會。還沒有人找我去工作。
關於這位女士的新工作，她說了些什麼？

(A) 工作本身和它聽起來一樣吸引人。
(B) 工作佔用她太多時間。 (C) 工作只是在初期。
(D) 這份工作已經使得一些人找她去工作。

* modeling〔ˈmɑdḷɪŋ〕*n.* 模特兒
career〔kəˈrɪr〕*n.* 工作；職業
sound〔saʊnd〕*v.* 聽起來　pretty〔ˈprɪtɪ〕*adv.* 非常
glamorous〔ˈglæmərəs〕*adj.* 吸引人的
take〔tek〕*v.* 上（課）；花費
workshop〔ˈwɝkˌʃɑp〕*n.* 研討會　***so far*** 到目前爲止
offer〔ˈɔfɚ〕*n.* 提供　***a job offer*** 求才
yet〔jɛt〕*adv.* 尚（未）　***take up*** 佔用
stage〔stedʒ〕*n.* 時期　***lead to*** 導致

52. (**B**) W：What did you say the title was?

M：The one over there on the shelf? It's *Philosopher's Crimes in the West*. I strongly recommend that you buy a copy.

Where does this conversation most probably take place?

女：你說書名是什麼？

男：妳是說書架上的那一本嗎？書名是西方哲學家之罪。我強烈推薦妳買一本。

這段對話最有可能發生在哪裡？

(A) 教室裡。 (B) 書店裡。

(C) 法庭裡。 (D) 警長的辦公室裡。

* title〔'taɪtl̩〕*n.* 書名 ***over there*** 在那裡

shelf〔ʃɛlf〕*n.* 書架

philosopher〔fə'lɑsəfɚ〕*n.* 哲學家

crime〔kraɪm〕*n.* 罪 west〔wɛst〕*n.* 西方

strongly〔'strɔŋlɪ〕*adv.* 強烈地

recommend〔,rɛkə'mɛnd〕*v.* 推薦

copy〔'kɑpɪ〕*n.* 本

conversation〔,kɑnvɚ'seʃən〕*n.* 對話

probably〔'prɑbəblɪ〕*adv.* 可能

courtroom〔'kort,rum〕*n.* 法庭

sheriff〔'ʃɛrɪf〕*n.* 警長

53. (**B**) W：What time did you get home last night?

M：I thought I'd get home around twelve at the latest. But the accident delayed my train for two hours and a half.

What time did the man get home?

女：你昨晚幾點回到家？
男：我原本以爲我最晚十二點左右會到家。但是，那場意外使我的火車誤點兩個半小時。
這位男士幾點回到家？

(A) 十二點半。　(B) 兩點半。
(C) 十二點。　(D) 九點半。

* ***at the latest*** 最晚　accident〔ˈæksədənt〕*n.* 意外
delay〔dɪˈle〕*v.* 延誤　half〔hæf〕*n.* 半小時

54. (**C**) W：Do you think Beth will get a raise?
M：Fat chance.
What does the man imply?
女：你認爲貝絲會被加薪嗎？
男：機會渺茫。
這位男士暗示？

(A) 貝絲會被加薪。　(B) 貝絲很笨。
(C) 貝絲不會被加薪。　(D) 貝絲超重了。

* raise〔rez〕*n.* 加薪　chance〔tʃæns〕*n.* 機會；可能性
(a) fat chance 機會渺茫　imply〔ɪmˈplaɪ〕*v.* 暗示
stupid〔ˈstjupɪd〕*adj.* 笨的
overweight〔ˈovəˈwet〕*adj.* 超重的

55. (**B**) W：Do you think Jennifer is attending today's club meeting?
M：I doubt it. I guess she's up to her neck in those reading assignments Dr. Finch gave her.
What does the man mean?
女：你認爲珍妮佛會出席今天的俱樂部會議嗎？
男：我懷疑。我猜她正埋頭在芬區博士給她的指定閱讀中。
這位男士的意思是？

(A) 她弄傷自己的脖子。　　(B) 她太忙了。

(C) 她無法閱讀。　　(D) 閱讀是她的工作。

* attend [əˈtɛnd] *v.* 出席　　club [klʌb] *n.* 俱樂部
  meeting [ˈmitɪŋ] *n.* 會議　　doubt [daʊt] *v.* 懷疑
  guess [gɛs] *v.* 猜測　　neck [nɛk] *n.* 脖子
  be up to** one's **neck in 埋頭於
  assignment [əˈsaɪnmənt] *n.* 指定作業
  Dr. [ˈdɑktɚ] *n.* 博士（= *doctor*）
  hurt [hɝt] *v.* 使受傷

56. (**B**) W：I'd like to go out tonight.

M：That's fine with me.

What would the woman like to do?

女：我想今天晚上出去。

男：我沒問題。

那位女士想要做什麼？

(A) 今晚待在家裡。　　(B) 今晚出門。

(C) 今晚煮晚餐。　　(D) 休假。

* cook [kʊk] *v.* 烹調　　vacation [veˈkeʃən] *n.* 休假
  take a vacation 休假

57. (**B**) W：I would like to send this by airmail and I'd also like ten five-dollar stamps.

M：Let me weigh the package first and then I'll get your stamps.

Where does the conversation take place?

女：我想要用航空郵件來寄這封信，而且我還要買十張五元郵票。

男：先讓我量一下這個包裹的重量，然後再把郵票給妳。

這段對話發生在哪裡？

(A) 在圖書館。　　　(B) <u>在郵局。</u>
(C) 在健身房。　　　(D) 在文具店。

＊ send (sɛnd) *v.* 寄；送　　airmail (ˈɛr,mel) *n.* 航空郵件
by airmail 以航空郵寄　　stamp (stæmp) *n.* 郵票
weigh (we) *v.* 稱重　　package (ˈpækɪdʒ) *n.* 包裹
library (ˈlaɪ,brɛrɪ) *n.* 圖書館　　***post office*** 郵局
gymnasium (dʒɪmˈnezɪəm) *n.* 健身房
stationery (ˈsteʃən,ɛrɪ) *n.*【集合名詞】文具

58. (**D**) W : It's really humid outside. It's difficult to breathe.
M : Yes, and there's no relief in sight.
What does the man imply?
女：外面眞潮濕。令人難以呼吸。
男：是的，而且濕氣沒有馬上減輕的可能。
這位男士暗示？
(A) 這星期會比較涼爽。
(B) 它會非常幽默。
(C) 天氣不適合觀看。
(D) <u>同樣的天氣還會持續一會兒。</u>

＊ humid (ˈhjumɪd) *adj.* 潮濕的
outside (ˈaʊtˈsaɪd) *adv.* 在外面
breathe (brið) *v.* 呼吸　　relief (rɪˈlif) *n.* 減除；減輕
sight (saɪt) *n.* 看見　　***in sight*** 在望；立即
There's no relief in sight. 字面意思是「情況沒有馬上改善的可能。」，在這段對話中，是作「濕氣沒有馬上減輕的可能。」解 (= *The weather is expected to continue.*)。
cool (kul) *adj.* 涼爽的
humorous (ˈhjumərəs) *adj.* 幽默的
viewing (ˈvjuɪŋ) *n.* 觀看　　same (sem) *adj.* 相同的
weather (ˈwɛðɚ) *n.* 天氣　　while (hwaɪl) *n.* 短暫的時間
for a while 一會兒

59. (C) M：Please read the directions carefully. There are 20 tablets and you get no refills.

W：You mean I'll have to get a new prescription after these? What a bother!

Where does this conversation take place?

男：請仔細地閱讀說明書。這裡有二十顆藥，而且妳不能再配一次藥。

女：你的意思是說吃完這些藥之後，我必須再去拿一張新的處方？眞麻煩！

這段對話發生在哪裡？

(A) 在救火站。 (B) 在超級市場。
(C) 在藥房。 (D) 在圖書館。

* direction (dəˈrɛkʃən) *n.* 說明書
tablet (ˈtæblɪt) *n.* 藥片 refill (ˈri,fɪl) *n.* 再配藥
prescription (prɪˈskrɪpʃən) *n.* 處方
bother (ˈbɑðɚ) *n.* 麻煩 ***fire station*** 救火站
pharmacy (ˈfɑrməsɪ) *n.* 藥房

60. (D) M：This is great. What is it?

W：I'm not sure but it's too hot for my taste. The seasoning is really spicy.

What are the people talking about?

男：眞好吃。這是什麼啊？

女：我不確定，但是它對我來說太辣了。這調味料眞辣。

這些人在談論什麼？

(A) 一個季節。 (B) 氣候。 (C) 衣服。 (D) 食物。

* hot (hɑt) *adj.* 辣的 taste (test) *n.* 味覺
seasoning (ˈsiznɪŋ) *n.* 調味料
spicy (ˈspaɪsɪ) *adj.* 辣的 season (ˈsizn̩) *n.* 季節
climate (ˈklaɪmɪt) *n.* 氣候 clothes (kloz) *n. pl.* 衣服

LISTENING TEST ⑪

- *Directions for questions 1-25. You will hear questions on the test CD. Select the one item A, B, C or D which answers the question correctly, and mark your answer sheet.*

1. A. He saw the picture twice.
   B. He wanted to see the picture again.
   C. He saw the picture once and that was enough.
   D. He liked the picture, so he saw it again and again.

2. A. the front B. the back
   C. the side D. underneath

3. A. never B. always
   C. sometimes D. every Tuesday

4. A. the way it got crazy
   B. the way it looked for food
   C. the way it got bigger
   D. the way it got smaller

5. A. She will be taught how to do the job.
   B. She will be fired from her job.
   C. She will look for a new job.
   D. She will quit her job.

6. A. in the rest room B. in a visitor's room
   C. in the family room D. in a concert hall

7. A. a doctor B. a mechanic
C. a teacher D. a clown

8. A. summer B. spring
C. winter D. fall

9. A. It's coming in from Osaka.
B. In about twenty minutes.
C. Gate number three. D. platform B.

10. A. I enjoy the movie. B. I don't like going away.
C. It's tiring. D. We plan to visit our uncle.

11. A. in her car B. by bus
C. on foot D. by taxi

12. A. She was praised. B. She was promoted.
C. She was reprimanded.
D. She was complimented.

13. A. people who didn't come
B. people who buy things
C. people who buy nothing
D. people who work in the shop

14. A. quit smoking. B. cut off a cigarette.
C. stop to smoke. D. give himself to smoking.

15. A. It rained suddenly. B. It rained heavily.
C. It has rained over. D. It rains all the time.

16. A. She took off all of it.
    B. She took off some of it.
    C. She cooked some of it.
    D. She sold some of it.

17. A. It had begun to hide.
    B. It had begun to show up.
    C. It had begun to wither.
    D. It had begun to point out.

18. A. a very large typewriter
    B. a very heavy typewriter
    C. a light typewriter that's easy to carry
    D. a typewriter that can't type

19. A. go to class
    B. stay away from the class
    C. clean the classroom
    D. be the class leader

20. A. paintings
    B. drawings
    C. writings
    D. scriptures

21. A. shower
    B. brush his teeth
    C. swallow his pride
    D. take medicine

22. A. I prefer fiction.
    B. I saw it on TV.
    C. Facts are everywhere.
    D. Yes, it is true.

23. A. There were many trees close together.
    B. There were only little trees in the forest.
    C. There were very few trees.
    D. There was a thick fog in the forest.

24. A. milk B. juice
C. a soft drink D. alcohol

25. A. She has ten feet. B. She has ten hands.
C. She has two feet. D. She has two hats.

- *Directions for questions 26-50. You will hear statements on the test CD. Select the one answer A, B, C, or D which comes closest to the meaning of the statement and mark your answer sheet.*

26. A. The voices are distinct.
B. The voices are too loud.
C. The voices are indistinct.
D. The voices are shrill.

27. A. She lent money to the bank.
B. She borrowed money from the bank.
C. Her bank credit is poor.
D. She earns a lot of money for the bank.

28. A. Please, take a nap.
B. Please, sign this registration form.
C. Please, change your name.
D. Please, sign your name.

29. A. He gets used to working.
B. He works for a company that sells vacuum cleaners.
C. He worked for an outfit that sold vacuum cleaners.
D. He never works for a company.

30. A. She has already tried her best.
    B. She works too hard.
    C. She has the excuse to do better.
    D. She has the potential to do better.

31. A. He will forget it.
    B. He will present it.
    C. He will ignore it.
    D. He will absorb it.

32. A. They must find the weapons.
    B. The must steal the weapons.
    C. They must return the weapons.
    D. They must make the weapons.

33. A. It is made of light methane.
    B. It is made of heavy metal.
    C. It is made of wood.
    D. It is made of light metal.

34. A. A good teacher distinguishes students.
    B. A good teacher introduces students.
    C. A good teacher punishes students.
    D. A good teacher encourages students.

35. A. They were unfriendly.
    B. They met in a meeting.
    C. They arranged an appointment.
    D. They met unexpectedly.

36. A. One must prove who one is.
    B. One must join the army.
    C. One must dedicate oneself.
    D. One must be able to see.

37. A. They will be evaluated.
    B. They will be outfitted with special weapons.
    C. They will be admired. D. They will be special.

38. A. He is a man of integrity.
    B. He is very faithful to his wife.
    C. He is an honest civilian.
    D. He is a principal of a school.

39. A. It will do you harm. B. It will not work.
    C. It won't hurt you. D. It might hurt you.

40. A. Only some students like him.
    B. He teaches jokes.
    C. He knows interesting stories.
    D. His style of teaching is interesting.

41. A. They should not touch. B. They should be covered.
    C. They should be cut.
    D. They should be taken away.

42. A. The two files are the same.
    B. The two files are prime.
    C. The two files are distinct.
    D. The two files are competent.

43. A. She glanced at the program last night.
B. She didn't like last night's program.
C. She commended the program last night.
D. She fell asleep early last night.

44. A. He always makes a lot of noise.
B. There is constant noise from his neighbors.
C. He doesn't know where the noise is coming from.
D. His neighbors are moving away.

45. A. The plastic was inside the weapon.
B. The weapon was used to cut plastic.
C. The weapon was covered with plastic.
D. The weapon was colorful.

46. A. The wind and the wheat were damaged.
B. The wheat damaged the wind.
C. The wind did not hurt the wheat.
D. The wheat did not hurt the wind.

47. A. He flies for the airlines.
B. He flies occasionally.
C. He only flies for recreation.
D. He never flies on a Sunday.

48. A. He had a poor time.
B. He had an accident.
C. He enjoyed his trip.
D. He is going on a trip.

49. A. He bought a salad. B. He bought the store.
C. He bought a fish. D. He bought a fishing pole.

50. A. They took it to the warehouse.
B. They went and got it at the warehouse.
C. They brought it home from the warehouse.
D. They packed it up.

● *Directions for questions 51-60. You will hear dialogs on the test CD. Select the correct answer A, B, C, or D and mark your answer sheet.*

51. A. She wanted to exhibit her crafts.
B. She'd rather go somewhere else.
C. She saw the exhibition months ago.
D. She's sorry to have missed the exhibit.

52. A. Pay several bills. B. Phone the electric company.
C. Pay less rent. D. Make fewer telephone calls.

53. A. They would see better from a different row.
B. It isn't hard to see from his seat.
C. He would rather not move from his place.
D. He'll switch places with the woman.

54. A. He's sure the new chef is better.
B. He wonders whether the new chef is an improvement.
C. He hopes the new chef will stay longer.
D. He's going to see the new chef.

55. A. There's no more work for anyone to do.
B. No one is willing to work with them.
C. The woman knows several people on the committee.
D. The woman should be on the committee.

56. A. Her translations are good.
B. She isn't around today.
C. She can't see very well.
D. It would take her two days to do it.

57. A. She'll repeat what he said.
B. She'll tell the man how she feels.
C. She agrees with the man.
D. She plans to stay.

58. A. She couldn't get the right-sized jacket.
B. The skis were sold.
C. She wouldn't go outside without a jacket.
D. The shop was closed.

59. A. He hasn't eaten any sandwiches.
B. He's too thirsty to eat another sandwich.
C. He thinks the first sandwich was better than this one.
D. He'd like the same kind of sandwich as the last one.

60. A. There won't be enough chairs left.
B. They don't need any more chairs.
C. They're buying only what they need.
D. There is enough room for them both.

ECL 聽力測驗⑪詳解

1. (**A**) Mr. Robbins liked the movie so much that he went to see it again. What did he do?
羅賓斯先生非常喜歡這部電影，所以他又去看了一次？／他做了什麼？
(A) 他看了這部電影兩次。
(B) 他想要再去看一次這部電影。
(C) 他看過這部電影一次，而且這樣就夠了。
(D) 他喜歡這部電影，所以他一再地看這部電影。

* picture ['pɪktʃɚ] *n.* 電影
twice [twaɪs] *adv.* 兩次　　once [wʌns] *adv.* 一次
again and again 一再地

2. (**B**) The aircraft encountered a powerful tail wind. From which direction did the wind come from?
這架飛機遇到一陣很強的順風。／這陣風是從哪個方向吹來的？
(A) 前方。　　(B) 後方。
(C) 旁邊。　　(D) 下面。

* aircraft ['ɛr,kræft] *n.* 飛機
encounter [ɪn'kaʊntɚ] *v.* 遇到
powerful ['paʊɚfəl] *adj.* 強的
wind [wɪnd] *n.* 風　　***tail wind*** 順風
direction [də'rɛkʃən] *n.* 方向
front [frʌnt] *n.* 前面　　side [saɪd] *n.* 旁邊
underneath [,ʌndɚ'niθ] *n.* 下方

3. (**A**) My father never drinks tea. How often does he drink tea? 我父親從來不喝茶。／他多久喝一次茶？

(A) 從不。 (B) 總是。
(C) 有時候。 (D) 每個星期二。

* tea (ti) *n.* 茶 ***How often…?*** 多久…一次？

4. (**C**) The rat's growth was amazing. What was amazing about the rat?
這隻老鼠的成長速度驚人。／這隻老鼠的什麼很驚人？

(A) 牠發瘋的方式。
(B) 牠找食物的方式。
(C) 牠長大的方式。
(D) 牠縮小的方式。

* rat (ræt) *n.* 老鼠 growth (groθ) *n.* 成長
amazing (əˈmezɪŋ) *adj.* 驚人的
get (gɛt) *v.* 變得 crazy (ˈkrezɪ) *adj.* 瘋狂的
look for 尋找

5. (**A**) Tina will be shown how to do the work. What will happen to Tina?
有人會告訴緹娜如何做這份工作。／緹娜會發生什麼事？

(A) 有人會教她如何做這份工作。
(B) 她會從工作崗位上被開除。
(C) 她會去找一份新工作。
(D) 她會辭職。

* show (ʃo) *v.* 告知 happen (ˈhæpən) *v.* 發生
fire (faɪr) *v.* 開除 quit (kwɪt) *v.* 辭職

6. (**B**) Bob will stay in the guest room. Where will he stay?
鮑伯會住在客房裡。／他會住在哪裡？

(A) 在洗手間。 (B) 在訪客的房間。
(C) 在家庭娛樂室。 (D) 在音樂廳。

* stay〔ste〕*v.* 暫住 guest〔gɛst〕*n.* 客人
guest room 客房 visitor〔ˈvɪzɪtɚ〕*n.* 訪客
rest room 洗手間 ***family room*** 家庭娛樂室
concert〔ˈkɑnsɜt〕*adj.* 音樂會用的 hall〔hɔl〕*n.* 大廳

7. (**B**) Who is most likely to use a jack?
誰最有可能使用起重機？

(A) 醫生。 (B) 技工。
(C) 老師。 (D) 小丑。

* likely〔ˈlaɪklɪ〕*adj.* 可能的 jack〔dʒæk〕*n.* 起重機
doctor〔ˈdɑktɚ〕*n.* 醫生
mechanic〔məˈkænɪk〕*n.* 技工 clown〔klaʊn〕*n.* 小丑

8. (**C**) In what time of the year does it usually snow?
在一年中的哪個時候通常會下雪？

(A) 夏天。 (B) 春天。
(C) 冬天。 (D) 秋天。

* snow〔sno〕*v.* 下雪

9. (**C**) At what gate will flight 101 arrive?
班機一〇一會抵達哪個登機門？

(A) 它是從大阪來的。 (B) 大概在二十分鐘之後。
(C) 三號登機門。 (D) B 月台。

* gate〔get〕*n.* 登機門 flight〔flaɪt〕*n.* 班機
arrive〔əˈraɪv〕*v.* 抵達 ***come in*** 到來
Osaka〔oˈsɑkə〕*n.* 大阪 platform〔ˈplæt͵fɔrm〕*n.* 月台

10. (**D**) What are you gonna do this weekend?

你這個週末要做什麼？

(A) 我喜歡這部電影。 (B) 我不喜歡離開。

(C) 那是很累人的。 (D) 我們打算要去拜訪我舅舅。

* gonna〔'gɔnə〕等於 going to，是口語化的用法。

weekend〔'wik'ɛnd〕*n.* 週末 ***go away*** 離開

tiring〔'taɪrɪŋ〕*adj.* 令人疲倦的

plan〔plæn〕*v.* 打算 visit〔'vɪzɪt〕*v.* 拜訪

uncle〔'ʌŋkḷ〕*n.* 舅舅

11. (**D**) Mrs. Salomon went to town in a cab yesterday to see her therapist. How did she go?

索羅門太太昨天搭計程車到城裡去看她的物理治療師。／她怎麼去的？

(A) 在他的車上。 (B) 搭公車。

(C) 走路。 (D) 搭計程車。

* cab〔kæb〕*n.* 計程車

therapist〔'θɛrəpɪst〕*n.* 物理治療師

on foot 步行 taxi〔'tæksɪ〕*n.* 計程車

12. (**C**) Mary was called down for being habitually late. What happened to Mary?

瑪莉因為習慣性遲到而被嚴厲地責備。／瑪莉怎麼了？

(A) 她被稱讚。 (B) 她被升官。

(C) 她被嚴厲地譴責。 (D) 她被稱讚。

* ***call down*** 嚴厲責備

habitually〔hə'bɪtʃuəlɪ〕*adv.* 習慣性地

praise〔prez〕*v.* 稱讚 promote〔prə'mot〕*v.* 升遷

reprimand〔,rɛprə'mænd〕*v.* 嚴厲地譴責

compliment〔'kɑmplə,mɛnt〕*v.* 稱讚

13. (**B**) There are many patrons in the shop. Who is in the store?
有許多顧客在這家店裡。／誰在這家店裡？
(A) 不會來這家店的人。
(B) 買東西的人。
(C) 沒買東西的人。
(D) 在這家店工作的人。
* patron〔'petrən〕*n.* 顧客

14. (**A**) Tom has tried many times to give up smoking. What does Tom want to do?
湯姆已經試了很多次要戒煙。／湯姆想要做什麼？
(A) 戒煙。　(B) 切斷香煙。
(C) 停下來，去吸煙　(D) 沉溺於吸煙。
* ***give up*** 放棄；戒　smoking〔'smokɪŋ〕*n.* 吸煙
quit〔kwɪt〕*v.* 戒；停止　***cut off*** 切斷
cigarette〔'sɪgə,rɛt〕*n.* 香煙　smoke〔smok〕*v.* 吸煙
give** oneself **to 沉溺於

15. (**A**) All at once that sky became dark and it began to rain. What does the statement mean?
天空突然變暗，然後開始下雨。／這段敘述是什麼意思？
(A) 突然下起雨來。　(B) 下大雨。
(C) 雨停了。　(D) 經常在下雨。
* ***all at once*** 突然　dark〔dɑrk〕*adj.* 暗的
statement〔'stetmənt〕*n.* 敘述
suddenly〔'sʌdn̩lɪ〕*adv.* 突然地
heavily〔'hɛvɪlɪ〕*adv.* 猛烈地；大大地
all the time 經常；一直

16. (B) The nurse removed a part of the cast on his arm. What did she do to the cast? 護士把他手臂上的石膏拆掉一部份。／護士對石膏做了什麼？

(A) 她把石膏整個拆掉。 (B) 她把一些石膏拆掉。
(C) 她把一些石膏拿來煮。 (D) 她把一些石膏賣掉。

* nurse (nɝs) *n.* 護士 remove (rɪ'muv) *v.* 拆除
cast (kæst) *n.* 石膏 arm (ɑrm) *n.* 手臂
take off 除去 cook (kʊk) *v.* 煮 sell (sɛl) *v.* 出售

17. (B) The grass had begun to appear on top of the soil. What happened to the grass?
草開始出現在土壤上。／草怎麼了？

(A) 它開始躲藏。 (B) 它開始出現。
(C) 它開始枯萎。 (D) 它開始指出。

* grass (græs) *n.* 草 appear (ə'pɪr) *v.* 出現
on top of 在…的上面 soil (sɔɪl) *n.* 土壤
hide (haɪd) *v.* 躲藏 ***show up*** 出現
wither ('wɪðɚ) *v.* 枯萎 ***point out*** 指出

18. (C) One of the students bought a portable typewriter. What kind did he get?
有個學生買了手提式打字機。／他買了哪一種？

(A) 很大一台打字機。
(B) 一台很重的打字機。
(C) 一台很輕的打字機，而且方便攜帶。
(D) 一台不能打字的打字機。

* portable ('pɔrtəbl̩) *adj.* 手提式的
typewriter ('taɪp,raɪtɚ) *n.* 打字機
heavy ('hɛvɪ) *adj.* 沉重的 light (laɪt) *adj.* 輕的
carry ('kærɪ) *v.* 攜帶 type (taɪp) *v.* 打字

19. (**A**) Helen was ordered to attend class. What did she have to do? 海倫被命令要去上課。／她必須要做什麼？

(A) 去上課。 (B) 遠離班上同學。
(C) 打掃教室。 (D) 當班長。

* order〔'ɔrdɚ〕*v.* 命令 attend〔ə'tɛnd〕*v.* 上（課）
class〔klæs〕*n.* 課程；【集合名詞】班上的同學
clean〔klin〕*v.* 打掃 leader〔'lidɚ〕*n.* 領導者
class leader 班長

20. (**B**) Ms. Lee liked the cartoons in the comic book. What were they?
李小姐喜歡漫畫書裡的漫畫。／它們是什麼？

(A) 畫作。 (B) 圖畫。
(C) 著作。 (D) 聖典。

* cartoon〔kɑr'tun〕*n.* 漫畫；卡通
comic〔'kɑmɪk〕*adj.* 漫畫的
painting〔'pentɪŋ〕*n.*（一幅）畫
drawing〔'drɔ·ɪŋ〕*n.* 圖畫 writings〔'raɪtɪŋz〕*n. pl.* 著作
scriptures〔'skrɪptʃɚz〕*n. pl.*（基督教以外的）聖典；經典

21. (**D**) Peter must swallow a pill before breakfast. What must he do before breakfast? 彼得必須在早餐前吃一顆藥丸。／他在早餐前必須要做什麼？

(A) 淋浴。 (B) 刷牙。
(C) 抑制他的自尊心。 (D) 吃藥。

* swallow〔'swɑlo〕*v.* 吞下 pill〔pɪl〕*n.* 藥丸
shower〔'ʃauɚ〕*v.* 淋浴 brush〔brʌʃ〕*v.* 刷
teeth〔tiθ〕*n. pl.* 牙齒 pride〔praɪd〕*n.* 自尊心
swallow *one's* ***pride*** 抑制自尊心 take〔tek〕*v.* 吃
medicine〔'mɛdəsn̩〕*n.* 藥物

22. (**D**) Is that a fact? 那是眞的嗎？

(A) 我比較喜歡小說。 (B) 我在電視上看到它。
(C) 到處都是事實。 (D) 是的，那是眞的。

* fact〔 fækt 〕*n.* 事實 prefer〔 prɪ'fɝ 〕*v.* 比較喜歡
fiction〔'fɪkʃən 〕*n.* 小說

23. (**A**) They walked through a thick forest. What kind of forest was it?
他們走過茂密的森林。／那是哪一種森林？

(A) 有很多樹木緊靠在一起。
(B) 那座森林裡只有小樹。
(C) 沒什麼樹的森林。
(D) 森林裡有濃霧。

* thick〔 θɪk 〕*adj.* 茂密的；濃的 forest〔'fɔrɪst 〕*n.* 森林
close〔 klos 〕*adj.* 緊密的 fog〔 fɑg 〕*n.* 霧

24. (**C**) Jenny spilled her soda. What was spilled?
珍妮的汽水灑出來了。／什麼東西灑出來？

(A) 牛奶。 (B) 果汁。
(C) 清涼飲料。 (D) 酒。

* spill〔 spɪl 〕*v.* 灑出 soda〔'sodə 〕*n.* 汽水
soft〔 sɔft 〕*adj.* 不含酒精的 drink〔 drɪŋk 〕*n.* 飲料
soft drink 清涼飲料；不含酒精的飲料
alcohol〔'ælkə,hɔl 〕*n.* 酒

25. (**C**) How many feet does she have? 她有幾隻腳？

(A) 她有十隻腳。 (B) 她有十隻手。
(C) 她有兩隻腳。 (D) 她有兩頂帽子。

* feet〔 fit 〕*n.pl.* 腳 hat〔 hæt 〕*n.* 帽子

26. (**C**) The voices aren't very clear on the tape we recorded yesterday. We'll have to re-record it.
我們昨天錄的錄音帶，聲音不是很清楚。我們必須重錄。

(A) 聲音很清楚。 (B) 聲音太大聲。
(C) 聲音很模糊。 (D) 聲音很尖銳。

* voice〔vɔɪs〕*n.* 聲音　clear〔klɪr〕*adj.* 清楚的
tape〔tep〕*n.* 錄音帶　record〔rɪ'kɔrd〕*v.* 錄音
re- 表示「再次」的字首。　distinct〔dɪ'stɪŋkt〕*adj.* 清楚的
loud〔laʊd〕*adj.* 大聲的
indistinct〔,ɪndɪ'stɪŋkt〕*adj.* 模糊的
shrill〔ʃrɪl〕*adj.* 尖銳的

27. (**B**) Ruth owes the bank a large amount of money.
露絲欠那家銀行很多錢。

(A) 她借錢給銀行。 (B) 她從銀行借錢。
(C) 她的銀行信用不佳。 (D) 她替這家銀行賺了很多錢。

* owe〔o〕*v.* 欠　amount〔ə'maʊnt〕*n.* 數量
lend〔lɛnd〕*v.* 借（出）　borrow〔'bɑro〕*v.* 借（入）
credit〔'krɛdɪt〕*n.* 信用　poor〔pʊr〕*adj.* 欠佳的
earn〔ɝn〕*v.* 賺取

28. (**D**) I need your signature on this agreement.
我需要你在這份契約上面簽名。

(A) 請小睡一下。 (B) 請在這張註冊表格上簽名。
(C) 請改名。 (D) 請簽名。

* signature〔'sɪgnətʃɚ〕*n.* 簽名
agreement〔ə'grimənt〕*n.* 契約
nap〔næp〕*n.* 小睡　sign〔saɪn〕*v.* 簽名
registration〔,rɛdʒɪ'streʃən〕*n.* 註冊；登記
form〔fɔrm〕*n.* 表格

29. (**C**) I used to work for a company that sold vacuum cleaners. 我以前是在一家賣眞空吸塵器的公司工作。

(A) 他逐漸習慣工作。

(B) 他在一家賣眞空吸塵器的公司工作。

(C) 他以前替一家賣眞空吸塵器的公司工作。

(D) 他從未在一家公司工作過。

* ***used to V.*** 以前是⋯ vacuum (ˈvækjuəm) *n.* 眞空
cleaner (ˈklinɚ) *n.* 吸塵器 ***vacuum cleaner*** 眞空吸塵器
get used to 逐漸習慣 outfit (ˈaʊtˌfɪt) *n.* 公司；企業

30. (**D**) She has the ability to do better, but she must try a little harder. 她有能力做得更好，但她必須再努力一點嘗試。

(A) 她已經盡全力了。

(B) 她太努力工作了。

(C) 她有藉口可以做得更好。

(D) 她有潛力做得更好。

* ability (əˈbɪlətɪ) *n.* 能力 ***try one's best*** 盡全力
excuse (ɪkˈskjuz) *n.* 藉口 potential (pəˈtɛnʃəl) *n.* 潛力

31. (**B**) The manager will bring up the issue at the next conference.
經理會在下次開會時把這個問題提出來。

(A) 他會忘記它。 (B) 他會提出它。

(C) 他會忽視它。 (D) 他會吸收它。

* manager (ˈmænɪdʒɚ) *n.* 經理
bring up 提出 issue (ˈɪʃjʊ) *n.* 問題
conference (ˈkɑnfərəns) *n.* 會議
present (prɪˈzɛnt) *v.* 提出 ignore (ɪgˈnor) *v.* 忽視
absorb (əbˈsɔrb) *v.* 吸收

32. (**C**) The announcement on the bulletin board told all personnel to turn in their weapons.
佈告欄上的告示要全體人員歸還武器。
(A) 他們必許找到那些武器。
(B) 他們必須偷走那些武器。
(C) <u>他們必須歸還那些武器。</u>
(D) 他們必須製造那些武器。

* announcement〔əˈnaʊnsmənt〕*n.* 告示
bulletin〔ˈbʊlətɪn〕*n.* 告示
board〔bord〕*n.* 木板；佈告牌
bulletin board 佈告欄
personnel〔ˌpɝsn̩ˈɛl〕*n.* 全體人員 ***turn in*** 歸還
weapon〔ˈwɛpən〕*n.* 武器 steal〔stil〕*v.* 偷竊

33. (**D**) The case is made of aluminum.
這個盒子是鋁製的。
(A) 它是由輕沼氣製成的。
(B) 它是由重金屬製成的。
(C) 它是由木頭製成的。
(D) <u>它是由輕金屬製成的。</u>

* case〔kes〕*n.* 盒子 ***be made of*** 由…製成
aluminum〔əˈlumɪnəm〕*n.* 鋁
methane〔ˈmɛθen〕*n.* 沼氣 heavy〔ˈhɛvɪ〕*adj.* 重的
metal〔ˈmɛtl̩〕*n.* 金屬 wood〔wʊd〕*n.* 木頭

34. (**D**) A good teacher gives confidence to students so they won't give up trying.
好老師會給學生信心，所以學生們就不會放棄嘗試。
(A) 好老師會認出學生。
(B) 好老師會介紹學生。

(C) 好老師會處罰學生。

(D) <u>好老師會鼓勵學生。</u>

* confidence 〔'kɑnfədəns〕*n.* 信心　　***give up*** 放棄
distinguish 〔dɪ'stɪŋgwɪʃ〕*v.* 認出
introduce 〔,ɪntrə'djus〕*v.* 介紹
punish 〔'pʌnɪʃ〕*v.* 處罰
encourage 〔ɪn'kɝɪdʒ〕*v.* 鼓勵

35. (**D**) David and Lisa met accidentally.
大衛和麗莎偶然遇到。

(A) 他們不友善。

(B) 他們在一場會議中遇到。

(C) 他們安排了一場約會。

(D) <u>他們意外碰面。</u>

* accidentally 〔,æksə'dɛntḷɪ〕*adv.* 偶然地
unfriendly 〔ʌn'frɛndlɪ〕*adj.* 不友善的
meeting 〔'mitɪŋ〕*n.* 會議
arrange 〔ə'rendʒ〕*v.* 安排
appointment 〔ə'pɔɪntmənt〕*n.* 約會
unexpectedly 〔,ʌnɪk'spɛktɪdlɪ〕*adv.* 意外地

36. (**A**) In the army one must be able to identify himself.
在軍隊裡，一個人一定要能證明自己。

(A) <u>一個人必須要能證明自己。</u>

(B) 一個人必須要從軍。

(C) 一個人必須要奉獻自己。

(D) 一個人必須要能看得見。

* army 〔'ɑrmɪ〕*n.* 軍隊　　identify 〔aɪ'dɛntə,faɪ〕*v.* 證明
prove 〔pruv〕*v.* 證明　　join 〔dʒɔɪn〕*v.* 參加
dedicate 〔'dɛdə,ket〕*v.* 奉獻

37. (**B**) Before they go overseas, the soldiers will be equipped with special uniforms and weapons.
在士兵們出國之前，他們會穿上特殊制服，並配上特別的武器。

(A) 他們會被評估。
(B) 他們將配備特別的武器。
(C) 他們會被讚賞。
(D) 他們會是特別的。

* overseas 〔ˈovɚˈsiz〕*adv.* 到國外
soldier 〔ˈsoldʒɚ〕*n.* 士兵
equip 〔ɪˈkwɪp〕*v.* 使穿戴 <*with*>
special 〔ˈspɛʃəl〕*adj.* 特殊的
uniform 〔ˈjunəˌfɔrm〕*n.* 制服
evaluate 〔ɪˈvæljuˌet〕*v.* 評估
outfit 〔ˈautˌfɪt〕*v.* 配備　admire 〔ədˈmaɪr〕*v.* 讚賞

38. (**A**) The general is a man of honor and principle. He's very noble.
將軍是個既正直又有原則的人。他是個很高尚的人。

(A) 他是個正直的人。
(B) 他對他妻子很忠實。
(C) 他是個誠實的人民。
(D) 他是一所學校的校長。

* general 〔ˈdʒɛnərəl〕*n.* 將軍
honor 〔ˈɑnɚ〕*n.* 榮譽心；道義　***a man of honor*** 正直的人
principle 〔ˈprɪnsəpl̩〕*n.* 原則　noble 〔ˈnobl̩〕*adj.* 高尚的
integrity 〔ɪnˈtɛgrətɪ〕*n.* 正直
faithful 〔ˈfeθfəl〕*adj.* 忠實的　honest 〔ˈɑnɪst〕*adj.* 誠實的
civilian 〔səˈvɪljən〕*n.* 平民
principal 〔ˈprɪnsəpl̩〕*n.* 校長

39. (**C**) This is a harmless joke. 這是個沒有惡意的玩笑。

(A) 它會傷害你。 (B) 它不會有效。
(C) <u>它不會傷害你。</u> (D) 它可能會傷害你。

* harmless〔'hɑrmlɪs〕*adj.* 無惡意的
joke〔dʒok〕*n.* 玩笑；笑話
harm〔hɑrm〕*n.* 傷害 ***do sb. harm*** 傷害某人
work〔wɜk〕*v.* 有效 hurt〔hɜt〕*v.* 傷害

40. (**D**) All the students like Professor Roberts. He must have an interesting manner of teaching.
所有學生都喜歡羅伯茲教授。他的教學方式一定很有趣。

(A) 只有一些學生喜歡他。
(B) 他教笑話。
(C) 他知道有趣的故事。
(D) <u>他的教學風格有趣。</u>

* professor〔prə'fɛsɚ〕*n.* 教授 manner〔'mænɚ〕*n.* 方式
style〔staɪl〕*n.* 風格

41. (**A**) Those two wires should not come into contact with one another.
這兩條電線不該互相接觸。

(A) <u>它們不應該接觸。</u>
(B) 它們應該要被蓋住。
(C) 它們應該要被切斷。
(D) 它們應該要被拿走。

* wire〔waɪr〕*n.* 電線 contact〔'kɑntækt〕*n.* 接觸
come into contact with 與…接觸
one another 互相 touch〔tʌtʃ〕*v.* 接觸
cover〔'kʌvɚ〕*v.* 覆蓋 ***take away*** 拿走

42. (**C**) I don't know why Ron put these two reports together. They're two completely separate files.
我不知道爲什麼榮恩要把這兩份報告放在一起。它們是兩份完全不同的文件。

(A) 這兩份文件是相同的。
(B) 這兩份文件是最好的。
(C) <u>這兩份文件是不同的。</u>
(D) 這兩份文件是合格的。

* ***put together*** 把…放在一起
report (rɪ'pɔrt) *n.* 報告
completely (kəm'plitlɪ) *adv.* 完全地
separate ('sɛpərɪt) *adj.* 不同的
file (faɪl) *n.* 文件　　same (sem) *adj.* 相同的
prime (praɪm) *adj.* 最好的
distinct (dɪ'stɪŋkt) *adj.* 不同的
competent ('kɑmpətənt) *adj.* 合格的

43. (**C**) Mrs. Bronson remarked that she enjoyed last night's program very much.
布朗森太太說她很喜歡昨晚的節目。

(A) 她看了一眼昨晚的節目。
(B) 她不喜歡昨晚的節目。
(C) <u>她稱讚昨晚的節目。</u>
(D) 她昨晚很早就睡著了。

* remark (rɪ'mɑrk) *v.* 說
program ('progræm) *n.* 節目
glance (glæns) *v.* 看一眼
commend (kə'mɛnd) *v.* 稱讚；推崇
asleep (ə'slip) *adj.* 睡著的　　***fall asleep*** 睡著

44. (**B**) I'm moving away because I can't stand the continuous noise from my neighbors.

我要搬走了，因爲我受不了從鄰居那邊不斷傳來的噪音。

(A) 他總是製造很多噪音。

(B) 噪音不斷從他鄰居那邊傳來。

(C) 他不知道噪音是從哪來的。

(D) 他的鄰居要搬走了。

* stand (stænd) *v.* 忍受
continuous (kən'tɪnjuəs) *adj.* 連續的；不斷的
noise (nɔɪz) *n.* 噪音　　neighbor ('nebɚ) *n.* 鄰居
constant ('kɑnstənt) *adj.* 不斷的

45. (**C**) The weapon was wrapped in plastic.

武器被包在塑膠裡。

(A) 塑膠在武器裡。

(B) 這件武器被用來切割塑膠。

(C) 這件武器被塑膠覆蓋著。

(D) 這件武器的色彩豐富。

* wrap (ræp) *v.* 包；裹　　plastic ('plæstɪk) *n.* 塑膠
colorful ('kʌləfəl) *adj.* 色彩豐富的

46. (**C**) The wheat wasn't damaged by the wind.

這陣風沒有使小麥受損。

(A) 風和小麥都受損了。

(B) 小麥使風受損。

(C) 這陣風沒有使小麥受損。

(D) 小麥沒有使風受損。

* wheat (hwit) *n.* 小麥　　damage ('dæmɪdʒ) *v.* 受損
wind (wɪnd) *n.* 風

47. (**A**) Mr. Ron is a commercial pilot.
榮恩先生是民航飛行員。

(A) 他替航空公司駕駛飛機。
(B) 他偶爾駕駛飛機。
(C) 他只爲了娛樂而開飛機。
(D) 他從來沒有在星期日開過飛機。

* commercial (kə'mɜʃəl) *adj.* 商業的
pilot ('paɪlət) *n.* 飛行員 ***commercial pilot*** 民航飛行員
fly (flaɪ) *v.* 駕駛飛機 airlines ('ɛr,laɪnz) *n.* 航空公司
occasionally (ə'keʒənl̩ɪ) *adv.* 偶爾
recreation (,rɛkrɪ'eʃən) *n.* 娛樂

48. (**C**) Mary asked Joe if he had a nice trip. Joe answered yes. 瑪莉問喬旅行是否愉快。喬回答說是。

(A) 他玩得不愉快。 (B) 他發生意外。
(C) 他玩得很愉快。 (D) 他要去旅行。

* ***enjoy*** *one's* ***trip*** 玩得很愉快 ***go on a trip*** 去旅行

49. (**D**) Jack went to a sporting goods store to purchase a fishing rod.
傑克到運動用品店去買一根釣竿。

(A) 他去買一份沙拉。
(B) 他買下這間店。
(C) 他買了一條魚。
(D) 他買了一根釣竿。

* sporting ('spɔrtɪŋ) *adj.* 運動的 goods (gʊdz) *n. pl.* 商品
purchase ('pɜtʃəs) *v.* 購買 rod (rɑd) *n.* 釣竿
fishing rod 釣竿 (= *fishing pole*)
salad ('sæləd) *n.* 沙拉 pole (pol) *n.* 竿

50. (**B**) They picked up the package at the warehouse.
他們在倉庫撿到這個包裹。

(A) 他們把它拿到倉庫去。

(B) 他們到倉庫去拿這個包裹。

(C) 他們把這個包裹從倉庫帶回家。

(D) 他們把它打包。

* ***pick up*** 拿起；拾起　package〔ˈpækɪdʒ〕*n.* 包裹
warehouse〔ˈwɛr,haus〕*n.* 倉庫
pack〔pæk〕*v.* 打包　***pack up*** 打包

51. (**D**) M：The Native American Craft Exhibit closed this afternoon.
W：Oh no! I've wanted to see that for months!
What does the woman mean?
男：印第安人手工藝展到今天下午結束。
女：噢，不！我想去看這個展覽已經想了好幾個月！
這位女士的意思是？

(A) 她想要展示她的飛機。

(B) 她寧願去其他地方。

(C) 她幾個月前就看過這場展覽。

(D) 她很遺憾錯過這場展覽。

* native〔ˈnetɪv〕*adj.* 本土的
Native American 印第安人
craft〔kræft〕*n.*【不可數名詞】手工藝；【可數名詞】飛機
exhibit〔ɪgˈzɪbɪt〕*n.* 展覽會　*v.* 展示
close〔kloz〕*v.* 結束；停止
rather〔ˈræðɚ〕*adv.* 寧願　else〔ɛls〕*adj.* 其他的
exhibition〔,ɛksəˈbɪʃən〕*n.* 展覽會
miss〔mɪs〕*v.* 錯過

52. (**A**) M：Boy, it's the first of the month already! I'd better pay my phone bill.
W：Shouldn't you pay the rent and the electricity bill, too?
What does the woman suggest that the man do?
男：哇，已經是這個月的第一天了！我最好去繳我的電話費。
女：你是不是應該把房租和電費也繳一繳？
那位女士建議那位男士做什麼？
(A) 付幾張帳單。
(B) 打電話給電力公司。
(C) 少付一點房租。
(D) 少打幾通電話。

* boy〔 bɔɪ 〕*interj.* 哇　***had better*** 最好
phone〔 fon 〕*n.* 電話　*v.* 打電話
bill〔 bɪl 〕*n.* 帳單；帳款　rent〔 rɛnt 〕*n.* 租金
electricity〔 ɪ,lɛk'trɪsətɪ 〕*n.* 電
suggest〔 sə'dʒɛst 〕*v.* 建議
several〔'sɛvərəl 〕*adj.* 幾個的
electric〔 ɪ'lɛktrɪk 〕*adj.* 電的　call〔 kɔl 〕*n.* 打電話

53. (**A**) W：During intermission, let's change our seats.
M：It is hard to see from back here, isn't it?
What does the man imply?
女：我們休息時間來換個位子。
男：從後面這裡很難看到對不對？
這位男士在暗示什麼？
(A) 他們從別排可以看得比較清楚。
(B) 從他的位子不難看到。

(C) 他寧願不要從他的座位移開。
(D) 他會和那位女士交換位子。

* intermission (ˌɪntəˈmɪʃən) *n.* 休息時間
seat (sit) *n.* 座位 imply (ɪmˈplaɪ) *v.* 暗示
different (ˈdɪfərənt) *adj.* 不同的
row (ro) *n.* 一排 place (ples) *n.* 座席
switch (swɪtʃ) *v.* 交換

54. (**B**) W：There's a new chef at the restaurant in the shopping mall.
M：It remains to be seen whether the new one is any better than the old one.
What does the man mean?
女：購物中心裡的那家餐廳來了一位新廚師。
男：那還要看看新的廚師有沒有比舊的好。
那位男士的意思是？
(A) 他很肯定新的廚師比較好。
(B) 他想知道新的廚師是否比較好。
(C) 他希望新的廚師可以待久一點。
(D) 他要去看新的廚師。

* chef (ʃɛf) *n.* 廚師
restaurant (ˈrɛstərənt) *n.* 餐廳
mall (mɔl) *n.* 購物中心 ***shopping mall*** 購物中心
remain (rɪˈmen) *v.* 尚待
whether (ˈhwɛðə) *conj.* 是否
sure (ʃʊr) *adj.* 確定的
wonder (ˈwʌndə) *v.* 想知道
improvement (ɪmˈpruvmənt) *n.* 更進步者

55. (**D**) W：I wonder who'd be willing to work on this committee.

M：Well, you know more about it than anyone.

What does the man mean?

女：我想知道誰會願意在這個委員會工作。

男：嗯，妳比任何人都了解這個委員會。

這位男士的意思是？

(A) 沒有多餘的工作可以給任何人做了。

(B) 沒有人願意和他們一起工作。

(C) 那位女士認識委員會裡的幾個人。

(D) 那位女士應該去當委員會的委員。

* willing〔ˈwɪlɪŋ〕*adj.* 願意的

committee〔kəˈmɪtɪ〕*n.* 委員會

be on the committee 當委員之一

56. (**B**) M：Do you think Marcia would translate this paragraph for me?

W：I haven't seen her today.

What does the woman imply about Marcia?

男：妳認為瑪莎會幫我翻譯這段文章嗎？

女：我今天還沒看到她。

關於瑪莎，這位女士在暗示什麼？

(A) 她翻譯得很好。 (B) 她今天不在附近。

(C) 她看得不是很清楚。

(D) 她要花兩天的時間來做這件事。

* translate〔trænsˈlet〕*v.* 翻譯

paragraph〔ˈpærəˌgræf〕*n.* 文章

translation〔trænsˈleʃən〕*n.* 翻譯

around〔əˈraʊnd〕*adv.* 在附近 take〔tek〕*v.* 花費

57. (**C**) M：Doesn't this bright clear day make you feel wonderful?

W：I'll say.

What does the woman mean?

男：妳不覺得這晴朗無雲的日子很棒嗎？

女：我也有同感。

這位女士的意思是？

(A) 她會把他說的話重複一遍。

(B) 她會把她的感受告訴這位男士。

(C) 她同意這位男士的說法。　　(D) 她打算留下來。

* bright〔 braɪt 〕*adj.* 晴朗的
clear〔 klɪr 〕*adj.* 晴朗的；無雲的
wonderful〔ˈwʌndəfəl 〕*adj.* 很棒的
I'll say. 我也有同感。(= *You said it*.)
repeat〔 rɪˈpit 〕*v.* 重複　　agree〔 əˈgri 〕*v.* 同意

58. (**A**) M：Did you get the ski jacket you wanted?

W：They were all sold out of my size when I got to the shop.

What does the woman mean?

男：妳買到妳想要的滑雪夾克了嗎？

女：當我到那家店的時候，我的尺寸都賣光了。

那位女士的意思是？

(A) 她買不到尺寸正確的夾克。

(B) 滑雪板被賣掉了。

(C) 她不會不穿夾克就到外面去。

(D) 那家店關門了。

* ***ski jacket*** 滑雪裝；滑雪夾克　　***sell out*** 賣光
size〔 saɪz 〕*n.* 尺寸　　skis〔 skiz 〕*n. pl.* 滑雪板
closed〔 klozd 〕*adj.* 關門的

59. (**A**) W：Would you like another sandwich?
M：Another sandwich? I haven't had my first one yet.
What does the man say about the sandwiches?

女：你要不要再來一個三明治？
男：再一個三明治？我第一個三明治都還沒吃完。
關於那些三明治，這位男士說了什麼？

(A) 他還沒吃完任何三明治。
(B) 他太渴了，沒辦法再吃一個三明治。
(C) 他認爲第一個三明治，比這個三明治好吃。
(D) 他想要跟上一個一樣的三明治。

* ***would like*** 想要
sandwich ('sændwɪtʃ) *n.* 三明治
have (hæv) *v.* 吃　thirsty ('θɝstɪ) *adj.* 口渴的

60. (**B**) W：How many more chairs should we get for the meeting?
M：Don't we have enough by now?
What does the man imply?

女：我們還要再替這個會議拿幾張椅子？
男：現在已經有的椅子還不夠嗎？
那位男士在暗示什麼？

(A) 剩下的椅子不夠。
(B) 他們不需要更多椅子。
(C) 他們只買需要的東西。
(D) 有足夠的空間給他們兩個人。

* chair (tʃɛr) *n.* 椅子　***by now*** 現在已經
room (rum) *n.* 空間

LISTENING TEST ⑫

- *Directions for questions 1-25. You will hear questions on the test CD. Select the one item A, B, C or D which answers the question correctly, and mark your answer sheet.*

1. A. She goes on vacation.
   B. She eats food.
   C. She works at the base.
   D. She drinks water.

2. A. paper B. tree
   C. water D. food

3. A. Ignore it if you can. B. Repeat if you can.
   C. Answer it if you can. D. Ask it if you can.

4. A. Yes, I sometimes stay home.
   B. Yes, I do it because I must.
   C. Yes, I hate it.
   D. Yes, I am concerned.

5. A. He likes her teaching very much.
   B. He's not studying math these days.
   C. He doesn't like English at all.
   D. He's ready to leave school by four.

6. A. for eighty miles B. for twenty dollars
   C. for sixty minutes D. for a job

7. A. because of her remark
   B. because she is stupid
   C. because I am idiotic and lazy
   D. because she was angry

8. A. I'll carry the boxes.
   B. OK, but give it back to me later.
   C. I don't have one on me.
   D. My hands aren't here now.

9. A. how far the project had impressed
   B. how far the project had been approved
   C. when the project would take place
   D. how far the project had progressed

10. A. No, it was established over 100 years ago.
    B. One of the people from the Chicago office.
    C. Certainly, I would love to have company.
    D. Yes, he is a newcomer.

11. A. You look terrible. I'll call to get you an appointment.
    B. I saw him yesterday in the library.
    C. You can buy it in the convenience store.
    D. I feel much better now.

12. A. why he was hated
    B. why his commanding officer was late
    C. why he was late
    D. why he was so early

13. A. He is making use of it.
    B. He is taking advantage of it.
    C. He is joking about it.
    D. He is frowning at it.

14. A. A flight schedule.
    B. A Train.
    C. Lunch in a restaurant.
    D. A training schedule.

15. A. Joe asked for advice.
    B. Joe went home early.
    C. Joe went out to dinner.
    D. Joe answered his friend.

16. A. new B. yellow
    C. fast D. small

17. A. A plane departs.
    B. A plane accident happens.
    C. A plane lands.
    D. A planet explodes.

18. A. She takes mental training every week.
    B. She takes phonetics training every week.
    C. She takes physics training every week.
    D. She takes physical training every week.

19. A. medicine B. a bath
    C. a class D. a job

20. A. a place to put his car
    B. a place to live
    C. a place to work
    D. a place to keep his supplies

21. A. I think you can refuse it.
    B. Yes. You certainly deserve one.
    C. No. I think you're right.
    D. You should move it down.

22. A. for a short period of time
    B. for a long distance
    C. for a wrong period of time
    D. for a long period of time

23. A. the long one
    B. the correct one
    C. the usual one
    D. the revised one

24. A. with her baby sitter
    B. with no assistance
    C. with her mother
    D. with the help of her father

25. A. She wanted to leave.
    B. She wanted to rest.
    C. She wanted to wash.
    D. She wanted to walk.

● *Directions for questions 26-50. You will hear statements on the test CD. Select the one answer A, B, C, or D which comes closest to the meaning of the statement and mark your answer sheet.*

26. A. She will enter high school after April.
    B. She is through with high school.
    C. She is through with college.
    D. She has completed college.

27. A. The doctor will see her patient in a short time.
    B. The doctor will hit her patient in a short time.
    C. The doctor will yell at her patient in a short time.
    D. The doctor will see her patient tomorrow.

28. A. Did you find out why he didn't eat?
    B. Did you see him yesterday?
    C. Did you help him?
    D. Did you learn the reason for his lateness?

29. A. The factory exploded.
    B. The factory existed.
    C. The factory closed down.
    D. The factory expanded.

30. A. He was uncomfortable.
    B. He was unassuming.
    C. He was uncompromising.
    D. He was unbearable.

31. A. It is better. B. It is faster.
C. It is cheaper. D. It is lighter.

32. A. Shopping is easier at home.
B. Shopping is easier on the Internet.
C. Shopping is easier when the shops are close by.
D. Shopping is easier when the shops are far.

33. A. She doubts her classmate's honey.
B. She doubts her classmate's honesty.
C. She trusts her classmate's honesty.
D. She believes her classmate's honesty.

34. A. It's convenient. B. It's interesting.
C. It's modern. D. It's big.

35. A. A schedule was trained.
B. A meeting was organized.
C. A group was trained.
D. A schedule was established.

36. A. The ointment is not meant to be eaten.
B. The ointment is meant to be eaten.
C. The ointment is for babies only.
D. The ointment means animals.

37. A. She did not remember her classmate.
B. She reinforced her classmate.
C. She forgot her classmate.
D. She saw her classmate.

38. A. She came across a bus.
    B. She ran after a bus.
    C. She went across the road.
    D. She was hit and crushed by a bus.

39. A. She must go every day.
    B. She must go on Friday.
    C. She must go today.
    D. She must go tomorrow.

40. A. He united the order.
    B. He issued the order.
    C. He minimized the order.
    D. He broadcasted the order.

41. A. The descent was thrilling.
    B. The crowd watched their ascent.
    C. The balloons were excited.
    D. The crowd saw them exploded.

42. A. It was the ammunition tower area.
    B. It was the ammunition prison area.
    C. It was the ammunition storage area.
    D. It was the ammunition expense area.

43. A. He doesn't cry.
    B. He doesn't correct.
    C. He doesn't compete.
    D. He doesn't cooperate.

44. A. Bill hates going to the movies.
    B. Bill wants snacks whenever he goes to the movies.
    C. Bill wants company when he goes to the movies.
    D. Bill fears darkness.

45. A. It was easy for her to tie her sneaker.
    B. It was difficult for her to tie her sneaker.
    C. It was easy for him to tie his sneaker.
    D. It was difficult for her to lie her sneaker.

46. A. His car is in fine condition.
    B. His car is in air conditioning.
    C. His car is in rich condition.
    D. His car is in poor condition.

47. A. Plastic is made from insects.
    B. Plastic is made from insecticides.
    C. Plastic is made from petroleum.
    D. Plastic is made from products.

48. A. She won a pink car.
    B. She rented a pink car.
    C. She likes to talk about her pink car.
    D. Ann would rather have a pink car.

49. A. The train is on platform three.
    B. The train for Moscow is leaving.
    C. The number of the train to Moscow is 110.
    D. The train is leaving for Saint Petersburg.

50. A. People are being asked to leave the theater.
    B. The ticket office is going to be closed.
    C. People are being asked to return to their seats.
    D. The lounge is going to be closed.

- *Directions for questions 51-60. You will hear dialogs on the test CD. Select the correct answer A, B, C, or D and mark your answer sheet.*

51. A. an animal B. a fish
    C. some kind of bird D. a plant

52. A. Carol knows where it is.
    B. Carol can go there very easily.
    C. Carol likes the selection there.
    D. Carol has often gone there.

53. A. It is parked there.
    B. It is a Chevrolet.
    C. It has a license plate.
    D. It has its lights on.

54. A. It got very hot.
    B. The pipe broke.
    C. It got too cold.
    D. It ran out of water.

55. A. his birthday B. travel abroad
    C. immigration D. citizenship

56. A. He wants to be in contact with her.
    B. The woman should keep him in mind while on the trip.
    C. He wants the woman to have a good time.
    D. He wants the woman to comce back soon.

57. A. The man just finished making it.
    B. It is so soft that the man can't handle it.
    C. It is hard but the man doesn't mind.
    D. It is comfortable but the man doesn't like it.

58. A. She agrees with the administration's decision.
    B. She didn't know about the administration's decision.
    C. The administration is getting very strict with smokers.
    D. The administration is cracking down the walls of the smoking section.

59. A. The man should reconsider the date of the party.
    B. The man should invite twice as many people as before.
    C. The man should have a party on December 5th.
    D. The man should have a party today.

60. A. The man should deposit his money into a bank account.
    B. He should write down all his purchases.
    C. He should buy more things.
    D. He should buy less.

ECL 聽力測驗⑫詳解

1. (**C**) How did she make her living? 她如何維生？

(A) 她去渡假。 (B) 她吃食物。
(C) 她在基地工作。 (D) 她喝水。

* living ('lɪvɪŋ) *n.* 生活 ***make one's living*** 謀生
vacation (ve'keʃən) *n.* 休假 ***go on vacation*** 去渡假
base (bes) *n.* 基地

2. (**C**) What do theses pipes transport?
這些管子是運送什麼的？

(A) 紙。 (B) 樹。
(C) 水。 (D) 食物。

* pipe (paɪp) *n.* 管子 transport (træns'pɔrt) *v.* 運送

3. (**C**) What should you do when you're asked a question?
你被問問題的時候應該怎麼做？

(A) 如果可以就忽視它。 (B) 如果可以就重複它。
(C) 如果可以就回答它。 (D) 如果可以就問它。

* ignore (ɪg'nor) *v.* 忽視 repeat (rɪ'pit) *v.* 重複
answer ('ænsɚ) *v.* 回答

4. (**D**) Do you worry about your position?
你擔心你的工作嗎？

(A) 我有時候待在家裡。
(B) 是的，我會這樣做是因爲我必須這樣做。
(C) 是的，我討厭它。 (D) 是的，我很擔心。

* worry ('wɝɪ) *v.* 擔心 position (pə'zɪʃən) *n.* 工作
concerned (kən'sɝnd) *adj.* 擔心的

5. (**A**) What does your son think about his new math teacher? 你兒子對新來的數學老師有何看法？

(A) 他很喜歡她的教學。　(B) 他在那段日子沒有唸數學。
(C) 他一點都不喜歡英文。　(D) 他準備好四點要離開學校。

* math (mæθ) *n.* 數學　teaching (ˈtitʃɪŋ) *n.* 教學
not…at all 一點也不　ready (ˈrɛdɪ) *adj.* 準備好的
leave (liv) *v.* 離開

6. (**C**) How long a period of time may I study this book?
我應該唸這本書唸多久？

(A) 八十英哩。　(B) 二十元。
(C) 六十分鐘。　(D) 爲了一份工作。

* period (ˈpɪrɪəd) *n.* 時期　mile (maɪl) *n.* 英哩
job (dʒab) *n.* 工作

7. (**A**) Sara told me that I was stupid and lazy. Why was I angry at Sara?
莎拉說我又笨又懶。／我爲什麼對莎拉發脾氣？

(A) 因爲她說的話。　(B) 因爲她很笨。
(C) 因爲我又蠢又懶。　(D) 因爲她生氣了。

* stupid (ˈstjupɪd) *adj.* 笨的　lazy (ˈlezɪ) *adj.* 懶的
angry (ˈæŋgrɪ) *adj.* 生氣的　remark (rɪˈmark) *n.* 話
idiotic (ˌɪdɪˈatɪk) *adj.* 愚蠢的

8. (**A**) Could you give me a hand? 你可以幫我嗎？

(A) 我會搬這個箱子。
(B) 好的，但是以後要把它還給我。
(C) 我身上沒有手。　(D) 我的手現在不在這裡。

* hand (hænd) *n.* 幫助；手　***give sb. a hand*** 幫忙某人
carry (ˈkærɪ) *v.* 搬運　box (baks) *n.* 箱子
give back 歸還　later (ˈletɚ) *adv.* 以後

9. (**D**) Miss Madonna asked us what stage our project was in. What did she want to know?

瑪丹娜小姐問我們的計畫進行到哪個階段。／她想知道什麼？

(A) 這個計畫給人的印象有多深。

(B) 這個計畫得到何種程度的肯定。

(C) 這個計畫何時要舉辦。

(D) 這個計畫進行到什麼程度。

* stage (stedʒ) *n.* 階段
project (′prɑdʒɛkt) *n.* 計畫
How far…? …到什麼程度？
impress (ɪm′prɛs) *v.* 給（人）印象
approve (ə′pruv) *v.* 肯定　***take place*** 舉辦
progress (prə′grɛs) *v.* 進行

10. (**B**) Who is your company's new president?

你們公司的新董事長是誰？

(A) 不，它是在一百多年前創立的。

(B) 從芝加哥辦公室來的人之一。

(C) 當然，我很想要有同伴。

(D) 是的，他是新來的。

* company (′kʌmpənɪ) *n.* 公司；同伴
president (′prɛzədənt) *n.* 董事長
establish (ə′stæblɪʃ) *v.* 創立
Chicago (ʃɪ′kɑgo) *n.* 芝加哥【美國第二大城】
certainly (′sɝtn̩lɪ) *adv.* 當然
newcomer (′nju′kʌmɚ) *n.* 新來的人

11. (**A**) I got a fever. I should see a doctor.
我發燒了。我應該要去看醫生。

(A) 你看起來很糟糕。我幫你打電話去預約。
(B) 我昨天在圖書館看到他。
(C) 你可以在便利商店買到它。
(D) 我現在覺得好多了。

* fever ['fivɚ] *n.* 發燒
terrible ['tɛrəbl̩] *adj.* 很糟的
call [kɔl] *v.* 打電話
appointment [ə'pɔɪntmənt] *n.* 預約
library ['laɪ,brɛrɪ] *n.* 圖書館
convenience [kən'vinjəns] *adj.* 便利的
convenience store 便利商店

12. (**C**) Major Payne gave his commanding officer his reason for being tardy. What did Major Payne tell the officer?
沛恩少校把遲到的原因告訴他的指揮官。／沛恩少校告訴那位軍官什麼？

(A) 他被討厭的原因。
(B) 他延遲付款的原因。
(C) 他的指揮官遲到的原因。
(D) 他這麼早到的原因。

* major ['medʒɚ] *n.* 少校
commanding [kə'mændɪŋ] *adj.* 指揮的
officer ['ɔfəsɚ] *n.* 軍官
a commanding officer 指揮官
reason ['rizn̩] *n.* 理由　　tardy ['tardɪ] *adj.* 遲到的
payment ['pemənt] *n.* 支付

13. (**C**) He is making fun of her new hairdo. What is he doing?
他取笑她的新髮型。／他正在做什麼？

(A) 他在利用它。　(B) 他在利用它。
(C) 他在取笑它。　(D) 他對它皺眉頭。

* ***make fun of*** 嘲笑　hairdo〔'hɛr,du〕*n.* 髮型
make use of 利用　advantage〔əd'væntɪdʒ〕*n.* 好處
take advantage of 利用　joke〔dʒok〕*v.* 取笑
frown〔fraʊn〕*v.* 對…皺眉頭

14. (**B**) Train number 144 bound for New York has been delayed 40 minutes. What is this statement about?
開往紐約的 144 號火車延誤四十分鐘。／這段敘述是關於什麼？

(A) 班機時程表。　(B) 火車。
(C) 在餐廳的午餐　(D) 訓練時程表。

* bound〔baʊnd〕*adj.* 準備前往…的
delay〔dɪ'le〕*v.* 延誤
statement〔'stetmənt〕*n.* 敘述
flight〔flaɪt〕*n.* 班機
schedule〔'skɛdʒul〕*n.* 時程表
restaurant〔'rɛstərənt〕*n.* 餐廳
training〔'trenɪŋ〕*n.* 訓練

15. (**A**) Joe consulted his friend yesterday. What did Joe do?
喬昨天去徵求他朋友的意見。／喬做了什麼？

(A) 喬去請求建議。　(B) 喬很早回家。
(C) 喬出門吃晚餐。　(D) 喬回答他朋友。

* consult〔kən'sʌlt〕*v.* 徵求…的意見
advice〔əd'vaɪs〕*n.* 建議

16. (**B**) What color is James' card?
詹姆士的卡是什麼顏色？

(A) 新的。 (B) 黃的。
(C) 快的。 (D) 小的。

* yellow〔'jɛlo〕*adj.* 黃色

17. (**B**) When a plane accident occurs, most people are killed. What's the main cause of death?
當飛機失事時，大部分的人會喪生。／死亡的主因是什麼？

(A) 飛機起飛。 (B) 發生飛機失事。
(C) 飛機降落。 (D) 飛機爆炸。

* plane〔plen〕*n.* 飛機 accident〔'æksədənt〕*n.* 意外
occur〔ə'kɝ〕*v.* 發生 kill〔kɪl〕*v.* 使喪生
main〔men〕*adj.* 主要的 cause〔kɔz〕*n.* 原因
death〔dɛθ〕*n.* 死亡 depart〔dɪ'pɑrt〕*v.* 出發；離去
happen〔'hæpən〕*v.* 發生 land〔lænd〕*v.* 著陸；降落
explode〔ɪk'splod〕*v.* 爆炸

18. (**D**) Wilma spends two hours each week in physical training. What does Wilma do?
威瑪每星期花兩個小時作體能訓練。／威瑪做什麼？

(A) 她每星期作心智訓練。
(B) 她每星期作語音訓練。
(C) 她每星期作物理訓練。
(D) 她每星期作體能訓練。

* spend〔spɛnd〕*v.* 花費 physical〔'fɪzɪkḷ〕*adj.* 身體的
mental〔'mɛntḷ〕*adj.* 心理的；智力的
phonetics〔fo'nɛtɪks〕*n.* 語音學
physics〔'fɪzɪks〕*n.* 物理學

19. (**B**) Jenna takes a shower everyday. What does she take?
珍娜每天都淋浴。／她每天都做什麼？
(A) 吃藥。 (B) 洗澡。
(C) 上課。 (D) 工作。
* shower〔ˈʃauɚ〕*n.* 淋浴 medicine〔ˈmɛdəsn̩〕*n.* 藥物
bath〔bæθ〕*n.* 洗澡

20. (**B**) Mr. David is building a house. What is he building?
大衛先生正在蓋一棟房子。／他正在蓋什麼？
(A) 放車的地方。 (B) 住的地方。
(C) 工作的地方。 (D) 存放日常用品的地方。
* build〔bɪld〕*v.* 建築 keep〔kip〕*v.* 存放
supplies〔səˈplaɪz〕*n. pl.* 日常用品

21. (**B**) Do you think I should ask for a raise?
你覺得我應該要求加薪嗎？
(A) 我認為你可以拒絕它。
(B) 對。你當然值得被加薪。
(C) 不。我想你是對的。
(D) 你應該把它降級。
* raise〔rez〕*n.* 加薪 refuse〔rɪˈfjuz〕*v.* 拒絕
deserve〔dɪˈzɝv〕*v.* 值得 ***move down*** 降級

22. (**D**) Jenny will be working for an extended period of time. How long will she be working?
珍妮會長期工作。／她會工作多久？
(A) 短暫的時間。 (B) 長距離。
(C) 錯誤的時期。 (D) 長期。
* extended〔ɪkˈstɛndɪd〕*adj.* 長期的
distance〔ˈdɪstəns〕*n.* 距離 wrong〔rɔŋ〕*adj.* 錯誤的

23. (**B**) Be sure you use the proper form.

要確定你用的是正確的表格。

(A) 長的表格。 (B) 正確的表格。
(C) 經常用的表格。 (D) 改正過的表格。

* sure〔 ʃur 〕*adj.* 確定的
proper〔ˈprɑpɚ〕*adj.* 正確的；適當的
form〔 fɔrm 〕*n.* 表格
correct〔 kəˈrɛkt 〕*adj.* 正確的
usual〔ˈjuʒuəl〕*adj.* 經常的 revise〔 rɪˈvaɪz 〕*v.* 改正

24. (**B**) This pupil works independently of others. How does she work?

這名學生單獨工作，沒和別人一起。／她怎麼工作？

(A) 和她的臨時保母一起。
(B) 沒有任何協助。
(C) 和她媽媽一起。
(D) 她父親幫她。

* pupil〔ˈpjupḷ〕*n.* 學生
independently〔ˌɪndɪˈpɛndəntlɪ〕*adv.* 獨立地；單獨地
baby sitter 臨時保母
assistance〔 əˈsɪstəns 〕*n.* 協助

25. (**B**) Why did Mrs. White sit down?

懷特太太爲何要坐下？

(A) 她想要離開。 (B) 她想要休息。
(C) 她想要去洗手。 (D) 她想要走一走。

* rest〔 rɛst 〕*v.* 休息 wash〔 wɑʃ 〕*v.* 洗手

26. (**B**) Maggie has completed high school and will go to college in April. 瑪姬已經完成高中學業，即將在四月份進入大學。

(A) 她將在四月之後進入高中。

(B) 她完成高中學業。

(C) 她完成大學學業。

(D) 她完成大學學業。

* complete [kəmˈplit] *v.* 完成　college [ˈkɑlɪdʒ] *n.* 大學
April [ˈeprəl] *n.* 四月　enter [ˈɛntɚ] *v.* 進入
be through with 完成

27. (**A**) The psychiatrist told her patient that she'd see him in a moment. 精神病醫師告訴她的病人說，她會馬上幫他看診。

(A) 醫生不久就會替她的病人看診。

(B) 醫生不久就會打她的病人。

(C) 醫生不久就會對她的病人大吼。

(D) 醫生明天就會替她的病人看診。

* psychiatrist [saɪˈkaɪətrɪst] *n.* 精神病醫師
patient [ˈpeʃənt] *n.* 病人　moment [ˈmomənt] *n.* 分鐘
in a moment 很快；馬上　***in a short time*** 不久
hit [hɪt] *v.* 打　yell [jɛl] *v.* 大吼

28. (**D**) Did you discover what caused his tardiness?
你知道是什麼原因使他遲到嗎？

(A) 你知道他爲什麼不吃嗎？

(B) 你昨天有看到他嗎？

(C) 你有幫他嗎？

(D) 你知道他遲到的原因嗎？

* discover [dɪˈskʌvɚ] *v.* 發現；知道　cause [kɔz] *v.* 導致
tardiness [ˈtɑrdɪnɪs] *n.* 遲到　***find out*** 知道；發現
learn [lɝn] *v.* 知道　lateness [ˈletnɪs] *n.* 遲到

29. (**A**) The factory experienced an explosion.
這家工廠經歷了一場爆炸。

(A) 工廠爆炸了。　(B) 工廠存在。
(C) 工廠關閉了。　(D) 工廠擴大了。

* factory〔ˈfæktrɪ〕*n.* 工廠
experience〔ɪkˈspɪrɪəns〕*v.* 經歷
explosion〔ɪkˈsploʒən〕*n.* 爆炸
exist〔ɪgˈzɪst〕*v.* 存在　***close down*** 關閉
expand〔ɪkˈspænd〕*v.* 擴大

30. (**A**) The hot weather bothered the man very much.
炎熱的天氣使這位男士感到非常困擾。

(A) 他覺得傷腦筋。　(B) 他很謙虛。
(C) 他很頑固。　(D) 他令人難以忍受。

* weather〔ˈwɛðɚ〕*n.* 天氣　bother〔ˈbɑðɚ〕*v.* 困擾
uncomfortable〔ʌnˈkʌmfɚtəbl̩〕*adj.* 傷腦筋的；不舒服的
unassuming〔ˌʌnəˈsumɪŋ〕*adj.* 謙虛的
uncompromising〔ʌnˈkɑmprəˌmaɪzɪŋ〕*adj.* 頑固的
unbearable〔ʌnˈbɛrəbl̩〕*adj.* 難以忍受的

31. (**D**) Hot air is not as dense as cool air.
熱空氣的密度沒有冷空氣大。

(A) 熱空氣比較好。　(B) 熱空氣比較快。
(C) 熱空氣比較便宜。　(D) 熱空氣比較輕。

* dense〔dɛns〕*adj.* 密集的；濃厚的
cool〔kul〕*adj.* 涼的
cheaper〔ˈtʃipɚ〕*adj.* 比較便宜的
lighter〔ˈlaɪtɚ〕*adj.* 比較輕的

32. (**C**) It's more practical for everyone to shop near their homes. 對每個人來說，到住家附近購物是比較可行的。

(A) 在家裡購物比較容易。

(B) 在網路上購物比較容易。

(C) <u>當商店就在附近時，購物會比較容易。</u>

(D) 當商店很遠時，購物會比較容易。

* practical〔ˈpræktɪkl̩〕*adj.* 確實可行的
shop〔ʃɑp〕*v.* 購物　　Internet〔ˈɪntɚˌnɛt〕*n.* 網路
close by 在附近　　far〔fɑr〕*adj.* 遠的

33. (**B**) Jenny mistrusts her classmate.
珍妮不信任她同學。

(A) 她懷疑她同學的愛人。

(B) <u>她懷疑她同學的誠實。</u>

(C) 她相信她同學的誠實。

(D) 她相信她同學的誠實。

* mistrust〔mɪsˈtrʌst〕*v.* 不信任
classmate〔ˈklæsˌmet〕*n.* 同班同學
doubt〔daʊt〕*v.* 懷疑　　honey〔ˈhʌnɪ〕*n.* 愛人
honesty〔ˈɑnɪstɪ〕*n.* 誠實　　trust〔trʌst〕*v.* 相信

34. (**D**) We landed at the airport in New York. It's huge.
我們在紐約機場降落。那裡眞大。

(A) 它很方便。　　(B) 它很有趣。

(C) 它很現代化。　　(D) <u>它很大。</u>

* airport〔ˈɛrˌport〕*n.* 機場　　huge〔hjudʒ〕*adj.* 巨大的
convenient〔kənˈvinjənt〕*adj.* 方便的
interesting〔ˈɪntrɪstɪŋ〕*adj.* 有趣的
modern〔ˈmɑdɚn〕*adj.* 現代化的

35. (**D**) The group set up a meeting schedule.
這個團體提出會議時間表。

(A) 時間表被訓練。 (B) 會議籌畫好了。
(C) 一個團體被訓練。 (D) 建立了一個時間表。

* group〔 grup 〕*n.* 團體 ***set up*** 提出（計畫等）
schedule〔ˈskɛdʒul〕*n.* 時間表
train〔 tren 〕*v.* 訓練 organize〔ˈɔrgəˌnaɪz〕*v.* 籌畫
establish〔əˈstæblɪʃ〕*v.* 建立

36. (**A**) The ointment is for external usage.
這條藥膏是外用的。

(A) 這條藥膏不應該拿來吃。
(B) 這條藥膏應該拿來吃。
(C) 這條藥膏只限嬰兒使用。
(D) 這條藥膏的意思是動物。

* ointment〔ˈɔɪntmənt〕*n.* 藥膏
external〔ɪkˈstɝnl̩〕*adj.* 外部的
usage〔ˈjusɪdʒ〕*n.* 使用 mean〔 min 〕*v.* 意思是
be meant to V. 應該做

37. (**D**) Jane recognized her classmate at the circus.
珍在馬戲團認出她同學。

(A) 她不記得她同學。
(B) 她加強她同學。
(C) 她忘記她同學。
(D) 她看到她同學。

* recognize〔ˈrɛkəgˌnaɪz〕*v.* 認出
circus〔ˈsɝkəs〕*n.* 馬戲團
reinforce〔ˌriɪnˈfɔrs〕*v.* 加強

38. (**D**) The old woman was run over by a bus and killed.
這名老婦人被公車輾死。

(A) 她發現一輛公車。
(B) 她追一輛公車。
(C) 她穿越馬路。
(D) <u>她被公車壓死。</u>

* ***run over*** 輾過　***come across*** 偶然發現
run after 追逐　***go across*** 穿越
hit (hɪt) *v.* 撞到　crush (krʌʃ) *v.* 壓扁

39. (**C**) Mrs. Shelly has to go to the beach today.
雪莉太太今天必須到海邊去。

(A) 她必須每天去。
(B) 她星期五必須去。
(C) <u>她必須今天去。</u>
(D) 她必須明天去。

* beach (bitʃ) *n.* 海邊

40. (**B**) The order to attack was given out by the commander.
指揮官發布了攻擊的命令。

(A) 他統一命令。
(B) <u>他發布命令。</u>
(C) 他把命令縮到最小。
(D) 他廣播命令。

* order ('ɔrdɚ) *n.* 命令　attack (ə'tæk) *v.* 攻擊
give out 發布　commander (kə'mændɚ) *n.* 指揮官
unite (ju'naɪt) *v.* 統一　issue ('ɪʃju) *v.* 發布
minimize ('mɪnə,maɪz) *v.* 使…減到最小
broadcast ('brɔd,kæst) *v.* 廣播

41. (**A**) The colorful balloons' coming down were exciting to see. 看著五顏六色的氣球落下很令人興奮。

(A) 氣球下降令人興奮。　　(B) 人群看著它們落下。
(C) 氣球很興奮。　　(D) 人群看著它們爆炸。

* colorful ('kʌlɚfəl) *adj.* 五顏六色的
balloon (bə'lun) *n.* 氣球　　***come down*** 落下
exciting (ɪk'saɪtɪŋ) *adj.* 令人興奮的
descent (dɪ'sɛnt) *n.* 降下
thrilling ('θrɪlɪŋ) *adj.* 令人興奮的　　crowd (kraʊd) *n.* 人群
fall (fɔl) *n.* 落下　　explode (ɪk'splod) *v.* 爆炸

42. (**C**) The area was designated as the place to keep the ammunition. 這個區域被指定用來存放軍火。

(A) 那是軍火塔區域。
(B) 那是監禁軍火的區域。
(C) 那是保管軍火的區域。
(D) 那是花費軍火的區域。

* area ('ɛrɪə) *n.* 區域　　designate ('dɛzɪg,net) *v.* 指定 < *as* >
keep (kip) *v.* 存放　　ammunition (,æmjə'nɪʃən) *n.* 軍火
tower (taʊr) *n.* 塔　　prison ('prɪzn̩) *n.* 監獄；監禁
storage ('storɪdʒ) *n.* 保管　　expense (ɪk'spɛns) *n.* 花費

43. (**D**) This teacher has a negative attitude.
這名老師持反對的態度。

(A) 他不哭。　　(B) 他不改正。
(C) 他不競爭。　　(D) 他不合作。

* negative ('nɛgətɪv) *adj.* 反對的
attitude ('ætə,tjud) *n.* 態度　　correct (kə'rɛkt) *v.* 改正
compete (kəm'pit) *v.* 競爭
cooperate (ko'ɑpə,ret) *v.* 合作

44. (**C**) Bill doesn't like to go to the movies alone.
比爾不喜歡單獨去看電影。

(A) 比爾討厭去看電影。

(B) 比爾不論何時去看電影，都要有點心。

(C) 比爾去看電影時，要有同伴。

(D) 比爾怕黑。

* alone [ə'lon] *v.* 單獨地　snack [snæk] *n.* 點心
fear [fɪr] *v.* 害怕　darkness ['dɑrknɪs] *n.* 黑暗

45. (**B**) The woman had a problem when she tried to tie her sneaker. 那位女士在試圖綁運動鞋的鞋帶時碰到問題。

(A) 對她來說，綁運動鞋的鞋帶很容易。

(B) 對她來說，綁運動鞋的鞋帶有困難。

(C) 對他來說，綁運動鞋的鞋帶很簡單。

(D) 對她來說，欺騙運動鞋的鞋帶有困難。

* tie [taɪ] *v.* 綁鞋帶　sneaker ['snikɚ] *n.* 運動鞋
difficult ['dɪfə,kʌlt] *adj.* 困難的　lie [laɪ] *v.* 欺騙

46. (**D**) Donna's car is ready to fall apart.
多娜的車快要散了。

(A) 她的車狀況不錯。

(B) 她的車在空氣調節機裡。

(C) 她的車狀況富裕。

(D) 她的車狀況欠佳。

* ready ['rɛdɪ] *adj.* 快要…的　***fall apart*** 散開
condition [kən'dɪʃən] *n.* 狀況
air conditioning 空氣調節機
rich [rɪtʃ] *adj.* 富裕的　poor [pʊr] *adj.* 欠佳的

47. (**C**) Two well-known petroleum products are plastic bottles and bug spray.

大家都知道的兩項石油產品是塑膠瓶和殺蟲噴霧。

(A) 塑膠是由昆蟲製成的。

(B) 塑膠是由殺蟲劑製成的。

(C) 塑膠是由石油製成的。

(D) 塑膠是由產品製成的。

* well-known〔ˈwɛlˈnon〕*adj.* 著名的；眾所周知的
petroleum〔pəˈtrolɪəm〕*n.* 石油
product〔ˈprɑdʌkt〕*n.* 產品
plastic〔ˈplæstɪk〕*adj.* 塑膠的　bottle〔ˈbɑtl̩〕*n.* 瓶子
bug〔bʌg〕*n.* 蟲　spray〔spre〕*n.* 噴霧藥
be made from 由…製成的　insect〔ˈɪnsɛkt〕*n.* 昆蟲
insecticide〔ɪnˈsɛktəˌsaɪd〕*n.* 殺蟲劑

48. (**D**) Ann prefers a pink car. 安比較喜歡粉紅色的車。

(A) 她贏得粉紅色的車。

(B) 她租了粉紅色的車。

(C) 她喜歡談論她那輛粉紅色的車。

(D) 安寧願開粉紅色的車。

* prefer〔prɪˈfɝ〕*v.* 比較喜歡
pink〔pɪŋk〕*adj.* 粉紅色的　win〔wɪn〕*v.* 贏得
rent〔rɛnt〕*v.* 租　***would rather*** 寧願

49. (**B**) Attention all passengers. Train 101 for Moscow is now departing on track two. Please have your tickets ready. All aboard.

所有乘客注意。前往莫斯科的一〇一號火車現在在第二軌道要開車了。請準備好你的車票。請各位上車，火車要開動了。

(A) 火車在第三月台。

(B) 到莫斯科的火車要開了。

(C) 到莫斯科的火車是一一〇號。

(D) 火車將出發前往聖彼得堡。

* Attention〔ə'tɛnʃən〕*interj.* 注意
passenger〔'pæsn̩dʒɚ〕*n.* 乘客
Moscow〔'mɑsko〕*n.* 莫斯科【俄國首都】
depart〔dɪ'pɑrt〕*v.* 啓程　track〔træk〕*n.* 軌道
ticket〔'tɪkɪt〕*n.* 票　ready〔'rɛdɪ〕*adj.* 準備好的
aboard〔ə'bord〕*adv.* 上（車、船、飛機）
All aboard. 請各位上車，要開動了。
platform〔'plæt,fɔrm〕*n.* 月台
for〔fɔr〕*prep.* 前往
Saint Petersburg 聖彼得堡【俄國第二大城】

50. (**C**) Attention theatergoers. Act three is about to begin. The concession stand is now closed. Please return to your seat.
戲迷們注意。第三幕快要開演了。販賣處現在要關了。請回到你的座位上。

(A) 人們被要求離開戲院。

(B) 售票處要關了。

(C) 人們被要求回到位子上。

(D) 交誼廳要關了。

* theatergoer〔'θɪətɚ,goɚ〕*n.* 戲迷　act〔ækt〕*n.* 幕
about〔ə'baʊt〕*adj.* 即將的
concession〔kən'sɛʃən〕*n.* 場內販賣處
stand〔stænd〕*n.* 攤位　seat〔sit〕*n.* 座位
theater〔'θiətɚ〕*n.* 戲院　***ticket office*** 售票處
lounge〔laʊndʒ〕*n.* 交誼聽

51. (**D**) W：Did you remember to water this? The leaves are turning brown.

M：No, I didn't. I'll do it now.

What needs water?

女：你有記得幫這個東西澆水嗎？葉子都變棕色了。

男：不，我沒有。我現在就去做。

什麼東西需要水？

(A) 一隻動物。　　(B) 一條魚。

(C) 某些種類的鳥。　　(D) 一株植物。

* water〔ˈwɔtɚ〕*v.* 澆水　*n.* 水

leaves〔livz〕*n. pl.* 葉子【單數為 leaf】

turn〔tɝn〕*v.* 轉變　brown〔braʊn〕*n.* 棕色

plant〔plænt〕*n.* 植物

52. (**B**) M：Can you meet me at the department store, Carol?

W：Yes, it's a very convenient place.

Why will they meet at the department store?

男：卡洛，妳可以到百貨公司來跟我碰面嗎？

女：好的，那個地點很方便。

他們為什麼要在百貨公司碰面？

(A) 卡洛知道百貨公司在哪。

(B) 卡洛可以輕易到達那個地方。

(C) 卡洛喜歡那裡的精品。

(D) 卡洛常常去那裡。

* ***department store*** 百貨公司

convenient〔kənˈvinjənt〕*adj.* 方便的

selection〔səˈlɛkʃən〕*n.* 精選品

53. (**B**) W：There is a car with its lights on in the parking lot.
M：It's a blue Cadillac Eldorado with Florida license plates.
Which is NOT correct about this car?
女：停車場有部車的車燈開著。
男：那是藍色的卡迪拉克，車牌是佛羅里達州發的。
關於這部車，何者不正確？

(A) 它停在那裡。　(B) 它是雪佛蘭。
(C) 它有車牌。　(D) 它的燈是開著的。

* light〔 laɪt 〕*n.* 燈光　on〔 ɑn 〕*adv.* 開著
lot〔 lɑt 〕*n.* 土地　***a parking lot*** 停車場
Cadillac〔ˈkædḷˌæk 〕*n.* 凱迪拉克【美國高級汽車】
Cadillac Eldorado 凱迪拉克出產的一種車型
Florida〔ˈflɔrədə 〕*n.* 美國佛羅里達州
license〔ˈlaɪsṇs 〕*n.* 牌照　***license plate***　（汽車的）牌照
correct〔 kəˈrɛkt 〕*adj.* 正確的
park〔 pɑrk 〕*v.* 停（汽車）
Chevrolet〔ˌʃɛvrəˈle 〕*n.* 雪佛蘭【美國通用汽車公司製造的車】

54. (**C**) W：What's the problem?
M：The water in this pipe is frozen.
How did this happen?
女：有什麼問題？
男：這條管子裡的水結冰了。
這件事是怎麼發生的？

(A) 水變得很熱。　(B) 水管破了。
(C) 水變得太冷。　(D) 水用完了。

* pipe〔 paɪp 〕*n.* 管子　frozen〔ˈfrozṇ 〕*adj.* 結冰的
run out of 用完

55. (**C**) W：Were you born overseas?

M：No, but my parents were. They're from the Philippines.

W：They are very brave to move to another country.

What are they talking about?

女：你在國外出生的嗎？

男：不是，但我的父母是。他們是從菲律賓來的。

女：他們很勇敢，敢搬到別的國家住。

他們在談論什麼？

(A) 他的生日。

(B) 到國外旅行。

(C) 移民。

(D) 公民身分。

＊ overseas〔'ovə'siz〕*adv.* 在國外
parents〔'pɛrənts〕*n. pl.* 父母
Philippines〔'fɪlə,pinz〕*n. pl.* 菲律賓群島
brave〔brev〕*adj.* 勇敢的
abroad〔ə'brɔd〕*adv.* 到國外
immigration〔,ɪmə'greʃən〕*n.* 移民
citizenship〔'sɪtəzn̩,ʃɪp〕*n.* 公民身分

56. (**A**) W：I'm going away for three months.

M：Let's make sure we keep in touch.

What does the man imply?

女：我要離開三個月。

男：我們一定要保持聯絡。

這位男士在暗示什麼？

(A) 他要跟她保持聯絡。

(B) 那位女士在旅行時，也要記住他。

(C) 他希望那位女士玩得愉快。

(D) 他希望那位女士趕快回來。

* ***go away*** 離開 ***make sure*** 一定
keep in touch 保持聯絡 imply〔ɪm'plaɪ〕*v.* 暗示
be in contact with 與…聯絡 ***keep in mind*** 記住
trip〔trɪp〕*n.* 旅行 ***have a good time*** 玩得愉快

57. (**C**) W：How do you like your new bed?

M：Well, it's a little too firm and a little too short, but I'll make do with it.

What do we learn about the man's bed?

女：你喜歡你的新床嗎？

男：嗯，有點太硬而且有點太短，但是我會將就著睡。

關於這位男士的床，我們知道什麼？

(A) 這位男士剛把床鋪好。

(B) 床太軟了，這位男士無法搬運它。

(C) 床是硬的，但這位男士不介意。

(D) 床很舒服，但是這位男士不喜歡它。

* firm〔fɝm〕*adj.* 硬的 ***make do with*** 將就使用
finish〔'fɪnɪʃ〕*v.* 完成
make one's bed 整理床鋪；鋪床
soft〔sɔft〕*adj.* 柔軟的 handle〔'hændḷ〕*v.* 拿；搬運
hard〔hɑrd〕*adj.* 硬的 mind〔maɪnd〕*v.* 介意
comfortable〔'kʌmfətəbḷ〕*adj.* 舒適的

58. (**C**) M：Did you know that the administration just made this cafeteria non-smoking?

W：Yeah, they're really cracking down on smokers.

What does the woman imply?

男：妳知道管理部門剛把這家自助餐廳變成禁菸餐廳嗎？

女：是的，他們真的對吸煙者採取很嚴厲的手段。

這位女士暗示什麼？

(A) 她贊成管理部門的決定。

(B) 她不知道管理部門的決定。

(C) 管理部門對吸煙者變得很嚴格。

(D) 管理部門把吸煙區的牆打掉。

* administration〔ədˌmɪnəˈstreʃən〕*n.* 管理部門
cafeteria〔ˌkæfəˈtɪrɪə〕*n.* 自助餐廳
non-smoking〔ˌnɑnˈsmokɪŋ〕*adj.* 禁止吸煙的
crack down on 對…採取嚴厲手段
smoker〔ˈsmokɚ〕*n.* 吸煙的人
agree〔əˈgri〕*v.* 同意；贊成
decision〔dɪˈsɪʒən〕*n.* 決定　get〔gɛt〕*v.* 變得
strict〔strɪkt〕*adj.* 嚴格的　***crack down*** 使倒塌
wall〔wɔl〕*n.* 牆壁　smoking〔ˈsmokɪŋ〕*adj.* 吸煙的
section〔ˈsɛkʃən〕*n.* 區域

59. (**A**) M：I'm going to have a party on December 5th.

W：You should think twice about having it then. Exams start on December 6th.

What does the woman suggest?

男：我將在十二月五日舉辦宴會。

女：關於在那時候舉辦宴會，你應該再考慮一下。考試從十二月六日開始。

那位女士建議什麼？

(A) <u>那位男士應該重新考慮宴會的日期。</u>

(B) 那位男士應該邀請的人數是以前的兩倍。

(C) 那位男士應該在十二月五日舉辦宴會。

(D) 那位男士應該在今天舉辦宴會。

* have [hæv] *v.* 舉辦
December [dɪˈsɛmbɚ] *n.* 十二月
twice [twaɪs] *adv.* 兩次；兩倍地
exam [ɪgˈzæm] *n.* 考試　suggest [səˈdʒɛst] *v.* 建議
reconsider [ˌrikənˈsɪdɚ] *v.* 再次考慮
date [det] *n.* 日期　invite [ɪnˈvaɪt] *v.* 邀請

60. (**B**) M：How can I cut down on my spending?
W：Why don't you keep track of everything you buy?
What is the woman's advice?
男：我要怎麼樣才能減少開銷呢？
女：你爲什麼不隨時注意你買的每樣東西？
這位女士的建議是？

(A) 這位男士應該把他的錢存進銀行帳戶裡。

(B) <u>他應該把他買的所有東西寫下來。</u>

(C) 他應該買更多東西。

(D) 他應該少買一點東西。

* ***cut down*** 削減　spending [ˈspɛndɪŋ] *n.* 開銷
keep track of 隨時注意
advice [ədˈvaɪs] *n.* 建議
deposit [dɪˈpɑzɪt] *v.* 存（錢）
account [əˈkaʊnt] *n.* 帳戶
purchase [ˈpɝtʃəs] *n.* 購買的東西
less [lɛs] *n.* 較少量

LISTENING TEST ⑬

- *Directions for questions 1-25. You will hear questions on the test CD. Select the one item A, B, C or D which answers the question correctly, and mark your answer sheet.*

1. A. They will get hurt in a car accident.
   B. They will be careful when driving.
   C. They will become nervous.
   D. They might remain alive in a car accident.

2. A. Susie may go home.
   B. Susie may go for ice cream.
   C. Susie won't go to town.
   D. Susie may go to town.

3. A. They indulged themselves in the weather.
   B. They contributed themselves to the weather.
   C. They adjusted themselves to the weather.
   D. They devoted themselves to the weather.

4. A. the number of shirts　　B. the color of the shirt
   C. the size of the shirt　　D. the price of the shirt

5. A. Put them on whenever you go to a special occasion.
   B. Give them to your best friend as a gift.
   C. Throw them away.
   D. Wear them when they become fashionable again.

6. A. He had to catch the ball.
   B. He wanted to shave.
   C. He wanted to know the time.
   D. He had to wash his face.

7. A. no more　　B. many more
   C. a lot more　　D. a little more

8. A. He resigned.　　B. He signed.
   C. He assigned.　　D. He designed.

9. A. after she saw the sun
   B. after the sun went down
   C. long after midnight
   D. when her alarm went off

10. A. so everyone would find her right away
    B. so everybody would follow her
    C. nobody would like her
    D. so nobody would find her

11. A. They are full of regret for the food.
    B. They are happy with the food.
    C. They are apologetic for the food.
    D. They sympathize with the food.

12. A. in his pocket　　B. in a narrow hole
    C. in a cashier　　D. in his pants

13. A. watch movies.
B. beat the baby.
C. kiss the baby.
D. look after the baby.

14. A. ran away
B. fought on
C. surrendered
D. went home

15. A. its brakes
B. its color
C. its ability to pick up speed
D. its design

16. A. It was perfect.
B. It was parked.
C. It was unbalanced.
D. It was possessed.

17. A. He filled the car with gas.
B. He allowed John to use the car.
C. He insured the car.
D. He rented a car.

18. A. rebuild the engine
B. take the engine apart
C. report it to the boss
D. help our friend

19. A. She will make them operate together.
B. She will fake them to operate together.
C. She will dismiss them.
D. She will make them operate tomorrow.

20. A. the bats and the balls
B. the cats and the calls
C. the rats and the balls
D. the hats and the stalls

21. A. a policeman B. a conductor
C. a chef D. a store worker

22. A. the fish B. time
C. goods D. the total

23. A. a bakery B. a butcher's shop
C. a barbershop D. a bank

24. A. inside with an open door
B. in a hall
C. outside D. in a car

25. A. coldness B. dampness
C. heat D. rough handling

- *Directions for questions 26-50. You will hear statements on the test CD. Select the one answer A, B, C, or D which comes closest to the meaning of the statement and mark your answer sheet.*

26. A. You should ignore it.
B. You should take advantage of it.
C. You should advertise it.
D. You should not use a hand.

27. A. The park is next to the mall.
B. The park is across the street from the mall.
C. They are on different streets.
D. It's next to the pizzeria.

28. A. He bought an English book.
    B. He bought a sequence of English books.
    C. He bought books to learn Spanish.
    D. He bought a series of military books.

29. A. My friend took me to his house.
    B. My friend gave me his house number.
    C. My friend asked me to eat at his place.
    D. My friend gave me a present.

30. A. The bus stopped the train.
    B. The bus carried the train.
    C. The bus collided with the train.
    D. The bus ran after the train.

31. A. The box is not heavy.
    B. The box has lights.
    C. The box is easy.
    D. The box has a lift.

32. A. It can't be eaten.
    B. It can't be seen.
    C. It can't be sold.
    D. It can't be bought.

33. A. They will expose the crime.
    B. They will restrict the crime.
    C. They will extinguish the crime.
    D. They will investigate the crime.

34. A. He wants to know the exact leaning of it.
    B. He wants to know the ecstatic meaning of it.
    C. He wants to know the excited meaning of it.
    D. He wants to know the exact meaning of it.

35. A. She became award to it.
    B. She became awful because of it.
    C. She became aware of it.
    D. She became afraid of it.

36. A. Smoking is encouraged.
    B. Smoking is not allowed.
    C. Smoking is not taken seriously.
    D. Smoking is seen as a bad habit.

37. A. She had a good time.
    B. She was bored.
    C. She had a bad time.
    D. She had a key in her pocket.

38. A. We can go on an outing if the day is mice.
    B. We can go on an outing if the pay is nice.
    C. We can go on an outing if the day is nice.
    D. We can have a party if the way is nice.

39. A. She can't do any sleeping.
    B. She can't do any lifting.
    C. She can't do any eating.
    D. She can't do any exercise.

40. A. The teacher told the students how to build one.
    B. The teacher told the students how to blow it up.
    C. The teacher told the students how to get there.
    D. The teacher told the students to go home.

41. A. It was very cold.
    B. It was very warm.
    C. It was regularly hot.
    D. It was a little bit warm.

42. A. She can't be language qualified.
    B. She is language qualified.
    C. She was language qualified.
    D. She may be language qualified.

43. A. His book keeps correct time.
    B. His watch keeps correct rice.
    C. His clock keeps correct lime.
    D. His clock keeps correct time.

44. A. Comfort her. She's not happy.
    B. Send her away. She's not happy.
    C. Go on. She's not happy.
    D. Stop. She's not happy.

45. A. She was ungrateful. B. She was angry.
    C. She was grateful. D. She was violent.

46. A. He was told to do guard duty.
    B. He wanted to go guard duty very much.
    C. He asked to do guard duty.
    D. He forgot to do guard duty.

47. A. Each system is planned to do a prolific job.
    B. Each system is planned to do a particular job.
    C. Each system is planned to do a pathetic job.
    D. Each system is planned to do a pernicious job.

48. A. She knows Los Angeles.
    B. She knows Mr. Jones.
    C. She knows popcorn.
    D. She knows how many people live in Los Angeles.

49. A. It was burned out. B. It was burned off.
    C. It was turned on. D. It was turned off.

50. A. The building collapsed.
    B. The building crushed.
    C. The building exploded.
    D. The building fell asleep.

● *Directions for questions 51-60. You will hear dialogs on the test CD. Select the correct answer A, B, C, or D and mark your answer sheet.*

51. A. She has a cat. B. She doesn't like cats.
    C. The dogs hate cats. D. She likes cats.

52. A. change his socks B. put on a different shirt
    C. change his ways D. buy a shirt

53. A. making a report B. conducting an experiment
    C. looking for work D. studying for a test

54. A. It has many tall buildings.
    B. It's a place where ships come and go.
    C. You can see many famous people.
    D. It has good museums.

55. A. a gift shop
    B. a place to buy bread
    C. a place to buy flowers
    D. a pet shop

56. A. sunny B. windy
    C. snowy D. rainy

57. A. at a museum B. at a theater
    C. at a station D. at an airport

58. A. He admires Adam for being smart.
    B. He would like to spend more time reading books.
    C. He thinks Adam should spend less time reading.
    D. He doesn't think Adam is diligent.

59. A. She doesn't remember the trip.
    B. She remembers the man sleeping in the grass.
    C. She remembers slipping in the grass.
    D. She remembers the man slipping in the grass.

60. A. He will probably listen to the radio.
    B. He will probably clean his sweater.
    C. He will probably go outside.
    D. He will probably look out the window.

ECL 聽力測驗⑬詳解

1. (D) People have a better chance of survival in a car accident if they use seat belts. Why should people use seat belts?

如果人們有使用安全帶，在車禍中的生還機率就會比較大。／為什麼人們應該使用安全帶？

(A) 他們會在車禍中受傷。

(B) 他們在開車時會比較小心。

(C) 他們會變得緊張。

(D) 他們有可能在車禍中生還。

* chance〔 tʃæns 〕*n.* 機會　survival〔 sə'vaɪvḷ 〕*n.* 生存

accident〔'æksədənt 〕*n.* 事故

seat〔 sit 〕*adj.* 座椅的　belt〔 bɛlt 〕*n.* 安全帶

hurt〔 hɝt 〕*v.* 受傷　***get hurt*** 受傷

nervous〔'nɝvəs 〕*adj.* 緊張的

remain〔 rɪ'men 〕*v.* 保持；依舊是

alive〔 ə'laɪv 〕*adj.* 活的

2. (D) Betty said, "Susie might go to town." What did Betty say?

貝蒂說：「蘇西可能會去城裡。」／貝蒂說什麼？

(A) 蘇西可能會回家。

(B) 蘇西可能會去買冰淇淋。

(C) 蘇西不會去城裡。

(D) 蘇西可能會去城裡。

* town〔 taʊn 〕*n.* 城鎮　***go for*** 去買

3. (**C**) We adapted ourselves to the hot weather. What did they do?
我們適應了這種炎熱的天氣。／他們做了什麼？

(A) 他們沉溺於這種天氣。
(B) 他們把自己貢獻給這種天氣。
(C) 他們適應了這種天氣。
(D) 他們致力於這種天氣。

* adapt 〔ə'dæpt〕*v.* 使適應
adapt *oneself* ***to***… 使自己適應於…
weather 〔'wɛðɚ〕*n.* 天氣
indulge 〔ɪn'dʌldʒ〕*v.* 沉溺於 ＜*in*＞
contribute 〔kən'trɪbjut〕*v.* 貢獻
contribute *oneself* ***to***… 貢獻自己給…
adjust 〔ə'dʒʌst〕*v.* 調節；使適應
adjust *oneself* ***to***… 使自己適應於…
devote 〔dɪ'vot〕*v.* 致力於
devote *oneself* ***to***… 專心致力於…

4. (**D**) Liz said, "This shirt costs $12.96." What was Liz talking about? 麗茲說：「這件襯衫要價美金 12.96 元。」／麗茲在說什麼？

(A) 襯衫的數量。 (B) 襯衫的顏色。
(C) 襯衫的尺寸。 (D) 襯衫的價錢。

* shirt 〔ʃɝt〕*n.* 襯衫 number 〔'nʌmbɚ〕*n.* 數量
size 〔saɪz〕*n.* 尺寸 price 〔praɪs〕*n.* 價錢

5. (**C**) These socks are worn out. What should we do with them? 這些襪子都破了。／我們應該怎麼處理它們？

(A) 每當你到特殊場合去時，都穿上它們。
(B) 把它們當成禮物送給你最好的朋友。

(C) 把它們丟掉。

(D) 當它們又變流行的時候再穿。

* socks〔 sɑks 〕*n. pl.* 襪子
wear out 磨破了的；破舊的
do with 處理　***put on*** 穿上
whenever〔 hwɛn'ɛvɚ 〕*conj.* 不論何時
special〔'spɛʃəl 〕*adj.* 特別的
occasion〔 ə'keʃən 〕*n.* 場合
gift〔 gɪft 〕*n.* 禮物　throw〔 θro 〕*v.* 丟
throw away 丟棄　wear〔 wɛr 〕*v.* 穿
fashionable〔'fæʃənəbl̩ 〕*adj.* 流行的

6. (**C**) Why did Kevin look at his watch?
爲什麼凱文看著他的錶？

(A) 他必須接到球。
(B) 他想要刮鬍子。
(C) 他想知道時間。
(D) 他必須洗臉。

* catch〔 kætʃ 〕*v.* 接住　shave〔 ʃev 〕*v.* 刮鬍子
wash〔 wɑʃ 〕*v.* 洗　face〔 fes 〕*n.* 臉

7. (**D**) Lisa said she would have a bit more. How much did she want?
麗莎說她還想再多吃一點。／她要多少？

(A) 不再。　(B) 再多很多。
(C) 再多很多。　(D) 再多一點。

* have〔 hæv 〕*v.* 吃　***a bit*** 一點點
more〔 mor 〕*pron.* 更多的量　***no more*** 不再
many more 多很多

8. (**A**) He quit the position of President last week. What did he do last week?

他上週辭去了總統的職位。／他上週做了什麼？

(A) <u>他辭職了。</u>　(B) 他簽名了。
(C) 他指派了。　(D) 他設計了。

* quit (kwɪt) *v.* 辭職　position (pəˈzɪʃən) *n.* 職位
President (ˈprɛzədənt) *n.* 總統
resign (rɪˈzaɪn) *v.* 辭職　sign (saɪn) *v.* 簽名
assign (əˈsaɪn) *v.* 指派　design (dɪˈzaɪn) *v.* 設計

9. (**B**) Alice left the building after sunset. When did Alice leave?

艾莉絲在日落之後離開這棟大樓。／艾莉絲何時離開？

(A) 她看到太陽之後。　(B) <u>太陽下山之後。</u>
(C) 午夜過後很久。　(D) 當她的鬧鐘響起時。

* leave (liv) *v.* 離開　building (ˈbɪldɪŋ) *n.* 大樓
sunset (ˈsʌnˌsɛt) *n.* 日落　***go down*** 落下
midnight (ˈmɪdˌnaɪt) *n.* 午夜
alarm (əˈlɑrm) *n.* 鬧鐘　***go off*** 開始鳴響

10. (**D**) Janet went away to hide. Why did she go away?

珍娜去躲起來了。／她爲什麼要離開？

(A) 如此一來每個人都會立刻去找她。
(B) 如此一來每個人都會跟隨她。
(C) 沒有人會喜歡她。
(D) <u>如此一來就沒有人會去找她。</u>

* ***go away*** 離開　hide (haɪd) *v.* 躲藏
right away 立刻　follow (ˈfɑlo) *v.* 跟隨

11. (**B**) The students are very satisfied with their food in the cafeteria. What do the students do?
學生們對自助餐廳裡的食物很滿意。／學生們做什麼？
(A) 他們對食物充滿遺憾。
(B) 他們對食物感到滿意。
(C) 他們爲了食物道歉。
(D) 他們同情食物。

* satisfied〔'sætɪs,faɪd〕*adj.* 滿意的
cafeteria〔,kæfə'tɪrɪə〕*n.* 自助餐廳
be full of 充滿…的　　regret〔rɪ'grɛt〕*n.* 遺憾
happy〔'hæpɪ〕*adj.* 滿意的
apologetic〔ə,pɑlə'dʒɛtɪk〕*adj.* 道歉的
sympathize〔'sɪmpə,θaɪz〕*v.* 同情

12. (**B**) He put the money in the slot. Where did he put it?
他把錢放入投幣口。／他把錢放入哪裡？
(A) 他的口袋裡。　　(B) 一個狹窄的孔中。
(C) 小豬撲滿裡。　　(D) 他的褲子裡。

* slot〔slɑt〕*n.* 投幣口　　pocket〔'pɑkɪt〕*n.* 口袋
narrow〔'næro〕*adj.* 狹窄的　　hole〔hol〕*n.* 孔
cashier〔kæ'ʃɪr〕*n.* 收銀機　　pants〔pænts〕*n.* 褲子

13. (**D**) He must take care of the baby in the evening. What must he do in the evening?
晚上他必須照顧嬰兒。／晚上他必須做什麼？
(A) 看電影。　　(B) 打嬰兒。
(C) 親吻嬰兒。　　(D) 照顧嬰兒。

* ***take care of*** 照顧　　beat〔bit〕*v.* 打
look after 照顧

14. (**C**) The army gave up to the superior forces. What did the army do?
軍隊向佔優勢的部隊投降了。／軍隊做了什麼？

(A) 逃跑。　(B) 繼續奮戰。
(C) 投降。　(D) 回家。

* army [ˈɑrmɪ] *n.* 軍隊　***give up*** 投降
superior [səˈpɪrɪɚ] *adj.* 較優秀的；佔優勢的
force [fɔrs] *n.* 軍事力量；部隊
run away 逃跑　***fight on*** 繼續戰爭
surrender [səˈrɛndɚ] *v.* 投降

15. (**C**) Jerry liked the acceleration of the car. What did he like? 傑瑞喜歡這部車的加速性能。／他喜歡什麼？

(A) 它的煞車。　(B) 它的顏色。
(C) 它的加速能力。　(D) 它的設計。

* acceleration [æk,sɛləˈreʃən] *n.* 加速性能
brake [brek] *n.* 煞車　ability [əˈbɪlətɪ] *n.* 能力
speed [spid] *n.* 速度　***pick up speed*** 加速
design [dɪˈzaɪn] *n.* 設計

16. (**C**) What made the bicycle wheel wobble?
是什麼使得腳踏車的車輪搖搖晃晃？

(A) 它很完美。　(B) 它停好了。
(C) 它不平衡。　(D) 它著魔了。

* bicycle [ˈbaɪ,sɪkḷ] *n.* 腳踏車　wheel [hwil] *n.* 車輪
wobble [ˈwɑbḷ] *v.* 搖晃　perfect [ˈpɝfɪkt] *adj.* 完美的
park [pɑrk] *v.* 停車
unbalanced [ʌnˈbælənst] *adj.* 不平衡的
possessed [pəˈzɛst] *adj.* 著魔的

17. (**B**) Fred gave John permission to drive the car. What did Fred do?

弗瑞德准許約翰開那輛車。／弗瑞德做了什麼？

(A) 他爲汽車加油。 (B) 他准許約翰使用那輛車。

(C) 他爲汽車投保。 (D) 他租了一輛車。

* permission〔pəˈmɪʃən〕*n.* 許可 fill〔fɪl〕*v.* 裝入
gas〔gæs〕*n.* 汽油 allow〔əˈlaʊ〕*v.* 准許
insure〔ɪnˈʃʊr〕*v.* 將…投保 rent〔rɛnt〕*v.* 租

18. (**B**) We'll have to disassemble the engine. What will we have to do?

我們必須把引擎拆開來。／我們必須做什麼？

(A) 改造引擎。 (B) 拆卸引擎。

(C) 向老闆報告。 (D) 幫助我們的朋友。

* disassemble〔ˌdɪsəˈsɛmbl̩〕*v.* 拆卸；分解
engine〔ˈɛndʒən〕*n.* 引擎 rebuild〔riˈbɪld〕*v.* 改造
apart〔əˈpɑrt〕*adv.* 分開地 ***take apart*** 拆卸
report〔rɪˈpɔrt〕*v.* 報告 boss〔bɔs〕*n.* 老闆

19. (**A**) Jenny will coordinate the maneuvers. What will she do about the maneuvers?

珍妮將會協調軍事演習。／她將會對軍事演習做什麼？

(A) 她將會使它們一起運作。

(B) 她將會欺騙它們一起運作。

(C) 她將會解散它們。

(D) 明天她將會使它們運作。

* coordinate〔koˈɔrdn̩ɪt〕*v.* 使協調
maneuvers〔məˈnuvəz〕*n. pl.* 軍事演習
operate〔ˈɑpəˌret〕*v.* 行動；運作
fake〔fek〕*v.* 假裝；欺騙 dismiss〔dɪsˈmɪs〕*v.* 解散

20. (**A**) Donna told us to bring the baseball equipment. What did Donna tell us to bring?
唐娜叫我們帶棒球裝備過來。／唐娜叫我們帶什麼？

(A) 球棒和球。 (B) 貓和哨子。
(C) 老鼠和球。 (D) 帽子和馬廄。

* baseball ('bes,bɔl) *n.* 棒球
equipment (ɪ'kwɪpmənt) *n.* 裝備
bat (bæt) *n.* 球棒
call (kɔl) *n.* (模仿鳥獸叫聲的) 哨子
rat (ræt) *n.* 大老鼠 stall (stɔl) *n.* 馬廄

21. (**D**) Linda always asks the clerk to get the things she wants. Who does Linda ask?
琳達總是要求店員去拿她想要的東西。／琳達要求誰？

(A) 警察。 (B) 車掌。
(C) 主廚。 (D) 店員。

* clerk (klɝk) *n.* 店員
policeman (pə'lismən) *n.* 警察
conductor (kən'dʌktɚ) *n.* 車掌
chef (ʃɛf) *n.* 主廚

22. (**D**) Gina added up the digits. What did she calculate?
吉娜把數字加起來。／她在算什麼？

(A) 魚。 (B) 時間。
(C) 商品。 (D) 總數。

* add (æd) *v.* 加 ***add up*** 把…加起來
digit ('dɪdʒɪt) *n.* 阿拉伯數字
calculate ('kælkjə,let) *v.* 計算
goods (gʊdz) *n. pl.* 商品 total ('totl̩) *n.* 總數

23. (**C**) Where does Peter go for a haircut?
彼得去哪裡理頭髮？

(A) 麵包店。 (B) 肉店。
(C) 理髮店。 (D) 銀行。

* haircut〔ˈhɛr,kʌt〕*n.* 理髮　bakery〔ˈbekərɪ〕*n.* 麵包店
butcher〔ˈbʊtʃɚ〕*n.* 肉販
barbershop〔ˈbɑrbɚ,ʃɑp〕*n.* 理髮店
bank〔bæŋk〕*n.* 銀行

24. (**C**) Ryan changed in the open. Where did he change?
萊恩在戶外換衣服。／他在哪裡換衣服？

(A) 在門打開的室內。 (B) 在大廳。
(C) 在室外。 (D) 在車裡。

* change〔tʃendʒ〕*v.* 換衣服
open〔ˈopən〕*n.* 戶外 *adj.* 打開的
in the open 在戶外　inside〔ˈɪnˈsaɪd〕*adv.* 在室內
hall〔hɔl〕*n.* 大廳
outside〔ˈaʊtˈsaɪd〕*adv.* 在室外

25. (**B**) Books should be kept away from moisture. What should they be kept away from?
書應該要放在遠離潮濕的地方。／它們應該遠離什麼？

(A) 寒冷。 (B) 濕氣。
(C) 熱氣。 (D) 粗魯地拿。

* keep〔kip〕*v.* 存放；保存　***keep away from*** 使遠離
moisture〔ˈmɔɪstʃɚ〕*n.* 潮濕
coldness〔ˈkoldnɪs〕*n.* 寒冷
dampness〔ˈdæmpnɪs〕*n.* 濕氣　heat〔hit〕*n.* 熱氣
rough〔rʌf〕*adv.* 粗魯地　handle〔ˈhændḷ〕*v.* 拿

26. (**B**) A chance like that is not to be sneezed at.
像那樣的機會不容輕忽。

(A) 你應該忽略它。 (B) <u>你應該利用它。</u>
(C) 你應該宣傳它。 (D) 你不應該用一隻手。

* sneeze〔sniz〕*v.* 噴嚏 ***not to be sneezed at*** 不可輕視
ignore〔ɪg'nor〕*v.* 忽略 ***take advantage of*** 利用
advertise〔'ædvə˞,taɪz〕*v.* 宣傳

27. (**B**) The park is opposite the mall. 公園在購物中心對面。

(A) 公園在購物中心旁邊。
(B) <u>公園和購物中心的對街。</u>
(C) 它們在不同條街上。
(D) 它在比薩店旁邊。

* opposite〔'ɑpəzɪt〕*prep.* 在…的對面
mall〔mɔl〕*n.* 購物中心 ***next to*** 緊鄰著
across from 在…對面 different〔'dɪfrənt〕*adj.* 不同的
pizzeria〔,pitsə'riə〕*n.* 比薩店

28. (**B**) The major bought a set of books to help him learn English. 少校買了一套書來幫助他學英文。

(A) 他買了一本英文書。
(B) <u>他買了一系列的英文書。</u>
(C) 他買書來學西班牙文。
(D) 他買了一系列的軍用書。

* major〔'medʒə˞〕*n.* 少校 set〔sɛt〕*n.* 一套
sequence〔'sikwəns〕*n.* 一系列；一連串
Spanish〔'spænɪʃ〕*n.* 西班牙語
series〔'sɪrɪz〕*n.* 一系列
military〔'mɪlə,tɛrɪ〕*adj.* 軍事的

29. (**B**) My pal has given me his address.
我朋友給我他的住址。

(A) 我朋友帶我去他家。
(B) 我朋友給我他的門牌號碼。
(C) 我朋友邀我到他家吃飯。
(D) 我朋友送我一個禮物。

* pal (pæl) *n.* 朋友　address (əˈdrɛs) *n.* 地址
take (tek) *v.* 帶領　***house number*** 門牌號碼
ask (æsk) *v.* 邀請　place (ples) *n.* 住所
present (ˈprɛzn̩t) *n.* 禮物

30. (**C**) The bus crashed into the train. 公車撞上火車。

(A) 公車使火車停駛。　(B) 公車載著火車。
(C) 公車和火車相撞。　(D) 公車追逐火車。

* crash (kræʃ) *v.* 撞上　carry (ˈkærɪ) *v.* 載；運送
collide (kəˈlaɪd) *v.* 相撞　***run after*** 追逐

31. (**A**) This box can be lifted easily because it is very light.
我們可以輕易地拿起這個箱子，因爲它很輕。

(A) 箱子不重。　(B) 箱子有燈。
(C) 箱子很簡單。　(D) 箱子有升降機。

* lift (lɪft) *v.* 舉起 *n.* 升降機　easily (ˈizɪlɪ) *adv.* 輕易地
light (laɪt) *adj.* 輕的 *n.* 燈　heavy (ˈhɛvɪ) *adj.* 重的

32. (**B**) The air we inhale is invisible.
我們吸入的空氣是看不見的。

(A) 它不能吃。　(B) 它是看不見的。
(C) 它不能賣。　(D) 它不能買。

* inhale (ɪnˈhel) *v.* 吸入
invisible (ɪnˈvɪzəbl̩) *adj.* 看不見的

33. (**D**) The police are going to find out about the crime.
警方將會查明這起犯罪事件。

(A) 他們將會揭發犯罪事件。
(B) 他們將會限制犯罪事件。
(C) 他們將會消滅犯罪事件。
(D) <u>他們將會調查犯罪事件。</u>

* police〔pə'lis〕*n. pl.* 警方　　***find out*** 查明
crime〔kraɪm〕*n.* 犯罪
expose〔ɪk'spoz〕*v.* 暴露；揭發
restrict〔rɪ'strɪkt〕*v.* 限制
extinguish〔ɪk'stɪŋgwɪʃ〕*v.* 消滅
investigate〔ɪn'vɛstə,get〕*v.* 調查

34. (**D**) Joe wants to understand the literal meaning of this vocabulary word. 喬想要了解這個單字字面上的意義。

(A) 他想要知道它確切的嗜好。
(B) 他想要知道它狂喜的意義。
(C) 他想要知道它興奮的意義。
(D) <u>他想要知道它確切的意義。</u>

* understand〔,ʌndɚ'stænd〕*v.* 了解
literal〔'lɪtərəl〕*adj.* 字面上的　　meaning〔'minɪŋ〕*n.* 含義
vocabulary〔və'kæbjə,lɛrɪ〕*adj.* 單字的
exact〔ɪg'zækt〕*adj.* 確切的
leaning〔'linɪŋ〕*n.* 嗜好
ecstatic〔ɪk'stætɪk〕*adj.* 欣喜若狂的

35. (**C**) After a while, Samantha realized the error.
過了一會兒，莎曼珊明白了那個錯誤。

(A) 她變成錯誤的獎賞。
(B) 她因犯錯而變得很糟。

(C) 她察覺到了那個錯誤。
(D) 她對錯誤感到害怕。

* ***after a while*** 片刻之後
realize〔ˈriəˌlaɪz〕*v.* 了解；明白
error〔ˈɛrɚ〕*n.* 錯誤　award〔əˈwɔrd〕*n.* 獎賞
awful〔ˈɔfʊl〕*adj.* 很糟的
aware〔əˈwɛr〕*adj.* 察覺的
afraid〔əˈfred〕*adj.* 害怕的

36. (**B**) Smoking at work is prohibited.
工作時禁止抽煙。

(A) 抽煙是被鼓勵的。
(B) 抽煙是不被允許的。
(C) 抽煙沒有被認眞看待。
(D) 抽煙被視爲壞習慣。

* smoke〔smok〕*v.* 抽煙
prohibit〔proˈhɪbɪt〕*v.* 禁止
encourage〔ɪnˈkɝɪdʒ〕*v.* 鼓勵
take〔tek〕*v.* 以爲；把…看作
seriously〔ˈsɪrɪəslɪ〕*adv.* 認眞地　habit〔ˈhæbɪt〕*n.* 習慣

37. (**A**) Amanda enjoyed her visit.
亞曼達有趟愉快的旅行。

(A) 她玩得很盡興。
(B) 她很無聊。
(C) 她玩得不開心。
(D) 她口袋裡有一把鑰匙。

* visit〔ˈvɪzɪt〕*n.* 遊覽；旅行
have a good time 玩得愉快
bored〔bord〕*adj.* 感到無聊的　pocket〔ˈpɑkɪt〕*n.* 口袋

38. (**C**) If the weather clears up, we can have an outing.
如果天氣放晴，我們就可以去郊遊。

(A) 如果那一天是老鼠，我們就可以去郊遊。
(B) 如果薪水很高，我們就可以去郊遊。
(C) 如果天氣很好，我們就可以去郊遊。
(D) 如果方式很好，我們就可以舉辦一個派對。

* ***clear up*** 放晴　outing〔ˈaʊtɪŋ〕*n.* 郊遊
go on an outing 去郊遊
mice〔maɪs〕*n. pl.* 老鼠（mouse 的複數）
pay〔pe〕*n.* 薪水

39. (**B**) Since her illness, she can't do any heavy work.
因爲生病，她無法做任何粗重的工作。

(A) 她完全無法入眠。　(B) 她無法舉起任何東西。
(C) 她完全無法進食。　(D) 她無法做任何運動。

* since〔sɪns〕*conj.* 因爲　illness〔ˈɪlnɪs〕*n.* 患病
heavy〔ˈhɛvɪ〕*adj.* 粗重的　sleeping〔ˈslipɪŋ〕*n.* 睡眠
exercise〔ˈɛksɚˌsaɪz〕*n.* 運動

40. (**C**) The teacher told the students how to reach the compound. 老師告訴學生們要如何到達場地。

(A) 老師告訴學生們要如何建造場地。
(B) 老師告訴學生們要如何炸毀它。
(C) 老師告訴學生們要如何到達那裡。
(D) 老師叫學生們回家。

* reach〔ritʃ〕*v.* 到達
compound〔ˈkɑmpaʊnd〕*n.*（有圍牆的）場地
build〔bɪld〕*v.* 建築　blow〔blo〕*v.* 吹
blow up 炸毀　get〔gɛt〕*v.* 到達

41. (**B**) The weather was unusually hot. 天氣異常炎熱。

(A) 很冷。 (B) <u>很溫暖。</u>

(C) 天氣經常很熱。 (D) 有點溫暖。

* **unusually** (ʌn'juʒuəlɪ) *adv.* 異常地；非常地
warm (wɔrm) *adj.* 溫暖的
regularly ('rɛgjələ·lɪ) *adv.* 經常地 ***a little bit*** 有點

42. (**D**) If this pupil gets over 90 on the test, she will be language qualified.
如果這位學生考試超過九十分，她就通過語言檢定了。

(A) 她無法通過語言檢定。 (B) 她通過語言檢定。

(C) 她通過語言檢定了。 (D) <u>她有可能通過語言檢定。</u>

* **pupil** ('pjupḷ) *n.* 學生 **language** ('læŋgwɪdʒ) *n.* 語言
qualified ('kwɑlə,faɪd) *adj.* 有資格的；經過檢定的

43. (**D**) Peter's clock keeps accurate time. 彼得的鐘很準。

(A) 他的書時間正確。 (B) 他的錶維持正確的米。

(C) 他的鐘維持正確的萊姆。 (D) <u>他的鐘時間正確。</u>

* **keep** (kip) *v.* 維持；保持 ***keep time*** （鐘、錶）走得準
accurate ('ækjərɪt) *adj.* 準確的
correct (kə'rɛkt) *adj.* 正確的 **rice** (raɪs) *n.* 米
lime (laɪm) *n.* 萊姆

44. (**D**) Back off. She is not comfortable. 算了吧。她不太自在。

(A) 安慰她。她不高興。 (B) 把她送走。她不高興。

(C) 繼續做。她不高興。 (D) <u>停下來。她不高興。</u>

* ***back off*** 放棄；讓步
comfortable ('kʌmfə·təbḷ) *adj.* 舒服的；自在的
comfort ('kʌmfə·t) *v.* 安慰 ***send away*** 送走
go on 繼續下去

45. (**C**) Emma thanked the man for his help.
艾瑪謝謝那位男士的幫忙。

(A) 她忘恩負義。 (B) 她很生氣。
(C) <u>她很感激。</u> (D) 她很兇暴。

* ungrateful〔ʌn'gretfəl〕*adj.* 忘恩負義的
grateful〔'gretfəl〕*adj.* 感激的
violent〔'vaɪələnt〕*adj.* 兇暴的

46. (**A**) Private Carson was assigned to guard duty.
二等兵卡森被派去站哨。

(A) <u>他被叫去站哨。</u> (B) 他非常想去站哨。
(C) 他要求去站哨。 (D) 他忘記去站哨。

* private〔'praɪvɪt〕*n.* 二等兵
duty〔'djutɪ〕*n.* 責任；職責 ***guard duty*** 哨兵勤務

47. (**B**) All systems in a car are designed to do a specific job.
車子裡的所有裝置，都是被設計爲執行特定任務的。

(A) 每樣裝置都是設計爲執行豐富任務的。
(B) <u>每樣裝置都是設計爲執行特定任務的。</u>
(C) 每樣裝置都是設計爲執行可憐的功能的。
(D) 每樣裝置都是設計爲執行有害功能的。

* system〔'sɪstəm〕*n.* 機械裝置
specific〔spɪ'sɪfɪk〕*adj.* 特定的
job〔dʒɑb〕*n.* 任務；作用
plan〔plæn〕*v.* 設計
prolific〔prə'lɪfɪk〕*adj.* 豐富的
particular〔pɚ'tɪkjələ˞〕*adj.* 特定的
pathetic〔pə'θɛtɪk〕*adj.* 可憐的
pernicious〔pɚ'nɪʃəs〕*adj.* 有害的

48. (**D**) Ms. Jones knows what the population of Los Angeles is. 瓊斯女士知道洛杉磯的人口總數有多少。

(A) 她知道洛杉磯。

(B) 她認識瓊斯先生。

(C) 她知道爆米花。

(D) 她知道有多少人住在洛杉磯。

* population [ˌpɑpjəˈleʃən] *n.* 人口總數
Los Angeles 洛杉磯【美國加州西南部一港市】
popcorn [ˈpɑpˌkɔrn] *n.* 爆米花

49. (**D**) After the typhoon, the power was cut off for two hours. 颱風過後，電力中斷了兩個小時。

(A) 它被燒光了。 (B) 它被燒光了。

(C) 它被開啓了。 (D) 它被關掉了。

* typhoon [taɪˈfun] *n.* 颱風 power [ˈpaʊɚ] *n.* 電力
cut off 切斷；中斷 burn [bɝn] *v.* 燃燒
burn out 燒光 ***burn off*** 燒盡
turn on 打開開關 ***turn off*** 關掉

50. (**A**) The explosion caused the building to fall down suddenly. 爆炸使得建築物突然倒塌。

(A) 建築物倒塌了。 (B) 建築物被壓壞了。

(C) 建築物爆炸了。 (D) 建築物睡著了。

* explosion [ɪkˈsploʒən] *n.* 爆炸
cause [kɔz] *v.* 導致 ***fall down*** 倒塌
suddenly [ˈsʌdn̩lɪ] *adv.* 突然地
collapse [kəˈlæps] *v.* 倒塌 crush [krʌʃ] *v.* 壓壞
explode [ɪkˈsplod] *v.* 爆炸
asleep [əˈslip] *adj.* 睡著的 ***fall asleep*** 睡著

51. (**B**) M：Do you have any pets at home?

W：Yes, I have two dogs.

M：Don't you have any cats?

W：No, I hate cats.

What does the woman mean?

男：妳家有養寵物嗎？

女：有，我有兩隻狗。

男：妳沒有養貓嗎？

女：沒有，我討厭貓。

這位女士的意思是？

(A) 她有一隻貓。 (B) 她不喜歡貓。

(C) 狗討厭貓。 (D) 她喜歡貓。

* pet〔pɛt〕*n.* 寵物

52. (**B**) W：Are you ready to go?

M：I will be as soon as I change my shirt.

What is the man going to do?

女：你準備好要出發了嗎？

男：等我換好襯衫就好了。

這位男士將要做什麼？

(A) 換襪子。

(B) 穿上不同件襯衫。

(C) 改變他的做法。

(D) 買一件襯衫。

* ready〔ˈrɛdɪ〕*adj.* 準備好的

as soon as 一…就…

shirt〔ʃɜt〕*n.* 襯衫　　***put on*** 穿上

53. (**B**) W：What do you need?
M：I need more of this chemical.
What is the man probably doing?
女：你需要什麼？
男：我需要多一點這種化學藥劑。
這位男士可能正在做什麼？
(A) 做報告。 (B) 做實驗。
(C) 找工作。 (D) 爲了考試唸書。

* chemical ('kɛmɪkḷ) *n.* 化學藥品
probably ('prɑbəblɪ) *adv.* 可能
report (rɪ'port) *n.* 報告 conduct (kən'dʌkt) *v.* 進行
experiment (ɪk'spɛrəmənt) *n.* 實驗 ***look for*** 尋找

54. (**B**) W：What is your city famous for?
M：It's a seaport.
What is his city known for?
女：你的城市以什麼聞名？
男：它是個海港。
他的城市以什麼聞名？
(A) 有很多高樓。
(B) 它是一個船隻來往的地方。
(C) 你可以看到很多名人。
(D) 有很好的博物館。

* famous ('feməs) *adj.* 著名的
seaport ('si,port) *n.* 海港
be known for 因…而聞名
ship (ʃɪp) *n.* 船 ***come and go*** 來來去去
museum (mju'ziəm) *n.* 博物館

55. (**B**) W：May I help you, sir?

M：Is there a bakery in this shopping mall?

W：Yes, it's on the second floor.

What is the man trying to find?

女：先生，需要我幫忙嗎？

男：這間購物中心有麵包店嗎？

女：有的，在二樓。

這位男士試著找什麼？

(A) 禮品店。 (B) 買麵包的地方。

(C) 買花的地方。 (D) 寵物店。

* ***shopping mall*** 大型購物中心 floor〔 flɔr 〕*n.* 樓

bread〔 brɛd 〕*n.* 麵包

56. (**D**) M：Look at me. I'm soaking wet.

W：Me too. It's terrible outside, isn't it?

What is the weather like now?

男：看看我。我全身溼透了。

女：我也是。外面天氣糟透了，不是嗎？

現在天氣如何？

(A) 晴朗。 (B) 刮風。

(C) 下雪。 (D) 下雨。

* soaking〔'sokɪŋ〕*adv.* 溼淋淋地

wet〔 wɛt 〕*adj.* 濕的

terrible〔'tɛrəbḷ〕*adj.* 很糟的

sunny〔'sʌnɪ〕*adj.* 晴朗的

windy〔'wɪndɪ〕*adj.* 多風的；刮風的

snowy〔'snoɪ〕*adj.* 下雪的

rainy〔'renɪ〕*adj.* 下雨的

57. (**B**) M：Are there any tickets left for tonight's show?
W：I'm sorry. All tickets are already sold out.
Where does this conversation take place?
男：今晚的表演還有剩下票嗎？
女：抱歉。所有的票都已經賣完了。
這段對話發生在哪裡？
(A) 在博物館。 (B) 在戲院。
(C) 在車站。 (D) 在機場。

* ticket (ˈtɪkɪt) *n.* 門票 leave (liv) *v.* 剩下
show (ʃo) *n.* 表演 ***sell out*** 賣光
conversation (ˌkɑnvəˈseʃən) *n.* 對話
take place 發生 theater (ˈθiətɚ) *n.* 戲院
station (ˈsteʃən) *n.* 車站 airport (ˈɛrˌport) *n.* 機場

58. (**C**) W：Adam is so smart. He always has the right answer.
M：That's because he spends all his time reading books.
What is the man's opinion of Adam?
女：亞當眞是聰明。他總能想出正確答案。
男：那是因爲他把所有的時間都拿來唸書。
這位男士對亞當有什麼看法？
(A) 他欽佩亞當的聰明才智。
(B) 他想要多花點時間唸書。
(C) 他認爲亞當應該少花點時間唸書。
(D) 他不認爲亞當很勤奮。

* smart (smɑrt) *adj.* 聰明的 answer (ˈænsɚ) *n.* 答案
opinion (əˈpɪnjən) *n.* 看法 admire (ədˈmaɪr) *v.* 欽佩
would like to V. 想要 diligent (ˈdɪlədʒənt) *adj.* 勤奮的

59. (**D**) M：Do you remember the time we went to the animal park?
W：Wasn't that the time you slipped in the grass?
How well does the woman remember the trip to the animal park?
男：你記得我們去動物園那一次嗎？
女：不就是你在草地上滑倒的那次嗎？
這位女士對於那次去動物園旅遊記得多少？
(A) 她不記得那次的旅遊。
(B) 她記得那位男士在草地上睡覺。
(C) 她記得她在草地上滑倒。
(D) 她記得那位男士在草地上滑倒。

* remember〔 rɪ'mɛmbɚ 〕*v.* 記得　***animal park*** 動物園
slip〔 slɪp 〕*v.* 滑倒　grass〔 græs 〕*n.* 草地
trip〔 trɪp 〕*n.* 旅遊

60. (**C**) M：Do I need to wear a sweater?
W：I think you had better. They announced on the radio that it is going to snow.
What will the man probably do?
男：我需要穿毛衣嗎？
女：我想你最好穿上。收音機播報說將會下雪。
這位男士可能會做什麼？
(A) 他可能會聽收音機。　(B) 他可能會洗他的毛衣。
(C) 他可能會外出。　(D) 他可能會看窗外。

* sweater〔'swɛtɚ 〕*n.* 毛衣
announce〔 ə'naʊns 〕*v.* 播報
clean〔 klin 〕*v.* 清洗　***look out*** 從…往外看

LISTENING TEST ⑭

- *Directions for questions 1-25. You will hear questions on the test CD. Select the one item A, B, C or D which answers the question correctly, and mark your answer sheet.*

1. A. the rear B. the front
   C. the side D. the top

2. A. She sat down outside the theater.
   B. She sat down in the last row.
   C. She sat down in the front row.
   D. She sat down on stage.

3. A. about ten pockets B. about ten dollars
   C. about two dollars D. about twenty dollars

4. A. roses, tulips, and sunflowers
   B. spoons, knives, and forks
   C. cake, tea, and sugar
   D. balloons, lights, and cards

5. A. The temperature is staying the same.
   B. The temperature is going down.
   C. The temperature is rising.
   D. The temperature is fluctuating.

6. A. from and to B. up and down
   C. left and right D. here and there

7. A. He took it off the rim.
   B. He filled the tire with air.
   C. He repaired it.
   D. He let air out of the tire.

8. A. The water is polluted.
   B. The water is sluggish.
   C. The water is restricted.
   D. The water is purified.

9. A. provide the cure.
   B. deceive the symptoms.
   C. preview the cure.
   D. relieve the symptoms.

10. A. She had too many drinks.
    B. She had a dog.
    C. She had on a dark skirt.
    D. She doesn't like to dress up.

11. A. registration.
    B. reservation.
    C. accommodations.
    D. confirmation.

12. A. Give him a call.
    B. Go ask him a question.
    C. Ask someone to follow him.
    D. Steal his cell phone.

13. A. It's impossible to me.
    B. It's important to me.
    C. It's imposing to me.
    D. It's immature to me.

14. A. 10 blocks
    B. 2 blocks
    C. 12 blocks
    D. 20 blocks

15. A. She's not doing it. B. She's doing line.
C. She's doing fine. D. She's doing nine.

16. A. one he can count on.
B. one he can hurt.
C. one who can take care of the meals.
D. one who can do accounting.

17. A. Surgeons. B. Dentists.
C. Physicians. D. Experts.

18. A. attack them B. attach them
C. attract them D. attain them

19. A. an insolent change B. an important change
C. an intolerable change D. an unimportant change

20. A. at home B. in the city
C. in the mountains D. at the ocean

21. A. a difference of opinion B. a date
C. an agreement D. a huge, yellow plant

22. A. Yes, they like one another.
B. Yes, they like students.
C. Yes, they look the same.
D. Yes, they like number 2.

23. A. solar energy. B. lunar energy.
C. star energy. D. Mars energy.

24. A. a fireman B. a psychologist
C. a policeman D. a doctor

25. A. She always spends a lot. B. a quarter
C. four times the amount D. half the amount

● *Directions for questions 26-50. You will hear statements on the test CD. Select the one answer A, B, C, or D which comes closest to the meaning of the statement and mark your answer sheet.*

26. A. He had been gone only a minute before she called.
B. He left only a few minutes after she called.
C. He was just going to leave when she called.
D. He didn't leave after she called.

27. A. I go to work at six p.m.
B. I begin to work at six p.m.
C. I finish work at six p.m.
D. I come back from work at six p.m.

28. A. The road is wider after a kilometer.
B. The road is not so wide after a kilometer.
C. There is no road after a kilometer.
D. The road is dangerous after a kilometer.

29. A. I knew her before.
B. I'm looking after her.
C. I'm late to meet her.
D. I am eager to meet her.

30. A. Their resistance was strong.
    B. They were lacking in petroleum.
    C. They were defeated.
    D. They were ali captured.

31. A. She goes to the movies occasionally.
    B. She goes to the movie regularly.
    C. She goes to the movie steadily.
    D. She goes to the movie specially.

32. A. Janet and Paul sold the pen.
    B. Janet is using Paul's pen.
    C. Janet hid Paul's pen.
    D. Janet and Paul kept the pen.

33. A. They took prisoners.
    B. They took towers.
    C. They took petroleum.
    D. They took tanks.

34. A. They will meet in the post office.
    B. They will meet now.
    C. They will meet later.
    D. They met yesterday.

35. A. We were going to Madrid.
    B. We were going to Madrid first.
    C. We were going to Paris.
    D. We weren't going to Madrid.

36. A. He studies medicine.
    B. He purchases medicine.
    C. He anticipates medicine.
    D. He searches for medicine.

37. A. He will eat something.
    B. He will be angry.
    C. He will want some water.
    D. He will cry.

38. A. Wear your jacket. B. Burn your jacket.
    C. Ride your jacket. D. Hang up your jacket.

39. A. There is no bus going there.
    B. He doesn't ride the bus there.
    C. He doesn't like to take the bus.
    D. He never takes the bus to go anywhere.

40. A. She broke her pencil.
    B. She didn't understand the idea.
    C. She missed her exit.
    D. She stopped for some food.

41. A. He gave out the solution.
    B. He can't solve it.
    C. He never has problem.
    D. He worked it out.

42. A. It is dangerous. B. It is in bad condition.
    C. It is not wide. D. It has many turns.

43. A. He doesn't have the money to buy new shoes.
    B. He had his shoes repaired.
    C. He doesn't have time to buy new socks.
    D. He has the time but not the money.

44. A. They decided to fight off the exercises.
    B. They decided to issue the exercises.
    C. They decided to take on the exercises.
    D. They decided to escape the exercises.

45. A. Yesterday the bookstore was closed.
    B. The bookstore ran into Mr. Nolan.
    C. I met Mr. Nolan yesterday.
    D. I'll meet Mr. Nolan today.

46. A. He did something weird.
    B. He did something correct.
    C. He did something right.
    D. He did something wrong.

47. A. The group had to stay late.
    B. The group split up.
    C. The group was permitted to leave early.
    D. The group traveled together.

48. A. Tom and Jim rode the bus together.
    B. Jim got on the wrong bus.
    C. Both Tom and Jim rode the wrong bus.
    D. Tom and Jim like buses.

49. A. The trip to town was long.
    B. The bus was late.
    C. Standing up is tiring.
    D. All seats on the bus were taken.

50. A. They must fill out a blue form.
    B. They wish to take French.
    C. Only twenty students can take Japanese.
    D. The form has to be returned by Monday.

● *Directions for questions 51-60. You will hear dialogs on the test CD. Select the correct answer A, B, C, or D and mark your answer sheet.*

51. A. He is very occupied.
    B. She likes his watch.
    C. She doesn't know what time it is.
    D. He borrowed the watch from her.

52. A. take a break   B. eat lunch
    C. find out how much it costs
    D. find out how big it is

53. A. The ending was disappointing.
    B. The book ended happily.
    C. She thought the ending was sudden.
    D. She thought the book was good.

54. A. He is speaking softly.   B. He is yelling.
    C. He is planning ahead.   D. He is telling a secret.

55. A. clothes B. stationery
    C. toys D. tableware

56. A. She doesn't want to take breaks.
    B. She has too many chores to do.
    C. She doesn't have enough chores to do.
    D. The man wants her to take breaks.

57. A. It was a silly thing to do.
    B. The matter is not important.
    C. It was appropriate to do this.
    D. It was a good thing to do.

58. A. He should eat later.
    B. He should go to bed earlier.
    C. He should eat less before going to bed.
    D. He should eat different foods.

59. A. John's family will take him swimming.
    B. The son will be given some water.
    C. No one in John's family can swim.
    D. The son is on a different side of the beach.

60. A. He's not sure if the manager will be good or not.
    B. He agrees with her opinion that the manager will be good.
    C. He thinks the manager should run the company differently.
    D. He's not sure who the manager really is.

ECL 聽力測驗⑭詳解

1. (**A**) The tail of the aircraft was broken. What part of the aircraft was broken?
   這架飛機的機尾故障了。／這架飛機的哪個部分故障了？
   (A) 尾部。 (B) 前面。
   (C) 旁邊。 (D) 頂端。
   ＊ tail〔 tel 〕*n.* 機尾　aircraft〔ˈɛr,kræft〕*n.* 飛機
   broken〔ˈbrokən〕*adj.* 故障的　rear〔 rɪr 〕*n.* 尾部

2. (**C**) Wilma took a seat in the front row at the theater. What did she do?
   威瑪坐在戲院的前排。／她做了什麼？
   (A) 她坐在戲院外面。 (B) 她坐在最後一排。
   (C) 她坐在前排。 (D) 她坐在舞台上。
   ＊ seat〔 sit 〕*n.* 座位　***take a seat*** 坐下
   row〔 ro 〕*n.* 排　theater〔ˈθiətɚ〕*n.* 戲院
   outside〔ˈaʊtˈsaɪd〕*prep.* 在外面
   stage〔 stedʒ 〕*n.* 舞台

3. (**B**) We had approximately 10 dollars in our pockets. How much money did we have?
   我們的口袋裡大約有十元。／我們有多少錢？
   (A) 大約十個口袋。 (B) 大約十元。
   (C) 大約兩元。 (D) 大約二十元。
   ＊ approximately〔əˈprɑksəmɪtlɪ〕*adv.* 大約
   pocket〔ˈpɑkɪt〕*n.* 口袋

4. (**B**) Sam bought some tableware for his wife. What did he buy her? 他買了一些餐具給他妻子。／他買給她什麼？

(A) 玫瑰、鬱金香和向日葵。

(B) 湯匙、刀子和叉子。

(C) 蛋糕、茶和糖。

(D) 汽球、燈和卡片。

* tableware ('tebḷ,wɛr) *n.* 餐具　wife (waɪf) *n.* 妻子
rose (roz) *n.* 玫瑰　tulip ('tulɪp) *n.* 鬱金香
sunflower ('sʌn,flauɚ) *n.* 向日葵　spoon (spun) *n.* 湯匙
knife (naɪf) *n.* 刀子【複數爲 knives】
fork (fɔrk) *n.* 叉子　sugar ('ʃugɚ) *n.* 糖
balloon (bə'lun) *n.* 氣球

5. (**B**) The weather is getting colder. What's happening to the weather? 天氣變更冷了。／天氣怎麼了？

(A) 溫度保持不變。　(B) 溫度下降。

(C) 溫度上升。　(D) 溫度在變動。

* weather ('wɛðɚ) *n.* 天氣　happen ('hæpən) *v.* 發生
temperature ('tɛmpərətʃɚ) *n.* 溫度
same (sem) *adj.* 相同的；不變的　rise (raɪz) *v.* 上升
fluctuate ('flʌktʃu,et) *v.* 上下移動

6. (**B**) The picture had many vertical lines. Which direction did the lines go?
這張圖裡有很多條直線。／這些直線的走向是？

(A) 從和到。　(B) 上下。

(C) 左右。　(D) 到處。

* vertical ('vɝtɪkḷ) *adj.* 垂直的　line (laɪn) *n.* 線
direction (də'rɛkʃən) *n.* 方向　left (lɛft) *n.* 左邊
right (raɪt) *n.* 右邊　***here and there*** 到處

7. (**B**) I took the tire to the gas station and had an attendant inflate it. What did the attendant do?

我把這個輪胎拿到加油站去讓服務生充氣。／服務生做了什麼？

(A) 他把輪胎從輪框中取下。

(B) 他替輪胎充滿氣。

(C) 他修理輪胎。

(D) 他讓空氣從輪胎中跑出來。

＊ tire〔taɪr〕*n.* 輪胎　gas〔gæs〕*n.* 汽油
station〔ˈsteʃən〕*n.* 站　***gas station*** 加油站
attendant〔əˈtɛndənt〕*n.* 服務生
inflate〔ɪnˈflet〕*v.* 使鼓起；充氣　***take off*** 取下
rim〔rɪm〕*n.*（安裝車輪輪胎的）輪框
fill〔fɪl〕*v.* 裝滿　repair〔rɪˈpɛr〕*v.* 修理

8. (**A**) The area is roped off because the water is contaminated. Why did they rope off this area?

這個區域被用繩子隔開了，因為水受到污染。／他們為什麼要用繩子隔開這個區域？

(A) 水被污染。

(B) 水流得很慢。

(C) 水受限制。

(D) 水被淨化。

＊ area〔ˈɛrɪə〕*n.* 區域　rope〔rop〕*v.* 用繩隔開
contaminate〔kənˈtæmə͵net〕*v.* 污染
pollute〔pəˈlut〕*v.* 污染
sluggish〔ˈslʌgɪʃ〕*adj.*（流水等）緩慢的
restricted〔rɪˈstrɪktɪd〕*adj.* 受限制的
purify〔ˈpjʊrə͵faɪ〕*v.* 淨化

9. (**D**) The drugs could only alleviate the symptoms, not provide a cure. What can the drug do?
這種藥只能緩和症狀，不能提供治療。／這種藥能做什麼？

(A) 提供治療。 (B) 欺騙症狀。
(C) 預習治療。 (D) 緩和症狀。

* drug〔 drʌg 〕*n.* 藥
alleviate〔 əˈlivɪˌet 〕*v.* 緩和
symptom〔 ˈsɪmptəm 〕*n.* 症狀
provide〔 prəˈvaɪd 〕*v.* 提供
cure〔 kjʊr 〕*n.* 治療 deceive〔 dɪˈsiv 〕*v.* 欺騙
preview〔 priˈvju 〕*v.* 預習
relieve〔 rɪˈliv 〕*v.* 緩和

10. (**C**) What did your sister wear to the club?
你妹妹穿什麼到俱樂部去？

(A) 她喝了太多飲料。
(B) 她有一隻狗。
(C) 她穿一條深色的裙子。
(D) 她不喜歡盛裝打扮。

* wear〔 wɛr 〕*v.* 穿；戴 club〔 klʌb 〕*n.* 俱樂部
have〔 hæv 〕*v.* 吃；喝 drink〔 drɪŋk 〕*n.* 飲料
on〔 ɑn 〕*adv.* 穿著 dark〔 dɑrk 〕*adj.* 深色的
skirt〔 skɝt 〕*n.* 裙子 ***dress up*** 盛裝打扮

11. (**C**) The rooms and meals at the Spring Hotel were not only adequate but also inexpensive. What is adequate and inexpensive at the Spring Hotel?
春天旅館的房間和餐點不但充足，而且便宜。／春天旅館的什麼充足又便宜？

(A) 登記。　　(B) 預訂。
(C) <u>住宿設備。</u>　　(D) 確認。

* meal〔 mil 〕*n.* 餐飯　***not only…but also*** 不但…而且…
adequate〔'ædəkwɪt〕*adj.* 充分的
inexpensive〔,ɪnɪk'spɛnsɪv〕*adj.* 便宜的
registration〔,rɛdʒɪ'streʃən〕*n.* 登記
reservation〔,rɛzə'veʃən〕*n.* 預訂
accommodation〔ə,kɑmə'deʃən〕*n.* 住宿設備
confirmation〔,kɑnfə'meʃən〕*n.* 確認

12. (**A**) Give the captain a ring after you land. What should you do after landing? 等你降落之後，打個電話給指揮官。／你降落之後應該做什麼？

(A) <u>打電話給他。</u>　　(B) 去問他問題。
(C) 要求某人跟著他。　　(D) 偷走他的手機。

* captain〔'kæptən〕*n.* 指揮官　ring〔 rɪŋ 〕*n.* 打電話
land〔 lænd 〕*v.* 登陸；降落　steal〔 stil 〕*v.* 偷走
cell phone 手機

13. (**B**) Are you serious about your work?
你有認眞看待你的工作嗎？

(A) 對我而言，那是不可能的。
(B) <u>對我而言，工作很重要。</u>
(C) 它讓我印象深刻。
(D) 對我而言，那是尙未成熟的。

* serious〔'sɪrɪəs〕*adj.* 認眞的
impossible〔ɪm'pɑsəbl̩〕*adj.* 不可能的
important〔ɪm'pɔrtn̩t〕*adj.* 重要的
imposing〔ɪm'pozɪŋ〕*adj.* 給人深刻印象的
immature〔,ɪmə'tʃʊr〕*adj.* 未成熟的

14. (**C**) Johnny is at the shop. He wants to go back to his house. It is necessary for him to walk twelve blocks. How far is it from the shop to Johnny's house?

強尼在這家店裡。他要回家去。他必須走十二個街區。／從這家店到強尼的家有多遠？

(A) 十個街區。 (B) 兩個街區。
(C) 十二個街區。 (D) 二十個街區。

* necessary〔ˈnɛsəˌsɛrɪ〕*adj.* 必須的
block〔blɑk〕*n.* 街區 far〔fɑr〕*adj.* 遙遠的

15. (**C**) How is Miss Smith getting along with her new job?

史密斯小姐的新工作進展如何？

(A) 她現在沒在做了。 (B) 她在做線。
(C) 她做得不錯。 (D) 她在做九。

* ***get along with*** （工作）進展

16. (**A**) Every director needs an assistant that he can trust to take care of problems. What kind of assistant does a director need?

每個導演都需要一位可以信任的助理，來幫他處理問題。／導演需要哪一種助理？

(A) 他可以依賴的助理。 (B) 他可以傷害的助理。
(C) 可以負責餐點的助理。 (D) 會記帳的助理。

* director〔dəˈrɛktɚ〕*n.* 導演
assistant〔əˈsɪstənt〕*n.* 助理 trust〔trʌst〕*v.* 信任
take care of 處理；負責
count on 依賴 hurt〔hɝt〕*v.* 傷害
accounting〔əˈkaʊntɪŋ〕*n.* 會計；記帳

17. (**B**) Who can take care of people's teeth and treat diseases of the mouth?
誰可以照顧人們的牙齒，並治療口腔疾病？
(A) 外科醫生。 (B) 牙醫。
(C) 內科醫生。 (D) 專家。

* ***take care of*** 照顧　teeth〔 tiθ 〕*n. pl.* 牙齒【單數爲 tooth】
treat〔 trit 〕*v.* 治療　disease〔 dɪ'ziz 〕*n.* 疾病
mouth〔 maʊθ 〕*n.* 嘴巴　surgeon〔'sɝdʒən 〕*n.* 外科醫生
dentist〔'dɛntɪst 〕*n.* 牙醫
physician〔 fə'zɪʃən 〕*n.* 內科醫生
expert〔'ɛkspɝt 〕*n.* 專家

18. (**B**) Please fasten the two parts of your seatbelt. What should we do?
請將安全帶的兩側扣好。／我們應該做什麼？
(A) 攻擊它們。 (B) 繫上它們。
(C) 吸引它們。 (D) 獲得它們。

* fasten〔'fæsn̩ 〕*v.* 扣住；繫牢
seatbelt〔'sit'bɛlt 〕*n.* 安全帶　attack〔 ə'tæk 〕*v.* 攻擊
attach〔 ə'tætʃ 〕*v.* 繫上　attain〔 ə'tɛn 〕*v.* 獲得

19. (**B**) Miss Vivian made a major change in her attitude. What kind of change was it?
薇薇安小姐的態度有重大的轉變。／那是哪一種轉變？
(A) 無禮的轉變。 (B) 重要的轉變。
(C) 無法忍受的轉變。 (D) 不重要的轉變。

* major〔'medʒɚ 〕*adj.* 重大的　attitude〔'ætə,tjud 〕*n.* 態度
insolent〔'ɪnsələnt 〕*adj.* 無禮的；傲慢的
intolerable〔 ɪn'tɑlərəbl̩ 〕*adj.* 無法忍受的
unimportant〔,ʌnɪm'pɔrtn̩t 〕*adj.* 不重要的

20. (**D**) Kelly got knocked over by a big wave. Where was she? 凱利被大浪給撞倒。／她在哪裡？

(A) 在家裡。 (B) 在城裡。
(C) 在山裡。 (D) 在海裡。

* knock〔nɑk〕*v.* 敲打；撞倒 ***knock over*** 撞倒
wave〔wev〕*n.* 波浪 ocean〔'oʃən〕*n.* 海洋

21. (**A**) Jane and Marc had an argument. What did they have? 珍和馬可吵架了。／他們有什麼？

(A) 意見不合。 (B) 約會。
(C) 協定。 (D) 又大又黃的植物。

* argument〔'ɑrgjumənt〕*n.* 爭吵
difference〔'dɪfərəns〕*n.* 不同
opinion〔ə'pɪnjən〕*n.* 意見 date〔det〕*n.* 約會
agreement〔ə'grimənt〕*n.* 協定
huge〔hjudʒ〕*adj.* 巨大的 plant〔plænt〕*n.* 植物

22. (**C**) Are those two girls alike? 那兩個女孩長得像嗎？

(A) 是的，她們互相喜歡。 (B) 是的，她們喜歡學生。
(C) 是的，她們看起來很像。 (D) 是的，她們喜歡二號。

* alike〔ə'laɪk〕*adj.* 相似的 ***one another*** 互相
same〔sem〕*adj.* 相似的

23. (**A**) What do you call the power of the sun's light and heat? 你怎麼稱呼太陽的光能和熱能？

(A) 太陽能。 (B) 月球的能量。
(C) 星星的能量。 (D) 火星的能量。

* heat〔hit〕*n.* 熱 solar〔'solɚ〕*adj.* 太陽的
energy〔'ɛnɚdʒɪ〕*n.* 能量 lunar〔'lunɚ〕*adj.* 月球的

24. (**D**) The student has a broken arm. Who should he see?
這名學生的手臂骨折了。／他應該去看誰？

(A) 消防員。 (B) 心理學家。
(C) 警察。 (D) <u>醫生。</u>

* broken ['brokən] *adj.* 骨折的 arm [ɑrm] *n.* 手臂
fireman ['faɪrmən] *n.* 消防員
psychologist [saɪ'kɑlədʒɪst] *n.* 心理學家
policeman [pə'lismən] *n.* 警察

25. (**B**) Mary spent a fourth of her money. How much of it did she spend?
瑪麗花了四分之一的錢。／她花了多少錢？

(A) 她總是花很多錢。
(B) <u>四分之一。</u>
(C) 這個數目的四倍。
(D) 這個數目的一半。

* spend [spɛnd] *v.* 花費
fourth [forθ] *n.* 四分之一
quarter ['kwɔrtɚ] *n.* 四分之一
time [taɪm] *n.* 倍 amount [ə'maʊnt] *n.* 數量
half [hæf] *adj.* 一半的

26. (**A**) He had just left my house when she called.
她打電話來的時候，他才剛離開我家。

(A) <u>她打電話來前一分鐘他才離開。</u>
(B) 他在她打來幾分鐘之後就離開。
(C) 她打來的時候，他正準備要離開。
(D) 她打來之後，他沒有離開。

27. (**C**) I get through work at six p.m. every day.
我每天下午六點做完工作。

(A) 我下午六點去上班。
(B) 我下午六點開始工作。
(C) 我下午六點完成工作。
(D) 我下午六點下班回家。

* ***get through*** 完成　finish [ˈfɪnɪʃ] *v.* 完成
come back 回來

28. (**B**) That road narrows to one lane after a kilometer.
那條路在一公里之後變窄爲一個車道。

(A) 那條路在一公里之後比較寬。
(B) 那條路在一公里之後就沒這麼寬。
(C) 一公里之後就沒路了。
(D) 那條路在一公里之後很危險。

* **narrow** [ˈnæro] *v.* 變窄　**lane** [len] *n.* 車道
kilometer [ˈkɪlə,mitɚ] *n.* 公里
wide [waɪd] *adj.* 寬的
dangerous [ˈdendʒərəs] *adj.* 危險的

29. (**D**) I'm looking forward to meeting her.
我期待見到她。

(A) 我以前就認識她了。
(B) 我正在照顧她。
(C) 我跟她見面時遲到了。
(D) 我渴望見到她。

* ***look forward to*** 期待　meet [mit] *v.* 見面
look after 照顧　late [let] *adj.* 遲到的
eager [ˈigɚ] *adj.* 渴望的

30. (**A**) The enemy put up a great deal of opposition to the forces. 敵人大力反抗軍隊。

(A) 他們強烈反抗。　(B) 他們缺乏石油。
(C) 他們被打敗了。　(D) 他們全都被俘虜了。

* enemy〔'ɛnəmɪ〕*n.* 敵人　***put up*** 表示（抵抗）
a great deal of 許多的　opposition〔,ɑpə'zɪʃən〕*n.* 反抗
forces〔'fɔrsɪs〕*n. pl.* 軍隊
resistance〔rɪ'zɪstəns〕*n.* 反抗
lack〔læk〕*v.* 缺乏　petroleum〔pə'trolɪəm〕*n.* 石油
defeat〔dɪ'fit〕*v.* 打敗　capture〔'kæptʃɚ〕*v.* 俘虜

31. (**A**) She doesn't go to the movies very often—just off and on. 她沒有很常去看電影——只是有時候去看。

(A) 她偶爾去看電影。　(B) 她經常去看電影。
(C) 她經常去看電影。　(D) 她專門去看電影。

* ***off and on*** 有時　occasionally〔ə'keʒənḷɪ〕*adv.* 偶爾
regularly〔'rɛgjələlɪ〕*adv.* 定期地；經常地
steadily〔'stɛdəlɪ〕*adv.* 經常地
specially〔'spɛʃəlɪ〕*adv.* 專門地

32. (**B**) Janet borrowed a pen from Paul.
珍娜向保羅借了一隻筆。

(A) 珍娜和保羅賣了那隻筆。
(B) 珍娜在用保羅的筆。
(C) 珍娜把保羅的筆藏起來。
(D) 珍娜和保羅保存那隻筆。

* borrow〔'bɑro〕*v.* 借（入）
sell〔sɛl〕*v.* 販賣【過去式及過去分詞爲 sold】
hide〔haɪd〕*v.* 隱藏【過去式爲 hid】
keep〔kip〕*v.* 保存

33. (**A**) The soldiers captured many of the enemy troops.
士兵俘虜了許多敵軍。

(A) 他們抓到俘虜。　(B) 他們抓到塔。
(C) 他們抓到石油。　(D) 他們抓到坦克。

* soldier〔'soldʒɚ〕*n.* 士兵
enemy〔'ɛnəmɪ〕*adj.* 敵國的
troops〔trupz〕*n. pl.* 軍隊
prisoner〔'prɪznɚ〕*n.* 囚犯；俘虜
tower〔'tauɚ〕*n.* 塔　tank〔tæŋk〕*n.* 坦克車

34. (**C**) Fanny has postponed her meeting with Belinda.
芬妮把她和布蘭達見面的時間延後。

(A) 她們會在郵局碰面。
(B) 她們現在會碰面。
(C) 她們晚點才會見面。
(D) 她們昨天見過面了。

* postpone〔post'pon〕*v.* 延期
meeting〔'mitɪŋ〕*n.* 會面　***post office*** 郵局
later〔'letɚ〕*adv.* 較晚地

35. (**A**) We had to land in Paris while en route to Madrid.
我們在到馬德里的途中，必須在巴黎降落。

(A) 我們前往馬德里。
(B) 我們先去馬德里。
(C) 我們去巴黎。
(D) 我們不去馬德里。

* Paris〔'pærɪs〕*n.* 巴黎
en route〔ɑn'rut〕*adv.* 在途中
Madrid〔mə'drɪd〕*n.* 馬德里

36. (**A**) My brother is studying medicine in college.

我弟弟在大學唸醫科。

(A) <u>他唸醫學。</u> (B) 他買藥。
(C) 他期待藥。 (D) 他找藥。

* medicine〔'mɛdəsn̩〕*n.* 醫學；藥
college〔'kɑlɪdʒ〕*n.* 大學
purchase〔'pɝtʃəs〕*v.* 購買
anticipate〔æn'tɪsə,pet〕*v.* 期待
search〔sɝtʃ〕*v.* 尋找

37. (**C**) He will be thirsty when he comes back.

當他回來的時候，他會很渴。

(A) 他會吃一些東西。
(B) 他會很生氣。
(C) <u>他會想要一些水。</u>
(D) 他會哭。

* thirsty〔'θɝstɪ〕*adj.* 口渴的
angry〔'æŋgrɪ〕*adj.* 生氣的

38. (**A**) Here, put on your jacket.

好了，穿上你的夾克。

(A) <u>穿著你的夾克。</u>
(B) 燒掉你的夾克。
(C) 騎著你的夾克。
(D) 把你的夾克掛好。

* here〔hɪr〕*interj.* 好了【用於喚起別人的注意或告誡孩子】
put on 穿上 burn〔bɝn〕*v.* 燒掉
ride〔raɪd〕*v.* 騎 hang〔hæŋ〕*v.* 懸掛
hang up 吊；掛

39. (**B**) Tom jogged to the Base Exchange. He never takes the bus there.
湯姆慢跑到基地消費合作社。他從來沒搭過那裡的公車。

(A) 沒有公車到那裡。
(B) 他沒有搭那裡的公車。
(C) 他不喜歡搭公車。
(D) 他從來沒有搭公車到任何地方去。

* **jog** (dʒɑg) *v.* 慢跑　　base (bes) *n.* 基地
exchange (ɪks'tʃendʒ) *n.* (消費)合作社
base exchange 基地消費合作社　　take (tek) *v.* 搭乘
ride (raɪd) *v.* 搭乘

40. (**B**) Miss Key missed the point. 綺小姐錯過重點。

(A) 她把鉛筆摔斷。
(B) 她不了解那個觀念。
(C) 她錯過她的出口。
(D) 她停下來買一些食物。

* **miss** (mɪs) *v.* 錯過　　point (pɔɪnt) *n.* 重點
idea (aɪ'diə) *n.* 觀念;概念　　exit ('ɛgzɪt) *n.* 出口

41. (**D**) Carl kept studying the problem until he solved it.
卡爾一直研究這個問題,直到解出來爲止。

(A) 他公佈答案。
(B) 他解不出來。
(C) 他從來都沒有問題。
(D) 他解決了這個問題。

* **keep** (kip) *v.* 繼續　　solve (sɑlv) *v.* 解決;解答
give out 公佈　　solution (sə'luʃən) *n.* 解答
work out 解決(問題)

42. (**C**) The freeway in some places is very narrow.
有些地方的高速公路很窄。

(A) 高速公路很危險。 (B) 高速公路狀況不佳。
(C) 高速公路不寬。 (D) 高速公路有很多轉彎。

* freeway〔ˈfriˌwe〕*n.* 高速公路
narrow〔ˈnæro〕*adj.* 狹窄的
condition〔kənˈdɪʃən〕*n.* 狀況 turn〔tɝn〕*n.* 轉彎處

43. (**C**) Charles said, "I need to buy a pair of new socks, but I don't have the time."
查理說：「我需要買一雙新的襪子，但是我沒有時間」。

(A) 他沒有錢買新鞋。
(B) 他把鞋子送修。
(C) 他沒有時間買新襪子。
(D) 他有時間，但是沒有錢。

* pair〔pɛr〕*n.* 雙 socks〔sɑks〕*n. pl.* 短襪
shoes〔ʃuz〕*n. pl.* 鞋子 repair〔rɪˈpɛr〕*v.* 修理

44. (**C**) The commanders agreed to do the exercises.
指揮官同意要實施演習。

(A) 他們決定要擊退演習。
(B) 他們決定要發佈演習。
(C) 他們決定要開始演習。
(D) 他們決定要逃避演習。

* commander〔kəˈmændɚ〕*n.* 指揮官
agree〔əˈgri〕*v.* 同意 exercises〔ˈɛksɚˌsaɪzɪz〕*n. pl.* 演習
decide〔dɪˈsaɪd〕*v.* 決定 ***fight off*** 作戰而擊退
issue〔ˈɪʃjʊ〕*v.* 發佈 ***take on*** 開始做；開始處理
escape〔əˈskep〕*v.* 逃避

45. (**C**) I ran into Mr. Nolan yesterday in the bookstore.
我昨天在書店偶然遇到諾蘭先生。

(A) 昨天書店沒開。
(B) 書店偶然遇到諾蘭先生。
(C) 我昨天遇到諾蘭先生。
(D) 我今天會跟諾蘭先生碰面。

* ***run into*** 偶然遇到　　closed (klozd) *adj.* 關閉的

46. (**D**) Alex committed an error.
艾力克斯犯了錯。

(A) 他做了奇怪的事。　(B) 他做了正確的事。
(C) 他做了正確的事。　(D) 他做錯事。

* commit (kə'mɪt) *v.* 犯（罪、過錯等）
error ('ɛrɚ) *n.* 錯誤　　weird (wɪrd) *adj.* 奇怪的
correct (kə'rɛkt) *adj.* 正確的

47. (**C**) When the workers finished their project, they got time off for a job well done.
員工做完計畫之後，因爲做得很好而獲得休息時間。

(A) 這個團體必須留到很晚。
(B) 這個團體分裂了。
(C) 這個團體被允許早點離開。
(D) 這個團體一起去旅行。

* project ('prɑdʒɛkt) *n.* 計畫　　off (ɔf) *adv.* 休息
for (fɔr) *prep.* 爲了；由於
well done ('wɛl'dʌn) *adj.* 做得好的
split (splɪt) *v.* 分裂
permit (pɚ'mɪt) *v.* 允許

48. (**C**) Tom got on the wrong bus yesterday. **Jim did,** too.
湯姆昨天搭錯公車。吉姆也是。

(A) 湯姆和吉姆一起搭公車。

(B) 湯姆搭錯公車。

(C) 湯姆和吉姆兩個人都搭錯公車。

(D) 湯姆和吉姆都喜歡公車。

* ***get on*** 搭上

49. (**D**) We had to stand up in the bus on **the trip to town.**
到鎮上的途中，我們必須站著搭公車。

(A) 到鎮上的旅途很漫長。

(B) 公車晚來。

(C) 站著很累人。

(D) 公車上的所有座位都有人坐。

* full (ful) *adj.* 客滿的 tiring ('taɪrɪŋ) *adj.* 令人疲倦的
take (tek) *v.* 佔（位子）

50. (**C**) All students who wish to take **Japanese must fill out** the red form, only 20 students will **be permitted.**
所有想修日語的學生都要填紅色的表格。只有二十個學生可以修這堂課。

(A) 他們必須填藍色表格。

(B) 他們希望修法文。

(C) 只有二十個學生可以修日語。

(D) 表格必須在星期一前交回。

* take (tek) *v.* 修（課程）
Japanese (ˌdʒæpə'niz) *n.* 日語
fill out 填寫 form (fɔrm) *n.* 表格
French (frɛntʃ) *n.* 法語 return (rɪ'tɝn) *v.* 交回

51. (**C**) W：Excuse me, do you have the time?

M：My watch is out of order.

Which one is true?

女：抱歉，你知道現在幾點嗎？

男：我的錶壞了。

何者正確？

(A) 他非常忙。 (B) 她喜歡他的錶。

(C) <u>她不知道現在幾點。</u> (D) 他向她借錶。

＊ ***Do you have the time?*** 你知道現在幾點嗎？

(*cf. Do you have time?* 你有時間嗎？)

out of order 壞了 occupied〔'ɑkjə,paɪd〕*adj.* 無空閒的

52. (**D**) W：Is this all right?

M：I don't know. We need to measure it first.

What does the man want to do first?

女：沒問題吧？

男：不知道。我們需要先測量一下。

這位男士要先做什麼？

(A) 休息一下。 (B) 吃午餐。

(C) 查出要花多少錢。 (D) <u>查出它有多大。</u>

＊ ***all right*** 沒問題的 measure〔'mɛʒɚ〕*v.* 測量

break〔brek〕*n.* 休息 ***find out*** 找出；查出

53. (**C**) M：What did you think of the book?

W：The ending was very abrupt.

What did the woman think?

男：妳覺得這本書怎樣？

女：結局太令人意外。

這位女士怎麼想？

(A) 結局令人失望。 (B) 這本書有快樂的結局。
(C) 她認爲結局太出人意料。 (D) 她認爲這本書不錯。

* ending〔ˈɛndɪŋ〕*n.* 結局 abrupt〔əˈbrʌpt〕*adj.* 意外的
disappointing〔ˌdɪsəˈpɔɪntɪŋ〕*adj.* 令人失望的
end〔ɛnd〕*v.* 結束
sudden〔ˈsʌdn̩〕*adj.* 突然的；出乎意料的

54. (**A**) W：Why are you whispering?
M：My throat is very sore today.
What is the man doing?
女：你爲什麼要低聲說話？
男：我今天喉嚨很痛。
這位男士在做什麼？

(A) 他在輕聲說話。 (B) 他在大叫。
(C) 他在事先規劃。 (D) 他在說一個祕密。

* whisper〔ˈhwɪspɚ〕*v.* 悄悄說；低聲說
throat〔θrot〕*n.* 喉嚨 sore〔sor〕*adj.* 痛的
softly〔ˈsɔftlɪ〕*adv.* 輕聲地
yell〔jɛl〕*v.* 大叫 plan〔plæn〕*v.* 規劃
ahead〔əˈhɛd〕*adv.* 事先 secret〔ˈsikrɪt〕*n.* 祕密

55. (**B**) W：What are you getting Mary for her birthday?
M：I bought her a pink pencil case.
W：That's nice. I got her a new ballpoint pen.
What gifts will the speakers give Mary?
女：你要買什麼送瑪莉當生日禮物？
男：我買了粉紅色的鉛筆盒要給她。
女：那不錯啊。我買了一枝新的原子筆給她。
說話者要送瑪莉什麼禮物？

(A) 衣服。 (B) <u>文具。</u>
(C) 玩具。 (D) 餐具。

* pink〔pɪŋk〕*adj.* 粉紅色的　case〔kes〕*n.* 盒子
ballpoint pen 原子筆　gift〔gɪft〕*n.* 禮物
clothes〔kloðz〕*n. pl.* 衣服
stationery〔ˈsteʃən,ɛrɪ〕*n.*【集合名詞】文具
toy〔tɔɪ〕*n.* 玩具

56. (**B**) W：I never seem to be able to get all my chores done.
M：That's because you're always taking breaks.
What problem is the woman having?
女：我似乎永遠沒辦法把所有家事做完。
男：那是因爲妳一直在休息。
這位女士有什麼問題？
(A) 她不要休息。
(B) <u>她有太多家事要做。</u>
(C) 她沒有足夠的家事可做。
(D) 那位男士要她休息。

* seem〔sim〕*v.* 似乎　chore〔tʃor〕*n.* 家事；雜務
done〔dʌn〕*adj.* 完成的

57. (**A**) W：I slept all night with the air-conditioner on and the window open. I can't believe I did it.
M：You should have known better.
What does the man mean?
女：我整晚睡覺時都開著空調和窗戶。我眞不敢相信我做了這樣的事。
男：妳應該不會笨到做這種事。

這位男士的意思是？

(A) 這樣做很蠢。　　(B) 這件事不重要。
(C) 這樣做很適當。　　(D) 這樣做很好。

* air-conditioner〔'ɛrkən'dɪʃənɚ〕*n.* 空氣調節機
on〔ɑn〕*adv.* 開著
know better (than to V.) 不會笨到做…的地步
silly〔'sɪlɪ〕*adj.* 愚蠢的　　matter〔'mætɚ〕*n.* 事情
appropriate〔ə'proprɪɪt〕*adj.* 適當的

58. (**C**) M：I couldn't sleep at all last night. I think it may be my nerves.

W：Maybe you should not eat so much right before going to bed. It could keep you up.

What is the woman saying to the man?

男：我昨天整晚都睡不著。我覺得可能是因爲我很焦慮。
女：也許你不該在睡前吃太多東西。那會使你睡不著。
這位女士對那位男士說什麼？

(A) 他應該晚點吃東西。　　(B) 他應該早點睡。
(C) 他睡前應該少吃一點。　　(D) 他應該吃不同的食物。

* ***not at all*** 一點也不；完全不
nerves〔nɝvz〕*n.* 神經過敏；焦慮
keep *sb.* ***up*** 使某人睡不著
different〔'dɪfərənt〕*adj.* 不同的

59. (**C**) W：Do you think their son will ever learn to swim?

M：I doubt it. Nobody on John's side of the family has ever taken to the water.

What does the man say?

女：你認爲他們的兒子究竟能不能學會游泳？
男：我懷疑。約翰那邊的家族，從來沒有一個人能適應水。
這位男士說什麼？

(A) 約翰的家人會帶他去游泳。
(B) 人們會給這個兒子一些水。
(C) 約翰的家族沒有人會游泳。
(D) 兒子在海灘的另一邊。

* ever (ˈɛvɚ) *adv.* 究竟；從來　　doubt (daʊt) *v.* 懷疑
take to 適應

60. (**A**) W：The new manager is different. He's more relaxed and friendlier.
M：Time will tell. He's had no experience running a company. I'll wait before making my decision.
What does the man imply?

女：新來的經理很不一樣。他比較寬大和友善。
男：時間會證明一切。他沒有經營公司的經驗。我要等等再做決定。
這位男士在暗示什麼？

(A) 他不確定這位經理是好是壞。
(B) 他同意她的意見，認爲這位經理會是不錯的經理。
(C) 他認爲經理應該以不同的方式經營這家公司。
(D) 他不確定經理到底是誰。

* manager (ˈmænɪdʒɚ) *n.* 經理
relaxed (rɪˈlækst) *adj.* 寬大的
friendly (ˈfrɛndlɪ) *adj.* 友善的
Time will tell. 時間會證明一切。
experience (ɪkˈspirɪəns) *n.* 經驗　　run (rʌn) *v.* 經營
decision (dɪˈsɪʒən) *n.* 決定　　imply (ɪmˈplaɪ) *v.* 暗示
differently (ˈdɪfərəntly) *adv.* 不同地

LISTENING TEST ⑮

- *Directions for questions 1-25. You will hear questions on the test CD. Select the one item A, B, C or D which answers the question correctly, and mark your answer sheet.*

1. A. food B. coins
   C. toy D. presents

2. A. logistics B. cooking
   C. fighting D. writing

3. A. metal B. plastic
   C. glass D. wood

4. A. It was to his mother.
   B. It was to a teacher who lives in the suburbs.
   C. It was to another city.
   D. It was an expensive call.

5. A. Yes, I'm irritated.
   B. Yes, I went to bed late.
   C. Yes, I am a fast worker.
   D. Yes, I like to eat early.

6. A. what its uses are
   B. what its contents are
   C. what its characteristics are
   D. what its abilities are

7. A. in her fingers B. in her toes
   C. in her ears D. in her teeth

8. A. The sound became louder.
   B. The sound became softer.
   C. The sound became more irritating.
   D. The sound became more cheerful.

9. A. throw vegetables B. grow vegetables
   C. grind coffee beans D. fix appliances

10. A. It was moving. B. It was stopped.
    C. It was boring. D. It was alive.

11. A. to make it tidy. B. to keep it tidy.
    C. to make order. D. to keep order.

12. A. after delivery B. at the time of delivery
    C. before delivery D. yesterday

13. A. to slow down
    B. to return to the barracks
    C. to eat lunch
    D. to move quickly

14. A. on the roof B. in the yard
    C. in the house D. in the garage

15. A. anybody B. nobody
    C. ladies only D. no one

16. A. Jenny was sleeping. B. Jenny was hurt.
    C. Jenny was bored. D. Jenny went to school.

17. A. what is on his face
    B. what is in the place
    C. what is in the bone
    D. what is in the container

18. A. Of course. Take Moon Road and then turn left.
    B. It'll take you about ten minutes.
    C. You can buy tickets at this counter.
    D. There will be many people.

19. A. erase the table
    B. take the table away
    C. remove the tableware from the table
    D. place the tableware

20. A. It's about a ten-minute drive.
    B. It's about a ten-minute drink.
    C. It's about a ten-minute dream.
    D. It's about a ten-minute dance.

21. A. close the door B. stop talking
    C. turn off the radio D. turn off the light

22. A. in front of me B. behind me
    C. on me D. next to me

23. A. trap people's eyes
    B. catch the reader's eyes
    C. find the reader's eyes
    D. reach people's eyes

24. A. $ 14.00 B. $ 12.00
    C. $ 40.00 D. $ 20.00

25. A. arms B. toes
    C. eyes D. fingers

● *Directions for questions 26-50. You will hear statements on the test CD. Select the one answer A, B, C, or D which comes closest to the meaning of the statement and mark your answer sheet.*

26. A. Rita wrote the novel.
    B. Rita underlined the novel.
    C. Rita wants the novel.
    D. Rita hates the novel

27. A. She has to cut in her eating.
    B. She has to take up eating.
    C. She has to cut down on her eating.
    D. She has to enrich her diet.

28. A. He can guess it.
    B. He can authorize it to be done.
    C. He can grind it.
    D. He can guide it.

29. A. His mind is disturbed.
    B. His mind is healthy.
    C. His mind is normal.
    D. His mind is OK.

30. A. Pauline loves to see Frank.
    B. Pauline doesn't want to leave Frank.
    C. Pauline wants to talk to Frank.
    D. Pauline doesn't want to see Frank.

31. A. Donald was too little.
    B. Donald was too stupid.
    C. Donald was too good.
    D. Donald was too lazy.

32. A. Our vacation lasted five weeks.
    B. A long time has passed since our last vacation.
    C. Five people went on vacation together.
    D. We have never taken a vacation.

33. A. We dropped her off there.
    B. We went to see her there.
    C. We admitted her.
    D. We released her from there.

34. A. He is curious about what will happen.
    B. He is furious about what will happen.
    C. He is angry about what will happen.
    D. He is upset about what will happen.

35. A. He got his prescription. B. He has seen a doctor.
C. He is still waiting. D. He is still a nurse.

36. A. Now he has long hair. B. Now he has a beard.
C. Now he has a demand. D. Now he is bald.

37. A. They like to dye their hair.
B. They become bald.
C. Their hair turns gray.
D. They have their hair dyed.

38. A. Tom speaks loudly.
B. Tom's hearing is good.
C. Mary has hearing problems.
D. Mary was not speaking loud enough.

39. A. She's a housewife. B. She is hard-working.
C. She is unfriendly. D. She is demanding.

40. A. The weather is nice.
B. It's too hot to be outside.
C. The weather is very cold.
D. Eileen is bored.

41. A. There may be rain. B. It will be sunny.
C. It will rain much later. D. It will certainly rain.

42. A. She's long-haired. B. She's a brunette.
C. She's a character. D. She's blonde.

43. A. He was trying to find a pair.
    B. He was admiring one.
    C. He lost his pants.
    D. He changed into pants.

44. A. The student was late.
    B. The student was asked to solve the problem.
    C. The student finished the homework.
    D. The student didn't understand the problem.

45. A. He watches his employees.
    B. He demands his employees.
    C. He is fooling around.
    D. He punishes the students.

46. A. Don't rush.
    B. Use an alarm clock.
    C. Take a watch with you.
    D. Hurry up.

47. A. They eat different kinds of fruits daily.
    B. They beat different kinds of fruits daily.
    C. They eat distant kinds of fruits weekly.
    D. They eat dynamic kinds of fruits nightly.

48. A. He smokes a little.
    B. He doesn't smoke at all there.
    C. The library is a no smoking area.
    D. He smokes when he goes to the library.

49. A. She is free on Monday.
    B. She has a break on Thursday from two to three.
    C. She wants to play golf during her break.
    D. She has two hours free on Thursday.

50. A. I like skating.
    B. I want an opportunity to go skating.
    C. I want to go skating tomorrow.
    D. I wish I could skate.

- *Directions for questions 51-60. You will hear dialogs on the test CD. Select the correct answer A, B, C, or D and mark your answer sheet.*

51. A. She likes golf a lot.
    B. Tennis is the sport she likes the most.
    C. Golf is not a sport, but a favorite.
    D. She likes tennis only.

52. A. He doesn't know where Atlanta is.
    B. He doesn't see the bus.
    C. He is certain that the bus stops at Atlanta.
    D. He doesn't know if the bus stops at Atlanta.

53. A. She will say both are right.
    B. She will say her brother is right.
    C. She will say her brother is wrong.
    D. She will not say who is right.

54. A. if he has a house of his own.
    B. if he can drive a car.
    C. if he has a wife.
    D. if he has a job

55. A. managing money B. playing billiards
    C. fixing automobiles D. managing offices

56. A. He will be absent. B. He was very bored.
    C. He is unable to build it. D. He will be present.

57. A. The lady can't have a pay increase now.
    B. The lady should ask later.
    C. The lady should put her request in writing.
    D. The lady said he would be out of the office.

58. A. He received the approval easily.
    B. His new class schedule isn't very manageable.
    C. He hasn't received his advisor's approval.
    D. His advisor's opinion hadn't mattered before.

59. A. repairman B. banker
    C. chemist D. photographer

60. A. make a decision before applying
    B. decide on an order of preference
    C. attend the universities now
    D. apply to several universities now

ECL 聽力測驗⑮詳解

1. (**B**) The cashier returned my change to me. What did she give me? 收銀員把我的零錢找給我。／她給我什麼？

(A) 食物。 (B) 硬幣。

(C) 玩具。 (D) 禮物。

* cashier〔kæ'ʃɪr〕*n.* 收銀員 return〔rɪ'tɜn〕*v.* 歸還
change〔tʃendʒ〕*n.* 零錢 coin〔kɔɪn〕*n.* 硬幣
toy〔tɔɪ〕*n.* 玩具 present〔'prɛznt〕*n.* 禮物

2. (**A**) The private worked at supply and transportation. What did his job involve?
這名二等兵從事補給和運輸。／他的工作包括什麼？

(A) 後勤。 (B) 烹調。

(C) 戰鬥。 (D) 寫作。

* private〔'praɪvɪt〕*n.* 二等兵 ***work at*** 從事於
supply〔sə'plaɪ〕*n.* 儲備物資；補給
transportation〔,trænspɚ'teʃən〕*n.* 運輸
involve〔ɪn'vɑlv〕*v.* 包括 logistics〔lo'dʒɪstɪks〕*n.* 後勤
cooking〔'kukɪŋ〕*n.* 烹調 fighting〔'faɪtɪŋ〕*n.* 戰鬥

3. (**D**) The trunk was made of teak. What was it made of?
這個大皮箱是柚木製的。／它是由什麼製成的？

(A) 金屬。 (B) 塑膠。

(C) 玻璃。 (D) 木材。

* trunk〔trʌŋk〕*n.* 大皮箱 ***be made of*** 由…製成
teak〔tik〕*n.* 柚木 metal〔'mɛtl〕*n.* 金屬
plastic〔'plæstɪk〕*n.* 塑膠 glass〔glæs〕*n.* 玻璃
wood〔wud〕*n.* 木材

4. (**C**) Steve made a long distance call. What kind of call was it? 史蒂夫打了一通長途電話。／那是哪一種電話？

(A) 打給他媽媽。

(B) 打給住在郊區的老師。

(C) <u>打到另一個城市。</u>

(D) 很貴的電話。

* ***make a call*** 打電話　distance〔ˈdɪstəns〕*n.* 距離
suburbs〔ˈsʌbɝbz〕*n.* 郊區
expensive〔ɪkˈspɛnsɪv〕*adj.* 昂貴的

5. (**A**) Are you annoyed yet? 你已經厭煩了嗎？

(A) <u>是的，我覺得不耐煩。</u>

(B) 是的，我很晚睡。

(C) 是的，我是手腳俐落的工人。

(D) 是的，我喜歡早點吃。

* annoyed〔əˈnɔɪd〕*adj.* 厭煩的　yet〔jɛt〕*adv.* 已經
irritated〔ˈɪrə,tetɪd〕*adj.* 不耐煩的
fast〔fæst〕*adj.* 敏捷的

6. (**C**) The professor asked, "What are the properties of water?" What does he want to know?
教授問：「水的特性是什麼？」／他想知道什麼？

(A) 水的用途。　(B) 水的內容。

(C) <u>水的特性。</u>　(D) 水的能力。

* professor〔prəˈfɛsɚ〕*n.* 教授
property〔ˈprɑpɚtɪ〕*n.* 特性　use〔jus〕*n.* 用途
contents〔ˈkɑntɛnts〕*n.* 內容
characteristic〔,kærɪktəˈrɪstɪk〕*n.* 特性
ability〔əˈbɪlətɪ〕*n.* 能力

7. (**D**) Hanna's examination indicated that she has several cavities. Where were her cavities found?
漢娜的檢查指出她有幾顆蛀牙。／她的蛀牙在哪裡被找到？

(A) 在她的手指裡。
(B) 在她的腳趾裡。
(C) 在她的耳朵裡。
(D) 在她的牙齒裡。

* examination〔ɪg͵zæmə'neʃən〕*n.* 檢查
indicate〔'ɪndə͵ket〕*v.* 指出
several〔'sɛvərəl〕*adj.* 幾個的
cavity〔'kævətɪ〕*n.* 蛀牙（的洞）
finger〔'fɪŋgɚ〕*n.* 手指 toe〔to〕*n.* 腳趾
ear〔ɪr〕*n.* 耳朵
teeth〔tiθ〕*n. pl.* 牙齒【單數爲 tooth】

8. (**B**) Gradually, the sound of the music and laughter died down. What does the statement mean?
漸漸地，音樂聲和笑聲都消失了。／這段敘述是什麼意思？

(A) 聲音變更大。
(B) 聲音變更輕。
(C) 聲音變得更令人厭煩。
(D) 聲音變得更歡樂。

* gradually〔'grædʒuəlɪ〕*adv.* 逐漸地
sound〔saʊnd〕*n.* 聲音 laughter〔'læftɚ〕*n.* 笑聲
die down 逐漸消失 statement〔'stetmənt〕*n.* 敘述
mean〔min〕*v.* 意思是 loud〔laʊd〕*adj.* 大聲的
soft〔sɔft〕*adj.* 柔和的；輕的
irritating〔'ɪrə͵tetɪŋ〕*adj.* 令人不耐煩的
cheerful〔'tʃɪrfəl〕*adj.* 歡樂的；高興的

9. (**B**) Most people who reside in this area are engaged in agriculture. What do they do?
住在這個區域的人大多從事農業。／他們是做什麼的？

(A) 丟蔬菜。 (B) 種蔬菜。
(C) 磨咖啡豆。 (D) 修理電器用具。

* reside〔rɪ'saɪd〕*v.* 居住 area〔'ɛrɪə〕*n.* 地區
engage〔ɪn'gedʒ〕*v.* 從事 <*in*>
agriculture〔'ægrɪˌkʌltʃɚ〕*n.* 農業
vegetable〔'vɛdʒətəbḷ〕*n.* 蔬菜 grow〔gro〕*v.* 種植
grind〔graɪnd〕*v.* 磨；搗碎 bean〔bin〕*n.* 豆子
fix〔fɪks〕*v.* 修理 appliance〔ə'plaɪəns〕*n.* 電器用具

10. (**A**) The bus was in motion when I jumped on. What can you say about the bus?
我跳上這輛公車時，它正在走。／關於這輛公車，你可以說什麼？

(A) 它在移動。 (B) 它被攔下來。
(C) 它是令人厭煩的。 (D) 它是活的。

* motion〔'moʃən〕*n.* 移動 ***in motion*** 在運行中
boring〔'bɔrɪŋ〕*adj.* 令人厭煩的
alive〔ə'laɪv〕*adj.* 活的

11. (**A**) He's been trying to get his room in order. What does he want? 他試圖要整理他的房間。／他想要什麼？

(A) 使房間整齊。 (B) 保持房間整齊。
(C) 重整秩序。 (D) 維持秩序。

* order〔'ɔrdɚ〕*n.* 整理；秩序
get *one's* ***room in order*** 整理某人的房間
tidy〔'taɪdɪ〕*adj.* 整齊的
make order 重整秩序 ***keep order*** 維持秩序

12. (**C**) He paid for his car prior to delivery. When did he pay for it? 他在運送車子之前先付款。／他何時付款？

(A) 運送之後。 (B) 運送時。
(C) 運送之前。 (D) 昨天。

* prior〔'praɪɚ〕*adv.* 在前 ***prior to*** 在…以前
delivery〔dɪ'lɪvərɪ〕*n.* 運送

13. (**D**) Captain Green told his men to step on it. What did he order them to do?
格蘭上尉叫他的士兵加快速度。／他命令他們做什麼？

(A) 放慢速度。 (B) 回到兵營。
(C) 吃午餐。 (D) 動作加快。

* captain〔'kæptən〕*n.* 陸軍上尉
men〔mɛn〕*n. pl.* 士兵們 ***step on it*** 加快速度
order〔'ɔrdɚ〕*v.* 命令 ***slow down*** 放慢速度
return〔rɪ'tɝn〕*v.* 回到 barracks〔'bærəks〕*n.* 兵營

14. (**B**) They had to mow the lawn yesterday. Where did they work? 他們昨天必須割草坪的草。／他們在哪裡工作？

(A) 在屋頂上。 (B) 在院子裡。
(C) 在屋子裡。 (D) 在車庫裡。

* mow〔mo〕*v.* 割（草） lawn〔lɔn〕*n.* 草坪
roof〔ruf〕*n.* 屋頂 yard〔jɑrd〕*n.* 院子
garage〔gə'rɑʒ〕*n.* 車庫

15. (**A**) Who may use the public bathroom? 誰會使用公廁？

(A) 任何人。 (B) 沒有人。
(C) 只有女性。 (D) 沒有人。

* public〔'pʌblɪk〕*adj.* 公共的
bathroom〔'bæθ,rum〕*n.* 洗手間

16. (**B**) What was the consequence of the collision?
碰撞的結果如何？

(A) 珍妮在睡覺。 (B) 珍妮受傷了。
(C) 珍妮很無聊。 (D) 珍妮去上學。

* consequence〔'kɑnsəkwəns〕*n.* 結果
collision〔kə'lɪʒən〕*n.* 碰撞
hurt〔hɝt〕*v.* 使受傷
bored〔bɔrd〕*adj.* 感到無聊的

17. (**D**) Norman wants to know what the case contains. What does he want to know?
諾曼想知道盒子裡面裝什麼。／他想知道什麼？

(A) 他的臉上有什麼。
(B) 那個地方有什麼。
(C) 骨頭裡面有什麼。
(D) 那個容器裡面有什麼。

* case〔kes〕*n.* 盒子 contain〔kən'ten〕*v.* 包含；裝
bone〔bon〕*n.* 骨頭 container〔kən'tenɚ〕*n.* 容器

18. (**A**) Can you give me directions to City Hall?
你可以告訴我市政府怎麼走嗎？

(A) 當然。走月亮路，然後左轉。
(B) 那要花你十分鐘左右的時間。
(C) 你可以在這個櫃檯買票。
(D) 會有很多人。

* directions〔də'rɛkʃənz〕*n. pl.*（行路的）指引
city hall 市政府 moon〔mun〕*n.* 月亮
left〔lɛft〕*adv.* 向左邊 take〔tek〕*v.* 花費
ticket〔'tɪkɪt〕*n.* 票 counter〔'kaʊntɚ〕*n.* 櫃檯

19. (**C**) After dinner, Ruth cleared the table. What did Ruth do? 晚餐後，露絲清理桌子。／露絲做了什麼？

(A) 擦掉桌子。 (B) 把桌子拿走。
(C) 把餐具從桌上拿走。 (D) 把餐具放好。

* clear〔klɪr〕v. 清理　erase〔ɪ'res〕v. 擦掉
take away 拿走　remove〔rɪ'muv〕v. 移開
tableware〔'tebḷˌwɛr〕n. 餐具　place〔ples〕v. 放

20. (**A**) How far do we have to go to get to school?
我們必須走多遠才會到學校？

(A) 大約十分鐘的車程。 (B) 大約喝十分鐘的酒。
(C) 大約十分鐘的夢。 (D) 大約十分鐘的舞。

* far〔fɑr〕adv. 遙遠地　get〔gɛt〕v. 抵達
drive〔draɪv〕n. 車程　drink〔drɪŋk〕n. 飲酒

21. (**B**) The teacher told him to shut up and not say anything more about it. What did the teacher want?
老師叫他閉嘴，不要再說任何一句話。／老師想要什麼？

(A) 把門關上。 (B) 停止說話。
(C) 關掉收音機。 (D) 關燈。

* shut〔ʃʌt〕v. 關閉　***shut up*** 閉嘴　close〔kloz〕v. 關上
turn off 關掉　radio〔'redɪˌo〕n. 收音機

22. (**D**) Mr. Blue stood beside me on the bus. Where did he stand? 在公車上時，布魯先生站在我旁邊。／他站在哪裡？

(A) 我前面。 (B) 我後面。
(C) 我上面。 (D) 我旁邊。

* beside〔bɪ'saɪd〕prep. 在旁邊
behind〔bɪ'haɪnd〕prep. 在後面　***next to*** 在旁邊

23. (**B**) What is the first thing that an advertisement must do?
廣告的第一要務是什麼？

(A) 用陷阱捕捉人們的眼睛。 (B) <u>引起讀者的注意。</u>
(C) 發現讀者的眼睛。 (D) 達到人們的眼睛。

* advertisement (ˌædvɚˈtaɪzmənt) *n.* 廣告
trap (træp) *v.* 用陷阱捕捉 eye (aɪ) *n.* 眼睛；目光
catch** one's **eye 引起注意 reach (ritʃ) *v.* 達到

24. (**A**) Mary bought a pair of jeans for fourteen dollars plus 30 cents tax. How much did the pants cost without the tax? 瑪莉花十四元買了一條牛仔褲，外加三十分錢的稅。／不加稅的話，這條褲子要價多少？

(A) <u>十四元。</u> (B) 十二元。
(C) 四十元。 (D) 二十元。

* pair (pɛr) *n.* (長褲的)一條 jeans (dʒinz) *n. pl.* 牛仔褲
plus (plʌs) *prep.* 加上 cent (sɛnt) *n.* 一分錢
tax (tæks) *n.* 稅 pants (pænts) *n. pl.* 褲子

25. (**C**) Which one is a part of a person's face?
何者是人臉上的一部分？

(A) 手臂。 (B) 腳趾。
(C) <u>眼睛。</u> (D) 手指。

* arm (ɑrm) *n.* 手臂

26. (**C**) Rita said, "I'm going to keep his novel."
麗塔說：「我要把他那本小說留下來」。

(A) 麗塔寫了那本小說。 (B) 麗塔強調那本小說。
(C) <u>麗塔要那本小說。</u> (D) 麗塔討厭那本小說。

* keep (kip) *v.* 保留 novel (ˈnɑvl̩) *n.* 小說
underline (ˌʌndɚˈlaɪn) *v.* 強調

27. (**C**) Lori needs to lose weight. 羅莉需要減重。

(A) 她必須干預自己的飲食。

(B) 她必須開始吃。

(C) 她必須少吃。

(D) 她必須豐富她的飲食。

* lose〔 luz 〕*v.* 減少　　weight〔 wet 〕*n.* 重量
cut in 打斷；干預　　***take up*** 開始；從事
cut down on 減少
enrich〔 ɪn'rɪtʃ 〕*v.* 使豐富；提高…的營養價值

28. (**D**) The captain can steer that big ship.
那位海軍上校會駕駛這艘大船。

(A) 他可以猜到。　　(B) 他可以授權做這艘船。

(C) 他可以磨碎它。　　(D) 他可以駕駛這艘船。

* captain〔'kæptən 〕*n.* 海軍上校
steer〔 stɪr 〕*v.* 駕駛　　ship〔 ʃɪp 〕*n.* 船
guess〔 gɛs 〕*v.* 猜測
authorize〔'ɔθə,raɪz 〕*v.* 授權
guide〔 gaɪd 〕*v.* 引導；駕駛

29. (**A**) Andy is mentally deranged. 安迪精神錯亂。

(A) 他的精神錯亂。　　(B) 他的心理很健康。

(C) 他的心理正常。　　(D) 他的心理沒問題。

* mentally〔'mɛntḷɪ 〕*adv.* 精神上
deranged〔 dɪ'rendʒd 〕*adj.* 精神錯亂的
mind〔 maɪnd 〕*n.* 心理；精神
disturbed〔 dɪs'tɝbd 〕*adj.* 混亂的
healthy〔'hɛlθɪ 〕*adj.* 健康的
normal〔'nɔrmḷ 〕*adj.* 正常的

30. (**D**) Pauline's avoiding Frank.
寶琳在逃避法蘭克。
(A) 寶琳很喜歡看到法蘭克。
(B) 寶琳不想離開法蘭克。
(C) 寶琳想跟法蘭克說話。
(D) 寶琳不想見到法蘭克。

* avoid〔əˈvɔɪd〕*v.* 逃避　leave〔liv〕*v.* 離開

31. (**A**) The coach told Donald that he was too short to play basketball.
教練告訴唐納德說，他太矮了，不能打籃球。
(A) 唐納德太矮小了。
(B) 唐納德太笨了。
(C) 唐納德太棒了。
(D) 唐納德太懶了。

* coach〔kotʃ〕*n.* 教練　short〔ʃɔrt〕*adj.* 矮的
too…to 太…以致於不能　little〔ˈlɪtl̩〕*adj.* 矮小的
stupid〔ˈstjupɪd〕*adj.* 笨的　lazy〔ˈlezɪ〕*adj.* 懶惰的

32. (**B**) We took our last vacation five years ago. I can't remember much about it.
我們上一次去渡假是五年前。我不太記得那件事了。
(A) 我們的假期持續了五週。
(B) 從我們上次去渡假到現在，已經過了很長一段時間。
(C) 五個人一起去旅行。
(D) 我們從來沒有去渡過假。

* last〔læst〕*adj.* 上一個的　*v.* 持續
vacation〔veˈkeʃən〕*n.* 假期
remember〔rɪˈmɛmbɚ〕*v.* 記得　pass〔pæs〕*v.* 過去

33. (**B**) We visited her at the hospital.
我們到醫院探望她。

(A) 我們在那裡讓她下車。
(B) 我們去那裡看她。
(C) 我們讓她進來。
(D) 我們從那裡放了她。

* hospital ('hɑspɪtl̩) *n.* 醫院　***drop off*** 使下車
admit (əd'mɪt) *v.* 容許進入　release (rɪ'lis) *v.* 放走

34. (**A**) Alex wonders what will happen tomorrow.
愛力克斯想知道明天會發生什麼事。

(A) 他很好奇會發生什麼事。
(B) 他對於將要發生的事感到狂怒。
(C) 他對於將要發生的事感到生氣。
(D) 他對於將要發生的事感到不愉快。

* wonder ('wʌndɚ) *v.* 想知道
happen ('hæpən) *v.* 發生
curious ('kjʊrɪəs) *adj.* 好奇的
furious ('fjʊrɪəs) *adj.* 狂怒的
angry ('æŋgrɪ) *adj.* 生氣的
upset (ʌp'sɛt) *adj.* 不高興的

35. (**C**) He has not seen the nurse yet.
他還沒見到護士。

(A) 他拿到處方了。　(B) 他見過醫生了。
(C) 他還在等。　(D) 他還是一名護士。

* nurse (nɝs) *n.* 護士　yet (jɛt) *adv.* 尚(未)
prescription (prɪ'skrɪpʃən) *n.* 處方

36. (**B**) George hasn't shaved the hair on his face for two months. 喬治已經兩個月沒有剃臉上的毛髮了。

(A) 現在他的頭髮很長。

(B) <u>現在他有鬍鬚。</u>

(C) 現在他有需求。

(D) 現在他是禿頭。

* shave〔ʃev〕*v.* 剃去…上的毛髮
beard〔bɪrd〕*n.* 鬍鬚　　demand〔dɪ'mænd〕*n.* 需求
bald〔bɔld〕*adj.* 禿頭的

37. (**C**) When people become elderly, their hair changes color.
當人們變老，頭髮的顏色就會改變。

(A) 他們喜歡染髮。

(B) 他們變成禿頭。

(C) <u>他們的頭髮變灰白。</u>

(D) 他們染頭髮。

* elderly〔'ɛldɚlɪ〕*adj.* 稍老的　　dye〔daɪ〕*v.* 染色
turn〔tɝn〕*v.* 轉變　　gray〔gre〕*adj.* 灰色的

38. (**D**) Tom said, "I can hardly hear Mary."
湯姆說：「我幾乎聽不到瑪麗的聲音」。

(A) 湯姆大聲地說。

(B) 湯姆的聽力很好。

(C) 瑪麗有聽力問題。

(D) <u>瑪麗說得不夠大聲。</u>

* hardly〔'hɑrdlɪ〕*adv.* 幾乎不
loudly〔'laʊdlɪ〕*adv.* 大聲地
hearing〔'hɪrɪŋ〕*n.* 聽力

39. (**B**) Mrs. Handel has two jobs, one in the morning and one at night.
韓德爾太太有兩份工作，一份是白天的，一份是晚上的。

(A) 她是家庭主婦。 (B) 她很勤奮。
(C) 她不友善。 (D) 她很苛求。

* housewife〔'haus,waɪf〕*n.* 家庭主婦
hard-working〔'hɑrd'wɝkɪŋ〕*adj.* 勤勉的
unfriendly〔ʌn'frɛndlɪ〕*adj.* 不友善的
demanding〔dɪ'mændɪŋ〕*adj.* 苛求的

40. (**C**) Susan said, "Let's go in. I'm freezing." Eileen said, "I am too. Let's go"
蘇珊說：「我們進去裡面吧。我快冷死了。」愛林說：「我也是。我們走吧。」

(A) 天氣不錯。 (B) 待在外面太熱了。
(C) 天氣很冷。 (D) 愛林很無聊。

* ***go in*** 進去裡面 freezing〔'frizɪŋ〕*adj.* 極冷的
weather〔'wɛðɚ〕*n.* 天氣
outside〔'aut'saɪd〕*adv.* 在外面

41. (**A**) The meteorologist says, "There is a possibility of rain." 氣象學家說：「可能會下雨」。

(A) 可能會下雨。 (B) 天氣會是晴朗的。
(C) 再晚一點會下雨。 (D) 一定會下雨。

* meteorologist〔,mitɪə'rɑlədʒɪst〕*n.* 氣象學家
possibility〔,pɑsə'bɪlətɪ〕*n.* 可能
sunny〔'sʌnɪ〕*adj.* 晴朗的
certainly〔'sɝtn̩lɪ〕*adv.* 一定

42. (**D**) Jane's hair is the color of gold.

珍的頭髮是金色的。

(A) 她是長頭髮。 (B) 她的頭髮是深褐色的。
(C) 她是個傑出人物。 (D) 她的頭髮是金色的。

* gold〔gold〕*n.* 黃金；金色
long-haired〔'lɔŋ,hɛrd〕*adj.* 長髮的
brunette〔bru'nɛt〕*n.* 有深褐色頭髮的人
character〔'kærɪktɚ〕*n.* 傑出人物
blonde〔blɑnd〕*adj.* 金髮的

43. (**A**) Mr. Salomon was looking for new pants.

所羅門先生在找一條新褲子。

(A) 他試著要找一條褲子。
(B) 他欣賞一條褲子。
(C) 他弄丟一條褲子。
(D) 他變成褲子。

* ***look for*** 尋找 admire〔əd'maɪr〕*v.* 欣賞

44. (**B**) The teacher wrote the problem on the blackboard and asked the student to work it out.

老師把問題寫在黑板上，然後要求那名學生解答。

(A) 那名學生遲到了。
(B) 那名學生被要求解出這個問題。
(C) 那名學生寫完家庭作業了。
(D) 那名學生不懂這個問題。

* blackboard〔'blæk,bord〕*n.* 黑板
work out 解決（問題） solve〔sɑlv〕*v.* 解決
finish〔'fɪnɪʃ〕*v.* 做完

45. (**A**) The supervisor visits the classrooms to make observations. 督學巡視教室，並提出意見。

(A) 他監督他的員工。 (B) 他要求員工。

(C) 他在遊蕩。 (D) 他處罰學生。

* supervisor [ˌsupəˈvaɪzə] *n.* 督學
observation [ˌɑbzəˈveʃən] *n.* 言論；意見
make an observation 提出意見
employee [ˌɛmplɔɪˈi] *n.* 員工
demand [dɪˈmænd] *v.* 要求 ***fool around*** 鬼混；遊蕩
punish [ˈpʌnɪʃ] *v.* 懲罰

46. (**A**) Take it slow. 慢慢來。

(A) 不用趕。 (B) 用鬧鐘。

(C) 帶隻錶。 (D) 趕快。

* rush [rʌʃ] *v.* 匆促行事；趕緊 ***alarm clock*** 鬧鐘
hurry up 趕快

47. (**A**) They eat a variety of fruits every day. 他們每天吃各種不同的水果。

(A) 他們每天吃不同種類的水果。

(B) 他們每天打不同種類的水果。

(C) 他們每星期吃種類遙遠的水果。

(D) 他們每天晚上吃充滿活力的水果。

* variety [vəˈraɪətɪ] *n.* 變化 ***a variety of*** 各種的
different [ˈdɪfərənt] *adj.* 不同的
daily [ˈdelɪ] *adv.* 每天地
beat [bit] *v.* 打 distant [ˈdɪstənt] *adj.* 遙遠的
weekly [ˈwiklɪ] *adv.* 每週地
dynamic [daɪˈnæmɪk] *adj.* 充滿活力的
nightly [ˈnaɪtlɪ] *adv.* 每晚地

48. (**B**) The student refrains from smoking when he goes to the library. 那名學生到圖書館時，忍住不抽煙。

(A) 他抽一點煙。

(B) <u>他完全沒有在那邊抽煙。</u>

(C) 圖書館是禁煙區。

(D) 他到圖書館時抽煙。

* refrain〔rɪ'fren〕*v.* 忍住；避免
smoking〔'smokɪŋ〕*n.* 吸煙
library〔'laɪ,brɛrɪ〕*n.* 圖書館　　smoke〔smok〕*v.* 吸煙
not at all 一點也不；完全不　　area〔'ɛrɪə〕*n.* 區域

49. (**B**) I am whole free on Thursday from two till three. Could we play tennis then? 我星期四的兩點到三點完全自由。我們到時候來打網球好嗎？

(A) 她星期一有空。

(B) <u>她星期四從兩點到三點是休息時間。</u>

(C) 她要在休息時打高爾夫球

(D) 她星期四有兩個小時的空閒時間。

* whole〔hol〕*adv.* 完全；整個
free〔fri〕*adj.* 有空閒的；自由的
till〔tɪl〕*prep.* 直到　　tennis〔'tɛnɪs〕*n.* 網球
break〔brek〕*n.* 休息時間　　golf〔gɑlf〕*n.* 高爾夫球

50. (**B**) I'm hoping for a chance to go skating.
我希望有機會去溜冰。

(A) 我喜歡溜冰。　　(B) <u>我希望有機會去溜冰。</u>

(C) 我想明天去溜冰。　　(D) 我希望我會溜冰。

* chance〔tʃæns〕*n.* 機會　　skating〔'sketɪŋ〕*n.* 溜冰
opportunity〔,ɑpɚ'tjunətɪ〕*n.* 機會　　skate〔sket〕*v.* 溜冰

51. (**A**) M：Do you like sports?

W：Yes, I enjoy nearly all sports, but golf is my favorite.

What does the woman say about golf?

男：妳喜歡運動嗎？

女：是的，幾乎每一種運動我都喜歡，但是我最喜歡高爾夫球。

關於高爾夫球，那位女士說什麼？

(A) 她很喜歡高爾夫球。

(B) 網球是她最喜歡的運動。

(C) 高爾夫球不是一種運動，但是是她最喜歡的東西。

(D) 她只喜歡網球。

* nearly〔ˈnɪrlɪ〕*adv.* 幾乎

favorite〔ˈfevərɪt〕*n.* 最喜歡的事物

52. (**D**) W：Does the bus stop in Atlanta?

M：I guess it will.

What does the man mean?

女：這輛公車會停在亞特蘭大嗎？

男：我猜它會。

這位男士的意思是？

(A) 他不知道亞特蘭大在哪裡。

(B) 他沒看到那輛公車。

(C) 他確定公車會停在亞特蘭大。

(D) 他不知道公車會不會停在亞特蘭大。

* Atlanta〔ətˈlæntə〕*n.* 亞特蘭大【美國喬治亞州首府】

certain〔ˈsɝtn̩〕*adj.* 確定的

53. (**D**) M：Who do you believe is right? Your brother or me?
W：I believe I will stay neutral.
What is the woman telling the man?
男：妳認爲誰是對的？妳弟弟還是我？
女：我認爲我會保持中立。
這位女士告訴那位男士什麼？
(A) 她會說兩個人都對。 (B) 她會說她弟弟才對。
(C) 她會說她弟弟錯了。 (D) 她不會說誰是對的。

* stay〔 ste 〕*v.* 保持　neutral〔ˈnjutrəl〕*adj.* 中立的
wrong〔 rɔŋ 〕*adj.* 錯誤的

54. (**C**) M：My uncle moved to the city? Is he married?
W：I have no idea.
What does the man want to know about his uncle?
男：我叔叔搬到城裡去了？他結婚了嗎？
女：我不知道。
關於這位男士的叔叔，他想知道什麼？
(A) 他是不是有自己的房子。 (B) 他會不會開車。
(C) 他有沒有妻子。 (D) 他有沒有工作。

* uncle〔ˈʌŋkl̩〕*n.* 叔叔　married〔ˈmærɪd〕*adj.* 已婚的
have no idea 不知道　***of one's own*** 自己的
wife〔 waɪf 〕*n.* 妻子

55. (**C**) M：Do you think Jim could help me with my car troubles?
W：Well, he's had enough experience. He should know something about engines.
What does Jim know?

男：妳認爲吉姆會幫我解決車子的問題嗎？
女：嗯，他有足夠的經驗。他應該懂引擎方面的事。
吉姆知道什麼？

(A) 管錢。　(B) 打撞球。
(C) 修車。　(D) 管理辦公室。

* trouble〔ˈtrʌbḷ〕*n.* 問題；毛病
experience〔ɪkˈspɪrɪəns〕*n.* 經驗
engine〔ˈɛndʒən〕*n.* 引擎　manage〔ˈmænɪdʒ〕*v.* 管理
billiards〔ˈbɪljɚdz〕*n.* 撞球　fix〔fɪks〕*v.* 修理
automobile〔ˌɔtəməˈbil〕*n.* 汽車

56. (**A**) W：Will Mr. Jones be at the board meeting tonight?
M：I'm afraid he can't make it, but everyone else will be there.
What does the man say about Mr. Jones?
女：瓊斯先生會參加今晚的董事會議嗎？
男：他恐怕趕不上，但是其他人都會到。
關於瓊斯先生，那位男士說什麼？

(A) 他會缺席。　(B) 他很無聊。
(C) 他無法建造它。　(D) 他會出席。

* board〔bord〕*n.* 董事會　meeting〔ˈmitɪŋ〕*n.* 會議
make it 趕上　absent〔ˈæbsṇt〕*adj.* 缺席的
build〔bɪld〕*v.* 建造
present〔ˈprɛznṭ〕*adj.* 出席的；在場的

57. (**A**) M：Did you ask the boss for a raise?
W：Yes, but he said it was out of the question.
What did the boss say?
男：妳有要求老闆爲妳加薪嗎？
女：有的，但是他說不可能。

老闆說什麼？

(A) <u>這位女士的薪水現在無法調高。</u>
(B) 這位女士應該晚點問。
(C) 這位女士應該以書面提出要求。
(D) 這位女士說老闆將離開辦公室。

* boss〔 bɔs 〕*n.* 老闆　raise〔 rez 〕*n.* 加薪
out of the question 不可能　pay〔 pe 〕*n.* 薪資
increase〔 ɪn'kris 〕*n.* 增加　put〔 pʊt 〕*v.* 提出
request〔 rɪ'kwɛst 〕*n.* 要求　writing〔'raɪtɪŋ 〕*n.* 書面

58. (**C**) W：I imagine you've gotten your adviser's approval for your new class schedule.
M：As a matter of fact, I haven't.
What do we learn about the man from this conversation?
女：我猜你的新課程表已經得到指導教授的同意了。
男：事實上，我沒有得到他同意。
從這段對話，我們可以得知跟這位男士有關的什麼事？

(A) 他輕易就得到同意。
(B) 他的新課程表不是非常好用。
(C) <u>他沒有得到指導教授的同意。</u>
(D) 他指導教授的意見以前並不重要。

* imagine〔 ɪ'mædʒɪn 〕*v.* 想像；推測
adviser〔 əd'vaɪzɚ 〕*n.* 指導教授
approval〔 ə'pruvl̩ 〕*n.* 同意
schedule〔'skɛdʒul 〕*n.* 時間表
as a matter of fact 實際上　learn〔 lɝn 〕*v.* 得知
conversation〔,kɑnvɚ'seʃən 〕*n.* 對話
receive〔 rɪ'siv 〕*v.* 得到
manageable〔'mænɪdʒəbl̩ 〕*adj.* 可使用的
opinion〔 ə'pɪnjən 〕*n.* 意見　matter〔'mætɚ 〕*v.* 關係重要

59. (**C**) M：A few of the chemicals I need for today's experiment are missing from the shelf.

W：Better tell Mr. Adams about it.

What job does Mr. Adams most probably have?

男：我今天做實驗需要的一些化學藥品從架子上不見了。

女：最好把這件事告訴亞當斯先生。

亞當斯先生最有可能從事什麼工作？

(A) 修理工人。 (B) 銀行家。

(C) 化學家。 (D) 攝影師。

* chemical〔ˈkɛmɪkḷ〕*n.* 化學製品
experiment〔ɪkˈspɛrəmənt〕*n.* 實驗
miss〔mɪs〕*v.* 不見了 shelf〔ʃælf〕*n.* 架子
(***had***) ***better*** 最好 probably〔ˈprɑbəblɪ〕*adv.* 可能
repairman〔rɪˈpɛr͵mæn〕*n.* 修理工人
banker〔ˈbæŋkɚ〕*n.* 銀行家 chemist〔ˈkɛmɪst〕*n.* 化學家
photographer〔fəˈtɑgrəfɚ〕*n.* 攝影師

60. (**D**) M：Maria can't decide which university to attend.

W：Shouldn't she apply to several of them first before making a final decision?

What does the woman think Maria should do?

男：瑪麗亞無法決定要上哪一所大學。

女：她不是應該在做最後決定之前，先申請幾所學校嗎？

這位女士認爲瑪麗亞應該做什麼？

(A) 在申請之前先做決定。 (B) 按照喜歡的順序做決定。

(C) 現在就去上大學。 (D) 現在去申請幾所大學。

* decide〔dɪˈsaɪd〕*v.* 決定
university〔͵junəˈvɝsətɪ〕*n.* 大學 attend〔əˈtɛnd〕*v.* 上(學)
apply〔əˈplaɪ〕*v.* 申請 final〔ˈfaɪnḷ〕*adj.* 最後的
decision〔dɪˈsɪʒən〕*n.* 決定 order〔ˈɔrdɚ〕*n.* 順序
preference〔ˈprɛfərəns〕*n.* 喜歡

LISTENING TEST ⑯

- *Directions for questions 1-25. You will hear questions on the test CD. Select the one item A, B, C or D which answers the question correctly, and mark your answer sheet.*

1. A. It was sold. B. It was lent.
   C. It was stolen. D. It was borrowed.

2. A. Yes, his car broke down.
   B. Yes, he was driving too fast.
   C. Yes, he kept within the speed limit.
   D. Yes, he saw the traffic officer.

3. A. It processes air.
   B. It pumps blood.
   C. It fights infections.
   D. It processes food.

4. A. He has vegetables, fruit, and snacks.
   B. He has roses, tulips, and carnations.
   C. He has pigs, sheep, and a few horses.
   D. He has beans and corn.

5. A. The wire is not strong.
   B. The wire is not protected.
   C. The wire is not connected.
   D. The wire is not small.

6. A. They are very much different.
   B. They are not the same.
   C. They are very much alike.
   D. They are not related.

7. A. It ran on the floor.
   B. It smells like green tea.
   C. It fell on the floor.
   D. It fell on the ceiling.

8. A. empty streets
   B. railways
   C. crossroads
   D. downtown

9. A. in the card
   B. in the yard
   C. in the attic
   D. in the basement

10. A. his time
    B. his ideas
    C. his effort
    D. his knowledge

11. A. She prepares the decorations.
    B. She prepares the drinks.
    C. She goes hunting.
    D. She prepares the food.

12. A. time away from her sister
    B. time away from her brother
    C. time away from her work
    D. time away from her vacancy

13. A. garage
    B. refrigerator
    C. helicopter
    D. generator

14. A. eat breakfast with Bernie
    B. eat lunch with Bernie
    C. eat breakfast with Lisa
    D. eat dinner with Lisa

15. A. after the moon went down
    B. after the sun went down
    C. after the sky went down
    D. after the sun went up

16. A. He tied up the apple.
    B. He reached for the apple.
    C. He knocked on the apple.
    D. He swept away the apple.

17. A. 2 feet B. 10 inches
    C. 20 gallons D. 5 dollars

18. A. an astrology B. an astrologer
    C. an astronomy D. an astronaut

19. A. I put it on in the morning.
    B. I gave it to the eraser.
    C. I laid it on the bookcase.
    D. I stir-fried it and ate it.

20. A. animals and tools B. synthetic foods
    C. power stations D. nuclear weapons

21. A. It melts. B. It insulates.
C. It diminishes. D. It produces.

22. A. recovered B. revealed
C. worsened D. recycled

23. A. I wanted to watch some basketball games.
B. I had an accident while driving to the park three days ago.
C. I had to clean the bedroom.
D. I wanted to finish my work.

24. A. incorrectly B. indirectly
C. correctly D. criminally

25. A. Jim was self-controlled.
B. Jim could escape a fight.
C. Jim confessed his mistakes.
D. Jim recognized his anger.

● *Directions for questions 26-50. You will hear statements on the test CD. Select the one answer A, B, C, or D which comes closest to the meaning of the statement and mark your answer sheet.*

26. A. She is messy. B. She is responsible.
C. She is honest. D. She is careless.

27. A. They are comfortable. B. They are cheap.
C. They are available. D. They are costly.

28. A. We did all of it quickly.
    B. We scanned it.
    C. We omitted it entirely.
    D. We did it thoroughly.

29. A. I feel happy.
    B. I feel glad.
    C. I feel terrific.
    D. I feel sad.

30. A. She already had one.
    B. She didn't want a new one.
    C. She didn't have enough.
    D. She did have just enough.

31. A. He got to the top.
    B. He got to the bottom.
    C. He got to the pop.
    D. He got to the mop.

32. A. The bank has a pole in it.
    B. The container has a pole in it.
    C. The bank has a hole in it.
    D. The container has a hole in it.

33. A. It was cooked just right.
    B. It was too salty.
    C. It was not cooked long enough.
    D. It was delicious.

34. A. David will drink some milk.
    B. David will buy some milk.
    C. David doesn't like milk.
    D. David needs cookies with his milk.

35. A. It began to flower. B. It began to fly.
C. It began to spoil. D. It began to walk.

36. A. They have to decrease overtime work.
B. They'd better reduce the staff.
C. They have to train new staff.
D. They have to employ new staff.

37. A. We all have to go to the meeting.
B. It demands a lot.
C. Not all of us have to go.
D. No one can go to the meeting.

38. A. She was late. B. She was not lame.
C. She was fat. D. She was not late.

39. A. She lost it properly. B. She lost it gradually.
C. She lost it at night. D. She lost it quickly.

40. A. They loaded their guns.
B. They figured out how far the target was.
C. They hit the target.
D. Their range was not very far.

41. A. It seems that Janet was bored.
B. It seems that Janet was sleeping.
C. It seems that Janet had a good time.
D. It seems that Janet went on a trip.

42. A. She becomes disappointed in her friends.
    B. She becomes happy with her friends.
    C. She becomes annoyed with her friends.
    D. She becomes worried about her friends.

43. A. The recording takes 10 minutes to play back.
    B. The recording is 20 minutes long.
    C. The recording was made 20 minutes ago.
    D. The tape is not good, so it takes 30 minutes to record.

44. A. Soon another branch will be added.
    B. Never again will another branch be added.
    C. Sooner or later another branch will be added.
    D. Hopefully another branch will be added.

45. A. I like to eat snacks. B. I like to take a walk.
    C. I like to take a nap. D. I like to relax.

46. A. The corner is under construction.
    B. The building is not yet finished.
    C. The building needs a new roof.
    D. Construction has finished.

47. A. It was destroyed in Europe.
    B. It was made in Europe.
    C. It was played in Europe.
    D. It was sent to Europe.

48. A. They bought it off. B. They sawed it off.
    C. The fought it off. D. They cut it off.

49. A. We could wear jeans to the party.
    B. The president will attend the party.
    C. There is no form to fill out.
    D. Everyone has to dress up for the party.

50. A. Electric current is carried by wire.
    B. Wire is an electric thing.
    C. Electricity is weird.
    D. You need wire to pay for electricity.

● *Directions for questions 51-60. You will hear dialogs on the test CD. Select the correct answer A, B, C, or D and mark your answer sheet.*

51. A. selecting paint
    B. asking for directions
    C. trying on clothes
    D. looking for something he lost

52. A. Pull out her tooth.
    B. Wait a little longer.
    C. See the dentist for a while.
    D. Think about where she put the file.

53. A. They became more beautiful.
    B. They were picked.
    C. They died.
    D. They fainted.

54. A. It is a garbage dump.
    B. It is a place to deposit money.
    C. It is a place to build houses.
    D. It is a shopping center.

55. A. Mineral water
    B. Coffee and toast
    C. Cappuccino and a sandwich
    D. Groceries

56. A. searching for a doctor
    B. searching for an artist
    C. searching for an article
    D. searching for medicine

57. A. sad B. happy
    C. mad D. joyful

58. A. sew some cloth B. rip some cloth
    C. cut some cloth D. eat some cloth

59. A. buy the hotel B. leave the hotel
    C. sell the hotel D. enter the hotel

60. A. His wife gave him a present.
    B. He has just become a new uncle.
    C. His wife told him some good news.
    D. He has just become a new father.

ECL 聽力測驗⑯詳解

1. (**C**) A thief walked away with our new computer. What happened to the computer?
有個小偷偷走了我們的新電腦。／電腦怎麼了？
(A) 被賣掉了。 (B) 被借走了。
(C) <u>被偷了。</u> (D) 被借來了。

* thief〔θif〕*n.* 小偷 ***walk away with*** 偷走
happen〔ˈhæpən〕*v.* 發生
sell〔sɛl〕*v.* 出售【過去式及過去分詞爲 sold】
lend〔lɛnd〕*v.* 借（出）【過去式及過去分詞爲 lent】
steal〔stil〕*v.* 偷走【三態變化爲：steal-stole-stolen】
borrow〔ˈbɑro〕*v.* 借（入）

2. (**B**) Did the driver commit a traffic infraction?
這位駕駛人有違反交通規則嗎？
(A) 是的，他的車故障了。
(B) <u>是的，他開太快了。</u>
(C) 是的，他保持在速限之內。
(D) 是的，他看到那名交通警察。

* commit〔kəˈmɪt〕*v.* 犯（罪、過錯等）
traffic〔ˈtræfɪk〕*adj.* 交通的
infraction〔ɪnˈfrækʃən〕*n.* 犯規
break down 發生故障 keep〔kip〕*v.* 保持
within〔wɪðˈɪn〕*prep.* 在…以內
speed〔spid〕*n.* 速度 limit〔ˈlɪmɪt〕*n.* 限制
officer〔ˈɔfəsɚ〕*n.* 警官

3. (**B**) The heart is a vital organ. What does it do?
心臟是非常重要的器官。／它做什麼？

(A) 它對空氣進行加工。 (B) <u>它壓送血液。</u>
(C) 它對抗傳染病。 (D) 它對食物進行加工。

* vital〔ˈvaɪtl̩〕*adj.* 極爲重要的 organ〔ˈɔrgən〕*n.* 器官
process〔ˈprɑsɛs〕*v.* 對…進行加工
pump〔pʌmp〕*v.* 壓送；注入 blood〔blʌd〕*n.* 血液
fight〔faɪt〕*v.* 對抗 infection〔ɪnˈfɛkʃən〕*n.* 傳染病

4. (**C**) What kind of animals does Mr. Sharon have?
雪倫先生有哪幾種動物？

(A) 他有蔬菜、水果和點心。
(B) 他有玫瑰、鬱金香和康乃馨。
(C) <u>他有豬、綿羊和幾匹馬。</u>
(D) 他有豆子和玉米。

* vegetable〔ˈvɛdʒətəbl̩〕*n.* 蔬菜 snack〔snæk〕*n.* 點心
rose〔roz〕*n.* 玫瑰 tulip〔ˈtulɪp〕*n.* 鬱金香
carnation〔kɑrˈneʃən〕*n.* 康乃馨 sheep〔ʃip〕*n.* 綿羊
horse〔hɔrs〕*n.* 馬 bean〔bin〕*n.* 豆子
corn〔kɔrn〕*n.* 玉米

5. (**B**) Teresa said, "That wire is not insulated." What did Teresa mean? 泰瑞莎說：「這條電線不是絕緣的。」。
／泰瑞莎的意思是？

(A) 這條電線不堅固。 (B) <u>這條電線上沒有防護裝置。</u>
(C) 這條電線沒有連接著。 (D) 這條電線不小。

* wire〔waɪr〕*n.* 電線 insulated〔ˈɪnsəˌletɪd〕*adj.* 絕緣的
mean〔min〕*v.* 意思是 strong〔strɔŋ〕*adj.* 堅固的
protect〔prəˈtɛkt〕*v.* 在…上裝防護裝置以免傷害
connect〔kəˈnɛkt〕*v.* 連接

6. (**C**) This situation is comparable to the original one. What kind of situations are they?

這個情況跟原本的情況很類似。／它們是什麼樣的情況？

(A) 它們的情況很不一樣。　(B) 它們是不同的情況。

(C) 它們是非常相似的情況。　(D) 它們是無關的。

* situation (ˌsɪtʃʊˈeʃən) *n.* 情況
comparable (kəmˈpɛrəbḷ) *adj.* 類似的
original (əˈrɪdʒənḷ) *adj.* 原本的
different (ˈdɪfərənt) *adj.* 不同的
same (sem) *adj.* 相同的　alike (əˈlaɪk) *adj.* 相似的
related (rɪˈletɪd) *adj.* 相關的

7. (**C**) How did that teapot get smashed?

那只茶壺怎麼破掉的？

(A) 它在地板上跑。　(B) 它聞起來像綠茶。

(C) 它掉到地板上。　(D) 它掉到天花板上。

* teapot (ˈtiˌpɑt) *n.* 茶壺　smash (smæʃ) *v.* 打破；粉碎
floor (flor) *n.* 地板　smell (smɛl) *v.* 聞起來
ceiling (ˈsilɪŋ) *n.* 天花板

8. (**C**) Some collisions occur at intersections. Where do some collisions occur?

十字路口發生了一些碰撞。／哪裡發生了一些碰撞？

(A) 空蕩蕩的街上。　(B) 鐵路。

(C) 十字路口。　(D) 鬧區。

* collision (kəˈlɪʒən) *n.* 碰撞　occur (əˈkɝ) *v.* 發生
intersection (ˌɪntɚˈsɛkʃən) *n.* 十字路口
empty (ˈɛmptɪ) *adj.* 空的　railway (ˈrelˌwe) *n.* 鐵路
crossroad (ˈkrɔsˌrod) *n.* 十字路口
downtown (ˈdaʊnˌtaʊn) *n.* 鬧區

9. (**B**) She had to mow the lawn yesterday. Where did she work? 她昨天必須割庭院的草。／她在哪裡工作？

(A) 在卡片裡。 (B) 在庭院裡。
(C) 在頂樓。 (D) 在地下室。

* mow〔 mo 〕*v.* 割（草） lawn〔 lɔn 〕*n.* 草坪
yard〔 jɑrd 〕*n.* 庭院 attic〔ˈætɪk 〕*n.* 頂樓
basement〔ˈbesmənt 〕*n.* 地下室

10. (**B**) We asked for his opinion. What did we want?
我們尋求他的意見。／我們想要什麼？

(A) 他的時間。 (B) 他的意見。
(C) 他的努力。 (D) 他的知識。

* opinion〔 əˈpɪnjən 〕*n.* 意見 idea〔 aɪˈdiə 〕*n.* 意見
effort〔ˈɛfɚt 〕*n.* 努力 knowledge〔ˈnɑlɪdʒ 〕*n.* 知識

11. (**D**) Jessica cooks all our meals. What does she do?
潔西卡煮所有人的餐點。／她在做什麼？

(A) 她在準備裝飾品。 (B) 她在準備飲料。
(C) 她去打獵。 (D) 她在準備食物。

* cook〔 kʊk 〕*v.* 烹調 meal〔 mil 〕*n.* 餐；飯
prepare〔 prɪˈpɛr 〕*v.* 準備
decoration〔ˌdɛkəˈreʃən 〕*n.* 裝飾品
drink〔 drɪŋk 〕*n.* 飲料 hunting〔ˈhʌntɪŋ 〕*n.* 打獵

12. (**C**) Jane took a vacation. What did she take?
珍休假了。／她做了什麼？

(A) 暫時離開她姊姊。 (B) 暫時離開她弟弟。
(C) 暫時離開她的工作。 (D) 暫時離開她的空位。

* vacation〔 veˈkeʃən 〕*n.* 假期 ***take a vacation*** 休假
vacancy〔ˈvekənsɪ 〕*n.* 空位

13. (**B**) What can help you to keep food fresh?
什麼東西有助於保持食物的新鮮？

(A) 車庫。　(B) 冰箱。
(C) 直昇機。　(D) 發電機。

* fresh〔 frɛʃ 〕*adj.* 新鮮的
garage〔 gəˈrɑʒ 〕*n.* 車庫
refrigerator〔 rɪˈfrɪdʒə͵retɚ 〕*n.* 冰箱
helicopter〔ˈhɛlɪ͵kɑptɚ 〕*n.* 直昇機
generator〔ˈdʒɛnə͵retɚ 〕*n.* 發電機

14. (**D**) Bernie and Lisa are getting together for dinner. What will Bernie do?
伯尼和麗莎晚上要聚餐。／伯尼將要做什麼？

(A) 和伯尼一起吃早餐。
(B) 和伯尼一起吃午餐。
(C) 和麗莎一起吃早餐。
(D) 和麗莎一起吃晚餐。

* ***get together*** 聚會

15. (**B**) Ann quit studying after sunset. When did Ann stop?
安在日落之後就停止唸書。／安何時停止？

(A) 月亮落下之後。
(B) 太陽落下之後。
(C) 天空落下之後。
(D) 太陽升起之後。

* quit〔 kwɪt 〕*v.* 停止　sunset〔ˈsʌn͵sɛt 〕*n.* 日落
moon〔 mun 〕*n.* 月亮　***go down*** 落下
go up 上升

16. (**B**) The hungry boy tried to grab the rotten apple on the table. What did the boy do? 那名飢餓的男孩試圖抓住桌上的爛蘋果。／那名男孩做了什麼？

(A) 他把蘋果綁起來。 (B) 他伸手去拿蘋果。
(C) 他敲敲蘋果。 (D) 他把蘋果掃掉。

＊ hungry〔'hʌŋgrɪ〕*adj.* 飢餓的 grab〔græb〕*v.* 抓住
rotten〔'rɑtn̩〕*adj.* 腐壞的 tie〔taɪ〕*v.* 繫；綁
tie up 綁住 reach〔ritʃ〕*v.* 伸手去拿 <*for*>
knock〔nɑk〕*v.* 敲 sweep〔swip〕*v.* 掃

17. (**C**) What is the volume of this container?
這個容器的容量是多少？

(A) 兩呎。 (B) 十吋。
(C) 二十加侖。 (D) 五元。

＊ volume〔'vɑljəm〕*n.* 容量 container〔kən'tenɚ〕*n.* 容器
feet〔fit〕*n.* 呎【單數爲 foot】 inch〔ɪntʃ〕*n.* 吋
gallon〔'gælən〕*n.* 加侖

18. (**D**) What do you call a person who travels beyond the earth's atmosphere?
你怎麼稱呼到地球大氣層以外的人？

(A) 占星學。 (B) 占星家。
(C) 天文學。 (D) 太空人。

＊ travel〔'trævl̩〕*v.* 旅行；行進
beyond〔bɪ'jɑnd〕*prep.* 超過…的範圍
earth〔ɝθ〕*n.* 地球 atmosphere〔'ætməs,fɪr〕*n.* 大氣層
astrology〔ə'strɑlədʒɪ〕*n.* 占星學
astrologer〔ə'strɑlədʒɚ〕*n.* 占星家
astronomy〔ə'strɑnəmɪ〕*n.* 天文學
astronaut〔'æstrə,nɔt〕*n.* 太空人

19. (**C**) Where did you leave my pen yesterday?
你昨天把我的筆留在哪？

(A) 我早上穿上它。
(B) 我把它給了橡皮擦。
(C) <u>我把它放在書架上。</u>
(D) 我把它炒一炒，然後吃掉。

* ***put on*** 穿上
eraser〔ɪ'resɚ〕*n.* 橡皮擦
lay〔le〕*v.* 放置【過去式及過去分詞爲 laid】
bookcase〔'bʊk,kes〕*n.* 書架　stir-fry〔'stɝ,fraɪ〕*v.* 炒

20. (**A**) What is the earliest form of man's wealth?
人類最早的財富形式是什麼？

(A) <u>動物和工具。</u>　(B) 合成食物。
(C) 發電廠。　(D) 核子武器。

* form〔fɔrm〕*n.* 型式　man〔mæn〕*n.* 人類
wealth〔wɛlθ〕*n.* 財富
tool〔tul〕*n.* 工具　synthetic〔sɪn'θɛtɪk〕*adj.* 合成的
station〔'steʃən〕*n.* 站；廠　***power station*** 發電廠
nuclear〔'njuklɪr〕*adj.* 核子的　weapon〔'wɛpən〕*n.* 武器

21. (**A**) What happens when you take ice out of the refrigerator? 當你把冰塊拿出冰箱，會發生什麼事？

(A) <u>它會融化。</u>　(B) 它會孤立。
(C) 它會減少。　(D) 它會生產。

* ice〔aɪs〕*n.* 冰塊　melt〔mɛlt〕*v.* 溶化
insulate〔'ɪnsə,let〕*v.* 使孤立
diminish〔də'mɪnɪʃ〕*v.* 減少
produce〔prə'djus〕*v.* 生產

22. (**A**) After a month's rest he regained his health. How was the man?
經過一個月的休息之後，他恢復健康。／這個男人怎麼了？

(A) 恢復健康。　(B) 被揭發。
(C) 惡化。　(D) 回收再利用。

* rest〔rɛst〕*n.* 休息　regain〔rɪ'gen〕*v.* 恢復
health〔hɛlθ〕*n.* 健康　recover〔rɪ'kʌvɚ〕*v.* 恢復健康
reveal〔rɪ'vil〕*v.* 透露；揭發
worsen〔'wɝsn̩〕*v.* 惡化；變更糟
recycle〔ri'saɪkl̩〕*v.* 回收再利用

23. (**D**) Why did you stay so late at the office last Tuesday?
你上星期二爲什麼在辦公室待那麼晚？

(A) 我想要看幾場籃球賽。
(B) 我三天前開車去公園時發生意外。
(C) 我必須打掃臥房。　(D) 我想要把工作做完。

* accident〔'æksədənt〕*n.* 意外　clean〔klin〕*v.* 打掃
finish〔'fɪnɪʃ〕*v.* 完成

24. (**C**) Doctors must read their charts accurately. How must they read them?
醫生必須要正確地判讀病歷表。／他們必須怎麼讀病歷表？

(A) 不正確地。　(B) 間接地。
(C) 正確地。　(D) 犯法地

* chart〔tʃɑrt〕*n.*（病人的）病歷表
accurately〔'ækjərɪtlɪ〕*adv.* 正確地
incorrectly〔ˌɪnkə'rɛktlɪ〕*adv.* 不正確地
indirectly〔ˌɪndə'rɛktlɪ〕*adv.* 間接地
correctly〔kə'rɛktlɪ〕*adv.* 正確地
criminally〔'krɪmənl̩ɪ〕*adv.* 犯法地

25. (**A**) Jim was able to hold back his anger and avoid a fight. What is this statement about? 吉姆可以控制他的怒氣，並避免爭吵。／這段敘述是關於什麼？

(A) 吉姆是自制的。　　(B) 吉姆能逃離爭吵。
(C) 吉姆坦承錯誤。　　(D) 吉姆承認他生氣。

* ***hold back*** 抑制　anger〔ˈæŋgɚ〕*n.* 憤怒
avoid〔əˈvɔɪd〕*v.* 避免　fight〔faɪt〕*n.* 爭吵；打架
statement〔ˈstetmənt〕*n.* 敘述
self-controlled〔ˌsɛlfkənˈtrold〕*adj.* 能自制的
escape〔əˈskep〕*v.* 逃離　confess〔kənˈfɛs〕*v.* 坦承
mistake〔məˈstek〕*n.* 錯誤
recognize〔ˈrɛkəgˌnaɪz〕*v.* 承認

26. (**B**) Melanie always completes her work.
梅蘭妮總是能把工作做完。

(A) 她很混亂。　　(B) 她很負責任。
(C) 她很誠實。　　(D) 她很粗心。

* complete〔kəmˈplit〕*v.* 完成　messy〔ˈmɛsɪ〕*adj.* 混亂的
responsible〔rɪˈspɑnsəbl〕*adj.* 負責任的
honest〔ˈɑnɪst〕*adj.* 誠實的　careless〔ˈkɛrlɪs〕*adj.* 粗心的

27. (**D**) Brand-name clothes are expensive. 名牌衣服很貴。

(A) 它們很舒適。　　(B) 它們很便宜。
(C) 可以買得到它們。　　(D) 它們很貴。

* brand〔brænd〕*n.* 品牌　***brand-name*** *adj.* 名牌的
clothes〔kloðz〕*n. pl.* 衣服
expensive〔ɪkˈspɛnsɪv〕*adj.* 昂貴的
comfortable〔ˈkʌmfɚtəbl̩〕*adj.* 舒適的
cheap〔tʃip〕*adj.* 便宜的
available〔əˈveləbl̩〕*adj.* 買得到的
costly〔ˈkɔstlɪ〕*adj.* 昂貴的

28. (**C**) We had to skip chapter 5 since it was not important.
我們必須跳過第五章，因爲它不重要。

(A) 我們很快把第五章做完。
(B) 我們瀏覽一下第五章。
(C) 我們完全省略第五章。
(D) 我們把第五章整個做完。

* skip〔skɪp〕*v.* 跳過　chapter〔ˈtʃæptɚ〕*n.* 章
since〔sɪns〕*conj.* 因爲
important〔ɪmˈpɔrtn̩t〕*adj.* 重要的
scan〔skæn〕*v.* 瀏覽　omit〔oˈmɪt〕*v.* 省略
entirely〔ɪnˈtaɪrlɪ〕*adv.* 完全地
thoroughly〔ˈθɝolɪ〕*adv.* 完全地

29. (**D**) I regret that you had an accident.
我對你發生意外這件事感到很遺憾。

(A) 我很快樂。　(B) 我很高興。
(C) 我覺得很棒。　(D) 我很難過。

* regret〔rɪˈgrɛt〕*v.* 對…感到遺憾
glad〔glæd〕*adj.* 高興的
terrific〔təˈrɪfɪk〕*adj.* 極好的

30. (**C**) Fanny couldn't afford to get a new bike.
芬妮買不起一輛新的腳踏車。

(A) 她已經有一輛腳踏車。
(B) 她不想要一輛新的腳踏車。
(C) 她沒有足夠的錢。
(D) 她確實只有剛好的錢。

* afford〔əˈfɔrd〕*v.* 買得起　bike〔baɪk〕*n.* 腳踏車
do〔du〕*aux.* 一定；確實【強調肯定句】

31. (**A**) He finally attained the peak.
他終於抵達山頂。

(A) <u>他到達山頂。</u>
(B) 他到達山麓。
(C) 他到達流行歌曲。
(D) 他到達抹布。

* finally〔'faɪnḷɪ〕*adv.* 最後；終於
attain〔ə'ten〕*v.* 抵達　　peak〔pik〕*n.* 山頂
bottom〔'bɑtəm〕*n.* 底部；（山）麓
pop〔pɑp〕*n.* 流行歌曲　　mop〔mɑp〕*n.* 抹布

32. (**D**) The container is leaking.
這個容器在漏水。

(A) 這家銀行裡面有根柱子。
(B) 這個容器裡面有根柱子。
(C) 這家銀行裡面有個坑洞。
(D) <u>這個容器裡面有個洞。</u>

* leak〔lik〕*adv.* 漏水　　pole〔pol〕*n.* 柱子；棍子
hole〔hol〕*n.* 洞；坑洞

33. (**C**) The steak was too rare. 牛排太生了。

(A) 它被煮得剛剛好。
(B) 它太鹹了。
(C) <u>它煮得不夠久。</u>
(D) 它很好吃。

* steak〔stek〕*n.* 牛排
rare〔rɛr〕*adj.* 半生不熟的
salty〔'sɔltɪ〕*adj.* 有鹹味的
delicious〔dɪ'lɪʃəs〕*adj.* 美味的

34. (**B**) David told the clerk, "I want a carton of milk."
大衛告訴店員：「我要一盒牛奶」。

(A) 大衛會喝一些牛奶。
(B) <u>大衛會買一些牛奶。</u>
(C) 大衛不喜歡牛奶。
(D) 大衛需要一些餅乾來配牛奶。

＊ clerk (klɝk) *n.* 店員　carton (ˈkɑrtn̩) *n.* 紙盒

35. (**C**) The fruit began to rot.
水果開始腐爛。

(A) 它開始開花。　(B) 它開始飛起來。
(C) <u>它開始腐壞。</u>　(D) 它開始走路。

＊ rot (rɑt) *v.* 腐爛　flower (flaʊr) *v.* 開花
spoil (spɔɪl) *v.* 腐壞

36. (**D**) Either we'll have to increase overtime or take on new staff.
我們不是必須多加班，就是要雇用新職員。

(A) 他們必須減少加班工作。
(B) 他們最好裁掉那位職員。
(C) 他們必須訓練新職員。
(D) <u>他們必須雇用新職員。</u>

＊ ***either*** A ***or*** B 不是 A 就是 B
increase (ɪnˈkris) *v.* 增加
overtime (ˈovɚˌtaɪm) *n.* 加班　*adj.* 加班的
take on 雇用　staff (stæf) *n.* 職員
decrease (dɪˈkris) *v.* 減少　***had better*** 最好
reduce (rɪˈdjus) *v.* 裁減　train (tren) *v.* 訓練
employ (ɪmˈplɔɪ) *v.* 雇用

37. (**A**) Jackson said the meeting was mandatory.
傑克森說這場會議強制出席。

(A) 我們全都必須去開會。
(B) 它要求很多。
(C) 不是我們所有人都必須去。
(D) 沒有人可以去開會。

* **meeting** (ˈmitɪŋ) *n.* 會議
mandatory (ˈmændəˌtorɪ) *adj.* 必須的；強制的
demand (dɪˈmænd) *v.* 要求

38. (**D**) Jean came to school on time.
珍準時來到學校。

(A) 她遲到了。　(B) 她沒有跛腳。
(C) 她不胖。　(D) 她沒有遲到。

* ***on time*** 準時　**lame** (lem) *adj.* 跛足的

39. (**B**) Linda didn't lose weight overnight.
琳達沒有突然減重。

(A) 她適當地減重。
(B) 她慢慢地減重。
(C) 她在晚上減重。
(D) 她快速減重。

* **lose** (luz) *v.* 減輕
weight (wet) *n.* 重量
overnight (ˈovəˈnaɪt) *adv.* 一夜之間；突然
properly (ˈprɑpəlɪ) *adv.* 適當地
gradually (ˈgrædʒuəlɪ) *adv.* 慢慢地；逐漸地

40. (**B**) Before shooting at the target, the loaders computed the range. 在射擊目標之前，裝填器會先計算射程。

(A) 它們把槍裝上子彈。 (B) 它們算出目標有多遠。
(C) 它們擊中目標。 (D) 它們的射程沒有很遠。

* shoot〔ʃut〕*v.* 射擊 ***shoot at*** 向…射擊
target〔'tɑrgɪt〕*n.* 目標 loader〔'lodɚ〕*n.* 裝填器
compute〔kəm'pjut〕*v.* 計算 range〔rendʒ〕*n.* 射程
load〔lod〕*v.* 裝子彈於（槍砲） gun〔gʌn〕*n.* 槍
figure〔'fɪgjɚ〕*v.* 計算 ***figure out*** 算出
hit〔hɪt〕*v.* 擊中

41. (**C**) It sounds like Janet enjoyed herself at the party.
聽起來珍娜似乎在宴會中玩得很愉快。

(A) 珍娜好像很無聊。 (B) 珍娜好像在睡覺。
(C) 珍娜好像玩得很愉快。 (D) 珍娜好像去旅行。

* sound〔saʊnd〕*v.* 聽起來 ***enjoy oneself*** 玩得愉快
seem〔sim〕*v.* 好像 ***have a good time*** 玩得愉快
trip〔trɪp〕*n.* 旅行 ***go on a trip*** 去旅行

42. (**C**) Sometimes Jenny becomes irritated with her friends.
有時珍妮會對她朋友感到不耐煩。

(A) 她會對她朋友感到失望。
(B) 她會對她朋友感到滿意。
(C) 她會對她朋友感到厭煩。
(D) 她會爲她朋友擔心。

* irritated〔'ɪrə,tetɪd〕*adj.* 不耐煩的
disappointed〔,dɪsə'pɔɪntɪd〕*adj.* 失望的
happy〔'hæpɪ〕*adj.* 滿意的 annoyed〔ə'nɔɪd〕*adj.* 厭煩的
worried〔'wɝɪd〕*adj.* 擔心的

43. (**B**) It takes 20 minutes to record the video.
錄這卷錄影帶花了二十分鐘。

(A) 我們花了十分鐘來撥放這卷錄影帶。
(B) 這次錄影錄了二十分鐘長。
(C) 這卷錄影帶在二十分鐘前錄完。
(D) 這卷錄音帶不夠好，所以花了三十分鐘在錄音。

* take〔tek〕*v.* 花費
record〔rɪ'kɔrd〕*v.* 錄影；錄音
video〔'vɪdɪ,o〕*n.* 錄影帶
recording〔rɪ'kɔrdɪŋ〕*n.* 錄製；錄影帶
play back 播放　tape〔tæp〕*n.* 錄音帶

44. (**C**) The bank will eventually add another branch.
這家銀行最後會再加開另一家分行。

(A) 很快就會再開另一家分行。
(B) 再也不會開另一家分行。
(C) 遲早會開另一家分行。
(D) 有希望會開另一家分行。

* eventually〔ɪ'vɛntʃuəlɪ〕*adv.* 最後
add〔æd〕*v.* 增加　branch〔bræntʃ〕*n.* 分行
soon〔sun〕*adv.* 很快地　***sooner or later*** 遲早
hopefully〔'hopfəlɪ〕*adv.* 有希望地

45. (**D**) When I'm on vacation, I like to take it easy.
當我在渡假時，我喜歡放輕鬆。

(A) 我喜歡吃點心。　(B) 我喜歡散步。
(C) 我喜歡小睡一下。　(D) 我喜歡放輕鬆。

* ***take it easy*** 輕鬆一點　nap〔næp〕*n.* 小睡
relax〔rɪ'læks〕*v.* 放輕鬆

46. (**B**) On the corner, a new building is under construction.
轉角有一棟新的建築物正在蓋。

(A) 正在蓋轉角。
(B) <u>這棟建築物還沒蓋好。</u>
(C) 這棟建築物需要新的屋頂。
(D) 已經完成施工了。

* corner〔ˈkɔrnɚ〕*n.* 轉角　　building〔ˈbɪldɪŋ〕*n.* 建築物
construction〔kənˈstrʌkʃən〕*n.* 建築；施工
under construction 在建設中　　***not yet*** 尚未
roof〔ruf〕*n.* 屋頂

47. (**B**) The instrument was of European origin.
這個樂器來自歐洲。

(A) 它在歐洲被破壞。　　(B) <u>它在歐洲製造的。</u>
(C) 它在歐洲被演奏。　　(D) 它被送往歐洲。

* instrument〔ˈɪnstrəmənt〕*n.* 樂器
European〔ˌjurəˈpiən〕*adj.* 歐洲的
origin〔ˈɔrədʒɪn〕*n.* 起源；由來
destroy〔dɪˈstrɔɪ〕*v.* 破壞　　Europe〔ˈjurəp〕*n.* 歐洲
play〔ple〕*v.* 演奏　　send〔sɛnd〕*v.* 寄；送

48. (**C**) They repelled the attack. 他們抵抗攻擊。

(A) 他們花錢擺平它。
(B) 他們撐到攻擊停止爲止。
(C) <u>他們擊退它。</u>
(D) 他們切斷它。

* repel〔rɪˈpɛl〕*v.* 抵抗　　attack〔əˈtæk〕*n.* 攻擊
buy off 花錢擺平
see off 送別；撐到（敵人的）攻擊停止爲止
fight off 作戰而擊退　　***cut off*** 切斷

49. (**A**) George's party is very informal.
喬治的宴會非常不拘形式。

(A) 我們可以穿牛仔褲參加宴會。
(B) 總統會出席這個宴會。
(C) 沒有表格要填寫。
(D) 每個人都必須為了這個宴會盛裝打扮。

* informal [ɪn'fɔrml] *adj.* 不拘形式的
wear [wɛr] *v.* 穿戴　　jeans [dʒinz] *n.* 牛仔褲
president ['prɛzədənt] *n.* 總統
attend [ə'tɛnd] *v.* 出席　　form [fɔrm] *n.* 表格
fill [fɪl] *v.* 填寫　　***fill out*** 填寫
dress up 盛裝打扮

50. (**A**) Wire conducts electric current.
電線傳導電流。

(A) 電線傳送電流。
(B) 電線是一種帶電的東西。
(C) 電很奇怪。
(D) 你需要電線來付電費。

* conduct [kən'dʌkt] *v.* 傳導
electric [ɪ'lɛktrɪk] *adj.* 電的；帶電的
current ['kɝənt] *n.* 電流　　carry ['kærɪ] *v.* 傳送
electricity [ɪ,lɛk'trɪsətɪ] *n.* 電
weird [wɪrd] *adj.* 奇怪的

51. (**C**) M：How does it look?
W：The sleeves are a little too long, and the collar is too loose.
What is the man doing?

男：看起來如何？
女：袖子有點太長，而且領子也太鬆。
那位男士在做什麼？

(A) 選油漆。　(B) 問路。
(C) 試穿衣服。　(D) 找他弄丟的東西。

＊ sleeve〔sliv〕*n.* 袖子　collar〔'kalɚ〕*n.* 領子
loose〔lus〕*adj.* 鬆的　select〔sə'lɛkt〕*v.* 挑選
paint〔pent〕*n.* 油漆
directions〔də'rɛkʃəns〕*n.*（行路的）指引
try on 試穿　lose〔luz〕*v.* 遺失

52. (**B**) M：If your tooth aches, you really should make a dentist appointment.
W：I think I'll put it off for a while.
What is the woman going to do?
男：如果妳牙痛的話，眞的應該要去預約看牙醫。
女：我想我等一下就去預約。
這位女士即將做什麼？

(A) 拔牙。
(B) 等久一點。
(C) 看一下牙醫。
(D) 想想她把檔案放在哪。

＊ tooth〔tuθ〕*n.* 牙齒【複數是 teeth】
ache〔ek〕*v.* 疼痛
dentist〔'dɛntɪst〕*n.* 牙醫
appointment〔ə'pɔɪntmənt〕*n.* 預約
put off 延後；使等待　***for a while*** 一會兒
pull out 拔掉　file〔faɪl〕*n.* 檔案

53. (**C**) W：What happened to your gorgeous flowers?

M：The freeze killed them.

What happened to the flowers?

女：你那些美麗的花怎麼了？

男：寒流使它們枯死了。

那些花怎麼了？

(A) 它們變得更美。 (B) 它們被摘下來。

(C) <u>它們枯死了。</u> (D) 它們昏倒了。

* gorgeous〔'gɔrdʒəs〕*adj.* 很美的 freeze〔friz〕*n.* 寒流
kill〔kɪl〕*v.* 殺死 pick〔pɪk〕*v.* 摘；採
die〔daɪ〕*v.* 死；枯萎 faint〔fent〕*v.* 昏倒

54. (**A**) W：What are they building on the road out by Jeri's farm?

M：That's going to be a new city landfill.

In what way does the building serve the city?

女：他們要在傑利農場旁邊那條路上蓋什麼？

男：那將會是新的城市掩埋場。

這個建築物對城市有何用途？

(A) <u>它是個垃圾場。</u> (B) 存錢的地方。

(C) 蓋房子的地方。 (D) 它是購物中心。

* build〔bɪld〕*v.* 建築
…on the road out by… 在此等於 on the road near，加上 out 只是強調傑利的農場很遠。
landfill〔'lændfɪl〕*n.* 垃圾掩埋場
serve〔sɝv〕*v.* 當…用 garbage〔'gɑrbɪdʒ〕*n.* 垃圾
dump〔dʌmp〕*n.* 垃圾場
deposit〔dɪ'pɑzɪt〕*v.* 存（錢）
center〔'sɛntɚ〕*n.* 中心 ***shopping center*** 購物中心

55. (**C**) W : I'm going to get a cup of coffee. Would you like something?

M : Yes. Please. Cappuccino and a tuna sandwich.

W : I'll be back in a minute.

What has the man ordered?

女：我要去買一杯咖啡。你要什麼嗎？

男：好的。麻煩妳。卡布奇諾和鮪魚三明治。

女：我馬上回來。

那位男士點了什麼？

(A) 礦泉水。 (B) 咖啡和吐司。

(C) 卡布奇諾和三明治。 (D) 食品雜貨。

* Cappuccino〔ˌkɑpəˈtʃɪno〕*n.* 卡布奇諾【熱牛奶咖啡】

tuna〔ˈtunə〕*n.* 鮪魚 sandwich〔ˈsændwɪtʃ〕*n.* 三明治

order〔ˈɔrdɚ〕*v.* 訂購；點叫

mineral〔ˈmɪnərəl〕*adj.* 含礦物的

toast〔tost〕*n.* 吐司 grocery〔ˈgrosərɪ〕*n.* 食品雜貨

56. (**C**) W : I'm searching for an article on gun control.

M : There is one in this newspaper.

What is the woman doing?

女：我在找一篇關於槍枝管制的文章。

男：這份報紙上有一篇。

這位女士在做什麼？

(A) 找醫生。 (B) 找藝術家。

(C) 找文章。 (D) 找藥。

* search〔sɝtʃ〕*v.* 尋找 article〔ˈɑrtɪkḷ〕*n.* 文章

control〔kənˈtrol〕*n.* 管制 artist〔ˈɑrtɪst〕*n.* 藝術家

medicine〔ˈmɛdəsṇ〕*n.* 藥

57. (**C**) W：What did Emma do when the gas bill came?

M：She got kind of riled.

How did Emma feel?

女：當瓦斯費帳單來的時候，艾瑪做了什麼？

男：她變得有點生氣。

艾瑪覺得怎樣？

(A) 難過。 (B) 高興。

(C) <u>生氣。</u> (D) 快樂。

* gas〔gæs〕*n.* 瓦斯

bill〔bɪl〕*n.* 帳單 ***kind of*** 有點

riled〔raɪld〕*adj.* 生氣的；煩躁的

mad〔mæd〕*adj.* 生氣的

joyful〔ˈdʒɔɪfəl〕*adj.* 快樂的

58. (**C**) W：Would you please pass me the scissors?

M：Yes, of course.

What does the woman want to do?

女：請你把剪刀遞給我好嗎？

男：好的，當然沒問題。

這位女士想要做什麼？

(A) 縫布。 (B) 把布撕裂。

(C) <u>剪布。</u> (D) 吃布。

* pass〔pæs〕*v.* 傳遞

scissors〔ˈsɪzɚz〕*n. pl.* 剪刀

sew〔so〕*v.* 縫 cloth〔klɔθ〕*n.* 布

rip〔rɪp〕*v.* 撕裂 cut〔kʌt〕*v.* 剪

59. (**B**) W：We didn't know you stayed in this hotel.
M：Well, we're gonna check out now.
What is the couple going to do?
女：我們不知道你們住在這家旅館。
男：嗯，我們現在要去辦退房手續了。
這對夫婦要去做什麼？
(A) 買下旅館。　　(B) 離開旅館。
(C) 賣掉旅館。　　(D) 進入旅館。

＊ stay〔ste〕*v.* 投宿
gonna〔'gɔnə〕等於 going to，是口語化的用法。
check out 辦理退房手續
couple〔'kʌpl̩〕*n.* 夫婦　　leave〔liv〕*v.* 離開
enter〔'ɛntɚ〕*v.* 進入

60. (**D**) W：John certainly seems joyful.
M：Yes, he does. His wife recently gave birth.
Why is John happy?
女：約翰看起來一定很開心。
男：對啊，他很開心。他妻子最近剛生小孩。
約翰爲什麼開心？
(A) 他妻子送他一份禮物。
(B) 他剛當叔叔。
(C) 他妻子告訴他一些好消息。
(D) 他剛當爸爸。

＊ certainly〔'sɝtn̩lɪ〕*adv.* 一定　　seem〔sim〕*v.* 看起來
recently〔'risn̩tlɪ〕*adv.* 最近　　***give birth*** 生小孩
present〔'prɛzn̩t〕*n.* 禮物　　new〔nju〕*adj.* 剛成爲…的
uncle〔'ʌŋkl̩〕*n.* 叔叔

心得筆記欄

ECL 聽力測驗 II

主　　編／程　明
發 行 所／學習出版有限公司　☎ (02) 2704-5525
郵撥帳號／05127272 學習出版社帳戶
登 記 證／局版台業 *2179* 號
印 刷 所／裕強彩色印刷有限公司
台北門市／台北市許昌街 10 號 2 F　☎ (02) 2331-4060
台灣總經銷／紅螞蟻圖書有限公司　☎ (02) 2795-3656
本公司網址　www.learnbook.com.tw
電子郵件　learnbook@learnbook.com.tw

書 + MP3 一片售價：新台幣四百八十元正

2016 年 11 月 1 日新修訂

ISBN 957-519-895-6